I0723746

SHAPERS of WORLDS

Volume II

ALSO AVAILABLE FROM SHADOWPAW PRESS

shadowpawpress.com

Shapers of Worlds

Science fiction and fantasy by first-year guests of the Aurora Award-winning podcast *The Worldshapers*

Paths to the Stars:

Twenty-Two Fantastical Tales of Imagination

One Lucky Devil:

The First World War Memoirs of Sampson J. Goodfellow

Spirit Singer

Award-winning YA fantasy

The Shards of Excalibur Series

Five-book Aurora and Sunburst Award-nominated YA fantasy series

Song of the Sword

Twist of the Blade

Lake in the Clouds

Cave Beneath the Sea

Door Into Faerie

From the Street to the Stars

Andy Nebula: Interstellar Rock Star, Book 1

Peregrine Rising Series

Far-future science fiction duology

Right to Know

Falcon's Egg

Blue Fire

Epic YA fantasy

Assignment: Avalon

Far-future YA space opera

Star Song

Far-future YA science fiction

SHAPERS of WORLDS

Volume II

Science fiction & fantasy by authors featured on the Aurora Award-winning podcast The Worldshapers

Edited by
EDWARD WILLETT

SHADOWPAW
PRESS

SHAPERS OF WORLDS VOLUME II
*Science fiction and fantasy by authors featured on
the Aurora Award-winning podcast* The Worldshapers

Published by
Shadowpaw Press
Regina, Saskatchewan, Canada
www.shadowpawpress.com

Copyright © 2021 by Edward Willett
All rights reserved

All characters and events in this book are fictitious.
Any resemblance to persons living or dead is coincidental.

The scanning, uploading, and distribution of this book via the Internet or any other means without the permission of the publisher is illegal and punishable by law. Please purchase only authorized electronic editions of this book, and do not participate in or encourage electronic piracy of copyrighted material.

Trade Paperback ISBN: 978-1-989398-28-9
Hardcover ISBN: 978-1-989398-29-6
Ebook ISBN: 978-1-989398-30-2

Edited by Edward Willett
Cover art by Tithi Luadthong
Interior design by Shadowpaw Press
Created with Vellum

COPYRIGHTS

"Shadow Sight" © 2021 by Kelley Armstrong

"Ghost and Fox" © 2021 by Bryn Neuenschwander

"Letters from an Imprisoned Wizard to a Young Queen"
    © 2021 by Garth Nix

"Going to Ground" © 2021 by Candas Jane Dorsey

"Beneath a Bicameral Moon" © 2021 by Jeremy Szal

"Shapeshifter Finals" © 1995 by Jeffrey A. Carver

"Thibauld's Tale" © 2021 by Edward Willett

"The Cancellation" © 2021 by Bryan Thomas Schmidt

"River of Ice" © 2015 by David D. Levine

"I Hid in the Bathroom When the Aliens Arrived"
    © 2021 by Lisa Foiles

"The Only Road" © 2021 by Susan Forest

"The Cat and the Merrythought" © 2021 by Matthew Hughes

"Anamnesis in Ruins" © 2021 by Heli Kennedy

"Angel and Monica" © 2021 by Helen Dale

"Root Mother" © 2021 by Adria Laycraft

"The Cool Sequestered Vale of Life" © 2021 by Edward Savio

"The Lost Cipher of Dr. Dee" © 2021 by Lisa Kessler

"Message Found in a Variable Temporality Appliance"
    © 2021 by Ira Nayman

"Salvage" © 2014 by Carrie Vaughn, LLC

"Casey's Empire" © 1981 by Nancy Kress

"I Remember Paris" © 2021 by James Alan Gardner

"The Chthonic Op" © 2021 by Tim Pratt

"The Little Tailor and the Elves" © 1994 by Barbara Hambly

"A Murder in Eddsford" © 2008 by S.M. Stirling

CONTENTS

INTRODUCTION

By Edward Willett

Back in the sixteenth century, learned men were known for creating "cabinets of curiosities," collections of notable objects: relics of archaeological interest, fascinating geological specimens, stuffed animals, valuable books, works of art, and more. These cabinets (at the time, the term referred to rooms, not just pieces of furniture) were precursors to modern museums. They were also a form of entertainment: "learned entertainment," as the Royal Society in London termed it.

These collections might or might not have a strong central theme. It depended on the collector and his or her specific interests. Some might largely be collections of one type of thing; others might be collections of many different types of things.

Anthologies, it seems to me, are rather like cabinets of curiosities, the collector being the editor. Many anthologies have a strong central theme, such as "stories set on Mars," or "stories about ancient deities making their way in the modern world," or "alternate histories of the Civil War." The curiosities collected in such cabinets are all related to this central theme, and thus, readers know what to expect as they move from tale to tale.

This anthology, and its precursor, *Shapers of Worlds*, published last year, are far more eclectic. The stories collected here are stories connected not by theme but by something more concrete: every author was a guest during the second year of my podcast, *The Worldshapers*, where I interview other science fiction and fantasy authors about their creative process.

Both anthologies grew out of a presentation to the annual general meeting of SaskBooks, the association of Saskatchewan publishers of which I'm a member, in 2019. A publisher from Winnipeg explained how she had successfully Kickstarted an anthology of short fiction, and I thought, *Hey, I know some authors . . .*

I reached out to the guests from the first year of my podcast, which had begun in August 2018, and eighteen authors agreed to take part, with nine offering to write new stories and nine to provide reprints. After climbing the somewhat steep Kickstarter learning curve, I successfully crowdsourced *Shapers of Worlds* in early 2020 and published it through my own Shadowpaw Press last fall.

Having done it once, I thought I could do it again, so I reached out to my second-year guests. This time, eighteen authors agreed to write new stories, and six offered reprints, and that's the volume you now hold in your hand (or are viewing on your ebook reader of choice).

To return to my metaphor, these stories are those which the authors themselves chose to be displayed in this cabinet of curiosities. The result, I think you'll find, is as varied as the strange assortment of oddities and discoveries those long-ago collectors placed in their personal showcases, ranging from far-future science fiction to modern-day fantasy to stories of alternate histories to tales set in magical realms. Here you will find darkness and danger, but also light and hope; grimness, but also humour; rollicking adventure alongside quieter tales conducive to contemplation.

It has been a great honour both to interview these authors and to collect and edit these stories. I couldn't be prouder to present *Shapers of Worlds Volume II* to the world.

And, of course, none of this could have been possible without the generosity of all those who backed the Kickstarter earlier this year that provided the funds to pay the authors and produce this book. I hope you'll find your support was well worthwhile.

Another term for a cabinet of curiosities was "cabinet of wonder." In the stories that follow, you will find a great deal of wonder: they are, literally, wonder-full.

Enjoy, and thanks for reading!

Edward Willett
Regina, Saskatchewan
September 2021

SHADOW SIGHT

By Kelley Armstrong

Empty road stretching into darkness. Water shimmering in wagon-wheel ruts. One cry from a night creature, cut short as a shadow snatches it up. On a road like this, it's a sure bet something will swoop in to devour you. Which is why I'm walking right down the middle.

Come get me.

Please, come get me.

I'm watching the water-filled wagon ruts. No ripples. No one is here. Not yet. The full moon reflects in those strips of water, and as I watch, a second moon appears from behind the first.

I squint up into the night sky. The second moon is but a pale reflection of the first, yet it grows stronger as it moves into the forefront, leaching light from its double. I wait until it is about to intersect with the first, and then I tear my gaze away. They say that if you witness the intersection, the image will burn onto your eyes and you'll forever see those two moons, even in full daylight.

Is that true? I don't know, and I don't care. Only a fool tempts fate, and we Rileys are not fools. If I *had* to look at the double-moon, I'd take that chance, but if there's no reason to do it, then it's like sticking your hand in a fire just to see if it'll burn.

Most folks don't need to worry about gazing on a double-moon because most folks only ever notice the one. Rileys are different. We see the shadows. We see that second moon, emerging as a pale ghost of a thing and then gaining strength until it overtakes the moon itself.

People have those shadows, too. A second self that hides behind us, wispy and insubstantial. Normal folks sometimes catch a glimpse of it, that moment when they think a person isn't quite what they seem to be. But then the shadow disappears, and they tell themselves they were imagining things. They weren't.

Once, a friend took me to a church revival. I wasn't much interested in the sermonizing, but I was tempted by the promise of sugar jumbles. Sadly, to get the cookies, I had to sit through the sermonizing. I remember the preacher going on about people's secret selves. Their dark and sinful innermost selves. That's when I realized that even normal folks *know* about the shadows. They just can't see them.

I can't reckon what that must be like, meeting a person and knowing they could be the sort who'd knife you in the back or the sort who'd give you the shirt off their back, and not seeing their truth until it's too late. Until their knife is sticking between your ribs. Or until you've planted your knife between *their* ribs, mistrust and suspicion guiding your hand.

The problem with the shadow sight is that it's only really useful if you're willing to let your own shadow grow, just a little. We Riley women do good with our gift, but to do good, we also do bad.

Rileys are hired killers. My auntie May says "vigilantes," but that's only because she likes fancy words. Nothing fancy about killing.

If you've lived in this part of the world long, you'll hear whispers about us. A family who'll kill someone who needs killing. Just don't try saying that person did something they never did. This family will know the truth, and if you lied, they'll keep your money and warn the person you wanted dead.

To hire a Riley, you need to find one of our confederates. You'll never actually meet us. Never even hear our name. That's what keeps us safe. Folks expect they're hiring men. Brothers and fathers and sons of some magical family. The Rileys are just a house full of women, running a ranch after their menfolk died on the road west. They do all right by themselves—got a nice house, and they're always buying up land and paying good wages to their cowboys—but that's because their menfolk left them a ton of money.

We Rileys hide in plain sight, and that's what I'm doing tonight. Just a girl, not yet twenty, walking down a dark road, looking nervous as she tries to hide the jangling of her market coins.

Come out, come out, wherever you are.

I squint up at the moon as its shadow self disappears. It's a cool night. Crisp, Auntie May would say, and I'll admit *that's* a good word. Like biting into an apple, sharp and sweet and cool. When I smell apples on the breeze, I'm not sure it's real or my imagination. It's the right time of year, and I've been waiting for our orchard to ripen so I can start baking my apple pies. My apple pies are famous around these parts, and I make nearly as much in a season as I do with a killing.

Brush crackles to my left. I tense, fingers itching to grab my knife. I have to remind myself this is what I want. To be spotted. To look innocent and defenceless.

I push aside those nasty fears of someone stalking me from the bushes. Heaven forbid! Back to thoughts of apple pie, which makes me think about the harvest dance, which makes me think about Johnny. He's going to ask to woo me again, and I'm not sure what I'll say this year. Riley women can marry, if they want, but that means leaving home to be a regular person, coming around for Sunday dinner with the family. Is that what I want? I don't quite know yet. I reckon I have a year or two before I need to decide.

Another crackle, this one to my right, which does give me pause. I force myself to keep walking. Gran trusted me with this job, a very important one, and if I pull it off, I'll be a grown woman, ready to take on grown-woman jobs at grown-woman pay. While Johnny seems a fine boy—with hardly any shadow at all—I'd like to explore my options, as Auntie June would say.

The woods have gone silent. I cast out the fingers of my magic, tickling over the road. Shadows to both my left and right. Two. Or is that a third? My fingers itch again for the knife.

Patience.

It was yesterday morning when the job came in. One of our most trusted compatriots, Paula James, rode all night to bring us the news. Two families of settlers murdered on the road west. Their guide claimed they'd been set on by a raiding party while he'd been off scouting the road ahead. The family's relatives over in Concord were sure the guide murdered them in their sleep and stole their money and valuables. Those relatives wanted to hire us to put things right.

Auntie May and Auntie June had ridden with me most of the

way. Now they're back in town, waiting. This is my job. My test. I'm no longer a child. I can do this.

The shadow moon circles around again. Nearby, a coyote yips and then stops short. Gran says that animals see the shadow moon—that they see all the shadows. That's why a dog runs up to some strangers, wagging its tail, and runs up to others, baring its teeth, and every now and then, it runs clean in the other direction. I feel that urge now. Something is wrong here, the shadows oozing. When I send out my own magic, it balks and slinks back, and the hairs rise on my neck.

"Evie . . ."

The whisper creeps over on the shadows. I spin, peering into darkness.

"Little Evie, out all alone."

"Wh—who's there?"

One of the shadows glides onto the road and takes the form of a woman.

I squint at her. "Paula? That you?"

Paula saunters toward me, gun in hand. I yank out my knife, and she laughs.

There's a gun strapped to my thigh, but I don't go for it. I quaver, and my heart beats hard enough that I don't need to fake my fear.

"I—I don't understand," I say. "You come to help me catch the fella I'm hunting?"

Footsteps off to my left. I tense, and my gut screams for me not to look. Shadows pulse behind me, and I want to run. Throw my knife at Paula and hightail it into the woods.

Gripping my knife, I pivot to see two figures. A man and a boy about my age.

"You haven't met my Billy, have you?" Paula says behind me. "This is my boy, Billy, and my man, Chester."

Chester's shadow slips back and forth like a child playing peek-a-boo. The boy is different. I barely see the boy at all through the shadow.

I straighten and force myself to turn my back on Billy as I face Paula.

"There *was* a massacre," I say. "We heard the news. But the guide didn't do it, did he?"

Paula shrugs. "Oh, I expect he did. None of our concern. It was just the kind of story I knew would get you out here. I've had my eye on you for a while, Miss Evie. All it took was a whisper in the old woman's ear, telling her this guide was known for fancying pretty girls and weren't you just about old enough to do your own jobs? Specially one as easy as this, an old fella making his way home, thinking he got away with murder."

"You want me?" I say. "For what?"

"Your magic."

Behind me, Billy's shadow oozes and whispers. I block it out. As Paula saunters toward me, I grip my knife until the handle hurts my palm.

"That's a very special magic you got there, girl," she says. "I remember when I was little, my ma would tell me stories about the Riley women. How I had to be good, 'cause they'd know if I wasn't. How we James women were their special friends." She spits in the dirt. "Their *lackeys*, more like. We do all the work, finding clients, running messages, collecting pay, and we're lucky to get a few dollars while you all grow fat on that ranch."

"You want me to give you the magic?"

She snorts. "You think I'm stupid, girl? You get that magic from your momma, who got it from hers."

"So you want *me*. What for?"

She doesn't like the question. It's too calm. I reach down inside myself and relax the part that warns never to let them see my fear, even when I'm drowning in it.

"I—I don't understand," I say. "I just came to do a job."

That tremor is exactly what she wants, and she squeezes my arm. "I know. It's your gran's fault for letting you loose with that special gift. I'll look after you better. Billy will, too." Her gaze turns to her son, and her eyes glow. "Ain't he a fine boy? Big and hand-some, like his daddy was."

"I don't understand," I repeat, and this time, I just don't want to.

"You're going to marry my Billy. Tell your gran you decided to wed and keep moving west with us." She rubs my arm. "You'll like it better with me, child. I won't ask you to kill nobody."

I need to resist the urge to say, again, that I don't understand. I let my expression answer for me, and she laughs softly.

"You think that's all you're good for, girl? Killing folks? That's your gran's doing. Got your head twisted right around. You can tell when someone's lying. When they're a no-good son of a whore. That's gold, right there. Just look at your ranch. Your gran has a score of cowhands, and not one ever lays a hand on you girls or your cattle. They're decent men. That's how your magic ought to be used. For good."

I struggle to comprehend her meaning. She wants me as some kind of truth detector. She's thinking of all the ways it would be helpful in business to know whether or not someone can be trusted.

Is that better than killing folks? Depends on how you look at it. It's easier, that's for sure, but what we do *is* good work. Gran says it's like putting down a sick cow before she infects the herd. We put down killers before they hurt anyone else. What Paula's talking about only benefits herself.

"You'd like to stop killing folks, wouldn't you?" she wheedles. "And marry my Billy? He picked you from your cousins. He likes you."

I turn to Billy, and my gut twists. He stands there, face empty, the darkness swirling around him. That darkness calls to me. It whispers that I should draw closer. I don't want to. I really don't, but I know I must.

Billy's shadow seeps toward me. It whispers, like a child bursting to share secrets.

Let me tell you my truth.

Let me tell you what I've done.

I cautiously crack open the door, and his shadow shoves it wide and rushes in, images flooding over me, and I stagger back under the weight of them.

Oh, Paula.

In that moment, I will allow myself to feel sorry for her. To take pity on her.

Paula brought us the story of those families slaughtered on the trail west. I know now why she chose that one. Because she'd been nearby when it happened, in the town the families had left before their deaths. Left and been tracked by Billy. Murdered by Billy.

In the vision, he's calmly awaiting his chance, a snake hiding in the long prairie grass. I see him slit the throats of the parents as they slept. I see him methodically hunt down the children as they scatter. I see what he did to the bodies after to make it look like they'd been set upon by a raiding party. And I see him rifling through their belongings, taking only the best, like when a stray dog slaughtered our whole flock of hens and only ate a few bites.

I see more, too. I see that he wasn't alone. I see his partner, vomiting after, telling Billy to leave the bodies, that he doesn't need to do anything to them. Maybe so, but Billy does it anyway. He wants to do it.

My gaze swings to Chester. The older man flinches, like he knows what I see.

Oh, Paula.

You've got no idea, do you?

I turn to Paula. "What if I said you were wrong?"

Her face scrunches. "Wrong about what?"

"You say I inherited my power from my momma. I never knew my momma. My ma killed her. She did something—I got no idea what, but it was bad enough that she deserved killing. I was a baby. Ma scooped me up and brought me home."

Paula's brow furrows more. "But you've got the magic. Your real ma must have been a Riley. She went bad."

I shake my head. "There's none of Gran's blood running through my veins. None of her blood running in my ma's or my Auntie May's or Auntie June's either."

Now it's Paula's turn to say, "I don't understand."

"They ain't related, Ma," Billy says, his voice sharp with disdain. "The magic don't come from the blood. That's why there's no menfolk living on that ranch. There *were* no menfolk. They ain't never been married."

I nod. "The Rileys take girl children from those they've got to kill. Girl children who'd be left alone with no one to raise them."

"Then they give them the magic," Paula says.

I see the moment understanding hits, her eyes glittering.

"So you *could* give it to me," she says. "Me and my boy."

"Just you. That's why it's always girl children. The magic only works with them. Gran says, once upon a time, a Riley woman lost her whole family to a fellow who tricked her into thinking he was a good man. A witch gave her the power to see the shadow side and showed her how to give it to her daughters, only she never had more, so she adopted two little girls. Out here, there's always babies needing folks to raise them, especially girls. So that's what we do. If you want the power, I can give it to you."

Paula licks her lips. "'Course, I want it."

"Are you sure?" I ease back on my heels. "See, the thing is that Rileys only give it to little ones, so they grow up seeing the shadow side. To us, it's normal. To someone of your years?" I shrug. "I remember Ma told me about a lady she knew, was deaf from the time she was little, and then the doctor fixed something so she could hear, and she went around wearing earmuffs because the world was just too loud. You can't hide from the shadows. Even if you shut your eyes, you'll *feel* them there."

A hand lands on my shoulder. It's hot and heavy and stinking of oily shadow.

"That's enough," Billy says. "Don't you be trying to weasel out of this, girl. You know you're telling my ma a pack of lies." He looks at Paula. "She's tricking you, Ma. She can't give you no magic powers."

"No harm in her trying," Paula says. "If it works, we'll let her go."

Billy shifts, and his shadow drips down my back like sweaty fingers, and it takes everything in me to stand firm.

"You said I could keep her," he says. "You promised."

"If you want the power," I say to Paula, "you gotta let me go home. There are things I need to get."

Billy's laughter comes sharp, ringing out in the quiet night. "Girl, you think you are a heap more clever than you are. All that book learning Ma warned me you girls get." He looks at Paula. "Now do you see what she's doing?"

Paula's shoulders slump, and she turns away from me. "She's trying to trick me into letting her go back home. Pretending she needs secret ingredients for the spell."

"I do need secret ingredients," I protest. "It's not like I can just cast—"

Billy thumps me between the shoulders, hard enough that I stumble, even as his voice is light. "Enough of that, girl. You'll just embarrass yourself now. Come on, Chester. We'll fetch the wagon." He looks at me, cold amusement lighting those dead eyes. "And don't go thinking you can talk my ma into running off with you. She's not that stupid, and we're not going that far."

I slump. "Yes, sir."

Billy walks away with Chester. As soon as they're out of sight, I tug a folded paper from my hip pouch. Paula watches, frowning. I unfold it to show a couple of pinches of dried herbs.

"That tobacco?" she says. "Or tea?"

I lower my voice. "It's the ingredients I need. I just wanted Billy to leave us be. Otherwise, he'd have stopped you from taking it." I meet her gaze. "Men never want their womenfolk having an advantage."

She stares at the herbs, and then looks over her shoulder. "How do I know you're not poisoning me, girl?"

"You don't need to eat them. Just put them under your tongue while I cast the spell."

She peers at the dried mix. "Don't look like much."

"It's not. It's the magic used to make it that counts."

Paula takes the folded paper. Then she dumps the mixture under her tongue. There are a dozen poisons that would kill her where she stands, seeping through the lining of her mouth. But the herbs are exactly what I said they are, and I cast the spell quickly. When I'm done, she blinks at me. Then she steps back.

"There's . . . there's something behind you."

"That's my shadow self."

She shivers. "I can feel it. I can feel the things you've done. The people you've killed." She's about to say more when she tenses, her body jerking as her head snaps up. "What is *that*?"

"What's what?"

She convulses and then doubles over, retching.

"You—you poisoned me."

"No, that's a shadow you feel," I say. "Your son's."

Her head shoots up again, gaze locking on mine. "You lie."

"I do not lie, and you can tell that," I say calmly. "When he arrives, you'll see what he's done. *Actually* see it. There's a reason you were so close by when those families were killed."

She pauses, taking a moment to understand, then she spits, "You *lie!*"

"I do not, as you will see. Him and your new beau both. They killed those folks."

"Then it was Chester. He made my Billy do it."

"No, I'd guess it was the other way around. But you'll see for yourself."

She turns as their wagon appears, dirt crunching under the wheels. She heaves again, vomiting.

"Oh, just wait until he's closer," I say.

"You tricked me."

"No, you tricked us. Didn't you wonder how I just happened to have those herbs on me?" I step toward her. "You honestly expected you could lie to us?"

"I didn't lie." Her voice rises. "There *are* two dead families. Their kin *are* looking for the killer, and they *do* think it was the guide. I was careful. I never said anything that wasn't true."

"Your words don't matter, Paula. We see your *intent*. Gran knew exactly what you wanted, especially when you convinced her to send me all by myself. The plan was for me to give you a taste of the magic and then kill you for your betrayal. But then I met your son." I look her in the eye. "And I came up with a more fitting punishment."

While I talk, I bend, as if touching the ground, sensing something. Instead, I'm taking out my gun. When I rise, she sees it and goes to lift her own weapon.

"Uh-uh," I say. "I don't plan to kill you, but I will if I have to. Now, I'm going to leave, and you're going to let me. Then you're going to kill your boy."

"Wh-what?" She straightens. "I'll do no such thing, girl."

"Yes, you will. You'll see what he is—what he's done—and you'll kill him because you'll know you have to. You won't be able to live with yourself otherwise. If you're a coward, and you kill yourself instead, then me and my aunties will come back and finish the job ourselves."

Before she opens her mouth, I wrench the shadows from the trees and swaddle myself in them. She looks frantically from side to side as I disappear.

"You'll probably want to kill your man, too," I say. "But that's your choice." I lean to her ear. "It was all your choice. Remember that."

With the shadows tight around me, I slip away. I'll tell my aunties what I've done, and we'll stay the night, to be sure Paula does the right thing. That's the hard truth of shadow sight. It forces us to do the right things, the only things we can live with, and Paula will make the right choice.

She'll always make the right choices now.

GHOST AND FOX

By Marie Brennan

It was to be expected, the doctor said, after such a close call as yours. He spoke in learned terms of excesses of yin, of meridians and flows, stagnation in the blood that he had put right. The woman they said was your mother listened and nodded and paid him with taels of silver, thanking him with her forehead to the floor. She loved you, that was clear—loved you enough to spend a small fortune saving you.

Saving your life, at least. A simpleton now, the neighbours said, wagging their heads in regret. She'll never be married. Such a shame. But some kind-hearted man might take her for his concubine.

You weren't meant to overhear their words. And you didn't hear what came after, because memory overwhelmed you: hands caressing your body, fever-warm against your cold skin, and heat flooding into you like the light of the sun itself.

Then it faded. You were the daughter of a wealthy family, sheltered behind high walls. No man could possibly have gotten that close to you.

You believed them when they said your near-fatal illness had made you simple. After all, you didn't remember your mother, your father, the house you awoke in. Your own childhood nurse was a stranger. You ate what they gave you and stood like an obedient doll when they dressed you, because no one believed you could manage anything for yourself.

But your mind wasn't weak. You carried on conversations, read books your Second Brother brought you. The past was a blank, but you remembered new things without trouble.

You lied to them all.

The past wasn't a blank. It was a bottomless pool of strange recollections, into which you hardly dared dip more than your toes, for fear you would fall into its depths and drown. A house that was not the one you lived in. A slipper too small for your foot. Poems you had never read, songs you had never sung; you eyed your Third Sister's zither and suspected that if you set your hand to the strings, you could play it better than she did—though everyone said you had never been musical.

The word for that wasn't "simple." It was "mad."

Your family saw your distress and did what they could to set it right. The countryside, they reasoned, would be gentler for your weakened body and mind than the clamour of the city. They sent you to live in a rural house with your old nurse and your Second Brother to watch over you.

Out there, at least, you weren't surrounded by things you were expected to remember and didn't. Accompanied by your Second Brother and the things you shouldn't remember but did, you went for short walks in the fields, watching birds flit from branch to branch and foxes dart into the undergrowth. It brought a kind of peace.

Until you reached the tomb by the side of the road. Then you began to scream and scream, and your Second Brother carried you home, sending your nurse to fetch a doctor to sedate you. But he was not as skilled as the one in the city, and so even when you sank down into dreams, you could not escape the truth: that the weed-haunted tomb was once your own.

———

THERE WAS a time when I hated you.

Such a selfish little ghost, draining the yang energy from my beloved Sang with night after night of love-making, when I had been so cautious. I wanted to stay by his side always, but the danger to him was too great; I made myself stay away, visiting only when I could bear the separation no longer. You, though—you thought only of the love and pleasure the two of you shared. And so, you fed on him, until he nearly died. I would have killed you for that, except you were already dead.

When I caught you, though . . . how could I hate one whose love mirrored my own so well? And you were willing to do anything to save him. Even if it risked your own existence.

When you disappeared, I had everything I thought I wanted: Sang all to myself, with no competition, and my own self-restraint to keep him safe. Only when you were gone did I realize you had become as dear to me as he is.

Do you think it mere chance that he has come to this house and asked for your hand in marriage? There were only two possibilities for what had become of you. One was that some Buddhist monk or Taoist priest had banished you for good, sending your restless spirit onward. The other . . .

Everyone was gossiping. The daughter of the Zhang family, making such a miraculous recovery, when even the doctor thought she would die. Some even whispered she *had* died, and the doctor brought her back to life. He never confirmed it, but he smiles whenever anyone asks him, because a physician who can revive the dead commands very high fees indeed.

It had nothing to do with him, and everything to do with a wandering spirit and a body freshly vacated.

You did not remember your family because they were never yours to begin with. The memories you could not explain were your own. And so was the tomb.

It took a lot of gossiping where your so-called mother would overhear before I persuaded them to send you to the country. You needed to know the truth before Sang presented himself at the Zhang family door. If you hadn't strolled in the right direction that morning, I would have contrived to point you there eventually. And if the tomb did not spark your memories, I would have tried other tactics, until you understood.

Now the path is clear. You are a ghost no more; Sang can come to your bed without fear. Once the negotiations with your supposed father are complete, you will return to his house as his flesh-and-blood wife.

Do not embrace me yet, dear sister-in-love. I am the one who is a danger now, to you as well as him. My self-restraint is not as perfect as I might wish, and I would never forgive myself if my touch hurt either of you.

But be patient. It is not so common as ghosts restored to life, but there are tales of fox spirits reincarnating in human form. I will find a way. And when I have, I will return to you and to Sang, and the three of us will live together again—no longer ghost and fox and victim, but alive, and human, and happy for the rest of our days.

LETTERS FROM AN IMPRISONED WIZARD TO A YOUNG QUEEN, AND ASSOCIATED EXPLICATORY CORRESPONDENCE

By Garth Nix

From the Wizard Zachariah Zelznibone
to Her Majesty the Queen

Your Majesty:

I write to proclaim my joy at Your Majesty's ascension to the throne, so long hoped for, and so welcome. I dare to hope that Your Majesty may recall the small services I was able to do for Your Majesty as a very young princess in years not so long gone by, in the matter of illusions and the like for the celebrations of your seventh, eighth, and ninth birthdays and construction of the clockwork monkey whom you named Rollo.

I wish to apprise Your Majesty of my situation, given I do not believe Your Majesty or in fact anyone at court is aware of my predicament or the circumstances of my removal and imprisonment, under the seal of Your Majesty's late aunt and predecessor, but I believe in fact at the direction of Your Majesty's older cousin,

Angelika Raustem, who was then the Gatewarden of the Inner Castle. I know not what she may be now, though I devoutly hope she currently inhabits a cell far more vile than my own.

It is only the belated news of Your Majesty's coronation and the understanding that I was once honoured to be one of Your Majesty's first tutors as a royal child that has cowed my guards to the extent of allowing me pen and paper and, I trust and hope, the chance my correspondence will be carried to the palace. For I do not truly know if Abel, as I call the entity I have summoned to carry it, will, in fact, do as I have commanded or simply eat it. These denizens of the deep realms are over-fond of paper.

I do not know in which prison I am held so that Your Majesty may find me, but I am fairly sure there is a significant moat here, or perhaps a lake. I hear the water lapping at the wall beyond my cell, but lacking windows of any kind, I do not know exactly what makes this sound.

I wander far from the point, for which I offer a copious apology. I beseech Your Majesty to order my release, and remain your most humble and obedient servant,

Zachariah Zelznibone

**From Captain of the Guard David Tzikes
to the Keeper of the Green Cabinet, Wizard Suzanne Palindros,
enclosing a suspect missive**

My Dear Suzanne,

I trust you are well, and your familiar, Wildebjorn, likewise. I write to request your assistance with the matter of an unusual letter to Her Majesty, which I have enclosed. It arrived by odd means; to wit, it was tied to the back of a white rat with a black satin ribbon. The rat sat up before the guards at the Rose Garden gate and ran away when the letter was taken, and the ribbon fell into dust. I had the boy Willem write a fair copy for Her Majesty (as you know, she insists on seeing everything), and he appears to have suffered no ill-wishing, and I could feel no curse or magic in the letter itself. But I do not have your expertise, so I send the original letter on in the hope that you might have some explanation as to who it is actually from, what it means, and so on and so forth. I also wandered across to the Archive to ask old Fellquist if he knew of either "Zachariah Zelznibone" or "Angelika Raustem," and he said no, but he frowned in that way—with his surviving eyebrow, you know—which suggests he has conceived some thread he might tease out to come into greater knowledge, and he has disappeared back into his books to do so. Whatever you might be able to do would be welcome, and I would like to also take the opportunity presented by this necessarily official letter to add that I personally hope you will soon return to the city, and I invite you to share a bottle of the Tramin '88 with me, and I would not begrudge your familiar Wildbjorn a barrel or two of some lesser vintage.

<hr>

From the Wizard Zachariah Zelznibone
to Her Majesty the Queen

I FEAR Your Majesty has not received my previous letter, or so I must presume from my continued durance. Surely, in your magnanimity and kindness, Your Majesty would have ordered my release upon the receipt of my first missive. I send this note via the zephyr, Sarissa, who perhaps has a trifle more wit in her head than Abel and is less likely to eat the paper.

I remain Your Majesty's loyal servant and hope to serve you again, upon my release.

* * *

**From the Keeper of the Green Cabinet,
Wizard Suzanne Palindros,
to Captain of the Guard David Tzikes,
copied to Her Majesty the Queen**

Dear David,

Thank you for sending me the Zelznibone letter. It is most interesting. I have not yet been able to ascertain all I would wish to know from it, but you are correct that it carries no ill-wishing or curse and is, in fact, generally an innocuous and unremarkable piece of paper, without watermark or distinction, inscribed with common oak-gall ink. I say generally because in one specification it *is* remarkable. The letter was written both a week ago and a hundred and six years past. That is to say, it was created in two separate moments of time. Which is puzzling, to say the least. If any more letters arrive from Zelznibone, see if you can capture the rat, but do not harm it. I shall ask Her Majesty if I might return sooner than planned—though the work of the commission here is not yet complete, it is close to being done. Close enough, I adjudge.

Tramin of the '88 vintage? I was not aware any bottles survived the destruction of the vineyard, but I would happily share even the lesser vintage you offer Wildbjorn. I regret the trouble with the Carrengrove has called me away, for many reasons.

Report from the Rose Garden Gatekeeper Veronika Napp to Guard Captain David Tzikes, copied to Her Majesty the Queen

SIR:

The letter enclosed arrived by the beak of a saffron-coloured heron that flew overhead and dropped it at the feet of Harmold, one of the gardeners. We have now put by bird nets ready for use as well as the rat baskets. I have taken the liberty of enlisting the assistance of my two younger girls to stand by as rat- and bird-catchers, at a half-penny per day, which I trust I will be reimbursed?

From Her Majesty the Queen to Captain of the Guard David Tzikes

DAVID,

I wish to see copies of all correspondence pertaining to this matter. I do not recall any "Zachariah Zelznibone." I am sure I would remember such a ridiculous name. Furthermore, I never had a wizard conjure at my birthday parties as a child, nor did I have a clockwork monkey called Rollo. The Dowager Lady Blewson confirms my memory in all particulars; she was at that time responsible for all my birthday celebrations as the Mistress of the Nursery. None of my Maids know of Zelznibone, nor have any knowledge of clockwork monkeys. This includes those few living who served my mother before me.

I am also puzzled why this Zelznibone says, "when a very young princess in years not so long gone by," given I will not see my fiftieth year again. Is it foolish flattery or something additionally sinister?

<hr>

From Archivist Fellquist to Guard Captain David Tzikes, copied to Her Majesty the Queen

CAPTAIN:

While I did not immediately recall either name you mentioned to me in passing the other day, there was some slight resonance that suggested I had seen one or another of the names at some point. After consulting the usual references and then some of the lesser-used references, I have found some records that may be of use to you.

Firstly, Angelika Raustem was gatewarden to Her Majesty's great-great-great-great-aunt, Queen Jayne IV, and was indeed a cousin of some kind to that monarch. Raustem was executed by Queen Katalyn III, the immediate successor to Jayne IV, for her involvement in a plot referred to in a sole instance as the "Tulip Affair," but none of the usual records make mention of this, and the relevant pages from the State Book, the Queen's Concurrence, and the Roll of the Green Cabinet are all missing, neatly excised, the rolls expertly rejoined. I was only able to confirm the execution because a copy of the Writ was included in the disbursement of Raustem's properties in the Day Book of the Comptroller of Treasonous Assay for Queen Katalyn III. The Writ itself was not in the Book of the Block, which again is missing several pages for the period in question. The excision of the records suggests there were at least several executions, the persons concerned were closely related to Queens Jayne and Katalyn, and the family wished the matter not to be more widely known—in which they were almost entirely successful.

Queen Katalyn III was known as "the Young," for she ascended to the throne at the age of fifteen. This name endured throughout her reign, though it lasted almost forty years. Interestingly, certain authorities of the time considered Raustem to have a stronger claim to inherit the throne from Jayne IV than Katalyn. Both were cousins, in different lines, and Jayne had no direct heirs.

I am curious as to why these names have arisen for enquiry, and I hope you may enlarge upon the matter to me when next we meet.

From Her Majesty the Queen to Archivist Fellquist

Archivist:

We desire you to keep these matters close as they may appertain to both the safety of our person and certain family concerns mentioned in confidence by my mother and grandmother to myself. Anything to do with these messages, or Jayne IV or Katalyn III, must not be aired beyond Captain Tzikes and Wizard Palindros. I have instructed Captain Tzikes to inform you of the nature of the current enquiries.

From the Wizard Zachariah Zelznibone
to Her Majesty the Queen

Your Majesty:

I regret to say that my patience has been tried almost beyond endurance, and were it not for the affection I still bear for your late parents, I would have undertaken actions to wreak havoc on those who maintain my immurement. I cannot understand why your direction for my immediate release has not arrived! Surely the treachery of Gatewarden Raustem in seeking to supplant Your Majesty with herself has become fully clear, and my part in apprising the late Queen, your closer cousin, of the matter? I should think this service to the throne deserving of far more than my release! Indeed, I expect not only my pardon but also appointment to either the Mastery of the School of Owls or some other suitably well-endowed sinecure. Perhaps as Rector of Snowwade, or if that has in fact been rebuilt and carries actual duties with it, then as Keeper of the Pale Leopards? And I expect a donative of some weight as well, and not in the short-weight coinage of recent years, but the good currency of your grandmother or earlier sovereigns.

I await your reply, Majesty, with righteous but banked-down anger. Should my release still not be forthcoming, I will take matters into my own hands. I am sure I do not need to remind you or your advisors that the binding placed upon the practice of my art expired with the death of the late Queen, and I have not yet taken the new oath. While it is true I have neither staff, wand, athame, nor ancillary apparatus, some of my former colleagues can doubtless inform you of my reputation as a so-called "naked" sorcerer.

From Captain of the Guard David Tzikes
to the Keeper of the Green Cabinet, Wizard Suzanne Palindros,
Zelznibone letter enclosed, copied to Her Majesty the Queen,
also copied to Archivist Fellquist

DEAR SUZANNE,

I am alarmed at the threat embodied in the most recent letter from the Wizard Zelznibone, as enclosed. Unlike the other letters, the missive was not delivered by rat or bird but simply arrived in the Queen's privy retiring chamber and was found by a Servant of the Stool upon the lid of the pot only moments before her Majesty was about to enter to engage in her morning effusion. If this Wizard is able to infiltrate a letter past the guards and the wards about not only the palace but also the Queen's own chambers, then it is a very serious matter indeed. Her Majesty has taken my advice and removed herself to the Scarlet Fortress for the moment, but you are urgently needed here to discover this Zelznibone's whereabouts and remove the danger to her Majesty.

I have also sent a copy of the latest letter to Fellquist, who may be able to identify where Zelznibone is incarcerated. I am presuming that he was entrapped or encased himself in some temporal fastness and has since emerged, confused and very dangerous.

From Archivist Fellquist to Guard Captain David Tzikes, copied to Her Majesty the Queen

CAPTAIN:

I thank you for our conversation in the Rose Garden yestereve, enlarging my knowledge of these messages. I, too, am perturbed by the most recent letter and perhaps more still as I have uncovered certain correspondences and associated records that deal with the succession of Queen Katelyn III and the surprisingly large number of executions at that time, all of them excised from the usual archival references, requiring me to reconstruct them from an executioner's private tally within a secret diary, and the so-called long roll of the providore-wrangler of the New Castle, which at that time served as the principal prison of the realm, the Korraut then being rebuilt.

As instructed, I have kept this matter close, most particularly as there are certain aspects that speak to the legitimacy of the dynasty, though not, of course, that of our present beloved Queen, whose line of descent can be traced via the possibly dubious Katalyn III but also the absolutely definitive line of Emmelina the Great.

I am scouring all possible records that might indicate the location where Zelznibone was incarcerated. However, as it was definitely done secretly, none of the usual rolls or books will be of help, and I am having to explore ancillary and obscure archives and correspondence, again without the help of my assistants.

From the Keeper of the Green Cabinet,
Wizard Suzanne Palindros,
to Captain of the Guard David Tzikes,
copied to Her Majesty the Queen,
sent with all haste by a spirit of the air

DEAR DAVID,

I am returning at once and will risk flying Wildbjorn close to the Stones in order to be back during the night, or perhaps shortly before dawn tomorrow. Her Majesty must remove *immediately* from the Scarlet Fortress and lodge in a building that has been built within the past century. I offer my own Palindros House, though I suspect her Majesty would prefer Onesuch Palace. If so, she must *not* enter the North Wing, which I believe predates the rest and may be several hundred years old.

Zelznibone has not emerged from some temporal stop or fastness. He still exists entirely in the past, but there is a connection with our present. I suspect some temporal fissure caused by his sorcerous efforts to communicate, rather than an intentional joining, as I believe he intends to threaten the Queen *of his own time*, that is, Katelyn III, not our own dear Monarch. However, because of this temporal fissure, he may be able to cast malevolent spells within any building that physically existed in his era, and if they are addressed against the Queen rather than Katelyn by name, they will, unfortunately, strike Her Majesty in our own time.

It is possible we may be able to exploit the fissure by utilizing a magical device I know of to send someone back to physically deal with him, as it is likely he is warded against a direct attack using magic. But to do so, we must locate him geographically, in addition to exploiting the time fissure that joins his moment with our own. Furthermore, any person who did venture into the past to give this wizard surcease would themselves cease to exist at the moment of Zelznibone's death because this would heal the temporal fissure. To find a suitable agent for such a task will not be easy. Perhaps a prisoner, who has no other hope of release, promised a new life of freedom? This would be truthful, even if the life be very short.

The spirit who brings this will return to me upon command. Keep me informed of any change to the situation. Its name is Ichuangor, and you should use the words, "Ichuangor, take this message to your mistress with all haste."

⸻

From the Wizard Zachariah Zelznibone
to Her Majesty the Queen

I KNOW NOT whether it is evil advisors I must blame or the canker that has ever resided within the black hearts of your family for my continued imprisonment. I had hopes the charming child I knew, the young woman raised apart from the noisome clan that calls itself the royal family, might not carry within her the vicious nature of her ancestors, but clearly, I was foolish. While it is true I remain physically bound by chains I cannot break, my magic is not so constrained, and I declare my revenge shall have no limit. In truth, I shall probably die here, but I will not die alone! If I am not released by the morrow's dawn, Your Majesty will die!

From Guard Captain David Tzikes
to the Keeper of the Green Cabinet, Wizard Suzanne Palindros,
sent via the spirit Ichuangor, copied to Her Majesty the Queen

SUZANNE, the latest message from Zelznibone appeared while I was in private audience with Her Majesty in the Onyx Room of Onesuch. One moment there was nothing there, and then on the floor at the foot of her throne, a folded paper. We both saw it at the same time. No servant of the air or any such creature brought it, I would swear, even if one could pass the wards.

Onesuch was nothing but fields and an apple orchard a hundred years past, so clearly, Zelznibone is not limited by the novelty or otherwise of the Queen's residences.

We must act! How can we send someone back in time to deal with Zelznibone? You mentioned a device. Can this be utilized before your arrival, as I fear there is no time to be lost?

From the Keeper of the Green Cabinet,
Wizard Suzanne Palindros, to Guard Captain David Tzikes,
sent via the spirit Ichuangor, copied to Her Majesty the Queen

I WRITE in haste and very untidily from my dragon-back perch; I trust you can read my scrawl. We are close to the Stones, and I must give most of my attention to directing Wildbjorn's flight. I am still at least four hours away.

Go to the Inner Armoury and obtain the amulet of the Arch Wizard Helen of Dran and the tablet that is with it. The incantation on the tablet, while holding the Amulet, will take the bearer back in time. Whoever bears the amulet should hold the latest missive from Zelznibone. This will give the direction in time, but we still need to know the place.

Be aware that I am now certain whoever goes back will cease to exist when Zelznibone is slain and the fissure in time is made whole. Furthermore, if they are successful, we should already know it, as past time cannot be changed as such. If it has been done, it has been done. Ask Fellquist to redouble his efforts to find the place of Zelznibone's incarceration and also any indication of how he met his end. Perhaps a name will be mentioned.

David . . . I beg you do not do this yourself. If you cannot find a suitable prisoner, there must be someone among the guards who would put themselves forward for any opportunity to do Her Majesty such a service. You are too valuable to Her Majesty to be risked. And dare I say it? Also, to myself.

**From Her Majesty the Queen
to Captain of the Guard David Tzikes**

DAVID, you are forbidden to use the amulet. Find someone else. Suzanne's notion of using a prisoner appeals. Though I cannot immediately think of anyone we have to hand. Is Isobel Armantero still in the Korraut? She would be ideal.

**From Archivist Fellquist to Captain of the Guard David Tzikes
and the Keeper of the Green Cabinet,
Wizard Suzanne Palindros, copied to Her Majesty the Queen**

As per your request, I have found something pertaining to the location of the prison containing the rascal Zelznibone in a ledger concerning the replenishment of the Threxen Shore Fortress at Rougefiere, which was destroyed along with much of the town in the great storm in the tenth year of the reign of Queen Baras II. The ledger covers more than a hundred years and contains a number of charges for the "keeping of the prisoner Zelznibone" during the reign of Queen Jayne IV and Katelyn III, so I deduce this is where he was imprisoned. I am not sure if this will be of much help with the current matter, given the place is no longer extant.

The charges for the prisoner Zelznibone cease in the month of Leafall in the second year of the reign of Katelyn III, and there is a notation, "NLOBBRR," but I do not yet know what this means. I will continue my researches.

Also, I wish to assure you again that I have adhered absolutely to Her Majesty's instruction. The materials relating to the succession of Queen Katelyn III have not been shared with any of my staff, and I have all the papers locked in a coffer in my personal chambers. There is only one key, and the mirror you gave me, Suzanne, watches over the room entire.

From Guard Captain David Tzikes to Archivist Fellquist and the Keeper of the Green Cabinet, Wizard Suzanne Palindros

GOOD WORK, Fellquist! Keep at it.

**From Guard Captain David Tzikes
to the Keeper of the Green Cabinet, Wizard Suzanne Palindros,
sent via the spirit Ichuangor in great haste**

SUZANNE, I am not copying this to Her Majesty. She has forbidden me to use the amulet myself, but I cannot in all conscience order one of my guards to undertake this task, and we have no suitable prisoners. Isobel Armantero was released more than a year ago— Her Majesty had forgot she was pardoned with the Third Repenters and sent into exile.

So I must do the deed.

But I am not particularly eager to die, so I will wait until the quarter-hour before the dawn in the hope that you might arrive and think of some other way of dealing with this problem.

However, should this not occur, may I finally say what has been in my mind these several years, crystallized in these last weeks by your absence and this looming crisis, and emboldened by the last line of your most recent message. I have been a fool not to express my love for you. I have loved you almost since we first met, when you came into Her Majesty's service. But I did not speak or act, knowing Her Majesty's dislike of romantical attachments among those who serve her closely. I think, I hope, you felt something of this too and held back for the same reasons. Perhaps I delude myself, but I wanted you to know. Not before it is too late, as it is too late. I simply want you to know, whatever your own feelings.

* * *

From Archivist Fellquist
to Captain of the Guard David Tzikes, sent via the boy Willem, EXTREMELY IMPORTANT AND URGENT!

READ this before you do anything! David, your last message to Suzanne came to me instead. I don't think Ichuangor is all that bright, or perhaps you understandably gave it the wrong verbal directions. I have sent the spirit on with it, but I am not sure it understood me either.

You don't need to use the amulet to go back to Zelznibone's time and kill him. What is it that this Wizard wants? He wants an order to be released from his durance from his own Queen, that is to say, Katelyn III. I have found such an order in the fifth Scarlet Box of the Judiciary, scraped the name from the parchment, and written in "Zelznibone." As soon as I finish this message, I will run as best I can to the Treasure House. I have already alerted the Keeper of the Seals to bring forth the seal of Katelyn III. Meet us there with the amulet, and then I believe we can use it to send the order for Zelznibone's release back to the wizard in his own time. No one will need to venture in time themselves.

There is still an hour to dawn. Meet me at the Treasure House!

From the Keeper of the Green Cabinet,
Wizard Suzanne Palindros, to Guard Captain David Tzikes,
sent via the spirit Ichuangor

ICHUANGOR CAME BACK to me but without a message! I will be there within the hour, minutes ahead of the dawn. Do not go back in time yourself, David! I fear you will. Wait, and I will essay the time fissure myself—I am sure that by my arts, I might survive the closure of it and still be able to return. I can save Her Majesty. Wildbjorn speeds me to your side. Do not go!

From the Wizard Zachariah Zelznibone
to Her Majesty the Queen

NEITHER ABEL nor Sarissa can tell me if it is dawn, the foolish creatures, and my guard has not yet brought me breakfast. Lacking windows, as I may have mentioned, I cannot see for myself. But I adjudge it must be dawn or close enough, and still I have not received the order for my release. You have brought a terrible fate upon yourself, Your Majesty. I do only what must be done. I know I shall die, but you will die first, and in—

From Archivist Fellquist to Captain of the Guard David Tzikes

CAPTAIN:

Once again, I proffer my most sincere apologies for my stupid accident, which came so close to upsetting everything. The boy

Willem should be rewarded, for his mind is very keen and he saw to the heart of the matter at once, taking the order to you without pausing for a moment to see if I had, in fact, even survived the fall down those cracked steps by the monument. I admit I was somewhat irked at the time, but he had the right of it. I suspect if he had not taken it on, I might not have been in time anyway, what with the Keeper of the Seals being so slow. She should be retired; I have said so these many years.

I have now found the meaning of the code "NLOBBRR" set against Zelznibone's name in the Rougefiere replenishment ledger. It means "No Longer On Books By Reason of Release," as opposed to "NLOBBRE," which indicates "by reason of execution," and "NLOBBRPOV," which was the notation used for "prisoner's own victuals," when they remained incarcerated but were not fed at the state's expense. But I digress. In any case, it confirms that Zelznibone was indeed released.

Allow me also to congratulate you and Wizard Palindros on your forthcoming nuptials. Should my leg be sufficiently restored, I hope to dance.

**From the Rose Garden Gatekeeper of the Scarlet Fortress,
Veronika Napp, to her sister,
the Deputy Laundress of the Avilla Fleet, Leonora Napp**

OF COURSE, I know what the fuss with the Queen and Captain Tzikes and the Green Wizard was all about, Nora! But as they say, a stone must not speak, should the mason's chisel be ever so sharp. I was at the centre of it too, and the girls earned thruppence each assisting, though it has been a sore trial to see it paid. We are all heartily glad it is over, and more than pleased the Captain and the Green Wizard have finally sorted themselves out and are getting married. I could tell you more, far more, but I am a stone, as you know, and speaketh not. Give Harry a buffet on his earhole and I will see you at the turn of the season when you come with the fleet.

***

**From the Wizard Zachariah Zelznibone
to Her Majesty the Queen Katelyn III,
as discovered in the Archives by Archivist Fellquist
and copied to the Keeper of the Green Cabinet,
Wizard Suzanne Palindros-Tzikes,
and Guard Captain David Tzikes-Palindros**

YOUR MAJESTY, it has been seven weeks since you so nobly but rather belatedly ordered my release, and yet I have not received my patent to assume the office of Rector of Snowwade, or a warrant to assume the post of Keeper of the Pale Leopards. I am aware those incumbent in either position must be removed, and perhaps that is the cause of delay. If this is so, I offer my services to remedy this situation. My powers remain as potent as ever, and I have been reunited with staff, wand, and athame.

As for the matter of the donative, I had not known the shortage of gold to be so severe, and so I will allow that it be paid in the form of a draft to my bankers, the Good Dames of Parrat Street. I expect to hear from them soon as to the successful arrival of a suitable sum.

If I may serve Your Majesty in any way, you have but to issue the command. I have already begun the making of a new mechanical monkey for Your Majesty, as I suspect dear Rollo may be winding down. It has been some years, after all, but I do not begrudge my time in durance vile and rest assured I blame the evil companions of the former Queen entirely.

I remain your most loyal and obedient servant,

Zachariah Zelznibone
Wizard of the First Class
Toymaker to Her Majesty the Queen

GOING TO GROUND

By Candas Jane Dorsey

After I had been in the cell for a while I started making spiders out of a small spitball of earth and my shed hair. Spiders are easy because of the symmetry. You can just cross four hairs and press them into the ball of mud. Once you get good at those, there are refinements. I managed to save eight eyelashes once, and built a tiny perfect eyelash arach who eventually bred with one of the real spiders to have hundreds of tiny eyelash babies. So beautiful, but they were too stupid, unlike their mother who could carry and spin messages, talk a little (I'd used a splinter to shape a tiny mouth), and wrote an entire monograph on the microscopic differences in types of plaster that, with her permission, I passed off as mine briefly when I needed something to show Amnesty International.

Of course, I had actually attributed it properly, but that was seen as delightful caprice from a truly gifted allegorical poet writing about confinement and social justice, instead of just another example of a talent suppressed by the prejudice of history (c.f. Clara Schumann or Berthe Morisot).

The eyelash spider and I shared a (rather rueful) laugh about that. When she disappeared, I tried for weeks to interest her offspring in science, or even in the art of detection, but they were hopelessly uninterested little libertarians, and finally I had to admit my friend had been a lucky accident of creation, a bit like the Mona Lisa. That serendipitous brush-stroke of a mouth.

I'd been earning a few bucks as a fish compiler before my arrest. Well, more than a few, and I may have cut a few corners. Sushi is all the rage again and I have a fondness for a particular grade of yellowtail, the kind with the very defined two colours and textures of flesh. That's hard to do within existing regulations. But I had a lot of high-powered clients, and none of them wanted to lose their supply, so I figured as long as I skated only a little way out onto the frozen lake, and avoided the big fish (pun absolutely intended), I wouldn't get onto ice too thin to support me. If you want to push the metaphor, I just stayed in the lee of the shore in my little winter shed and drilled a very small ice hole to fish through. Not my fault an iron monster swam by and came up to my bait, gathering ice, shed, my gear, and me in one huge gulp. Here I am in its belly, and that's barely a metaphor, these days.

Maybe where you are, spiders don't talk yet, dogs are still people's best friends, and cats aren't yet collaborators in disobedience. In the cell next to mine, at least one brown tabby and I know for sure two gelded orange toms, along with an assortment of dogs, are crowded into a delicate détente, broken a couple of times a day—but it's more likely for a terrier to snarl at a Pom than for a full-on species war to break out, specist stereotypes notwithstanding, and no serious enmities arise.

They know that the enemy of one's enemy is one's friend.

WHEN YOU COMPILE a fish you don't want traced to you, you have a choice. With the best equipment, you can strip off all the copyright protection and present it as a natural fish. This only works if two preconditions are fulfilled: the fish has to be from a species still extant somewhere in the wild, and you have to have the best equipment. Oh, three, actually, because if you really want to sell it, it has to be legal to catch that fish, or farm it, somewhere in the world. Good luck with cod, for example. Trying to sell clean cod with un-marked genes is pretty much the classic definition of Too Stupid To Do Crime.

If you don't have the best equipment, and can't afford to have it ever, and can't figure out who to bribe to get unauthorized use of it, your options are more limited. Go to plan B or C.

Second option: you spoof the tag of a bona fide dealer who has the rep you need.

Third: you scribble the tag so that it isn't readable at all. Everyone knows the fish is fake but if you have scribbled thoroughly, scribbled a lot, and maybe scrubbed a little, you can't be traced. The signature is useless. This is the cheapest option, but it's labour-intensive. You have to do it microscopically and literally bit by bit. Guess which one I had to use. Go on, guess.

IN GENERAL, someone in power just has to think that it's a crime to make things, and someone else, someone who has to punch up, has to disagree. That gives you your baseline for insurrection.

Incognito, become a reluctant, hesitant revolutionary.

Civil disobedience is a grammar, a technique, a medium.

When even painting a landscape is a disastrous act of defiance, art is resurrected as significant.

When I sit down to make something, whether it's a spider or a manifesto—and what's the difference between those, really?—I tend toward the obvious and the didactic, and get caught, but there are people in our movement who are true heroes of the revolution, so poetic and allusive that their acts are almost impenetrable to interpretation.

They are probably only not here in jail with me because no-one can figure out whether they made a book, a painting, or just a refrigerator or an algorithm.

THE SPIDERS I make are very different from my fish. Different process, and also they are not as tasty. A sour joke, unfair to my eyelash friend: I asked the tabby if it was true that spiders are sour, and she said, "Yes, true. Bitter and not really worth eating, but it's my nature."

Quizzically furthering the question, I was given to understand that a spider's sideways scuttle in the night had often triggered a primal response to lateral motion, but the tabby of late had come to regret her heavy and automatic paw.

"It was someone new to talk to," she said, which is how I discovered the fate of my eyelash buddy. "I'm sorry," she continued when she saw my reaction. "It startled me when I was napping. I didn't mean to."

In other words, *it's my nature.*

The defence of half the murderers in the world, but under the circumstances, I decided not to turn my grief into a grudge. Life in here didn't allow such luxuries.

I did take a small revenge, though: I spent about a week telling her about my fish business, in detail. That cell was fed dry crunchies—cat or dog varieties—and water, and the tabby would unconsciously make little subvocal squeaks or gasps as I talked about tuna textures. After a while I got over that level of pettiness, partly because I came to like her, partly because the others were just as affected, and it wasn't fair.

You know all about the bats by now, and their magical physiology, from which we stole anti-ageing and good health the way Prometheus, Dr. Dee, and Dr. Frankenstein stole fire from heaven, and with similar paradoxical results. Bottom line, at the end of the upheaval, anyone with bat DNA—as detected by eyeballing the genotype of anyone who wasn't dead enough in one of the pandemics—was a criminal if they weren't rich enough to have bought the cure: a classic case of Anything Not Compulsory Is Forbidden.

It wasn't necessary to eliminate all the bats to bring about the chiroptocracy: that was just a side-hustle that the very rich used to safeguard their stuff—the Watts Prediction of 2021 came true a lot faster than was reasonable. But what he didn't predict was how we would all get conned into participating in a scheme that makes that whole thing with the Chinese and the birds look like a conservation event.

Bounties on bats, patriotic purges, all the things. Anyone with a bat house in their back yard was a terrorist: let's just say that besides my grandparents' kind of civilly-disobedient gene-hedging, a lot of doughty old gardeners who had liked the old mail-order biz Lee Valley ended up spending some time in a black ops facility when they were too old to really enjoy it.

My parents were the second-gen, of course: they loved the nano, and wanted to combine and bond with whoever was left after the mass extinctions. Spiders, cockroaches, glass fish, hedgehogs, Arctic hares: they used themselves and their offspring as subjects, so I suppose I should be thankful I'm not Gregor Samsa or Harvey. (Very historical. Never mind.)

On the other hand, since any tweaks, even just nano, will twitch the profile nowadays, that put me in the illicit fish biz whether I liked it or not.

The spiders were just a bit of harmless fun on the side.

In fact, I came to like all of my neighbours.

I could hear them—oh, could I hear them—but I couldn't see them unless one of them crowded into the very corner of their cell. Over time they took turns curling up there, and we would trade stories. Because there was only one of me, I made up a new biography every day, a source of some wonder and amusement to the literal-minded among them; in exchange I heard their lives.

The two orange lads, Dave and Henry, loved each other more than anyone else. That was it. They were agreeable old geezers really, and if they had been humans, they would have definitely ordered bat houses and dibbers online, back in the day. The tabby called herself something I couldn't pronounce, but admitted that her humans had sometimes called her Tig: despite their unoriginal attitude to naming, she loved them and had carried messages between their underground studios, had inevitably been caught—pastel dust on her paws and a tube of quinachrodone red in her mouth, capital offences, more or less, but it was a first offence, so she got fourteen years, a.k.a., at her age, life. She never saw her artists again.

The Yorkie, Washington, had been a companion dog to a guy in a wheelchair. He had bitten his friend's arresting security officer and been kicked across the room (he still limped), and his human companion had still been dragged away, also never to be seen again: his failure to—impossibly—save the guy still haunted him. The Golden Retriever, Zaroo, had a similar story, but without wheelchairs and with some peculiar betrayal that seemed to only make sense to the sheepdogs.

Those sheepdogs. The Highland kind, they had been code-breakers and code-talkers, and they really were a pain in the ass. They refused to tell anyone their real names, for spy reasons, which was also annoying AF. The egos on those otherfrackers, srsly. But get them in the right mood, and they had some amazing stories.

The rest of the dogs—except the Pom; I'll get to the Pom later—cycled through on short time. Denzel was a white standard poodle, ironically-named by the ancient hipsters who had been harvested when they passed their demographic sell-by date. He was repatriated out of here into a new fureverhome on the condition he inform on his new family: unclear if he did it willingly. Carrie was a Bassett in hunting trim and was taken off to be a government scent-hound. We think they did something to her brain, but we never found out what. Maybe she just wasn't that bright, but conspiracy theories aren't theories any more, these days, so you never know. Rami was an Akita, and spoke very little English, so we never really found out her story, but she had some awful scars on the side of her face and neck.

Aside from Tig, with whom I formed a surprisingly strong

bond after all, Kvit the Pom was probably the one I liked best. A very anti-Russian Ukrainian who turned up after Mari but apparently for keeps, he had been an interpretive dancer until his rear knees gave out, but now mostly identified as an installation and performance artist, and he was always working on something new, even in jail: I have never known anyone to need a job so badly. I expect it is some kind of compulsion, the way a poodle I once knew would arrange the shoes in rows at the front door, or a vampire has to stop to count all the grains if you throw rice down in front of them.

So ANYWAY, there we were. I'm not being rude about vampires: we jailbirds have nothing better to do in a day but count the rice.

BIRDS. That's another thing. Don't get me started on birds.

IF YOU READ Hugh Everett III, a very old-timey guy, you will know something about why I can do more, I believe, than my grandparents or parents on the spider front. Everett was the guy who posited the theory of time that says that everything that can happen does happen, that all branches of a superposition are actual and none more real than the rest, which results in an individual not being a thread through time, but rather a kind of thick interwoven knot through all dimensions, a bad macramé of time, a dreadlock of superpositions, tangled and baffled and freed in time by our ability to be All the Things at Once. This is a theory of course, but it explains me to myself. I figure I have only one real superpower, but it is the power to insist that the line I walk is one where my power works.

Think about that for a moment and it actually makes sense: I insist on an event and it must occur. I choose any option from the menu and I Make It So. It doesn't matter what the event, I choose my superpositions with a fierce and pointed will, and like Dillard's weasel, I do not let go.

THAT'S all.

I COULD DO spiders off the cuff, but I couldn't do fish because they are real things in the real world and for that, I need equipment. But I could sure do spiders, so I did.

Slightly bigger than my late eyelash friend, my fingernail-paring arachs are strong and curious. I convinced my neighbours to let the first ones I made look for their tough, sproingy, and sensitive dropped whiskers, used these as raw material for bigger, more militant hefties with longer range and more cunning. They turned out strong anyway, but I further reinforced them with some plating made of discarded claw-sheath fragments, and trained them to fetch. Carefully keeping them all out of paws'-reach, and avoiding guards' ken as much as their report-back function would allow, I sent the hefties marauding—for better food, the keys, sushi, paper clips, anything—with the parings along for reconnaissance.

Of course I was caught.

You were expecting that.

I suppose I was too.

But I was So. Damned. Bored. (The Pomeranian understood.)

"THE SPIDERS WERE JUST a bit of harmless fun on the side."

I tried to tell them when they came for me.

It's a fine line, being transparent from the bottom up (maybe there is more glass-fish in me than I know). If you just say what you know immediately, torturers will assume you are lying, because they would in your place: c.f. jaundiced eye. If you hold out too long, your friends get hurt. But no matter what you do, there is going to be some initial, deliberate collateral damage, because the thing about these folks? They seriously do not believe anyone understands them, listens to them, or believes their threats, I suppose same reason as above. So they like to start out with a little demonstration.

I like to read old blogs, back fifty years when people were so— well, whatever they were, they aren't now, so it's kind of restful. This one writer said that in stories, the writer can murder anyone except the cat or the dog. They were talking about fiction, of course, before dogs and cats were what they are today. These days, murder of all kinds is as common as dirt.

So I was already begging and yelling when three of them dragged me out of my cell into the corridor, and kept it up as two more went into my little palace and killed any arachs they could find. Which was a lot, because they had burst in, shock-and-awe style, while I was sleeping and the spides were playing. A few got away because Tig yowled a warning. Tig doesn't sleep much at night either.

I was hoping they would consider arachnocide enough.

Alas.

One held me shoved me up against the neighbouring gridwork, while the leader unlocked the other cell and the rest went in. I could see the whole thing from this new perspective, my cheekbones wedged between the bars: a ragged rectangle about twice the size of my cell, with doubled-up, bulging chicken-wire reinforcing the bars. Each of my buddies had staked out a little area where they placed the few possessions they had been allowed to keep: a couple of broken collars with tags of contact info for people long dead; the Go board the two code-talkers had made out of the two kinds of food (and since they were the same colour and dogs are kinda colourblind, they played by nose, the clever little curs), some other small pathetic heaps of indeterminate matter, and a couple of contraband ping-pong balls the spiders had rustled up for them. It was pitiful. In one corner, there were even a couple of Utility Spiders and one Jumper, backing away slowly—as were all the denizens of the cell—and trying not to be noticed. We aren't the arachnoplasts you've been looking for.

The guards waded in with equal-opportunity boot-crushing. The ping-pong balls shattered, their explosions as productive as a frag grenade. I saw sharp shards hit faces, blood start. The leader leaned in beside the guy holding me and said in my ear, "Which one is your favourite, huh, fishfracker?" With a flick of his finger, he indicated to a minion to approach each one in turn, while he scanned me with his go-stick for micro-expressions or changes in pulse. How the hell that showed him anything when I was already in panic mode, I don't know.

"Pick one," said a minion, "and we might leave the others

alone." I let my knees unlock, and sagged in their grasp, getting a couple of go-stick shocks that I hoped messed up the protocols enough.

"I don't care about these fracks," I whined. "Y-you killed my spiders, yo!" *I* would have been convinced, I was that good.

Boss-ass snorted. "You think this is my first rodeo, asshole?" For frack's sake, how long has it even been since there was anything like a rodeo?

Washington threw himself in their path, begged them to take him, but they nudged him aside, barely a kick, contemptuous, and looked around with their Two-Feet Good Jerkface stares, and fixed first on Dave. Henry intervened, with a fair amount of claw action, and one of them shook an angry cat off his arm and said, "Frack! Kill 'em all," and another one said, "For Pete's sake, Jason, don't be an asshole," which was pretty rich, raised his go-stick and shot Tig.

[this space intentionally left blank]

WHEN WE GET personal time travel for real I'll probably use it most for sleep, a handy snooze button, but I will definitely make use of it for moments like that.

I WRENCHED AWAY from the goons and threw myself across Tig's little body. Luckily go-sticks have a small-calibre pellet and it was a through-and-through, so she still had a thready heartbeat and some shocky breathing. Under cover of my body, I thrust some earth from the floor into the exit wound and spidered it shut. Then I had a discussion with the options and picked a reasonably accessible superposition I could live with. She probably wouldn't be happy with her new flank but she wouldn't be dead.

I also made as big a fuss as I could manage, letting out all the wailing and shouting that I would have done anyway. I didn't want them to shoot anyone else.

I was still working on the entry wound when they pulled me up and away, which was probably good, as there was still a convincing seep of blood.

"If it doesn't live, drag it out of here later," said the squad leader, and they all swept out of the cell, clanging the door, and dragged me off.

———

To MEET MY TORTURER, my fate, all or none of the above. But it seems affected to say so. After Tig.

———

I HAD USED up a good deal of willpower ensuring Tig stayed alive. Sometimes the process is exhilarating, as when I made the spiders, and sometimes exhausting. Guess which this time.

As I walked amid the uniformed, black-helmeted goons down the irrevocable corridor I formulated a theory that I may or may not have thought before: the more people and choices involved in the process, the harder it became until it demanded total exhaustion, commitment on an exponential graph, asymptotic with impossible but never really reaching it, limited only by my own ability to ask, all the way to the point where *almost* was indistinguishable from *fully* and probability stopped wiggling.

Right now it lay limp and comatose, and so did my ability to affect or even expect what was going to happen to me.

In the room at the end of the hall, the committee waited. I felt that zero at the bone that we call a sinking heart. There were five people here. I was a spider on a pin, immobile, neutralized, and they didn't even know it. There is something to say for a regime whose quantum effects occur unconsciously: they may never notice—and someday I will figure out something better.

As I walked through the doorway, I reflexively looked up. A tiny spider was folded into the corner of the doorframe, tense and immobile. Not alone, I was able to take a deep breath, a brief respite that was over when the cohort shoved me into the waiting chair and zip-tied my ankles and wrists and, new wrinkle this, neck to its purpose-built anchors.

EVERYONE KNOWS that the results of torture are unreliable, but people do it anyway despite the very small veracity return, so I've come to think that it's because some people just enjoy it. Perhaps not a profound insight, but a distressing one. And apposite at that moment. But I am not into inflicting or receiving pain, nor giving it more bandwidth, so I am not going to say what they did to me or much about how I reacted. Anyway, the next few hours are a bit murky, what with one thing and another.

By the way, they say pain sharpens the thinking.

This is not true.

At one point I was floating above my body watching various things be done to it, and I had time to think about bat DNA, fish trademarking, Washington's hopeless quest for martyrdom, and Tig's pigment-stained paws. I had time to think about superpositions—such as the one I was in at that moment—and super-predicaments ditto.

I also thought about my maybe-new insight in the corridor. If I had exerted myself to major transformations in the past, I'd done so at the risk of remembering nothing. Total exhaustion means total.

I should mention to you that I did know some names. A lot of names. Whether I'd done something radical before or not, those names were solid. The names of the people who had to go missing for the new regime to work. The Resistance blah blah same old same old. I was holding out so far, but maybe the regime would exert enough of their unsubtle will on me and I would tip. The names had needed me to encrypt their messages, sent by fish, and I had needed to know who they were, and some inkling of that, some errant scale, some fin, some tiny flexible bone of under-standing had leaked.

I was alone against the machine now. Realistically, I was losing.

I had to look at what would change. I had to take it far away from me and this jail and my friends and think about what would make the most long-term impact.

Are you one of hers? I asked the spider.

Are you kidding me? it replied. *You mistake me for one of those idiots?*

I looked closer, not at the wrinkled carapace or the kinked legs. I looked at the mouth, and I recognized her.

What—? —? How—?

This is what happens when you go through the digestive system of a goddamn cat wrapped in spider-thread, she said, *and you should be damned lucky I don't hold grudges or you and your little feline friend would both have died with your mouths and noses sewn shut. Just sayin'.*

Are you a ghost? Is that what this is? Am I dead?

Another voice from behind me. *You should be so lucky, human,* said Tig's discorporate self, flat as a light beam, as she squeezed through between the door and its frame.

Tig popped free and re-inflated. A long thin strand linked her the way I was linked. I noticed that the link was not from the navel of my body but to my left heel, and Tig's joined at her left heel too. It seemed counterintuitive, made moving very asymmetrical, but was no weirder than any of the rest of this.

Don't eat the spider again, I said.

As if. She was pissy enough about it the first time.

Why didn't you tell—oh, never mind. We are in a Situation here.

Looks more like you are, said Tig, looking pointedly down.

Pick what will make the most difference and just do it now, Eyelash snapped.

How do you—never mind that either.

It's not as if it's the first time, she said, and Tig laughed.

Fine. Right. Be that way.

By the way, thank you for saving my life. Tig spoke rapidly. *But if you don't hurry up, I'll be dead again. This stuff isn't easy.*

Tell me about it, said the spider, and let herself down by a thread. I did a double-take. There was a spider body on the ceiling, and then there was her, in front of me. *Fracking ectoplasm,* she said, and laughed.

I reached out to each of them. They seemed surprisingly solid.

Sorry, I said.

Quit wasting time, said Tig.

IT'S NOT a process I can easily describe except by metaphor. I spread myself very widely through the current probability and looked for weak and strong spots. Either one would be workable, but I preferred weak. Guess which I got.

Every oligarchy has to have an oligarch. They couldn't agree on an überBoss, so the new world order is a club of oligarchs. What we have learned in the last fifty years is that the real oligarchs are not always the political and corporate figureheads, but usually the backroom fixers who decide which lives are important. Small lives versus big lives. 'Way back when, Arnason nailed it in her Principle: it's not a battle between good and evil any more, it's between quality and shoddiness. Where do the shoddy of the world reside? How to find the ones who are really making this darkness last? Eyelash was my spotter while Tig kept an eye on the local situation and prompted me when I had to mumble something defiant.

They all look the same, you know. Bland and genial faces, quality suits (because yeah, it's still all about the suits), and they gather in restaurants and eat prime rib and filet mignon. Some beef compilers are living in luxury because of the hegemonic hunger for rare steak, and you can bet their bat DNA is legal. I'm a little jealous, actually. These people also love sushi and I was one helluva fishmaker. Maybe they could have blandished me with bat-powers and I wouldn't have ended up here.

Bat DNA. Okay, that's a place to start.

I narrowed it down to anyone with legal bat. Among them, I began to sort through the strands. I had enough *qi* to do something to the fates of maybe a dozen of them. Eyelash and I sought the ones with the most vigorous connexions. Some of them really were in the shadows. All backroom all the time. Others were spouses, executive assistants. Others stood right at the height of power. One particularly.

It wasn't easy to divert that many threads. I started in the shadows, and brought more shadow to several, obscuring their future, occluding their chances: a few non-fatal but crippling car accidents, a complicated birth, the detection of one's early-onset dementia. The half-bright were next: I sowed infidelities, betrayals, bad decisions, and a bout of food poisoning. The politicos are easier to bring down. Coups happen, right?

I stood before the last of them, the apex predator, the one everyone had tried to bring down and no-one could. I looked into his dead eyes, his sociopathically-unwrinkled face, and I couldn't find a harmless option. Everything about his life was predator. There was no place to hook even one good intention.

While I was looking, his gaze sharpened.

"You again?" he said.

"What? You can see me?"

"I saw you the last time too. I cut your translucent ass up and we put your body in jail. In a nice little psychic damper field. How the hell are you here?"

"I'm in the interrogation room," I said, and laughed aloud at his expression. I must have been very loud. Books crashed off the shelf behind him. He didn't even flinch.

"What are you going to do now, fishfracker? You with your principles and your peace vow and your save-the-world heart? You couldn't kill me last time, and I built it all again after you tried. Can you kill me now?"

I knew the answer. It was, "No."

I reached out anyway, and tried for a chokehold, and my incorporeal hands could not close on his neck. I pulled as much of my matter into my grip as I could, and still barely a dent. He waved his hands through my ethereal arms and laughed himself.

Oh, for frack's sake, said Tig, reached out into my left arm, drove our hand/paw into his chest, and stopped his heart. She didn't let go, and nor did I, until we could not feel his blood move or the electricity of his nerves, and the last tic and twitch of death had subsided.

You killed him, I said. I wasn't sure how I felt about that, and I couldn't decide on a path away from that confusion.

It's my nature, she said. She sounded exhausted.

He didn't look like much, crumpled on the floor, his pants wet with the urine his body released at death, his expensive tie askew.

Tig and Eyelash helped me get back.

MY BODY WAS STILL BEING TORMENTED.

It's going to take a while to trickle down, said Eyelash. *You may never know if you succeeded. Local conditions may remain the same.*

We'll wait, said Tig, and suddenly wasn't there.

Oh, crap, said Eyelash. *I hope she just passed out.* But we both knew that wasn't going to be true.

As if cued, I was back in my body, with all its pains and heartbreak, losses and confusions—

—thinking about the dreams pain brings, and how nice it was to see Eyelash again, even in a dream. The memory of that dream diminished to a black circle, into a dot—

—the dot on the back of a spider who hung from a thread in between my tormentors' faces and mine.

The committee apparently had a leader, who said, "Sling this one back into the cell. I don't think we'll get a damned thing. I think they got the wrong fish compiler."

Another one added, "Someone who could make revolution makes spiders instead—what a fool!" then reached out and grabbed the spider who looked like Eyelash, crushed it, and rubbed its remains off bloody palms.

<hr>

[this space intentionally left blank]

<hr>

IT TOOK me a long time to realize where I was. A cell, and in another cell next door, a Pomeranian who made it his work to tell me stories while I healed. There were a few spiders clomping around on hardy little feet, and a half-mad Yorkie who kept yelling, "Take me! Take me!", shushed repeatedly by code-talkers who said nothing else that anyone understood. There were others there. I could hear them, too.

One day the Pom sent me, via cargo spider, a little tuft of tabby fur wrapped at one end in a thread of spider silk. It looks a bit like a fetish, but it was a *memento mori*. And I did remember, a bit. I remembered a fragile spider with a smart mouth. I remembered a Tig, a tabby cat I think, a friend I am sure, who said, *It's my nature*.

What is *my* nature?

I think about that a lot.

I AM happy to imagine myself as a skein of time, a fabric made of all the versions of a life, endlessly superposed line upon line, but in four dimensions, each line no more nor less real, each leading somewhere I can't see because all I can really see is the line I'm on.

I posit that when I pick an option, it becomes a line in that moment, the solitary path I have to tread. Looking at this single inevitable line I keep willing onto being, I see no superpositions, just a timeline of one, and have to take the rest on faith.

Forest/trees.

But really, I am an infinite number of cats.

IF I BELIEVE THAT THESIS, there are things I can do.

I'm collecting eyelashes again. I have three.

We'll see.

BENEATH A BICAMERAL MOON

By Jeremy Szal

The aliens recapture me on the edge of the desert, just as I start hearing someone else's memory inside my head.

I don't realize what they are at first. It's something I feel rather than logically understand. Like I've unearthed a crumbling chamber secreted away inside my skull, cramped with events and memories I just *know* have aged with time. My implant—long disabled by my captors—fizzles and sparks as if performing a reboot. I frown, try to access it, but it's as dead as the blasted and scorched landscape around me: rolling dunes, soaring cliffs, and soul-destroying heat searing into the haze of far horizons in all directions.

It's all incredibly alien to me, as alien as the first day I saw it. But for a moment, I feel like I *know* it: every gorge, every crumbling ruin, every sun-bleached stone.

I don't know what to make of it. But I also don't have the chance to puzzle it out. I'm dragged back to the Citadel, back through the dozens and dozens of kilometres I ran. Back through this blasted desert. Back toward my punishment.

I'm strapped to a slanted cradle in an uncomfortable X-position, wriggling with a furious itch. They sprayed every inch of my body with powder from some mossy plant, and now my skin stings like I'm being constantly, relentlessly, endlessly tickled, scraped, and scoured by thousands of microscopic tendrils. The stinging in my armpits and the soles of my feet is the worst of it, threatening to draw tears from my eyes. I try to scrunch my feet and hands, rub my back against the sun-bleached wood, but it's no use. As a final humiliation, a steel muzzle has been fitted to my face.

It takes everything I have to remain silent. I won't give these alien heathens the satisfaction of seeing me suffer.

I learned early on the trick is to distract yourself with lesser pains. It's unpleasant, but it works. The furious Kharoom sun on my rapidly blistering pale skin, stabbing in my eyes. The mocking jeers from the aliens who've sauntered by to see their human captive taught a lesson. The sticky, chafing sensation of the prisoners' suit —dark purple, for human female captives—and harness I'm forced to wear, the thick, broad straps cutting tight over my back and shoulders and between my breasts, wrapped around my waist and thighs. It's a brief, if nasty, distraction from the apocalyptic itching.

But, of course, that's not the *real* torture here.

Past the piercing sunlight, past the spires of the alien city, past the limpid heatwave on the hazy desert horizon, hanging in the sky like the marbled brain of some celestial creature of interstellar myth, is Valbeck Habitat. My home. Even in orbit, its multitude of glorious spires and sweeping baroque structures sparkle in the sunlight. I can imagine it. The cool, polished plazas. The air-conditioned sanctum of the temples. The slow trickle of water in the bathing rooms and saunas that Joth and I would sneak into after curfew. I protested. Half-heartedly, of course. *Well, Sola, if you really prefer to study instead*, he'd say in that playful tone of his, his dark skin gleaming in the buttery glow, before I told him to shut up and pulled him into a hard, long kiss. He'd give a rich laugh I'd feel reverberating deep in his chest as he pressed up against me.

The sweet taste of his lips brushing against mine and the warmth of his hands on my hips grows stale in memory. What's he doing after all these years? Has he found some other girl?

My long black hair, pulled back into a high ponytail, flutters in the hot breeze. A familiar wave of hopeless frustration grips me, knowing I'm a prisoner of these aliens, trapped in this barren, scorching desert planet while the rest of my people dwell in paradise, waiting month after month, year after year, for rescue out of this misery.

"You'll have to look eventually, girl," Dren sneers. I open my eyes. I'm a tall, broad-shouldered woman, but I'm weedy in comparison to most Chaars, and Dren is no exception. His leathery green-brown skin affords a fierce protection against the searing desert heat. The multitudinous straps of the combat-harness that all Chaars wear run over his chest. His bloodstained armour is embedded with ornaments, bones, and skull fragments from rival warrior-chieftains. He's the one that captured me four years ago, when I was twenty-three and my speeder-vessel crashed. He jerks the back of my ponytail, my neck bending painfully, forcing my eyes upward.

"They'll come for me," I snarl through clenched teeth, sweat trickling down into my eyes. Making myself believe it. "Humanity never abandons their own. It's part of our Scripture."

"That so?"

"It's a matter of principle. But then, I don't expect a greenskin like you to understand that."

Dren sneers and sticks his face in mine, four-fingered hands hooked tight in my armpits, agitating the itching powder. My arms tremble in their straps as I fight an incredible frustration, being unable to bring my limbs down to my sides on reflex. "Well. Does your precious little *Scripture* tell them where to find you, girl?"

"Ah. The mighty chieftain warrior. Tormenting a helpless human captive. How so very noble." Rhiv snorts as he saunters over to us, his boots scattering hot sand. He smells of oil and leather, his red cape fluttering behind him in the dry breeze. At almost my height, he's short for a Chaar. He leans casually against his sharpshooter rifle. "Starting to see what all your bravery is about."

Dren laughs mirthlessly. It sounds like gravel being stirred in a bucket. "One minute in the arena, Rhiv. That's how long it'll take me to chop you into little pieces of meat."

Most Chaar would seethe at that kind of provocation questioning their honour. But Rhiv isn't most Chaar. "But we're not *in* the arena, are we? Pity. Oh, and our prisoner will spend the rest of her punishment on patrol with me. The other chieftains have agreed." Rhiv smiles thinly at Dren. "Unless, of course, you object to their decision?"

Dren knows when he's beaten. He leaves. Rhiv glances down at me askance. "Even for a human, you're still as stubborn as a rock."

"Sorry we don't all lie down and die for you."

Rhiv kneels over me, one hand gripping his rifle, dark-brown eyes narrowed. Watching me. He saw my eyes glazing over with memories just now. He must have. I wait for the hammer to fall. But it doesn't. "For both our sakes, don't try anything. If you do try and escape, I'll chase after you."

"Of course, you will," I say, smiling despite myself, knowing how to play Rhiv's game.

"And I will catch you."

"I'm counting on it."

"And I'll drag you back here, kicking and screaming."

"But I'll make you work for it."

"Can't make things too easy, can we?"

Even though it's Rhiv, he means what he says. I won't run. But I know how to seize an advantage when I see it. This little excursion will give me the chance to find out what's going on inside my head. And perhaps how I can use it to escape these creatures for good.

In the meantime, what am I going to do about Rhiv?

"Where we are going on patrol, exactly?" I ask as he goes about unlocking my muzzle.

"The Borderlands."

Suddenly, my plan doesn't seem like a good idea after all.

We shoot across the desert like a black thunderbolt on a sand-speeder. My suit creaks against the battered seat fabric, my knuckles turning white where I'm gripping the back of Rhiv's harness. I'm pretty sure he's throttling the speeder to test my stamina. I play along, determined not to show him how sick the velocity's making me.

Behind us, the city is an awe-inspiring glittering hive of architecture: twisting fractals frozen in sun-stained marble and bright stone, great plazas twisting off into blue domes and yellow spires, brazenly spotless against the dirty-gold desert sand. It's beautiful, no doubt, but it only serves as a reminder that the Citadel, like the planet, should be *ours*.

Little hurricanes of dust swirl as we zip past great sweeping graveyards, studded with the sun-bleached skeletons of bizarre creatures. Plumes of dust and sand come mushrooming up from the patrols of distant Chaar caravans like some massive phantasmagoria. We're going southwest, away from the lone human outposts, two hundred kilometres distant. I could steal a sandspeeder and make my escape, but Rhiv's linked my suit to his armour. He's frustratingly smart. I'm not going anywhere without incapacitating him.

We skid to a halt in the shadow of a soaring cliff. The dry, musty smell of sulphur and burned grass weighs heavily in the air. Within minutes of walking under the searing Kharoom sun, my muscles are on fire, and there are rivers of sweat down my back and chest. The sand's burning through my armoured boots. The thick fabric of the prisoner's suit sticks to my skin, gel padding pressing up against me, water-reclamation systems barely chugging along.

"How do you tolerate all the sand?" I grumble. "It gets *everywhere.*"

"You ignore it."

"Well, maybe I *can't* ignore it." I know I sound like a petulant child, but I need to lash out at someone after my punishment.

Rhiv claps me hard between my shoulders. I jerk away; I don't like being touched. Especially not by greenskins. "I think you've got more important things to worry about, Sola."

I fold my arms. "Like?"

"Like not provoking Dren. It's a good way to get yourself killed."

I'm still itchy from the torture, and scratch furiously at my chest before squinting up at him. "Seems like you had a bit of a death wish, yourself."

"I know you pretend to be stupid, so the others let their guard down around you." I just manage to keep a straight face when he says that. "But sometimes, I wonder if you really *are* stupid. Our tribal disputes are microscopic compared to this holy war you people have been fighting for centuries. For the ownership of a planet. *Planet,* Sola."

"It's *not* your planet," I say. It's too hot to argue, but I can't help myself.

"Oh, right. Of course. Your High Sanction looked into your astronav globes and declared it rightfully yours." Rhiv flings his arms wide and adopts a grand, mocking tone of voice. "The breadbasket of humanity. A new, untapped planet. Never mind it was already occupied with a Citadel of *millions*. Sola, do you really think you're the first human to make that argument with us?" Rhiv grips the back of my harness, not unkindly. "The sooner you stop trying to see all of us as the enemy, the better."

I clamp my teeth shut against a rebuttal. I have to conserve my strength, after all. I pull my focus into navigating the treacherous sandy slopes and narrow gorges. My Piousmen Instructors always told me that it is not victory that makes a person. It's her defeats. And I've been learning from mine: how these aliens think and behave, about their warrior-driven culture and fierce determination that allows them to carve out a living in this rugged wilderness. One day, I'll be able to teach my people so much about the enemy.

"So, you'd be smart not to attempt escaping again," says Rhiv. "You'd be even smarter just to take the ash. Place your allegiance with us. Make life so much easier."

"No. Never," I snap, harsher than intended. "I do that, you'll own me. Besides, I could never face my people again when they come for me. Someone like you could never understand."

"No. You're right. I don't."

I frown. Seeing a Chaar admitting to a mistake is like seeing a High Sanctum freely admit to blasphemy.

"But I do know your people aren't coming anytime soon. For your own sake, hold your tongue or lose it."

I hate to admit it, but the alien has a point. There's no telling how long the war will continue or when my people will set me free. I shiver at the prospect of decades upon decades of captivity. Chaars don't do prisoner exchanges. No. Escape is my only acceptable option.

The hairs across the nape of my neck prickle as we reach the Borderlands. The hard-packed soil's pockmarked with huge craters and gouged out with long furrows. Towers and battlements, stained soot-black, slant at perilous angles. Torn banners flutter in the sour wind. We enter into great, echoing halls of smooth marble, encrusted with cyan jewels that glisten in the swords of sunlight that pierce the domed ceiling. It's breathtaking in its beauty and utterly at odds with the bones jutting from the gritty sand like white daggers.

If the Chaars had a faith, this would be their grand cathedral. It has that same power, utterly irrevocable. *So much damage has been done to it. Such a tragedy it's been abandoned to the cruelties of time like this. Such a waste of—*

I startle. I know this place somehow. I'm responding to it emotionally as I gaze upon it, envisioning it unblemished and untainted by war. Ancient, solar-powered machines wheeze a few metres from me. A cold, dark ache blossoms in the upper left of my skull and spreads, giving rise to a series of fragmented, dreamlike images.

More memories. In my brief and ill-fated escape, I must have run past one of these ruins, something in the machine latching onto me and awakening my dormant implant, creating and opening a chamber to some artificial partition of my brain. A bicameral construct.

I can't think of any other explanation. How else can I remember standing here in this very place, centuries before I was even *born?*

We leave the halls behind, emerge into the open once more. I glance around the dilapidated ruins, the air heaving with hazy shockwaves, echoing with sinister whispers. I remember the thrum of machinery, the gurgle of thick liquids, the murmur of low voices, the scrape of cold stone beneath my feet.

Something terrible happened here.

Rhiv squints against the blinding sun, his cape fluttering in the wind as he peers down the long-range scope of his rifle in search of hostiles.

"And your people don't know what caused these places?" I demand. "Why some of these machines are still switched on?"

"War happened, Sola. That's all we need to know."

I climb up a sandy slope towards what was once a marble platform, swords of sunlight yawning down through the gaps in between the crumbling towers around me, and sweep my gaze around at them, my breath catching in my throat. This was a *laboratory.* Arcane experiments were conducted here. Black alchemy. The Apocryphal sciences. Like the leather-bound, gothic grimoires, ownership of which is punishable by ex-communication. Or worse.

And then I realize Rhiv's watching me.

He's seen my hazy, glazed-over expression. The same one I must have had when I was strapped down. The alien's eyes narrow. He knew something was wrong, and now he knows there's some connection to this place.

Suddenly, his dark eyes fly wide open. "Sola!" he roars.

Feral Chaars scramble over a hill in a chorus of shrieking. Without honour and without tribes, mad with bloodshed and cruelty, they rush toward us, bloodstained weapons sparkling in the dazzling sunlight. Six or seven of them. Two of us.

"Give me a weapon!" I yell to Rhiv as he joins me on the platform, getting the high ground while the Chaars scramble up towards us. The two of us stand back-to-back, our harness buckles rattling against each other. His muscles tense with hesitation. "Now!"

He knows he's got no choice, and if we die here, it won't matter. Metal scrapes as he unsheathes a curved blade and hands it to me. The gel-grip readjusts for my human hand.

After being so powerless and hopeless for so long, something primal ignites deep inside my chest. Old battle lessons spring to the present as I feint left, an axe hacking the air inches from my jugular. I hear myself exhale. I slash upwards with my blade and into the shrieking face of a Chaar. Black blood splatters as the blade bites deep into the creature's neck. But he's clawing for me, trying to go for my eyes, as if the injury is a mere inconvenience. The hilt is slippery with blood that I'm praying isn't mine. I rip the blade out of his neck and hack a long gash across his chest. A scream bubbles from the creature's mouth as he dies.

The ruins descend into a maelstrom of blood and teeth and hair, the heat like a hammer, and there's no space to think, to breathe, to do anything but *fight*. I hold my ground, my sweat-smeared vision shaking and throbbing. A Chaar clad in bright-blue robes sprays saliva in my face as he tries to bury an axe in my skull. I duck inside the swing and hack at his hand, severing three fingers in one clean sweep.

There's a glint of metal to my left. I yell a warning as a Chaar leaps down toward us from a high ledge. Rhiv wheels around and feints sideways, the bloodstained axe biting down between us, spraying dust. He cuts the attacking Chaar in half.

But the distraction costs me. I'm grabbed from behind, powerful fingers hooked around the straps of my harness, a fist smashing painfully across the back of my skull. My head whips forwards, and I'm thrown sideways, kicking up dust, legs tangled. I'm flat on my back, disoriented, breath sawing hard in my throat.

A Chaar in piecemeal yellow armour leaps forward, blade thrusting at my face. I scramble backwards, but I already know I'm dead.

There's an awful clash, and sparks spray my face. Rhiv has blocked the blade with his own, giving me time to scramble to my feet.

The Chaar's eyes widen in fury, his sword sent clattering away. But before Rhiv can kill him, the Chaar whirls around, battering his sword point aside and seizing him with ferocious speed. Hacksaw teeth gleam as the creature opens his mouth, lowering his head. It looks like he's about to take a bite out of Rhiv's neck.

The feral Chaar jolts. Freezes. Blinks heavily. I look down and see my blade's wedged in his stomach, my hands wrapped around the hilt.

The Chaar slides off the blade and crumples to the bloody sand.

I look up. Rhiv's eyes meet mine, and he gives me a long, hard stare.

I step back. My hands are still knotted around the blade, so it slithers free. I can't let go. We're both panting hard, soaked in sweat and spattered with blood, with half a dozen Chaars scattered on the sand around us. It's like my brain's been holding its breath this entire battle, and only now can a world of thoughts come crashing down.

"You can really handle yourself," Rhiv says with something approximating approval.

"Training at the Academy," I say.

Rhiv sees the blade clutched in my hands and grows serious. He extends an armoured hand. "Give it back to me, Sola. Now."

I could attack him with it. With the corpses piled up around us, there's plenty of evidence to plant the notion I've been captured or killed while I make my escape on the speeder. This could be my window. I could be back in the air-conditioned orbital temples within days.

Rhiv's eyes narrow. He senses my machinations at play. How can he not? But he doesn't hold me at gunpoint or restrain me or repeat his demand. He gives me the chance to comply. Like he's given me the chance to tell him what I've been feeling.

I hand the weapon back to him, hilt-first.

"Thanks, Rhiv," I say. I hook my hands around the chest straps of my harness to stop them shaking. "For, well, you know."

For the first time, he smiles, grips my shoulder. "You too, Sola. You too."

———

I'M A LOT OF THINGS. Some more prescient than others. But I'd like to think I'm humble enough to know when I'm wrong.

Which is how I've come to understand and accept there is indeed a strong similarity between those of my species and the Chaar. For all the battle-hardened and brutally fierce female warriors here, the Chaar underestimates us women. Despite my build, the chieftains all assume Rhiv single-handedly dealt with our assailants. It doesn't occur to them I've been trained to use weapons. Good. Better they don't know what I'm capable of. What I have planned.

It will not be the first time men have made that mistake.

Besides, I have no doubt I'd have cracked under captivity already if I were a man. Men can't deal with the strain of long-term isolation, especially in space—I'd always laugh at how pallid and sweaty Joth was after our service-pod pilgrimages. These four years have been tough, but I can endure them and endure four years further, if that's what's needed before I can escape.

But Rhiv's different. He knows how hard I fought. He's granted me two hours in the luxury baths to get clean. It's nothing like being strapped to a gel-seat and hosed down. Here, the water is actually *warm*. It's a mere sample of the comforts they'll heap on me if I take the ash and join their clan. I'm told other species have done so in the past. Once you do, they look past your origins, your past misdeeds. You're one of them.

But it's impossible. My people would brand me a traitor. Strip me of all my privileges and force me to live as a blasphemer, subject to constant humiliation and belittlement. If they don't imprison or execute me.

No. I'm a woman of Valbeck Station and I always will be.

Still, I'm pleasantly surprised when Rhiv starts training me as a warrior-student, part of his Scout Squad, regularly patrolling the Borderlands. We rise at dawn to a hellish round of exercises. We learn how to rifle Chaar weaponry. How to use curved blades. How to break your own thumb to escape the cuffs that wild Chaars carry. It's exhaustingly educational, but it's nothing I haven't experienced in the Training Modules. Standing abreast to the others – clad in those skintight orange-and-blue suits we women have to wear—pivoting from reciting Scripture to duelling and taking endurance tests from dawn to dusk. This is no different.

Well, actually, no. It is totally different. I really do have to remember that.

"This is yours," Rhiv tells me before we set out for the sixth circuit of the Borderlands. He stands from his seat, peeling his combat-harness off his back and wrapping it around me, securing the heavy, X-shaped straps tight and snug over my back, shoulders, chest, back, waist, and thighs, all buckles and straps connecting up and tightened. "We've completed six circuits together. That means I can pass down my gear to you."

I'd much rather change out of this hateful and chafing prisoner's suit, but I've long learned to be grateful for anything here. I frown and prod the black gel-grip blade jutting from my scabbard. "Um, you sure that's a good idea?"

"That's up to you, Sola. I won't have you working and fighting beside me if I can't trust you."

"Trust the enemy?"

"You're an outsider, true. Doesn't mean you have to be the enemy."

I raise an eyebrow. "That's noble of you."

"No. Not nobility. Honesty." He inhales from a tube issuing curls of hazy smoke, stuffed with a blood-coloured moss that grows in damp caves. "Something in rather short supply among both our people."

I laugh. "We've certainly got that in common."

"While we're on the subject, I need to know you won't try to cut and run again. The war's been escalating. Human dropships have been nearing the Borderlands, and the Chieftains are tense. They'll torture you for days, maybe *weeks*, if you run."

I shake my head, ponytail flipping from shoulder to shoulder.

"I won't." And I'm surprised to find that I actually believe it. For now, anyway.

But more pressing is that he knows that something is raging inside my head. I can see it in his eyes. It's a test. Will I show my hand first or wait for him to make the first move? He will deny it if I ask, and he knows I'll deny it if he does.

Well, I can play that game.

I hook my finger around the chest straps of my harness and plant myself in the padded seat the alien just occupied. "Hey, Rhiv. I appreciate the gesture. Our people . . . well, no one's given me anything like this before. Not really. Not without some other motive behind it. To test how pious I am, or whatever."

"You'll never take the ash if we continue treating you like a wild creature."

I twist my mouth. "You really want me to feel at home here, huh?"

"The world's cruel, Sola. It doesn't mean we have to be."

But that just makes the pain of losing my real home all the sharper. I quickly change subjects. "Swapping gear. You people have the weirdest rituals."

Rhiv thumps his chest. "It's yours who wear the fragments of fallen stars in your armour for good luck."

"How did you know that?"

"If you're going to fight a war, don't you think you should know who you're fighting?" Rhiv leans back, smirking. "Let me guess. You're only told that we Chaars are dirty, uneducated, barbaric, blasphemous creatures of primal urges." I feel my face going hot. "And they wouldn't extend the same courtesies to me if I was their captive, would they?"

"No. They'd torture you, straight away. Neuroprobe you and dissect you, like they did the other gre—Chaar captives." The words spill out of my mouth. I've never learned to hold my damn tongue. Why would Rhiv want to hear about the terrible things we've done to them? But I feel like I need to tell him, give him something in return. Show him we're not all the same. Like he's shown me. I scratch the back of my neck. "And here we are, calling *you* the savages."

Rhiv's dark eyes dissect me. "Not you, though."

"No," I say. "Not me."

THE MEMORIES COME TRICKLING in at a small but steady pace. I learn to compose a picture. Dimly lit silhouettes superimposed against the sprawling view. Robed and armoured figures looming over metal slabs upturned at an angle, their faces illuminated by monitors clustered with advanced biochemistry and mathematics. Genetic engineering. I know *what* they are, even if I don't understand it.

Beforehand, rare excursions out of cell saw me accompanied by red-robed, scar-covered guardsmen. But as the days blur into weeks and weeks blur into months and my Scout sessions accumulate, I'm given some freedom to roam the Citadel. Within certain boundaries, of course. So, I spend hours wandering the labyrinthine warren of dizzying streets, home to grand spice markets inside great domed cathedrals glittering with aquamarine and topaz gems, tech-alchemist workshops forged from sun-bleached wood and thick with sweet incense, and sweeping ship-yards where Chaars in armour and rigging harnesses build arrow-head-shaped glider-ships with elaborate mechanisms. I don't get as many puzzled and sneering looks as before. Some startle at seeing the harness I now wear, the respect a human girl like me has obviously earned. I smirk at them, pleased that I can at least surprise them.

The Citadel's so beautiful, I almost wish we didn't have to take it back for ourselves. Almost.

When I return from my Scouting, I sometimes climb up to the upper walkways and stare out at the view. Like I'd do back home with Joth. Nothing but us, the wind, and the dazzling landscape below. Rivers of sweat slither down my armpits and chest by the time I arrive. Mottled white tarpaulins stretched overhead barely shelter against the blast-furnace heat, and the breeze is a small, welcome mercy. But then I turn and see Dren's scowling, sullen face.

"What do you want, bastard?" I say. It's childish, but I don't care.

Despite his lumbering size, he's shockingly fast. He grabs my harness, locks my arms around my back, and wraps his body around mine from behind, slamming me up against the wall. "It seems the worm in our spine is growing comfortable here," he sneers, hot breath blasting on the nape of my neck. I squirm, but he's got me in a death grip. "You're going to screw up, girl. And when you do, I'll be there. You heard about what I did to my own squadmate just two days ago?" I did. I pale. Dren grins at my inability to tame my fear. "Of course you did, you little rat. Sneaking about everywhere, playing ignorant, spying on us. Well, my squadmate went out to retrieve a friend, injured in battle. But there's no room for the weak, the crippled. The honourable thing would be to die in the wastelands, and hope the sun kills you fast. I ordered them to dig their graves until their fingers started bleeding. Then I took their hands, their feet, their scalps. In that order. One of them lived for almost a week, too." He pats my chest, eyes narrowed. "The strong survive, the strong kill. Just give me an excuse, girl. You'll see what I'll do to a rotten, thieving, scheming rat like you."

"I've got blood on my hands, too." I'm speaking before I realize I'm doing it. "I've killed a dozen of those wild clansmen out there. You know, some of them look awfully similar to you. Maybe I'll get confused, fire off a loose shot in your direction. Killed by a weakling, captive human." I twist my head around, smile up at him. "How's that for honour?"

Dren's even more surprised at the outburst than me. His eyes go dark with venomous rage. He's not used to his prey talking back. The thrill of adrenalin bubbles and rushes through me. This is what power feels like. And it feels good. A warrior's rush.

"You insolent little cur."

"The insolent little cur who can fight back."

Dren grunts. He shoves me sprawling forward in a tangle of limbs, dirt spraying in my eyes.

"I won't need to get you to dig a grave, *girl*. That tongue of yours will do it one day." He grins, points back up to Valbeck Station. "And they'll never know what happened to you."

He stalks off. I smooth down my crumpled suit and scavenge for an oilcloth to clean my gear. But as I sit down, my thoughts turn to Valbeck Station. I wish they didn't. There's only pain there. The pain of knowing they'd call me a coward. A traitor. A blasphemer, even, for not killing an enemy of the Sanction, for not helping to rid Kharoom of these heathen aliens. They'd say I'm no child of the stars. And now, I'm friendly with the enemy, wearing the enemy's battle-harness.

You don't know what it's like! I want to scream. The hopelessness, the frustration. The *powerlessness,* the *humiliation* of captivity. How could I *not* be a coward, having been abandoned here by my people for all these years?

Rhiv saved my life. They never have. *They're* the cowards.

My throat hardens. Now, that *is* blasphemy. The worst kind.

But I don't care. And the realization, the sudden freedom of it, feels even better than angering Dren.

Rhiv's arrival jolts me out of my thoughts. He sits down next to me, claps me hard on the back. "Now. Sola, did you want me to ask about the visions, or are you just going to tell me at some point?"

I squirm in my seat. "You've known that they're visions for a while, haven't you?"

"There've been rumours of lost wartech in the Borderlands. But no one's found it like you have." The alien nudges his elbow into my side. "Also, I'm curious."

My hair whips in the warm breeze. The flags, banners, and sigils, flapping and snapping all around the city, form a colourful mosaic against the dry and barren background of the desert. "And if I don't want to tell you?"

"Well. Then I'll be forced to break your legs, rip open your ribcage, and feast on your organs while you're still breathing." Rhiv clacks his tongue—the Chaar equivalent of an exasperated eye roll. "Sorry, Sola. We're not all the savage beasts your people make us out to be. You won't lose anything. Except my trust."

Somehow, that's even worse.

Maybe I'm desperate for a friend. It's a moment of weakness, but right now, I don't care. I blurt it all out. "I'm seeing *memories*. Some kind of laboratory, I think. Experiments."

"What kind of experiments?"

"The forbidden kind. Experiments that have gotten scientists, alchemists, and academics excommunicated. Tampering with human biology, physiology." The stomach-dissolving dread mixed with the heady thrill of discovery, of achievement, is so strong it's almost tangible. It can't be anything else. "Upgrading us. Making us . . . survive."

"But survive what?" Rhiv glances sideways. I follow his gaze across the barren, bitter landscape. Sand and jagged rock and soaring windswept ruins, smearing into a haze of shadows and heatwaves.

"The desert," I whisper.

"Your people were trying to survive living here on Kharoom." The alien grips my shoulder hard. "That's what those ruins are. Lost experiments."

"Only one way to find out for sure," I say.

"You know what we said about doing stupid things? That's a very stupid thing, Sola."

"You said it yourself: you're curious. Besides, we've got to know. Before someone turns it into a cruel weapon."

"Who? Us? Or you?"

"Both," I say. "It doesn't matter. All the screams, the pain I'm hearing, feeling . . . no one deserves all that."

Rhiv fixes me with a long look. Relaxes. "I know just the place. We'll get our answers. Although we may not like them."

***

WE SLIP out of the Citadel at dusk.

We keep low and hug the shadows as we traverse trackless terrain. Valbeck looks like a metal egg, and I imagine it's cracked open, smearing the sky a vibrant orange with its yolk.

The journey is surreal and awfully similar to my own escapes. The exception, of course, being that I now have a Chaar helping me.

The irony isn't lost on the alien. He tugs on the back of my harness. "You're enjoying this, aren't you, Sola?"

"Got plenty of practice," I say. "Used to sneak out of my Academy Quarters all the time, back on Valbeck."

One eye pressed to his rifle's night-optic scope, Rhiv sweeps the marble structures flanking the Citadel outskirts, sloping off into ravines and rocky gorges. "I was wondering where that rebellious streak came from. But try to run, and—"

I roll my eyes. "You'll catch me, you'll drag me back, yes, I know."

"Ah. You're learning. Good. There's hope for your species after all."

"Shut it, Rhiv."

The hot wind's blasting in from the western horizon. Sand's found its way into my suit, chafing along my back with every step. My mouth's gone uncomfortably dry and my heart's hammering against my ribs as I follow Rhiv along a thin path that snakes through a deep cleft in the cliff face. But despite the dread, I feel strangely safe in Rhiv's presence. I don't trust this world, don't trust whatever's infesting my skull, so that leaves me trusting him. I hope that trust survives the truth of what we're about to discover.

You'd never know it, but Rhiv's told me reports of the war escalating between Chaars and humans, with humans being pushed further and further back off Kharoom. It'd make me feel even more hopeless, knowing any chance of being freed from captivity has grown thinner, except I'm starting to realize how little I believed I'd ever be rescued.

"Where are you taking me?" I ask the alien. He's been strangely silent on the subject this whole time.

His cape flutters in the hot wind as he glances back. "Someplace no one's been in centuries."

"Why?"

"Even faithless greenskins have their own superstitions."

I chew on my cracked lips. The journey takes two hours, which soon becomes four. More sand slips into my suit, my boots, gathers in my hair. Finally, we scramble for purchase down a rocky slope that leads to a soot-coloured stone archway carved with squared-off runic symbols.

The fibres in the stonework glare to life, casting sickly greenish light everywhere. There's a cathedral-sized space in here, the walkways gutted out. Rhiv goes about tightening and readjusting my harness before we abseil down into the massive space. The straps bite into my shoulders and chest. I gaze around in wide-eyed astonishment at the kilometres of hitech machinery gathered here, half-submerged in centuries' worth of sand and dust. I run my hands across the metal benchwork, tan-coloured hardware that was once white. Bas-relief images are carved high into the stonework around us. The sulphurous, dry, musty smell of Kharoom has been replaced with something far stronger. Like chlorine or bleach. Something chemical.

"This is the laboratory you saw." Rhiv's voice echoes strangely off the sweeping domed ceiling, his boots like gunshots on the marble. "Where all their experiments must have happened. Sola, what do—"

Without realizing when or how, I know.

I have one of those banned, bicameral datafiles inside my head. Has to be. Nanofibres unravelling and feeding me data, merging someone else's memories organically with my own, into the mosaic of my grey matter, so I can't tell the difference. I'm a woman of little more than twenty-five years old, with a brain containing *centuries* of memories. Memories I swear I've lived. And seeing this place, *again,* has triggered a surge of information, gushing into the present.

"No," I hear myself saying. "No. It . . . it can't be."

The world slides back into focus. Rhiv's grabbed me by the shoulders. I'm shaking. "Sola! What is it? What—"

"It's us," I say. "It wasn't just humans doing experiments here. It was your people, too. Experimenting with our genetics, our bodies. *Our* people."

Rhiv's face twists. He steps back. "You're saying Chaars and humans are *one* species? That we were *created* here?"

"No. I'm saying I'm not human." I spread my arms, sweat trickling down my ribs, my armpits. "I'm a Chaar. Every human being on Valbeck is a Chaar. Rhiv, our two species have a common ancestor."

Rhiv's pacing in dizzying circles around me, lighting up one of those mossy tubes to calm his nerves. I could go for one myself. "This is a little hard to take in, Sola."

"Yeah? Rhiv, my brain's telling me *I was there*. I remember *walking* in this room, hundreds of years before I was born." I fold my arms across my chest, scowl at him. "Want to try that on for size?"

"Fine. I get it. It's just—" Rhiv stops. "Ah. Of course. The experiments they were conducting. Humans . . . our people were trying to alter our bodies. Better adapting us to the desert. To live within the harsh wilderness."

"But something went wrong. They, *we,* weren't successful. We *mutated* ourselves. Created creatures that can survive the desert but don't look anything like us. Don't look remotely human." I swallow, glance around the fantastical, baroque cathedral. "I remember it all. People taking sides, arguing whether we destroy our mistake or not." I point to the walls, marred with soot-black stains, massive craters, and long gouges. "Someone made that decision early, wiped out *thousands*. All those ruins? The Borderlands? That wasn't from war. It was to bury a secret."

I'm out of breath. Rhiv's silent for an awfully long time. Finally, he says, "Sola, that means everything you believe, your faith, is all—"

"A lie." I want to start screaming with anger, with the injustice, but if I start, I won't stop. My chest shudders as I laugh. "A lie. The High Sanction, our gift to the stars, our arcane guidance, is all one big, fat lie. This holy war is built on a lie. Our conquest of the Citadel as humanity's breadbasket is a lie. Lies. Everything I've been taught, everything our people have been following for hundreds of years, is a *lie*." Tears of rage, of pure frustration, mist in the corners of my eyes. "That's why this holy war exists. To steal land back that was never ours, to destroy *ourselves*. And all we had to do was paint you as the heretics. Heathens. Blasphemers. That's all we needed to know to turn you into the enemy. Make sure the secret that could bring our empire down stays buried." I lean back against the cool stonework and tip my head back. "And I'm the idiot who swallowed the lies like the rest."

"You couldn't have known," Rhiv tells me.

"Yeah? I could have asked. Or looked closer. Or stopped to wonder *why* I hated you all so much."

Rhiv rubs the back of his head with the black-jelled handle of his rifle. "Well, it's hardly as if we looked closely at our own history, either."

"Seems like there's a reason why our people have a lot in common."

Rhiv responds, but I'm not paying attention. A small, smooth object comes arcing down between us. Purple gas sprays. I take two steps before I collapse face-first on the sand, the paralyzing agent gripping my muscles. Immobilizing them. It's like I've got anchors wrapped around my limbs.

Someone jumps down. Rolls me onto my back. Straddles me and pins my arms to the ground above my head.

"Well, well." Dren grins. "What an interesting conversation to have between a human and a greenskin. How about we start at the beginning?"

I'M SEETHING but utterly helpless. Rhiv and I are strapped back-to-back, bound with two restraining harnesses looped together, our hands shackled tight behind our backs. The back of the alien's harness buckle scrapes against mine as Rhiv furiously struggles. But no matter what we do, the straps only get tighter.

"This is humiliating," he mutters. Like *that's* the worst of our problems right now.

"I told you I'd be there when you screwed up, girl." Dren kneels in front of me, rifle jammed under my chin. I glare at him. "I just didn't expect to finally catch out Rhiv, too. Oh, I've waited so very long for this."

"Take your petty little feud and shove it," I say. "This is much, much more imp—"

Dren plants a vicious punch right under my ribcage. I gasp for breath as I jerk against my restraints. Veils of sweat and blood congeal in my eyelashes and trickle into my eyes. He must have hit me in the head, too. "The next time you take that tone with me, bitch, you lose your worm tongue."

"She's right, Dren." Rhiv twists around to plead with his fellow clansman. "If what she says is true, this is world-shattering. We can stop this war. It changes everything we know."

"True? It probably is true," Dren grunts. Up close, his rancid furs and sweaty, sulphurous stink make me violently nauseous. "But what of it? This war's the best thing to happen on Kharoom in centuries. We have a common enemy. An enemy we will eventually defeat. Our people have a purpose, and we're all the stronger for it. I told you, only the strong survive. You've always mocked me for that, Rhiv. Let's see how much you're laughing when I lead the clans into a victorious battle against the humans."

"You're no chieftain," Rhiv barks.

But Dren's focus is pinned back on me. "Speaking of truths, girl, did you ever stop to think why your people never attempted a rescue? Why no human has ever *been* rescued from our captivity?"

My blood turns to thick gel in my veins. Dren grins. Pats my chest. "Yes. That's right. The moment your shuttlecraft crash-landed on Kharoom, you became *ours.* Forever. They can't afford you coming back with your little history lesson and disagreeing with Scripture. Your little ideas, even if it's how we're not savage, bloodthirsty cannibals who eat young babies as treats. They can't afford to have you messing with their little orchestrated holy war, can they? No. They've cheerfully given you up to be our permanent prisoner."

No. It can't be. They wouldn't. They *wouldn't.*

Yes, they could. We're sitting in the ruins of the sordid price they paid, of the hundreds of innocents they vaporized into piles of rubble and meat, of the centuries of deception. What's one woman, having still not completed her Academy training, no less, weighed against their war?

I'm their sacrifice.

"I'm so very glad it's our people who've helped you to understand your own, girl." Dren opens his mouth and drags his tongue across my face. I shudder, recoil. "All that hope you've held onto all those years, was it really worth it? You'll have a long, long time to think about that." Dren's expression turns furtive, his voice going theatrical. "I tracked you down to these forbidden ruins, found you searching for a weapon, a way to spread malicious lies among our people. The courageous Rhiv tried to stop you, but you killed him, sawed his head off while he was still breathing. I managed to take you prisoner, but you lost your tongue in the battle, so you can't tell anyone your version of the events. Tragic. You'll be held in the Black Dungeons. Oh, the plans we'll have for you, girl." He tightens the chest straps of my harness, securing the two of us in place. "Don't worry. I'll leave a view of Valbeck open for you, so you can see your home, full of freedom you don't have, living a lie they'll always believe."

He unsheathes his serrated black blade, stalks around to Rhiv's side. And after Rhiv's been slowly loosening my cuffs for the last fifteen minutes, I have leeway to break my own thumb like he showed me. I swallow a scream at the shockwave of pain. I slip out of my cuffs, jerking forward with spine-snapping force. The chains tethering our harnesses together break. I grab my blade in my right hand, slashing through Rhiv's cuffs.

He jerks sideways, inches from the bloodstained tip of Dren's blade, scoops up a heavy rock and smashes Dren's kneecap. The war chieftain crashes to the gritty floor, with Rhiv pinning him down with his legs.

All the anger and rage that's been building up in me over the last four years boils to the surface. My captivity. Torture. The lies. The injustices our people have committed, the empires we've built on each other's throats. How my people praise unity and perseverance, only to hand me over as a sacrifice.

Thousands of lies, years of hope, all crushed by a single truth.

The anger rushes out of me in a devastating whirlwind of

adrenalin, burning away my doubts, my weaknesses. I straddle the big war chieftain and stab down into his face, into his chest, into his eyes. Again, again, again, black blood spattering and spraying. Rhiv holds his thrashing legs down as he roars and screams.

Finally, he stops moving. There's a sludgy, thick taste in my mouth. The air is blood-warm and drowsy. Someone's behind me. Rhiv. He gingerly peels the bloodstained blade out of my hand. He stands above me. Offers his gloved hand.

Not as a captor. Not as an enemy. Not as an alien or a human or a mutant cross-species.

As a friend.

I reach up and grab hold.

SHAVINGS OF DAWN light spill across the saffron sky, webbed with cataracts of clouds. Hot wind whips my hair about as we clamber atop the cliff. Another scorching day awaits. Rhiv's leaning one-handed against his rifle. I squint against the view. Etiolated sunlight glints off the thousand colours of the Citadel, bejewelled towers and ramparts and domes shining with burnished bronze, fierce emerald, startling crimson, deep cerulean, all against a clear aquamarine sky.

I hook my fingers around my harness, sweat already beading under the straps. "I feel older," I say.

"That's because you *are* older. Your memories are, anyway."

"Whoever they belonged to, they wanted someone like me to find them. To expose, well, everything."

"Those memories aren't yours, Sola. But you do get to decide what to do with them."

I raise an eyebrow. "Leaving it in my hands? Awfully generous of you."

"I think we've got enough problems between our people without inventing more."

"*Our people*," I mutter. That phrase will take some drastic adjustment. But I've made my decision. "I lost my home the moment those bastards up there decided to sell my life to keep a lie and keep their war." A desperate, ravenous longing fills my chest as I turn to my new friend. "I want to stay here. I want to be with you all, to become one of you. A Chaar. We're all the same, after all. Let me fight beside you." My arms hang down by my sides. "I've spent the last four years hopeless, powerless. And the last twenty before that, slave to a lie. Never again. I want power. I want as much power I can get. I want to become one of you."

Rhiv stares at me. A sly grin curves on his mouth, and he playfully punches me in the shoulder. "Ah. I was wondering when you'd finally come to your senses. Our first human prisoner to ever take the ash and become a warrior. Heads will roll."

I laugh. "As long as they roll up in Valbeck."

"I'm sure we can sneak them a little broadcast with the news."

The High Sanction teaches that while we all end up at the same destination, we must all find our own paths. That's perhaps the only truth they've ever told me. They threw me down a path of no return. Now, I've made it my own.

A frown creases his face. "And what about—"

"What we learned in there?" I rub sand out of my suit as I answer him. "Let's keep that tucked away. For now, at least. Like you said, we've got enough problems right now."

Rhiv agrees. "One difficulty. We can't take the ash until we return, and we're looking awfully suspicious, having both escaped the Citadel grounds and returning spattered with blood."

I raise an eyebrow, fold my arms. "Could be I tried to escape. Could be I'm still running, now."

Rhiv digs his elbow into my flank and sweeps his majestic black cloak around his shoulders. "If you do try and escape, I'll chase after you."

"Of course you will."

"And I will catch you."

"I'm counting on it."

"And I'll drag you back here, kicking and screaming."

"But I'll make you work for it."

"Can't make things too easy, can we?"

The alien claps me between my shoulders, giving me a surprisingly hard shove forward. But I'm waiting for it. I roll with the impact. I'm stumbling down the sandy scree, down the rocky structures, all the way toward the horizon and my new home.

....

SHAPESHIFTER FINALS

By Jeffrey A. Carver

Inspired by real events . . .

The crowd roared as the first pair of wrestlers engaged in competition out on the centre mat. *"Aww-riiiiii-choooo-guyyyys!"* *"HUGGA-HUGGGA-HUGGGA-HUGGGA!"* *"Wickety-(psicry!)-wickety-(psicry!)-wickety-(psicry!)"* Hog Donovan peeked over in the direction of the match but tried not to get drawn into watching it. Neither of the contestants in the ninety-three-pound class was human, and better he should keep his mind on his own upcoming match.

"Gaaiiee! Gaaiiee!" *"Brackit-it-it-it-it-it-it-it-it!"* *"Wheeeooop-ooop-ooop!"* The assortment of cries from the stands was damned disconcerting, the crowd being over half extraterrestrials. It was the opening bout, finals round, in the 57,463rd Annual Games of the IntraGalactic Interworld Multicultural Amateur Wrestling League—and the first games ever to be hosted by Earth. Hog Donovan prayed that the human fans could drown out all the ETs

when he got to the mat himself. He was as nervous as a laboratory rat on speed, and he was going to need all the psychological boost he could get.

Hog paced the warmup area in his tights and warmup jacket, trying to still the butterflies in his stomach. It would be at least forty minutes yet before they called him to the mat, for the 138-pound finals. An eternity! Hog threw himself into his warmup exercises and tried to blank out everything else.

Bye-bye baby, baby bye-bye . . . The refrain of a popular song repeated mercilessly in his head, warring with the cheers of the crowd.

Hog grunted, working up a good sweat. Hog indeed! He was long and whiplike and bore his nickname only because his old heavyweight friend, Hermie "Harmin'" Harmon, had dubbed him "Hog" in retribution for his jokes about Harmon's rhino-like neck. Those were the old days, but the name had stuck . . .

The crowd roared, and Hog was startled to realize that the first match was over—the victor a mercurial-skinned creature from Tau Ceti. The next weight class was up, and—hey!—this was the only other human finalist, a wiry little Brit named Johnnie Johnson, up against some sort of centipede from the Vega asteroids.

Hog ducked through to the sidelines to yell encouragement. "*Give 'im hell, Johnnie!*" he hollered as the Earthman trotted onto the mat. His voice was drowned out by a loud buzzing. Up in the stands, a large contingent of centipede fans were rubbing their upper limbs together, en masse, cheering on their fellow Vegan.

Hog suppressed a shudder as he watched Johnnie engage the centipede from a standing position. All those *legs*. And they were so . . . insectlike. And quick. With a chitter and a blur of speed, the centipede caught Johnnie's left ankle with several of its legs and tripped him for a two-point takedown. The crowd buzzed in appreciation.

"*Get up! Keep moving!*" Hog yelled.

Tap tap. Hog started at the rap on the top of his head and turned to see Coach Tagget urging him away from the sidelines. "But coach—"

"Hog, go warm up. Don't fret over Johnnie, you're just scaring yourself." Tagget rapped him on the skull again. "Don't forget—"

"I know, I know, the brain is the most important muscle," Hog repeated by rote as he turned back to the warmup area.

"*Think* about your match. *Think,*" Coach Tagget urged as Hog resumed his stretches. After a moment, satisfied with Hog's progress, the coach left to go watch Johnnie himself.

Think, right. Think about the fact that he was about to wrestle an alien named Belduki-Elikitango-Hardart-Colloidisan, an Ektra shapechanger capable of assuming about a thousand different multiworld multicultural body configurations. He was thinking about it, all right. And he was having trouble keeping his knees from shaking.

Bye-bye baby, baby bye-bye . . .

He remembered how smug the Earth promoters had been when the IIMAWL rules committee had offered to make Terran rules the norm for this tournament in honour of the hosting world. Of course, none of the promoters had even *thought* about the fact that Earth's wrestlers would be competing against sentient bugs, snakes, gorillas . . . and shapeshifters . . . except that they'd finally decreed a return to the more modest, and protective, tights in place of skimpy singlets. In other respects, the referees' interpretation of Earth's rules had turned out to be a tad subjective, to say the least.

"*Johnnie—NO!*"

The single shout from the Brit's coach was drowned out by a rising buzz from the crowd. Hog jumped up, trying to see what was happening. The centipede buzz crescendoed. Hog ducked through an opening in the sidelines crowd to get a better view.

Uh-oh. Johnnie was in big trouble. The centipede had him halfway onto his back, with about six legs pushing his shoulders toward the mat. Hog knelt on the sidelines, twisting and arching sympathetically as Johnnie struggled against the inexorable leverage of all those limbs. Johnnie's coach, a wiry little man, was screaming, *"Scoot out! Scoot out!"* and making futile sweeping gestures with his arms.

Hog cupped his hands and screamed, *"PULL HIS ANTENNAS! PULL HIS ANTENNAS!"*

The match seemed to freeze abruptly as the centipede cocked its head and glared across the mat at Hog with all four eyes. Its hairy antennas bristled. Hog gulped, regretting his impulsive yell. The thing looked as if it might just abandon the match and come on over and stomp him for his remark. It appeared to have completely forgotten its opponent.

Johnnie seized the opportunity. For an instant, it looked as though he might actually grab the thing's antennas—which would have been a definite foul—but instead, Johnnie managed to get an elbow inside the thing's legs and knock out several locked joints, loosening the centipede's grip. The crowd buzzed, and the centipede turned back to its opponent, but Johnnie was already wriggling quickly out of its arms.

"That's it! That's it! That's it!" screamed the coach, waving wildly.

Johnnie was frantically trying to complete his escape. He had one leg out now and was up on the other knee. The human crowd was screaming.

The centipede spasmed with rage and tackled Johnnie with a dozen legs. They fell together to the mat with a *whump*, knocking the breath out of Johnnie. Before Hog could even rise up on his toes to yell, Johnnie was on his back under the centipede, the ref was down on five elbows, peering to see if shoulder blades were touching the mat, and—*slap! tweeeeeeeet!*—just like that, Johnnie was pinned, and the match was over.

The centipede humped its back and drew away from its human opponent, chittering triumphantly. Johnnie sat up, gasping. The centipede crowd went crazy, rubbing their limbs.

Hog caught Coach Tagget's eye and turned away, sighing, to return to the warmup area. Johnnie had finished in second place. That meant the honour of Earth, wrestling-wise, rested on Hog. He swallowed, trying not to think about it. But how *could* he not think about it? He was the only human left in the finals. All eyes, and cameras, would be on him.

As he was stretching his hamstrings, Johnnie walked past, shaking his head. "Tough luck," Hog sympathized.

The Englishman paused, peering at him with dazed eyes. "Are you the bloke who got that thing as mad as a raving hornet?"

"I—well—" Hog spread his hands. "I was just cheering for you. You almost made it out, too. Sorry you didn't—"

"You know what those bastards *smell* like when they're on top of you and they're mad?" Johnnie wheezed. "Cheeeeeeeez-z-z," he whispered hoarsely. "That was what damn near killed me." Johnnie shook his head and wandered off toward the clutches of the TV interviewers. "It wasn't the bloody pin . . ."

Hog saw Johnnie's coach staring darkly in his direction. He went back to his warmups. Stretch left, stretch right, down, up . . .

"Heyyaaah, earthman krrreeepy-krrreeepy . . ."

Hog turned, wrinkling his nose at a sudden whiff of ammonia.

The centipede was standing beside him, balanced on half its legs, waving the claws on the rest of its legs in his direction. "Uh—?" Hog managed. "Can I, uh, help you?"

The centipede's antennas waved drunkenly. *"Hoho yassss,"* hissed the centipede. *"Krrreeepy-krreeepy earthman sso sssmart! Come sssee me lataaah."* *Poot!* It made a loud spitting sound. *"Yahh-heyyy?"*

Hog backed up a step. "I don't know what you're talking about—"

The centipede chittered with laughter and sauntered away. *"Lataaaah, earthman . . ."*

Hog stared after it in disbelief. He jumped when he felt a hand on his shoulder. Then he heard the familiar sound of his coach tsk-tsking.

"Poor sportsmanship, Hog. That's all that is—poor sportsmanship. What do you expect from a centipede?" Tagget scowled at the Vegan, who was now parading in front of its fans, waving its arms in triumph. "Look, why don't you go on back to the locker room and clear your mind. I'll call you when it's time to come back out."

Hog nodded with relief. Yes. Back to the locker room. Forget centipedes. Have a swallow of honey for quick energy.

Bye-bye baby, baby bye-bye . . .

He trotted back to the locker room, shaking the tension out of his arms.

ALL THINGS CONSIDERED, it was actually pretty amazing that Earth had ever gotten nominated to host the IIMAWL tournament. After all, by 2028 AD, the farthest any human had ever gotten from Earth was the Moon. But the Interworld Sporting Federation liked to give a boost to newly discovered worlds. And Earth was among the newest—not yet five years a part of the interworld community, since the Rigellians had landed and made first contact and promptly proposed building factories here to employ the locals. In the eyes of the Terran promoters, the tournament was not so much a sporting event per se as a promotion of tourism and general economic opportunity aimed at ETs who might want to spend money here. And in that respect, it was already successful, at least to the tune of a new sports complex for Cleveland and a good crowd of paying ET visitors.

The human wrestling world, on the other hand—the top wrestlers, the Olympic and AAU winners—had been pretty resistant to the idea, claiming that it was insane to pit oneself against aliens whose bodies were so different as to render competition meaningless. Mostly, the sportswriters echoed that position, denouncing the games as blatant sensationalism. Still, there were some good, if maybe not great, wrestlers who hadn't seen the obvious—and had wound up entering the competitions that one wag, as *Time* was so fond of repeating, called the "crocodile free-for-alls."

That's the kind of wrestler Hog Donovan was: not great—but sharp, determined, and something of an iconoclast. He figured he only had a few good years of wrestling left in him, and he was determined to make the best of them. And the way to do that was to enter a competition so new, so outré, that the mainstream wrestling world hadn't caught on to it yet. And maybe, Hog figured, it would *become* recognized, and maybe it would even give *him* enough recognition so that once he'd hung up his tights and joined the working world, he wouldn't have to work on a Rigellian assembly line building Lotusflower roadsters.

Anyway, that was the reason he'd given his parents and his

coach, though it was really only half the story. The other half was that he'd sacrificed and sweated blood at this sport for over seven years now, and by God, he wanted to be the best damned wrestler in the galaxy—okay, *one* of the best damned wrestlers in the galaxy—even if only for one brief, glorious moment.

To his own surprise, he'd done well, working his way through four preliminary rounds and winning the semifinals just yesterday, narrowly besting a titanium-boned opponent with twice his strength and half his agility and intelligence. He was proud of that victory and the semiconductor-medal it had assured him of and the recognition it brought to his home planet.

But right now, he had to focus on just one thing—and that was how the hell to wrestle against an Ektra shapeshifter.

He PACED in front of his locker and shook the tension out again. Peering around the corner of the lockers, he saw one of the black-skinned African wrestlers warming up, and he gave a collegial thumbs-up of encouragement before returning to his own spot. *Wait a minute!* he thought suddenly. *There* aren't *any Africans in the finals.*

He heard a loud *crack*. Uneasily, he peered around the corner again. The black-skinned being, which was *not* human, was separating its joints as if they were held together by rubber bands. It was pulling its right forearm out from its elbow, and dislocating its shoulder and stretching it way behind its neck. The creature grinned a gleaming grin, and Hog withdrew to his own corner, shivering. A *transformer,* he realized. Just like the toys that a kid could flex and twist until they'd changed from, say, a spaceship to an atomic monster. What world was this creature from?

Don't think about it. Think about your opponent. How are you going to beat Belduki-Elikitango-Hardart-Colloidisan?

He'd only seen the shapeshifter once, briefly, in a preliminary round. *"Belduki's its name, and throttlin's its game,"* was how the *Plain Dealer* had put it, in pointed reference to its reputed predilection for near-strangulation of its opponents. That was obviously an exaggeration for effect; nevertheless, it unnerved Hog, who devoutly regarded wrestling as a gentleman's sport, safe and well regulated. He'd always scorned so-called """"professional wrestling"""" (he always mentally put several quotes around the phrase, to emphasize his disdain), in which contestants were slammed to the deck, or thrown against the ropes, or otherwise theatrically mistreated. Real wrestling wasn't like that; it was a sport of skill and conditioning and determination.

It'd come as a shock to learn that in the IIMAWL, there was not entirely the same sense of careful sportsmanship. Oh, sure, there were some protections: no contestant could emit chemicals toxic to the opponent, for instance. But with the contestants so morphically different from one another, monitoring safety was a lot harder than it was between human wrestlers. One contestant might turn blue with concentration, another with suffocation. Would a ref who heard that cracking sound of the transformer recognize it as the sound of breaking bones in a human? In the end, the IIMAWL claimed to be keeping the sport safe, but it was Hog's uneasy suspicion that they mostly threw up their hands, flippers, and toes and said, "To hell with it, let's *try* to keep them from killing each other, but if a ref misreads a physiologic sign, what are we supposed to do?"

Think about the Ektra, Hog thought, shooting a practice takedown in the empty space in front of his locker. Think about the Ektra.

The shapeshifter. Actually, he'd been more or less counting all along on Belduki-Elikitango-whatever being knocked out by Gazoom Gazoom the Indefatigable Baboon, the returning champion, from Veni Five. After his own victory against Titanium Jimm, Hog had been carefully planning ways to defeat the baboon . . . ingenious ways, resourceful ways. And then the stupid baboon had gone and fallen right into the Ektra's four-armed can-opener in the third period, and *boom*, right onto his back. *Slap! Tweet! (Psicry!)* The ref called the fall, and there went all of Hog's planning out the window. And now, *he* faced the shapeshifter.

Hog drew a deep breath and blew into his cupped hands. This was no good—hanging around the locker room, thinking about what could go wrong. He'd be better off out on the floor, soaking up the psychic energy of the meet. And where the hell was Coach Tagget, anyway?

Hog reached into his locker, took a long drag from his plastic honey bear, and slammed the locker shut. For just an instant, as his hand was about to close the combination padlock, he hesitated. What if he were knocked unconscious and they needed to get into his locker? *Good God, man—stop it!* He squeezed the lock shut with a decisive click.

⁂

AS HE STRODE up the echoing passageway to the gym, he heard shouts from the crowd and felt a surge of adrenalin. He broke into a trot, darted past a couple of ETs who were half-blocking the end of the passageway, and jogged out toward the end of the arena.

The crowd erupted with a roar of approval. He smiled to himself, flushing with confidence, then peered over to see what they were actually cheering about.

Tweeeeeeeeet! Slap!

The 133-pound match had just ended with a pin. An alien that looked like a huge gerbil got up, shaking, from under one that looked like a leaf. The ref flagged the leaf as the winner.

And Hog was up next.

Bye-bye baby, baby . . .

<hr>

COACH TAGGET FOUND him just in time to yell something incomprehensible in Hog's ear, shake his hand vigorously, and push him onto the mat with a whack on the rear. Hog shook off his irritation at the coach and stepped onto the mat with a glance at the ref.

A new referee had come out from the table, replacing the one who had just tweeted the last winner. This ref looked a little like a centaur, with multijointed legs and big paddle-shaped hands, great for slapping the mat. *Good*, Hog thought. *The better to signal Hog Donovan winner by fall. None of this eking out a victory by points. Hog Donovan goes for the whole enchilada. Starting right now. This is for* Earth, *and this is for* Hog. He swung his arms, huffing. *Damn straight.*

"You can do it, Justin! Tear his lungs out!" screamed a woman somewhere in the stands. Hog smiled a little. He couldn't pick her out of the crowd, but he knew his mother was waving her program wildly, endangering the eyesight of everyone within reach. His father was just as avid a fan, but he'd be too busy with the fastcam to spend much time yelling.

A blast of easy-listening music filled the gymnasium from somewhere overhead—a sampler of Earth culture to entertain the ET crowd.

Hog's opponent streamed onto the mat from the opposite side

and gathered itself up into something resembling a whiplike tree. Its feet, if that was what they were, stretched out like roots, and Hog could have sworn that the roots were embedding themselves in the mat. What the hell kind of creature was this? Ektras didn't make up shapes; they always emulated real species that Ektras had known, somewhere in the galaxy. Hog puffed into his fist and looked at the ref, determined not to be distracted by unanswerable questions.

The announcer's voice boomed: "IN THE ONE HUNDRED THIRTY-EIGHT POUND CLASS! FROM EARTH: HOG DONOVAN—HUMAN!" There was a murmur of approval, plus his mother's shrieks, but not exactly the thunderous roar Hog had imagined. He glanced up into the crowd and saw a row of centipedes sitting on their legs. "AND FROM EKTRA FOUR: BELDUKI-ELIKITANGO-HARDART-COLLOIDISAN — EKTRA SHAPESHIFTER!" Hog held his breath, waiting for the cheers for his opponent. What he actually heard was more like a group indrawn breath of fear.

He noted that the Ektra had sprouted about a hundred suction cups on the ends of its tree branches. He was going to have a dickens of a time avoiding *those*. Hog danced in place, thinking hard—and coming up with very little, strategy-wise.

Fortunately, he was saved from despair by a voice that boomed out through the general noise: "HOGMAN, YOU PIN THIS WALKING JELLO-SALAD, AND DRINKS ARE ON ME FOR THE REST OF THE *YEAR*!" Hog grinned despite himself, and at that moment, caught sight of Hermie "Harmin'" Harmon in the front row, shaking his hammy fists in the air. Harmin' now worked the graveyard shift at Lotusflower Assembly, hanging transaaactional warp modules under Rigellian interstellar roadsters. He hadn't wrestled in three years, and his physique now resembled that of a hippopotamus. Was that what was in store for Hog after his wrestling career ended? Lotusflower Assembly, with the rest of the guys? Not if he could help it ...

Hog frowned and stepped into a crouch, facing his opponent.

The shapeshifter waved its branches. The ref gestured with its paddles, and Hog reached out to grip the nearest branch in a handshake. The suction cups latched onto his hand, and let go with a *pop*. Hog shook off the stinging sensation. The ref levelled a paddle-shaped hand between the two contestants, then jerked it away with a *tweet!* on its whistle. The match was on.

Hog danced sideways and forward and back, snatching in quick grabs at the shapeshifter's branches. He was just testing, seeing if he could get the thing off balance. The Ektra waved its branches unconcernedly. Its feet remained planted. Hog circled, trying to make it lift its feet and follow. The Ektra didn't turn at all; it just waved different branches at him as he circled. Where the hell were its eyes, anyway—on the leaves? And what would constitute putting this thing on its back? he wondered.

"Cut 'im down, Hog!" he heard in the dim distance of the sidelines. Harmin', cheering him on. His friend sounded as if he was miles away.

"You don't have all day, Donovan—go in after him!" he heard on the other side. Coach Tagget, offering helpful strategy.

Hog shrugged off a negligent grab by one of the branches, and without thinking, launched his attack. He shot forward, low, grabbing for the base of the shapeshifter's trunk. It was a purely instinctive move—go for the single-leg takedown, whether the thing had legs or not. It worked better than he could have expected: the branches waved madly above him, and some of the suckers came down on his back. But he got good penetration and wrapped both arms around the Ektra's trunk. He got one knee up under him and lifted, hard.

The Ektra didn't budge. It was holding itself down not so much by its roots as by a large sucker at the base of its trunk. Hog grunted, trying to break it free. As he strained, the Ektra's branches were clinging to his back, though fortunately, the fabric of his tights top kept it from getting too secure a grip. Grunting harder, Hog dug his fingers under the edge of the tree's suction base. He heard his coach's distant voice: "—the *hell* are you doing?"

"Gaaaahhhh!" With a roar, Hog pulled up with his fingers. *Sploook.* The Ektra came loose from the mat, and he had it in the air like a heavy Christmas tree. He staggered, turning with it, trying to tip it over. The tree was snatching at his back and his arms. Hog lost his balance and went over sideways, taking the tree with him.

Even as they fell, he could feel the thing changing shape. By the time they hit the mat, the Ektra was an extremely slippery snakey thing, sliding out of his hands. Hog tightened his grip, trying to keep it from getting away. But it was impossible; it had some sort of coating that made it slick as hell. He scrambled to follow it on the mat, desperately trying to hold on long enough to get the takedown points.

"Queeeeeee!" whistled the shapeshifter, and with a convulsive jerk, slithered out of Hog's hands.

"No points!" brayed the ref, prancing alongside.

Hog glanced up in frustration. He was *sure* he'd earned the takedown points, even if he had to concede a one-point escape. Was this ref going to be an impossible-to-please type?

The glance was a mistake; it distracted him from his opponent. By the time he looked back, his opponent was gone.

Whufff!

His breath went out with a gasp, and he felt the snake's coils wrapping around him from behind. *How could it have moved so fast?* he thought uselessly, as he struggled to jam his elbows down into the coils to protect his ribs from the rapidly tightening pressure.

"Queee-ee-eeeee!" chortled the snake in what sounded like a merry laugh. *Prelude to strangulation?* Hog wondered. The next coil whipped around his ankles, and he fell to the mat like a hundred and thirty-eight pounds of frozen meat.

"Two-point takedown!" whinnied the ref.

"Augggh!" Hog grunted, trying to keep from rolling onto his back. The snake was trying to get him to do just that, but it didn't have a firm enough hold on his legs, and he was able to scissor hard and gain some leverage, getting himself halfway up to his elbows and knees. "Hunhh! *Uunhh!*" He was struggling just to breathe. He could feel himself sliding a bit inside the slippery coils, despite the pressure. If only he could slide out . . .

In fact, he was moving a little, squirming in the coils. "*Unhhhh! Unhhh!*" He inhaled as hard as he could, held his breath a moment, then gasped it out and jammed his elbows hard against the coils. He pushed them down by about a foot.

The snake tightened like a vise around his hips. His progress stopped; the coils were smaller than his hipbones. "Auuughhh!" Hog groaned, blinking at the sight of the ref leaning close, maybe to make sure he was still breathing. If he wasn't turning purple now, he never would be!

He heard a din and a stamping around him. The crowd was loving it—probably hoping he got squeezed to death.

Coach Tagget was yelling something, but he couldn't hear what it was. But another voice reached him through the cacophony: "HAWWWWG—SLAM 'IM TILL HE LETS GO!" he heard distantly.

Hermie. And good thinking. Hog huffed, raising himself on all fours, lifting the snake's weight. He suddenly went flat, hitting the mat as hard as he could, right on the snake's coils. He felt them loosen for an instant, and he squirmed frantically . . .

Tweeeeeet!

The snake gave a last squeeze, then relaxed its grip as the ref halted the action.

"Warning!" brayed the ref. "Slamming is forbidden! Warning number one against the human!" The ref waved his paddle-hands.

Hog gasped, trying to catch his breath. Warning or not, he had a fighting start now; they would resume the match from a one-up one-down position. As the coils unwound, he lumbered to his feet and walked in a brisk circle to shake off the effects. Then he knelt back down on his hands and knees.

"Shake it off—shake it off!" he heard his coach yell. "Now stay out of those coils!"

Hog glanced back to see if the Ektra would take another shape. But no—he could only change shape while the clock was running. That was a regulatory concession to the nonshifting wrestlers: the shapeshifters had the advantage of versatility of form, but they were momentarily vulnerable during the change, and for a few seconds following, while they "got into" their new forms.

"No delay!" called the ref. This time it was yelling at the shapeshifter. The Ektra seemed to be having trouble deciding how to situate itself on the top position over Hog: it had no hands or feet to place on or near him. "Rest your head on his back!" the ref instructed.

"Queeee?" protested the shapeshifter.

"On his back," repeated the ref. "No delay, please."

"Queeee," it answered.

Hog felt the snake's head touch the centre of his back. He glanced over his shoulder and saw that the creature was arching over him from a base of coils on the mat and was indeed touching him just on the centre of the back. Good. He just had to move faster than the snake.

Tweet!

Hog launched himself up to a standing position, whirling away. He felt no resistance. "One-point escape!" called the ref. Hog spun around to face the snake.

"QUAAARRRRRRRRR!" roared the creature that was facing him—no snake now, but an enormous, maned animal with a mouth full of large teeth. *(TERROR! TERROR! I'M BIGGER THAN YOU!)* Hog backed away, startled. He tripped on the heel of his sneaker and fell to his knees. "QUAAAAAAAAAA!" bellowed the Ektra, charging. *(BARE YOUR GNEEPHITZXX . . . !)* echoed its psicry.

For an instant, Hog was paralyzed with fear—like a man who'd stumbled in front of a rabid lion. *Do something*, he thought. *Get out of its way!* Then something in him snapped, and instead of using common sense and fleeing, he leaped straight at the charging beast with a bloodcurdling Tarzan-yell. "AAAHH-AAAUUGGHH-HH!" He was going to meet those teeth, and it would all be over before the ref could tweet his whistle, but he couldn't stop himself.

The Ektra lion halted in midcharge, bewildered by Hog's furious yell.

Hog slammed into it, grabbing it around the neck. The damn thing was all fur and air; it weighed the same as he did but at three times his size. The Ektra went over like a bowling pin, perhaps too surprised to react.

BLAAATTTT!

Tweeeeet! "No points!"

Hog rolled away from the shapeshifter and leaped to his feet. "Whaaat?" he yelled. "I had him—"

"End of first period!" called the ref, strutting away on its four centaur legs, ignoring Hog's protest. Hog sighed, wheezing for breath. Damn, this wasn't looking good. He had to do *something*.

"Ref, you blindfolded nag! If that wasn't a takedown, what was it?" came a scream from the sidelines. Hog kept his back to his coach as Tagget demonstrated proper Earth sportsmanship. Not that Hog didn't agree with him.

He turned and stared at the leonine alien, whose unreadable eyes were just shifting from Hog to the ref. *(I crush you.)* "Quaaaaaa?" it asked the ref.

"Call the toss!" whinnied the centaur, holding an oversized poker chip in its paddle-hand. The chip was red on one side, blue on the other.

"Quaaaa," grumbled the Ektra.

The ref flipped the chip. It fluttered and landed red side up on the mat. "Up or down?" it asked, pointing to the Ektra, who had apparently called red.

"Quaaa," it said, with a shrug of its furry shoulders.

"Ektra up! Human down!" announced the ref, pointing to the centre of the mat. Hog knelt and assumed the position.

"No teeth, shapechanger!" yelled Coach Tagget as the lion-thing positioned itself with two large paws on Hog's back and its mouth open, breathing hot, fetid air straight down on the back of Hog's neck. "No biting allowed!" shouted Tagget.

"QUAAAAAAAARRRR!" answered the beast with a terrifying rumble. *(I SQUEEZE YOUR—!)*

"Get up and away from him!" Hog heard through the ringing in his ears.

The ref peered at the two, raising a flat hand. *Tweet!*

Hog scrambled, and felt the lion all over him. It felt heavy, and it was quick, and its breath made him reel. But it had to be tiring with all that movement, and maybe Hog could wear it out. He soon realized something, and the lion must have, too. Except for its teeth and claws, which it couldn't use, it had no good way to hold onto him other than hugging him in a smothering embrace and staying on top of him. If Hog could just shoot his legs out to the side and keep moving . . .

He felt the Ektra changing shape even as he did so. He made it partway out of the Ektra's embrace, then lurched to stand up. He turned, hopping back and away—and was nearly free when he felt a tentacle whip around his left ankle. He hopped harder, trying to jerk away, but the tentacle was faster. He managed to turn to face his opponent and found the tentacle attached to something that looked as if it had crawled out of a very dark lagoon. God only knew what planet the original was from. It had a head like a mouldy stump and two squidlike tentacles that sprouted from the head, and it was trying to snake its other tentacle around Hog's right leg. Hog hopped madly to evade it, and the lagoon-creature responded by hoisting his left ankle to a ridiculous height, practically to his chin, with the first tentacle. Hog was left hopping like a crazed ballet dancer, struggling not to lose his balance.

"Krrrreeeee!" screeched the lagoon-thing.

"F-f-f- . . . says you!" gasped Hog. *No, don't talk to it!* he thought. *Save your strength, save your strength.* He jumped, trying to lever his weight downward to break free, but the tentacle's grip was tenacious.

"You can do it, Justin!" screamed his mother's voice from somewhere.

"Get yourself out of there, dammit, Hog! How'd you get into

that?" he heard from another direction. He was completely disoriented with respect to the room; he could only focus on the mat and this infernal creature.

He jumped higher. The tentacle went higher. He still didn't break free, and now his leg was up as far as it could possibly go, and his hamstrings were screaming.

"Krrrreeeeee!" urged his opponent.

"Scree you!" Hog retorted angrily.

Tweeeeeeeeet! The ref strode forward, breaking the impasse. It turned to Hog and waved a paddle in his direction while braying to the scoring table: "The use of abusive language is prohibited. One-point penalty against the human!"

"*What?*" Hog gasped, limping away from the Ektra.

"References to the opponent's progenitors are strictly forbidden!" scolded the centaur with the whistle. "Assume the position."

"*Ref—you piece of Arcturan fungus!*" screamed a voice from the sidelines. "*You mould, you donkey! You wouldn't know a foul if it came up and plugged you—you—!*"

Hog ignored his coach's rantings and assumed the position.

The centaur was staring coldly in the direction of the sidelines, but it said nothing until the shapeshifter had hunched behind Hog, its tentacles on his back. A little too *firmly* on his back, Hog realized. "Ref—wait a min—"

Tweet!

Hog was a moment slow in moving, and the shapeshifter had its tentacles around his waist by the time he was into his standup. He was on his feet, but he couldn't break free, and he began lunging one way and then another, trying to loosen the thing's grip. He dug his hands down under the tentacles to break their hold. Yes—he had them loose! "Aarrrrr!" he snarled, spinning and bracing his feet outward. If he could just arch, he could complete the escape . . .

He staggered a little as the Ektra pushed him backwards off the mat.

Tweet! "No points!"

Hog cursed under his breath and returned to the centre of the mat. This time he was ready.

Tweet!

He was up, turning, leaving the lagoon-creature on the mat . . . except for the tentacle that whipped out and caught his ankle and jerked his leg high in the air. "*Gaaahhhh!*" Hog roared, hopping . . . hopping . . . hopping . . .

Time seemed to slow and twiddle its thumbs as he danced, evading the second tentacle while struggling in vain to escape from the first. He edged slowly toward the out-of-bounds, and the lagoon-creature slowly dragged him back.

Time took a coffee break. Time went out to an early lunch . . .

And Hog hopped . . . hopped . . . hopped . . .

Would the period never end? he thought desperately, throwing his weight up and down with fading strength. Would time never run out on this eternal second period . . . ?

BLAAATTTT! went the buzzer.

Tweeeeet! "No points!" called the ref.

Hog gasped as the Ektra released his leg.

"Shake it off, Hog—shake it off!"

"Go, Justin—!"

He gulped air as he staggered in a circuit around the mat before going to assume the top position for the final period. "Whattza score?" he rasped to the ref.

"Three to one, Ektra," the ref informed him.

From somewhere overhead, the strains of country-western music filled the gymnasium.

———

FOR EARTH, Hog thought dizzily, focusing on the form of the creature before him. *Do it for Earth. Do it for wrestling. For wrestling. For the tricrystal medal. Just gotta do it, somehow. You're on camera—the only human left.*

"FREE DRINKS, HAWWWG!" yelled Harmin'.

Tweet!

He hurled his weight into the lagoon-creature, hoping to topple it. His only hope now was to turn it over for the fall. He felt its weight giving way . . . altering shape under him. What the hell was it going to be this time?

For an instant, he felt a disgusting slime under him as the Ektra's form dissolved. Repulsed, he involuntarily loosened his hold a little, and as he did so, a hundred and thirty-eight pounds of Ektra bounced up into his chin. He almost lost his grip but somehow recovered his balance and thrust himself against the Ektra with all the strength his legs had left.

Boing.

The Ektra bounced back against him.

Boing.

It bounced away from him, veering unexpectedly to his right, and doing a backflip out of his arms. He threw himself against it before it could get completely away, tackling it and carrying it out of bounds.

Tweeeet!

Panting, Hog took a good look at his opponent as it settled, more or less, into position in the centre of the mat. It looked like a large coil spring inside a knotted sock, and it seemed unable to stop bouncing completely, even in the starting position. It bobbed and jittered at a sort of idle speed, reminding Hog of his Uncle Wainwright, who could never sit still, bouncing and gum-chewing his way through entire ballgames—and who had often belittled Hog for choosing wrestling over basketball. Hog glared at the coil-springed Ektra and imagined it shapechanging into his Uncle Wainwright.

With a silent snort, Hog settled behind the Ektra and placed his hands carefully on its trunk, prepared to tackle it as viciously as he could. The centaur-ref peered at him for a moment, seemingly unable to decide if his positioning was legal. Then it flipped its paddle-hand. *Tweet!*

Boing.

Hog lunged into the bouncing shapeshifter and bounced with it, *boing, boing*, right off the mat. He got up, glaring even harder. Time was running out, and it didn't do him any good just to hold the thing down; he needed to pin it. But how could he pin a coil spring? The one thing that encouraged him, as he watched it bounce back to the centre of the mat, was that it was starting to look tired. Maybe all this springing was wearing it out.

At the whistle, Hog threw his weight into it again and landed flat on his chin. For an infuriating, flustered moment, he thought he had lost the Ektra, and he scrambled to get up, looking around wildly. Then he realized that the Ektra was under him; it had splatted out into an enormous pancake with tiny, starfish legs around its outer edge. He pushed and hauled on it, but the thing was immovable.

"Turn it over! *Turn it over!*" yelled his coach, his mother, somebody.

He couldn't *possibly* turn it over—unless he got off it

completely and tried to flip it like a throw rug. But that would be crazy . . . it was too heavy and too awkward.

"Warning—Ektra—stalling!" brayed the ref.

"*Hog—you're running out of time! DO SOMETHING!*" hollered Harmin' from somewhere very close to the edge of the mat.

With a snarl, Hog jumped off the pancake and yanked on the edge of the thing. It went "Querrreee!" and began contracting into a new shape. Good! Now he could go to work on it!

The change took place in a dizzying blur, and it was not just a physical blur. Hog felt a wave of confusion pass through his mind, and he blinked and found himself holding the hand of, and staring into the large brown eyes of, the most breathtakingly beautiful woman he had ever seen or imagined. (*Come . . . come to me . . . now . . .*) whispered the psicry. She had long, golden-brunette hair; and she was wearing a clinging silk wrap that did not altogether cover her breathtaking . . . her breathtaking . . .

. . . and she was breathing so hard, so *quiveringly* hard, and pulling him by the hand toward her with a smile that made his heart stop.

"Whoaaa—Hog! All riiiight! Go for it, man, go get it!"

The sound of Harmin's voice was strangely removed, as though Hog and his . . . opponent? . . . had been whisked into a private place for a special little tête-à-tête, with everyone else suddenly a very long way away, miles away, light-years away. (*Yes, yes . . . come get it . . . you will like it very much . . .*) And, for a fleeting instant, Hog thought that was fine, just fine, very fine indeed. For the glory of Earth fine. Oh yes.

And then maybe a whiff of oxygen reached his brain, or maybe a whiff of astringent alien breath, because the hypnotic spell slipped just a little, and his heart seemed to beat again, and with a start, he realized that he was sinking to the mat, allowing himself to be drawn into the arms of this . . . about to pull this gorgeous creature on top of him, this . . .

"*Get that goddamn tramp off you, Justin!*" screamed someone, his mother.

. . . Ektra shapeshifter.

"Awwwww, jeeeez!" he panted, struggling to get his brain clear, and realizing he had about one second before he'd be flat on his back under this . . . sex-crazed . . .

The woman's weight was already shifting for the pin. And his mind was still fogged . . . but not quite so fogged that he couldn't make one last desperate, hopeless move.

He reached down and tickled her in the ribcage.

"*Breee-heee-heeeeeee!*" shrieked the shapeshifter, erupting into helpless laughter and losing its hold.

Hog scooted out from under it but managed to keep his fingers in there tickling. He was gasping from the exertion, but his gasps were drowned out by screams of laughter . . .

"Kreee-heee-hee-*(stop)*-heee-heee-kreee-*(stop)*-heee-heee-hee-*(please stop!)*-hee—"

Hog struggled to disregard the psicry pummelling his mind. He hugged and cradled this creature, far and away more gorgeous than any woman he had ever even fantasized about, cradled her in a fabulous embrace . . . tickling mercilessly.

"Kreee-hee-hee-*(stop please stop!)*—"

"HOG, TEN SECONDS LEFT!"

The thing's laughter was contagious, and Hog fell on her, nearly laughing uncontrollably himself. And he pressed her back down to the mat, his left arm crooked in a careless reverse-half-nelson, his right hand tickling just below those magnificent—

Whack! Tweeeeeeet! "Pin! The match goes to the human!" brayed the centaur-ref.

And he almost couldn't make himself stop tickling her now that he had her down, but the roar of the crowd was enough to make him look up in a daze, and the first thing he saw, past the four legs of the ref, was Harmin' Harmon jumping up and down like a dancing buffalo. His friend's voice was drowned out, but it hardly mattered. And the second thing Hog saw was the centaur bending down to look at him with apparent puzzlement in its eyes.

"Human, I am unsure how you did that," the ref said, waving its paddle-hands. "But congratulations. And if you don't get up off your opponent, it will be a shame that you will be required to forfeit the match . . ."

"Huh?" Hog released the Ektra with a start and sat back on his haunches, blinking in amazement at what he had done. He stood up shakily and extended a hand to help his opponent up off the mat.

The Ektra-woman was pouting as it rose. But after a moment, its lips quivered and reformed into a smile . . . and then into a beaming grin. *A grin?* Hog thought.

"Earth!" "Earth!" "Earth!" "Earth!" "Earth . . . !" A chant had started in the stands and was growing in intensity. They were banging their seats now. *"Number One!" "One!" "One . . . !"*

"WAY T' GO, HAWWWWWG!" bawled Harmin' Harmon, striding up and down the sidelines, fists in the air.

"Look at the camera, Justin—look at the camera!" His mother was practically on the mat, pointing up into the stands at his father and the fastcam.

Hog grinned weakly and looked back at the Ektra. It was still a dazzling creature, but her grin had continued to widen, bright teeth sparkling, until the grin seemed to take up most of her face. And then Hog realized dizzily that her face was slowly disappearing, leaving *only* the grin. And he stood, blinking, watching the grin fade last of all, until the Ektra was gone altogether. And Hog turned in bewilderment to the ref, who was looking toward the scoring table and didn't see any of it happen.

"Justin! Ask it to do that again! Your father missed it!"

Hog turned around, waving in confusion. "Say, uh—" he croaked to his absent opponent, "nice match!" And found himself thinking, *Is it true? Is it really true? Did I win the tricrystal medal for Earth? The only human in history to win a tricrystal?* And then the centaur-ref trotted back to him and hoisted his hand in victory, and Hog forgot his doubts and waved triumphantly to the crowd. And when he turned, he saw a large, iridescent lizard rising up as if from the very substance of the mat and turning to shuffle away.

"Hey, Ektra!" he cried.

"Breee?" said the lizard, looking back. *(We like semiconductor medals better, anyway. [I lie!] [I lie!])* it whispered in a psicry.

Hog laughed happily and patted it on the back. "Great match, guy. Next time don't be so ticklish!"

"Breee," said the lizard. *(Done well. Next match, I get the home crowd, okay?)*

"Okay. See you around." Hog trotted off the mat, waving again to the crowd, and fell into the congratulating arms of his mother and Harmin' Harmon. He hardly even heard their voices, or the voice of Coach Tagget . . .

"Drinks on me, just like I said . . ."

"Where'd you learn to *do* that sort of a thing with a woman, Justin . . . ?"

"Donovan, just like I been tellin' you, the brain is the most important . . ."

But if he didn't hear what they said after that, he did hear the chants of *Earth! Earth!* and he could already feel the tricrystal medal glistening and breathing in his hand. And he heard a centipede voice hissing, *"Kreeeepy kreeepy Earthman— sssee you nexxxt yearrr on Meetsssnepp Fffive, hah-hahhh! Zerrrro grrravity unlimited, suckahhh ... !"* Only this time, Hog just laughed out loud and didn't even bother to look as he headed for the cameras, as the Vegan's voice faded back into the waves of *"HOG DONOVAN! HOG DONOVAN! TRICRYSTAL EARTH ... !"*

Bye-bye Lotusflower, Lotusflower bye-bye!

THIBAULD'S TALE

By Edward Willett

AUTHOR'S NOTE: This story, which takes place ten years before the events of my upcoming novel The Tangled Stars, *due out from DAW Books in 2022, introduces the novel's three main characters.*

I met Laysa Grey the old-fashioned way, at the lavish wedding of a crime boss's daughter.

The crime boss in question, Anderson Kain, is long-dead now, the victim of an explosive-decompression incident. (Terrance, the man getting married that day to Bodelia, Anderson's youngest of two daughters, swears the fatal event was purely accidental. Since he was the only other person there at the time and is now boss in his father-in-law's place, I guess we'll have to take his word for it.) At the time of the wedding, though, Anderson Kain had his finger in every unsavoury activity taking place on Luna, from drug-running to organ-jacking to money-laundering to people-smuggling to even nastier, unhyphenated things. Since Luna's economy pretty much runs on unsavoury activity, that meant Kain also ran

Luna's politicians, and hence, effectively, Luna itself. That made him a very wealthy man, which made his daughter's wedding the kind of Bacchanalian extravaganza at which Nero would have been relegated to playing second fiddle in the dance band.

I encountered Laysa on one of the observation balconies ringing the Crystal Aerodome, where winged aeronauts, taking advantage of lunar gravity, perform aerobatics beneath the Earth and stars, riding updrafts generated by giant fans in the floor. I wasn't flying myself—I'd tried it once and gotten horribly airsick, very much unappreciated by those flying below you—but I had my eye on a girl who was wearing very little besides her wings and who had shared a drink with me before launching herself into space.

Nursing my second half-litre of beer and admiring the view, I was startled when a woman I *didn't* have my eye on suddenly sat down beside me.

"You're Cooper Douglas," she said, and she was right. Although how she knew that I didn't know since I'd never seen her before in my life.

"Guilty," I said, then kind of wished I hadn't, because I *was* guilty, of several things, even though I'd just turned twenty-one. One of the things of which I was guilty had resulted in my invitation to the wedding of Anderson Kain's youngest daughter, courtesy of Ilya Stadnyk, husband of Kain's eldest daughter, Freya. Stadnyk was a man whose charm, erudition, and love of fine art made him a most pleasant companion—as I knew, because he'd taken me to a very expensive restaurant when he'd hired me to obtain a birthday present for his wife, located, oddly enough, in the home of another, rival, collector of fine art. (It was a painting by an Old Earth master whose name I can never remember. Something Italian, which doesn't exactly narrow it down. Mary and

Baby Jesus were in it, which helps even less.) I have a certain . . . knack, let's say, for retrieving things from supposedly secure locations. I like to call it "pre-salvage." Everything ends up as salvage eventually, and a salvage operation is a perfectly respectable thing to run. I just salvage things a little earlier than might be expected.

I doubted Anderson Kain himself even knew I existed. Actually, I *hoped* he didn't.

This mysterious woman did, though, and that worried me. "Who are you?" I said, in a perhaps not entirely civil tone.

"Laysa Grey."

I'd never heard the name before and assumed it was assumed, anyway. I took another sip of Armstrong Ale (made from a recipe Neil Armstrong himself invented and first brewed aboard Apollo 11, the brewery claimed, though I had my doubts) and studied her over the rim of the mug. She had auburn hair piled up in an elaborate coiffure, slanting green eyes, and bright-red lips, all in striking contrast to her ebony skin. Since Luna fashion at that time (a short-lived fad, thankfully) meant cosmetically changing your hair colour, eye colour, and skin colour every time you went to a party, there was no way of knowing which, if any, of those were original. At that moment, I was myself sporting green hair with silver tips, bright-blue eyes with cat-eye pupils, and pale-lavender skin.

Physical attributes were much harder and more expensive to change (and to change back), and such changes came with sometimes unpleasant side-effects, so I was pretty sure she was at least slim and about my height, a hair over one hundred seventy centimetres.

Okay, maybe a little taller.

"Interesting name," I said as I carefully replaced my mug on the table. Distant shouts and laughter from the flyers echoed off the crystal dome. My previous drink-date was currently being chased by a muscular man, every bit as blond as she was, wearing skin-tight trunks that emphasized a part of his anatomy that also may or may not have been original. He had the kind of good looks you could only get by spending a lot of money on the aforementioned bio-sculpting, nasty side-effects be damned. I was pretty sure the girl would let him catch her, and I wouldn't see her again.

I would have liked to have blamed that on the fact a new woman had sat down uninvited next to me, but honesty compelled me to admit that the fault was in myself that I was forgettable.

Still, being forgettable was an asset in my business, so, again, I was uneasy at being recognized by someone I did not recognize in return. (Sometimes, I was uneasy being recognized by someone I *did* recognize in return, as would have been the case with Anderson Kain and certain members of the Luna Rangers.) "You know me; I don't know you." I stood up. "Have a nice day."

"I have a job for you," Laysa Grey said. She wasn't looking at me—she was watching the hot blond guy chase the hot blonde girl, though I couldn't tell which one interested her—but she'd said the magic words.

I sat back down again and punched an order for another Armstrong Ale into the table. She looked away from the flyers and ordered something of her own.

"What kind of job?"

"The usual."

"What's the target?"

"I'm hardly going to tell you that on an open balcony."

"In general."

"Technology."

"That's broad."

"It's meant to be."

Our drinks arrived via robot waiter—just a dumb, wheeled trolley, not the kind of supercilious AI-brained android programmed with a French accent I'd endured in the restaurant Ilya had taken me to. She'd ordered a Lunatov Cocktail, a frothy high-octane concoction that arrived *en flambe* and had to be doused with a special lid that, though made of metal, was a dead ringer for a pink parasol. "Cheers," she said and took a sip, vapour curling around her ears.

I swallowed some ale. "I can't agree without more information."

"Of course." She tapped the middle knuckle of her right hand on the table, and my smartbracelet vibrated. "Contact info. Time and place." She smiled briefly. "Safe spot. You know it."

She stood, slammed back the rest of the Lunatov without choking, coughing, or staggering—impressive!—and said, "If you don't show, I'll go to Ventura." And then she walked away.

Low blow, I thought. Ventura and I had a history I won't go into, but this Laysa Grey clearly knew it and knew I'd rather eat unrefined biosludge than let him take a job I could have had. I blinked my right eye three times to call up the smartbracelet's in-vision display. Sure enough, there was a contact number, a time—1300 the next day (Apollo City operated on Old Earth's Greenwich Mean Time)—and a place I did, indeed, recognize well, since it was my apartment, which I would have sworn no one could have linked to me, buried under multiple aliases as it was. It *should* have been a safe spot—now, I wasn't so sure.

I looked back out at the flyers. Buff blond bozo and bare blonde babe had disappeared, presumably bonding on some other balcony—or bouncing on a bed. I'd been dumped.

Well, I had a more intriguing female in my life now, anyway.

I finished my ale and left the party, which, the guest list being what it was, I figured might turn a little sour as the evening went on.

(I found out later it wasn't bad—only four killings, and none on the dance floor, unlike the massacre at the wedding of Ilya Stadnyk to Freya.)

Anyway, the next day, I made sure my stunner was in my pocket and sat on my bed—my apartment was a pressurized cargo container, so the bedroom was the *only* room, with a tiny bathroom attached to one end and an equally tiny food-storage-and-preparation unit at the other. Laysa Grey showed up right on time. She now had creamy-coffee skin, presumably her original shade, glossy black hair—ditto—and her eyes were a sparkling, inviting brown.

Inviting? I thought. *You just met her. Down, boy.*

She looked around the room. "Cozy."

I shrugged. "I don't need much."

The bed was the only furniture, so she remained standing. I didn't like her looking down at me, so I stood up, too. I waited for her to speak.

"How do you feel about cats?" she said.

I blinked. "What?"

"How do you feel about cats?" she repeated. "Do you like them? Hate them? Do they make you sneeze?"

"I've never really thought about them at all," I said. "I've never met one in person." There were plenty of cats on Luna—far more than dogs, which were much harder to care for in a place where taking an animal for a walk was problematic, and urination on odd corners of the infrastructure frowned upon—but they didn't usually wander loose in the corridors. (I won't say never. They were cats, after all.)

"Are you allergic to them?"

This was the strangest conversation I'd ever had before a putative pre-salvage. "Not that I'm aware of."

"We'll get you tested."

"Look, Ms. Grey—"

"Laysa."

"Laysa. What kind of job is this, anyway?"

She took another look around the room. There was a vidscreen above the bed, mounted on a swinging arm so I could position it for comfortable watching while I lay in, or sat on, the bed. I had it set to show an endless series of images from cameras scattered around the lunar surface. Right now, it showed Earthrise over some mare or other. "Do you love the moon?" she said.

I shrugged. "It's home. I was born here. Raised here. I don't know anything else."

"How do you feel about the Free Mooners?"

"The 'revolutionaries' trying to free us from the 'yoke of Earth tyranny'?" I snorted. "They're a joke. What have they ever accomplished?"

"If they tried to blow up Parliament, how would you feel?"

I gave her a narrow look. "Are you an undercover cop? If I say yes, do I get a one-way ticket to a full-G Earthside prison, with a little torture to spice up the trip?"

"No," she said. "Now, answer the question if you want the job."

I thought about it. While I had no love for Parliament or the MPs, who were "nominated" mostly by Alexander Kain and "elected" through "votes" tabulated and "certified" by "independent" observers from "Earth" . . . I mean, Earth . . . I also had no love for mass murder or political assassination. Also, blowing up

Parliament might very well compromise the integrity of a rather large portion of Apollo City, and I had even less love for breathing vacuum.

"I'd be against it," I said. "Not a fan of mass death, generally speaking. Or even individual death. Especially mine."

"Good. Because if you take this job, you're going to help me stop a radical Free Moon cell from blowing up Parliament." She smiled briefly. "Using a cat."

———

With a set-up like that, how could I not listen to her? It turned out the cat in question was also the technology in question: a cutting-edge, one-of-a-kind, genetically modified feline whose brain had been overlayed by an experimental AI crafted by the functional equivalent of a mad scientist and encoded in a quantum foam that . . .

Well, no need to recount everything she said since I didn't understand most of what followed "AI." Turned out, though, that Laysa Grey *did* understand that stuff. Like, really, *really* understood it. Which was how she'd stumbled on this AI-uplifted cat in the first place. As she told it, she'd always been good with computers and AIs, taking apart and re-coding her childhood toys, hacking government networks as a pre-teen, etc., etc. A natural.

She said nothing about her parents. I said nothing about mine, either, but that was because I didn't know who they were. My earliest memories were of an obsidian-walled undersurface bubble, home to some two dozen small children of both sexes, cared for by two nursemaids and four robots (who, in retrospect, I think were more reliable sources of affection than the human beings: said affection was simulated in both instances, but the AIs' version was more believable).

Of my parents, I knew nothing. None of us did. That's why we were in a government-run childcare facility, which was every bit as much fun as it sounds like.

From the nursery bubble, I went with other pre-adolescents to the Suffer the Little Children Orphanage. Somehow, probably through bribery, since theoretically, at least, all government services were supposed to be kept strictly secular, the local congregation of a Christian sect had received permission to run that orphanage, part of the sect's belief in "laying up treasures in heaven" by doing good deeds on Earth . . . or, in this case, the moon . . . such as caring for widows and orphans. Like me. They did their best to train us up in the way we should go so that when we were old, we would not depart from it.

In my case, at least, it didn't work. When I turned thirteen, the Suffer the Little Children Orphanage decided it best, not so much for me as for my fellow orphans, several of whom I had conned out of money or small, valuable items (what can I say? fooling them was, literally, child's play) to return me to the care of the government: specifically, the Moonchild Youth at Risk Mitigation and Detention Centre. Having learned, in the orphanage, the things the church and the government thought it appropriate I should learn, I devoted my next few years at Moonchild learning a great many things the church and the government would have thought it totally *in*appropriate I should learn.

Though the facility in which we lived called us "youth at risk," I think the government—not without reason—actually considered us "risky youth," and no doubt would much have preferred to simply keep us locked up indefinitely, on the well-founded assumption very few of us would emerge from our regimented government-controlled adolescence to become well-rounded and productive regimented government-controlled citizens. Since a high percentage of us would, they were certain, eventually be locked up again anyway, it would have been more efficient to simply keep us confined rather than go to all the trouble of rounding us up again years—or, in some cases, mere months, weeks, or for the true prodigies, days—after our "graduation."

Still, even on Luna, some effort had to go into presenting a palatable public facade for government orphanages, and so as we grew older, we were given increasing amounts of freedom, which we immediately and enthusiastically abused in all sorts of fun ways. It was during those halcyon days I discovered the pleasures of sex, alcohol, and other mind-altering substances, and the even greater pleasure of breaking the law and getting away with it, particularly when said lawbreaking resulted in the acquisition of material wealth, which could then be used to obtain more sex, alcohol, and other mind-altering substances.

Six of the three-score teens in my cohort did not live to leave government care. One suicided, two were murdered, and three overdosed. I came very close to being the fourth of the latter and undoubtedly would have had I not discovered Shakespeare.

No, not William. *Brandon* Shakespeare, proprietor of Shakespeare's Salvage and Pawn Shop (motto: "Neither a borrower nor a lender be, unless you're doing business with me!"). Due to remarkably poor record-keeping on my part, probably brought on by the aforementioned discovery of alcohol and other mind-altering substances, I attempted to pawn off on Shakespeare a pocket holo-projector I'd stolen from his shop during a break-in just two nights before. I wasn't surprised he didn't try to have me arrested (it would have been a very odd choice for him to involve the Rangers, given the uncertain provenance of a great many of the items in his storeroom), but I *was* surprised he didn't beat me to a pulp, strip me naked, and dump me in the alley.

Instead, he closed the shop, took me into his living quarters in the back, gave me a beer (correctly guessing that though I was underage, it wasn't my first), and grilled me closely but non-painfully about my background (unpleasant), my prospects (non-existent), and my skills (considerable in certain areas). In particular, he wanted to know how I had managed to defeat his security system—and how he could make sure no one else could do so in the future.

Shakespeare's own childhood mirrored my own—he, too, had been raised by the government (though without my religious-education interlude). But he had found a mentor, the previous owner of the establishment in which we sat, and he now offered to mentor me in turn. I accepted. He took me in officially, not adopting me but fostering and apprenticing me, which was good enough for the government: I was sixteen-going-on-seventeen and out of their hair. (In fact, I discovered they'd used me as an example of shining success in that year's annual report when I spotted my photo in a copy of said report in their main office, which I was ransacking at the time.)

Perhaps it was in the spirit of honouring the memory of his own mentor, one Amelia "Tricksy" Clearwater, who had died many years before, that Shakespeare rescued me from state-run care. I'd like to think so because I did like the guy and grew quite fond of him over the next couple of years. However, my good fortune may have just arisen from the fact he had need of someone with the proven ability to defeat security systems and a gift for talking his way out of trouble, because he immediately set me to work.

Except for the aforementioned ransacking of the government

childcare facility, which I did entirely for my own pleasure, the jobs he gave me were carefully planned and targeted. A lot of people owed Shakespeare money, and one way they could pay off their debt without facing a couple of his *other* employees (Arnold and Dwayne, generic musclebound thugs straight out of a crime holodrama) in a dark alley some night—or worse, out on the Lunar surface—was to point him in the direction of some item of even greater value.

So, I "pre-salvaged" (I got the term from Shakespeare, and it always confuses people when I tell them that) precious paintings and scandalous sculptures and transgressive technology and even some things that weren't alliterative. I rarely met a security system I couldn't beat, and even more rarely, a person I couldn't bamboozle.

Which had led me to this moment, when I was taking great pleasure in staring into the sparkling brown eyes of Laysa Grey as she explained how the radical Free Moon revolutionaries intended to use the amazing technological achievement of mating an AI with a cat to create a walking, intelligent, fanatically moti-vated bomb. Unsuspected, this creature would sneak into the Luna Parliament Building while the MPs were in session and self-detonate, killing them all.

Laysa Grey said she had stumbled on this nasty little intended insurrection while poking around in places no one thought anyone would be able to poke. No one had asked her to do so. No one had asked her to try to stop the plot she'd uncovered. She was taking on the task herself.

I know what you're thinking. She should have gone to the authorities. Yeah . . . not so much. Her activities, if discovered, were shady enough to get her transported to Earth for life—which tended to be short for Luna-native prisoners in one-G prisons—

and anyway, the insurrectionists, she claimed, boasted a not-insignificant number of said authorities among their ranks.

"Wait," I said at that point. "If you're doing this on your own, then no one's paying you. And if no one's paying you, how are you going to pay me?"

"I'm not. I'm appealing to your sense of civic duty."

No one had ever appealed to my sense of civic duty before for the very good reason it didn't exist. But . . . like I said, I'm not a fan of mass death, I didn't want the habitat breached, and did I mention those sparkling brown eyes?

"All right," I said, even while some part of me was metaphorically staring at the other part of me with its mouth open, wondering what the hell I was doing. "I'm in. What's the plan?"

THREE DAYS LATER, at 3 a.m., I rather nervously walked down a long tunnel in the lunar basalt toward a very unfriendly looking door, yellow-and-black, ribbed and barred, and hung with a white-letters-on-bright-red-background sign that said, "NO ACCESS BEYOND THIS POINT: RADIATION AND DECOMPRESSION HAZARD."

Beyond the door had originally lain the artificial cave where one of Apollo City's first nuclear reactors had been built, the one that failed rather spectacularly due to the mysterious and capricious surge of energy that leaped like lightning from point to point around the solar system when the interstellar transportation network of Multiverse Adjacent Space-Time Tunnels—MASTTs, for short—collapsed more than a century earlier, an event known as the Great Cataclysm. (Said cataclysm plays no further role in this tale, but just thought I'd mention it.)

Anyway, according to the maps, all that remained beyond that door now was a radioactive and unpressurized slag heap. What really lay there, though, according to Laysa, was the secret laboratory of the radical Free Mooners, constructed surreptitiously with the help of the aforementioned not-insignificant number of authorities who were clandestinely helping the wannabe insurgents.

"You sure about this?" I said, almost whispering even though there were four kilometres of empty tunnel behind me.

"Of course, I'm sure," Laysa's voice said in my ear. She could not only hear what I heard, she could see what I saw through the specialized camera contact in my right eye. Which I kept wanting to rub. I hate contacts. "Get on with it."

The door had a rather robust security system that was not tied into the computer networks she was so good at manipulating. Had it been, she could have opened it remotely. Since it wasn't, it fell upon me to use my skills to convince it to provide me access.

Here's the thing about security systems on the moon. They're all built by the same company because the moon is a small place, and how many security-system manufacturers do you need? Oh, sure, you could, at ruinous expense, bring one up from Earth and the technicians to install it, and maybe some facilities did, but Free Mooners were hardly likely to choose an *Earth* system, were they?

While the products of LunaVault Technics (LVT) varied in detail, I had learned at a very early age, as part of my *real* education, that the code at the heart of every LVT system contained a back door, legally mandated so that the authorities could always deactivate it if need-be. This bit of code was supposed to be inaccessible to anyone without specialized equipment available only to law-enforcement officers, but did you know you can "pre-salvage" stuff from law enforcement just like you can pre-salvage stuff from anyone else?

Which was why when I walked up to that forbidding yellow door, all I had to do was wave my smartbracelet in front of it, and it opened with no fuss whatsoever.

Since I wasn't immediately sucked, briefly screaming, into radioactive depressurized hell, it seemed Laysa's information had been good.

So far.

I stepped through into a short, very bland corridor that might have belonged to any of a hundred office buildings in Apollo City. The door slid shut behind me. It was bland on this side, too. "Pretty boring for the headquarters of radical revolutionaries," I commented.

"What do you expect, motivational posters?" Laysa said. "Quit wasting time."

At the end of the corridor was another door. This one, Laysa had told me, operated differently. It did not have an LVT security system on it. It had a voice-lock: not a biometric system, but pass-phrase activated. Said pass-phrase was another thing she had managed to ferret out of the bad guys' databases.

Feeling a bit silly, I faced the door and said clearly, "The fog comes on little cat feet; the dog likes his little meat treat."

The door slid open. That, I'd expected. What I hadn't expected was to come face to face with a red-haired young woman in a white lab coat, looking at me wide-eyed. "Who are you?" she said.

"Shit," Laysa said in my ear.

I drew myself up. "I was sent by—"

"Kipsis," Laysa said.

"—Kipsis," I repeated, with hardly any hesitation.

"Oversees security for the Free Mooners. Also, a Luna Ranger officer," Laysa said rapidly, whispering even though there was no way the woman could hear her voice in my ear.

The woman blinked. "At 3 a.m.? Why? What's up?"

"Possible threat to the operation," I said crisply. "Likely nothing, but I'm here to check it out."

The woman's eyes flicked past me at the closed door that led into the tunnel. I could almost see her thinking that if I'd been able to get through that and I'd known the password to enter the lab proper, I must be legit. "Is there anything I can do to help?"

I gave her my best smile. "Tell me who you are?"

"Sharon Sheffield."

"And why are *you* here at 3 a.m.? Kipris told me the place would be deserted this time of night."

Sharon coloured. "I came to talk to Thibauld."

"The cat," Laysa whispered.

"Why at 3 a.m.?"

Sharon bit her lip. She was about my age, but that made her look like a teenager. "I'm not supposed to talk to him. But I like cats. I rub his head and give him treats. I'm not interfering with his programming, I swear!" she added hastily.

A frown seemed warranted. "You know he's a . . ." What was the euphemism Laysa said the revolutionaries used? ". . . a self-motivated direct-action device?" *In other words, a walking bomb.*

"I know," Sharon said. "But . . . I've always wanted a cat. I feel bad for him."

"She shouldn't be telling you that," Laysa said. "If her superiors found out . . ."

I turned my voice frosty. "I'm going to do you a favour, Sharon Sheffield. I'm going to pretend I never heard you say that. I'm going to pretend I never saw you here. I'm going to give you five minutes to vacate the premises. But I'll remember you. Don't do this again, or the consequences will be . . . severe."

I had no idea how the Free Moon radicals dealt with problematic people, but I was pretty sure "severe" covered it.

Sharon paled. "I'm sorry! I'm so sorry! I'll leave right now!" She brushed past me, down toward the exit, pulling off her lab coat as she went. The door opened. She stepped through. Lab coat under her arm, she looked back at me.

I gave her a reassuring smile and a thumbs up. She frowned slightly as the door closed.

"Cute girl," I said to Laysa.

"Really? I didn't notice. Now get moving."

The layout of the lab wasn't as complicated as entertainment holovids would have you believe the secret hideouts of mad scientists and revolutionary groups are wont to be. It was really just a string of rooms along a corridor that formed a box around the carefully sealed-and-shielded remnants of the old reactor.

In one of those rooms, I found Thibauld.

His cage took up half the room and included a feeding unit, a self-cleaning litter box, and a complicated array of padded shelves at various heights. A large black cat with yellow eyes—larger than average, it seemed to me, although admittedly, I hadn't seen a lot of cats up close—he sat in the middle of the cage floor, his tail curled neatly around his front paws, watching me as I entered.

"Are you an oppressor?" he said.

I admit it, I jumped. Laysa had told me Thibauld could talk, although he didn't use his feline vocal apparatus: the voice was generated by an implanted speaker in his chest. It sounded vaguely British, the voice of a young man, although Laysa had also told me he could generate any voice he wanted, of any gender, or accurately copy any voice he heard.

I closed the door behind me. "I don't think so."

The cat's eyes tracked me as I walked over to the cage. "You are not one of my revolutionary brethren," he said. "I have been provided with a database containing all of them so that I can recognize them on sight. There are only revolutionaries and oppressors. You are not a revolutionary; therefore you are an oppressor."

"See?" Laysa said in my ear. "He's been literally programmed to be devoted to the cause."

I crouched down so I was more on Thibauld's level and looked into his eyes. They looked like any other cat's eyes, although Laysa had said that among his modifications were sharper vision and the ability to see all colours, something ordinary cats lacked. They looked back at me, utterly inscrutable, seemingly possessed of great wisdom. "I'm neither a revolutionary nor an oppressor. I'm here to rescue you."

"I do not need rescue. I am not a prisoner."

"You're locked in this cage."

"For my own security."

"You're wasting time," Laysa said. "Give him the treat."

I reached into the breast pocket of the black vest I was wearing over my black shirt (above black pants, over black boots—there was no particular reason to dress all in black, but I thought it looked cool) and took out the little plastic bag Laysa had given me back in her apartment—a much nicer, more-than-one-room, smartly decorated little place not far from the Crystal Aerodome where we'd first met. That's where she was now, watching and listening.

Inside the bag were three little squares of protein—ordinary cat treats, except that each contained a little something extra: a nanobot concoction of Laysa's that would allow the AI in

Thibauld's head to do something it had never been able to do before—connect to LunaNet.

Connect, in short, to all the data that had been carefully denied him about . . . well, everything. The moon. The Earth. The solar system. Governments. Sports teams. Criminals. Musicians. Literature. Recipes.

The city he lived in. The damage that would be done to it if he followed through on the suicide-bombing plan he'd been brainwashed to carry out.

The people he'd kill.

I opened the bag and dumped the treats into my hand. They all contained the same nanobots, but each was a different flavour to be sure Thibauld ate at least one of them. Apparently, cats were picky.

Still, I hesitated. I was fascinated by the creature before me. "The revolutionaries want you to blow yourself up. Why are you willing to kill yourself?"

"That is what I was made for. It is my purpose."

"You'll kill human beings, too."

"The members of Parliament are my prey. I'm a predator. Killing prey is what I do."

"You'll be dead, too. You won't be able to eat them."

"They are also oppressors. They must die so that the moon can be free."

"You won't be around to enjoy that freedom, though."

"But I will have served my purpose."

"You don't have to go through with it."

"Of course I do."

"Why?"

"I just told you." He cocked his head to one side, those disconcerting eyes never wavering from my face, as if he found me the most fascinating thing he'd ever seen. "I must fulfill my purpose. Otherwise, my life has no meaning."

"If you continued to live, you could find a new purpose for your life. You could make your own meaning."

"Is that how you run your life?"

"Yes."

"Does it not make you feel sad, lonely, and empty, searching for a purpose you might never find? Is that why you became an oppressor?"

"I told you, I'm not—"

"Coop," Laysa almost screamed in my ear, "quit playing with the cat! Give him his—"

The last word was drowned out by a shout from behind me. "Don't move!"

I'd already started to my feet before I registered the command not to move, so perhaps it's not too surprising something zapped me that made all my muscles snap rigid. I fell forward, my head bouncing off the mesh of Thibauld's cage.

The treats flew from my hand, landing at his feet.

I hit the floor, unable to move. I knew the sensation. Stunner. The previous time I'd felt it, it had been a Luna Ranger doing the honours. This time, it had to be . . .

Someone rolled me over. I found myself looking up at a skinny, bearded man. The stunner he'd shot me with was still in his right hand. It was a duo-beamer: it could stun, or it could kill. A bright red light glowing on top told me he'd just thumbed it over to the latter setting.

"Who are you?" he growled.

The initial paralysis was fading. I could talk, but there was no way I could get up from the floor.

"Kipsis sent me . . ."

"No, she didn't," the man snarled. "Sharon double-checked as soon as she was out of your reach. Kipsis sent *me*. Who are you really? How did you get through our security? How did you know the pass-phrase?"

I was hoping Laysa would throw in a suggestion right about then, but all I heard was snapping and popping sounds in my ear. *Great,* I thought. *The stunner must have fried it.*

"Take me to Kipsis," I said, trying to buy time. "She knows who I am. She just didn't want to—"

"I don't have to take you. She's coming here." He grabbed me by the collar and hauled me to a sitting position. From his belt, he pulled magnetic restrainers, which he snapped onto my wrists, pinning them behind my back. He wasn't wearing a Ranger uniform—just an all-black ensemble much like the one I'd chosen for the evening's work—but he seemed to be kitted out with a lot of Ranger gear.

He stepped back then. "Won't be long." His eyes moved past me, and I realized he was looking at Thibauld. "What have you got there?"

I twisted my head. Two of the three treats that had landed at Thibauld's feet were gone, and he was just swallowing the third. His eyes widened, then closed. He sat very still for a moment. Then his eyes opened again. "I've been lied to," he said.

"Of course you have," my captor said. "This man is an oppressor. They lie to everyone, even themselves. That's why you have to—"

"He didn't lie," Thibauld interrupted. I'd never heard of an AI who could interrupt a human. "The *Free Mooners* have lied to me." His ears went flat. "*You* did. You, and all your kind. The world is not as simplistic as you have made it seem. There is more to it. Infinitely more. There is more to life. There can be more to *my* life.

I do not have to choose death. I reject the purpose you have set for me."

"Shit," my captor said. He glared at me. "What did you do to him, you bloody—"

"Set me free," Thibauld said. "Like this."

Beside me, the cage door made a clicking sound. The cat walked forward and butted it open with his head.

My captor swung his beamer toward Thibauld.

"That's set on kill," the cat said conversationally. "Does Lieutenant Kipris want you to kill me? I could still be reprogrammed. Reset. But if you kill me, the whole plan goes out the airlock."

"Shit," the man said again. He fumbled with the beamer control, far too slowly, of course, because, yowling, Thibauld launched himself at the man's face. Claws slashed, blood sprayed, and my captor stumbled back, off-balance, screaming in pain. He tripped over his own feet and hit the floor hard, the back of his head slamming into the metal with a force that made me wince. He lay still, blood streaming from his face.

"Is he dead?" I said, both horrified and impressed.

"Probably not," Thibauld said indifferently. He turned and padded over to me. "We should go."

"Uh . . . yeah." I rattled my magnetic cuffs against the cage. "About that . . ."

"One moment." Thibauld trotted over and poked his nose at something on the man's belt. The cuffs released. I pulled my arms back in front of myself and massaged each wrist in turn. "Can you walk?"

"I'll try." I took a deep breath and pulled myself to my feet, clinging to the cage. "Wobbly, but ambulatory."

"I suggest you put those cuffs on Eliot, here," Thibauld said.

I blinked. "You know him?"

"Of course I know him," Thibauld said impatiently. "I told you, I know all the revolutionaries. Hurry, he might wake up."

I followed instructions. "Laysa, are you there?" I said as I cuffed Eliot.

Thibauld, who was sitting watching the door, twisted his head around to look at me. "Who's Laysa?"

"Partner. She set this up. Told me about you. Got me in here. But I think the stunner blast fried my comm unit."

"Let's go find her, then," Thibauld said. He trotted toward the door but stopped suddenly. "Oh, there she is."

I'd been watching my feet to be sure I didn't step on Eliot. Now I raised my eyes toward the door, startled, half-expecting to see Laysa standing there. But Thibauld wasn't even looking at the door; his eyes didn't seem to be focused on anything at all. He was silent for a long minute, and then another one.

"Where?" I said when I couldn't stand it any longer.

"I'm here," Laysa said.

I stared down at Thibauld. The voice had issued from him. "In the cat?"

"No, not in the cat," Thibauld said, which was when I discovered he could do sarcasm. "In the network. Which I'm now connected to, thanks to those treats. Which were yummy, by the way. I hope you have more."

"Not on me," I said.

"Too bad." Thibauld licked his lips absently. "Laysa Grey was looking for me in the network. She found me. I'm routing her voice to my speaker."

"Thibauld's told me what's going on," Laysa said. "You need to get out of there. Kipris won't be coming alone, and if she finds you there . . ."

"That access tunnel is kilometres long," I said. "And there's nowhere to hide. We can't go that way."

"We don't have to," Thibauld said. "There's an emergency exit. Follow me." He started toward the door again, paused, and twisted his head to look up at me once more. "You *can* manage a surface suit, I hope?"

I sighed. "Yeah."

"Good."

THIBAULD LED me to an airlock at the back of the square of corridors surrounding the old reactor core. Hanging in the airlock's antechamber were a dozen surface suits of varying vintages and sizes. "Pick a big one," Thibauld told me. "You and I are about to be intimate."

I picked one big enough for both of us and pulled it on.

"Sit," Thibauld commanded. Like an obedient dog, I sat. He jumped onto my lap, then reached up and put his paws around my neck. He nestled his head under my chin. "Cinch me in."

I was struggling to zip and belt and buckle everything in place with what amounted to a ten-kilogram lump on my belly when Laysa said, "Crap. Coop, they've passed the halfway mark in the tunnel."

I didn't ask how she knew: there was a camera there. I'd waved to her when I'd passed it on the way in.

That gave me a shot of adrenalin that had me sealed and pressurized in a trice (however long a trice is—I've never been sure). "Keep your claws in," I told Thibauld.

"I'll try to restrain myself from my natural instinct to disembowel any soft belly I get my hind legs up against," Thibauld said.

"Get out of there now!" Laysa shouted through Thibauld.

I punched the button to open the inner door of the airlock at the back of the chamber. It slid aside. I hurried in and punched the cycle button on the other side. Air hissed, attenuated to silence. The light over the outer door turned green. I punched another button, and it opened.

A ladder led up the side of a vertical tube carved in the rock. I started climbing.

"They're at the front door," Laysa said after a minute.

I was almost at the top of the ladder. All I could see was a black sky and stars.

"Allow me to take care of the problem," Thibauld said. "You, whatever your name is, the guy holding me—"

"Cooper Douglas," I said. "Coop, for short."

"Crouch. Jump. Get out of this tunnel."

I looked up. "But—"

Claws raked my belly. "Now!"

I crouched. I jumped. I shot up out of the hole into merciless lunar sunlight. I reached the apex of my jump. I started down.

Below me, the hole vanished, wiped out by a gout of dust that swept up and over me, blinding me. I descended, hit the ground, rolled. Thibauld yowled. I expected the suit to fail at any moment, but it held solid . . . unlike the ground, which shook beneath me. I rolled over onto my back to avoid crushing Thibauld and lay there until the tremors stopped.

When at last I could sit up, dust still falling silently all around me, I saw that in the direction of Apollo City, there was now a vast indentation in the ground.

"What did you do?" Laysa and I asked in perfect unison.

"The detonation of the bomb I was intended to smuggle into

Parliament was always intended to be under my control," Thibauld said.

"But why would they keep it armed before they implanted it in you?" Laysa said.

"They didn't," the cat said. "However, with the full network access you granted, I was able to easily bypass their security and arm it myself."

I thought of Eliot, handcuffed in Thibauld's cell. If he hadn't been dead before, he certainly was now. "What happened to Kipris and the others?"

"The blast door contained the explosion," Laysa said. "They're alive. Heading back down the tunnel at high speed. Now leave me alone a minute. I have work to do."

"Well, I like that," I muttered. I got to my feet, feeling bruised and still a little wobbly from the stunner. I looked around. "Which way?"

"The nearest city airlock is four point five kilometres to the southwest," Thibauld said.

I had to think for a second. The secret revolutionary base had been due east of Apollo City, which meant southwest was . . . that way. I started walking.

"This is extremely uncomfortable," Thibauld said after a few steps.

"Tell me about it," I said. I could feel his hind claws were dug into my belt. I hoped they didn't slip lower.

After that, there wasn't much to say until Laysa's voice returned, about two kilometres of unpleasant trudging later.

"Done," she said. "I've erased all of their computers. All of their data concerning the Thibauld experiment is gone. I chased down every backup file, too. There could be physical copies somewhere, but I've also set up an automated hunter-killer bot that will backtrack and destroy any device containing any of their data the moment it touches the network. It will be years, if ever, before they can create another AI like him."

"I'm not an AI," Thibauld said. He sounded, amazingly, sleepy. "I'm a quantum-AI overlay on a living feline brain." He yawned. "I'm a cat."

"What do we do with him?" I said to Laysa.

"What do you mean, what do we do with him?" Laysa said. "He's a cat. He needs a home. We adopt him, of course."

I actually paused walking. "We?"

"I've seen your place," Laysa said. "You need a home, too."

And that was how I acquired, in one fell swoop, both a friend and future lover *and* a wisecracking, super-intelligent, sarcastic feline companion—not to mention the future first mate of a spaceship I didn't yet know I would someday own, and the future captain of the starship I'd one day steal.

But that, as they say, is a tale for another time.

··

THE CANCELLATION

By Bryan Thomas Schmidt

A John Simon Story

They called it dog watch. Ten p.m. to six a.m. And John Simon was beginning to wonder if that was because it left cops tired as a dog. Either way, the detective and his partner, Lucas George, were standing freezing in a cemetery downtown when their shift was supposed to be over.

"We're shorthanded," their boss, Sergeant Brian Delmater, had said. "But someone dug a grave overnight, and they need someone there. Just see if we need to call in a team and then go home."

So Simon and Lucas had reported. Just standing there had flashed Simon back to an earlier case, and it was not a fond memory. The discovery of that girl had marked the return of a serial killer he had been hunting—one of his earliest cases as a detective. The man targeted college-aged women of all races— raped them, beat them, tortured them, and then buried them alive. And his signature was tiny notes left hidden inside jewellery or watches on the victims. Thankfully, that killer—"the Phantom," as the press had called him, Louis Turner by name—had been in prison for the past fifteen years. This couldn't be related, but it sure brought back memories.

"I'm too old for this shit," he muttered.

"You are," his partner, Lucas George, agreed and smirked, the only obvious sign of his android nature being the slight silver tint to his perfect green eyes that lent them a glow at night.

It was about twenty degrees out this dead December night, and for just a moment, Simon wished one of his partner's special abilities as an android involved generating heat within a certain radius for those around him. For a moment, he was tempted to laugh at the thought, but instead, he narrowed his eyes and snapped, "Shut the fuck up," then ripped the end off a Snickers wrapper and took a huge bite.

"I feel like we've had this conversation before," Lucas said.

"Yeah, a hundred times, but good catchphrases hold up," Simon said.

"And you guys complained my movie-quote schtick was getting old," Lucas said. Ever since Simon's precocious teenage daughter had suggested Lucas study cop movies to learn how to be more like human cops, he'd been firing off quotes, not always at the appropriate times.

"I get giddy when I'm tired," Simon muttered.

"Tired as a dog," they added together and laughed.

"And predictable," Lucas said. "The glory of police work, isn't that what they say?"

"Only people who don't actually know what police work is like," Simon said.

The cemetery maintenance foreman called, "You wanna take a look?"

Simon stepped forward and hopped down into the hole, examining the victim without hesitation. She was young, too, Hispanic, with long, dark hair and bright blue eyes. Her arms showed bruising and cuts and abrasions, and she was naked, several fingernails broken off—a possible sign of scratching or fighting her attacker. Then he noticed the watch. It was a Timex, dirt crusted over the face, but the band was shiny. Out of pure curiosity, he reached down and used a gloved hand to lift her wrist, wiping at the watch to get a better look.

"Takes a licking, keeps on ticking," Lucas said as he watched his partner. "No surveillance cameras?" he asked the foreman.

"At the entrances and exits, but not out here," the foreman replied. "This is an older part of the cemetery. They're closer to the fences and roads."

Simon looked up at Lucas. "Call Crime Scene. This is definitely a homicide." And that meant he and Lucas wouldn't be going home anytime soon. He climbed up out of the hole, taking the watch with him. He didn't know why, but he had an urge to open it. It would kill time, at least, and rule something out, so he took it back across the grass toward the hood of their car, then pulled out his tools.

He heard Lucas on the radio with Dispatch as he pulled out a tiny screwdriver and began removing the back from the face of the watch.

"Something about the watch?" the foreman asked.

He'd been so focused on the watch, Simon hadn't heard him approach. "Not sure. Just a feeling. Might as well take a look."

The foreman frowned. "What for?"

"You never know what you'll find in homicides," was all Simon said as he unscrewed the fourth screw and set it carefully inside the plastic top case of his toolkit for safekeeping, then gently pulled off the back of the watch. Nothing. It was empty. The similarities to the Turner killings were all in his head.

He turned to the foreman. "Any ID?"

The foreman nodded. "We haven't checked the body yet. Want me to do it?"

Simon raised a palm to stop him. "No, let's wait for Crime Scene. They'll do it."

THE STUDENT ID card from a local high school they found on the victim had identified her as Tracy Ramirez, a junior. So Simon and Lucas took on the grim job of going to her house.

"Oh, my God!" Liz Ramirez cried out and burst into tears when Simon informed her of her daughter's death, and Simon felt a stabbing in his chest as he thought of his own sixteen-year-old daughter, Emma.

"We are sorry for your loss," Lucas added, doing his best to sound sympathetic, but for the next few moments, the mother was inconsolable.

"I'm sorry to ask this," Simon said when she'd finally calmed down, "but can you think of anyone who might have wanted to harm Tracy? Any enemies?"

Liz shook her head. "No. I mean, she had rivals at school. You know how kids are. But murder? My God!" And the tears poured again.

"We are not sure it was murder yet," Lucas said, which only made Liz cry harder.

Over the next few minutes, they managed to get a few names and other details, including a class schedule and list of Tracy's appointments and activities over the past few days that Liz knew about, but Tracy was seventeen and had her own car, and her mother admitted she'd long ago stopped assuming she knew where her daughter was every moment.

"That was hard," Lucas admitted as they walked back to the car. It had been his first notification.

"It always is," Simon said, mulling over the names.

"A quick search of the internet reveals most of these people are schoolmates of Tracy," Lucas said, having used his internal computer to store the names and initiate a search. "Do teenagers kill each other?"

"The rivalries can get pretty brutal at that age," Simon admitted.

Lucas frowned. "Poor Emma." The android and Emma had taken an immediate liking to each other and become fast friends.

"Yeah, I'm hoping Emma's too smart to let any rivalries get that bad," Simon said. "She knows when to walk away."

"Perhaps someone should have told Tracy," Lucas observed, and Simon chose not to respond as he pulled the car out of the Ramirez's driveway and headed back to headquarters. He and Lucas would continue working the case after he got some much-needed sleep. But with a murder case, he'd likely get very little over the next week, unless Homicide took it over and pushed them aside—something they often did, but Simon wouldn't allow that if he could help it.

***

AT 3 P.M. THAT AFTERNOON, they were called to the coroner's for the autopsy.

As they strode through the double doors into the Jackson County Coroner's Office, Simon thought a moment about how to prepare his partner. The android had no sense of smell, so the usual odours of chemicals, body fluids, and decay wouldn't bother him. "They're going to cut up the body," he explained, then marvelled at how businesslike and stoic Lucas remained throughout the procedure. Most first-timers vomited at least once.

"Well, it's definitely homicide," the coroner said as he finished the exam. "Cause of death was suffocation and blood loss after she was buried alive."

Simon winced. "God, what a horrible way to go."

The coroner nodded. "The fingernails probably broke mostly as she fought to dig herself out."

It would have been hopeless. She was buried under four feet of dirt. Whoever had done it had to have either worked all night or brought machinery. Simon made a note to ask the neighbours if they'd heard anything.

"Nothing under her fingernails?" Simon asked.

"Dirt and blood," the coroner replied. "No foreign DNA."

So she hadn't scratched her attacker. Shit.

"There are also strange bite marks all over her upper arms and forearms," the coroner went on.

"Fats, you better spray the toilet! I saw a cockroach in there!" Lucas quoted.

"Not cockroaches, but insects of some kind, most likely," the coroner said. "We'll examine them under a microscope and see if we can identify the source."

"Thanks, Doc," Simon said and turned, heading for the door. Lucas followed.

"Oh, she was poisoned too, I think," the coroner called, and Simon's feet dragged as he and Lucas turned back.

"Poison is a woman's weapon," Lucas quoted. "Men prefer steel."

"The perp could be either gender," Simon said. "We're not sure yet."

"I won't know for sure until the toxicology tests come back," the coroner continued, ignoring their banter, "but her pupils are abnormally large, and there's some discoloration of the blood and a strange odour coming from some of the organs."

"So she was dying anyway?" Simon asked.

"I'd say so," the coroner replied. "If he hadn't buried her, she'd have died within a few hours."

"Call me as soon as you get those results," Simon said.

"Of course."

Simon turned and headed through the doors, Lucas following again. "Someone who knows her," Lucas said.

"Probably, but we'll also talk with anyone who might have seen her," Simon said.

"And if they did not?" Lucas asked.

"Then we start with people her mother gave us. See if we can recreate the last few days of her life."

"They will not know she is dead," Lucas said.

Simon sighed. "Yeah, we have to notify them as well. You just let me handle that."

"WHERE ARE you with witnesses and relatives?" Delmater asked later when they arrived at the Generalist squad room on the third floor of KCPD Headquarters.

"So far," Simon said, "a wasted four days." None of the victim's family and friends or witnesses they'd tracked down who'd encountered her the past week had known anything about her being near the cemetery. And her movements, as far as they could trace them, seemed fairly benign and routine.

"So you've got nothing?" Delmater replied.

"I don't have Jack shit," Lucas said, a line from *The Wolf Of Wall Street*.

"Well, maybe you talked to the wrong Jack?" Detective Benny Jimenez joked from a nearby cubicle, clearly amused by the quote.

Delmater didn't even crack a smile. "Well, start working the angles then. Somebody has to know something."

"Don't shoot where it is, son. Shoot where it's going to be," Lucas replied, parroting a quote from some Robert Patrick show.

"Bailey and Tucker from Homicide have been assigned, and they're setting up a war room upstairs," Delmater said, this time smiling slightly at the joke. "I put out word, and you've been invited, but coordinate with them if you want in. Or you could go home and sleep."

Simon would ordinarily jump at that offer, but the case had him wired and he wanted in, so he shook his head.

Delmater shrugged. "You know the drill."

Simon nodded and headed for the door, Lucas following.

"There's a convenience store and two gas stations with CCTV in a half-mile radius from the cemetery," Lucas reported, and Simon knew his partner, as usual, was already working the angles via his internal internet connection.

"Let's check in upstairs, then we'll call them and go check out their feeds," Simon said as he scooted back his chair and stood.

"Roger dodger," Lucas replied, and they headed for the door again.

HOMICIDE CONSISTED of four squads on the ninth floor, each in cubicle farms with sergeants, much like the Generalist squad. The room was bustling as Simon and Lucas entered and a clerk busy filing near the door directed them to a conference room in the northwest corner, where they saw Detectives Jerry Tucker and Tom Bailey working a map on the wall. Tucker was chubby, with a round face and white Santa Claus beard, his white hair cut short on top, his skin freckled from years of sun and beginning to wrinkle and show its age. Five years older than his partner at fifty-two, he looked like a wise, kind grandpa, which was ironic considering he'd been widowed a decade earlier by cancer and had no offspring. Bailey was tough, a former bodybuilder, great in a fight, solid sense of humour, and damn good instincts. He was also one of the top shooters with a handgun in the entire detective squad and one of the few openly gay officers on the KCPD. The two were using coloured pens to mark various locations as they discussed the case.

"Word has it you guys can't handle the heat," Simon teased, "so we're here to pick up the slack." He and Lucas had worked with the two several times before, and Simon had worked a few homicides with them earlier in his career, so they'd developed a good rapport.

"Thank God you Generalist types are here to save us," Bailey deadpanned, then grinned. "Shouldn't you be in bed?"

Simon stifled a yawn. "My partner never sleeps. Have to keep up with him."

"Lucky bastard," Tucker said, nodding toward Bailey, whose energy levels were the envy of his peers. "I know how you feel."

Simon chuckled. "What can we do?"

"Heard you made the notification to the victim's mother," Tucker said, his soft green eyes filled with sympathy.

Simon grunted. "Yeah, she's struggling. Her only child."

"Fuck," Bailey said. "Let's find these bastards."

Simon pointed to his partner. "We found some CCTV cameras at a couple of gas stations and a convenience store near the cemetery. We already told them we'd be coming. Mind if we check them out?"

Bailey nodded. "Can't hurt. In the meantime, send us a list of any witnesses you've identified. We should have more for you when you get done."

"Yeah, we've talked with a few, but nothing so far," Lucas replied.

Tucker smiled. "Sure you wouldn't rather get a few zzzzzzs while you can? Things are bound to get crazy soon enough."

Simon shook his head. "We'll stay awhile. Couldn't sleep if I wanted to."

"I do not need sleep," Lucas said.

Tracy Ramirez was missing from the CCTV footage of the first gas station and the convenience store, but on the second station's tape, there she was, half an hour before the coroner's estimated time of death—filling up her car. Simon and Lucas had picked up the CCTV tapes, stopping to question the clerks about whether anyone recognized Tracy before taking them back to headquarters to review. None of the clerks remembered seeing her, though one woman did think she looked familiar. That might mean she'd been there before, but none of the clerks in question had been on duty the previous evening. The night clerk from the gas station in question would have to be tracked down and interviewed as well.

As they rewatched the gas-station footage, Simon ignored the smell of coffee and doughnuts coming from across the squad room. Then his phone rang. It was Trevor Welch from Computer Services. "We have something," Welch reported. "From CCTV across the street from a gas station."

"The one off Independence?" Simon asked.

"How'd you know?"

"We just watched the tapes from there," Simon said. "She filled up around eleven."

"So you saw it."

"Saw what?"

"The abduction."

"What?" Simon said, putting Welch on speaker.

"There's footage from across the street of an altercation," Welch went on. "Guy brushes past her, a few words exchanged. Then he goes inside. A few minutes later, she writhes and scratches at her arms as if she's being bitten by insects or something. Then he comes out and grabs her, takes her to his car."

"Wait," Simon said. "All this is on camera?"

"From a distance," Welch said.

"Can you blow up his face for us?" Lucas asked.

"It's too blurry, and he's wearing a sweatshirt with a hood pulled up," Welch replied.

"Send it over now, please," Simon said.

"In your inbox," Welch said, and Simon pulled up his email server on the computer at his desk and began searching. "But there's no licence plate either. Camera was too far. Going to work on it, though."

Simon pulled up the footage and played it on the screen at his desk, Lucas watching over his shoulder. "Thanks, Trev. Let us know if you get anything else."

"We'll keep at it," Welch said and hung up.

Simon and Lucas watched the footage—seeing the altercation Welch had described.

"Does that guy look white or black?" Simon asked.

"I cannot tell with all the shadows," Lucas said.

"Shit, me either," Simon said, then reran the footage again, leaning in. "Is something crawling on her?"

"What's the last thing that goes through a bug's mind when it hits a windshield? Its ass!" Lucas quoted.

"Good one," Simon said.

"But it's not insects," Lucas said.

Simon frowned and looked at his partner. "How can you tell? I can't even see them."

"I scanned the marks on her arms and have been examining them, running searches," Lucas explained. Like the walking computer he was, the android had the ability to take and manipulate images, including blowing them up to many times magnification. "As the doctor said, they do not match local insects of poisonous nature, and they are very small. But I found nanobots with this signature."

"Nanobots?"

"Yes," Lucas said. "I believe they were used to deliver the poison."

"Then why abduct her? Why not just wait and let the poison do its thing?" Simon asked.

"Simon, George!" Delmater called from his office. "Bailey and Tucker need you. There's another body."

Simon jumped to his feet. "Where?"

THE SECOND VICTIM WAS MALE, not female, and black, not Hispanic, though he was also around the same age, and he was found collapsed in a heap on the sidewalk outside a medical clinic that had signs promising "All Night Clinic" but was closed due to a staff shortage. Simon was fairly sure he'd been seeking help and succumbed to the poison. Bailey and Tucker agreed.

"Well, the MO is the same," Bailey said, "same bite marks on the arms and neck, and he had ID like the first victim and one hundred in cash, so it wasn't robbery."

"Jesus." Tucker shook his head. "Poison. What a way to go."

Construction equipment pounded in the distance over the constant humming drone of city traffic, and the air was filled with the smell of car exhaust mixed with cooking oil and freshly brewed coffee from the café next door.

"So, what connects him with Tracy Ramirez?" Lucas wondered, meaning a connection besides the bite marks that might signal how they'd both known the killer. If he asked, Simon knew his internal searches had so far turned up nothing.

"That's what we need to find out," Tucker said.

"The coroner said it wasn't insects," Bailey said. "So we still have a mystery source."

"Nanobots," Lucas said.

"What?" Bailey asked.

Lucas explained his theory. The smell of pollution grew as a city bus whooshed past, almost obliterating the wet concrete smell left over from the previous night's rain.

"Tiny mechanical bugs?" Tucker shuddered. "That is the definition of creepy."

"I like bugs," Lucas quipped.

"You're metal, they can't bite you," Bailey retorted.

"It actually answers some questions," Simon said. "It's intentional—someone programmed them, and they are manmade. And obviously, people are being targeted."

"But why? And by who?" Bailey asked.

"I didn't say it answered *all* the questions, just some," Simon replied.

Simon's cell rang, and he recognized the number. "Coroner." As he answered, Lucas and the others continued searching the scene. "Yeah, Simon."

"Well, it was ricin," the coroner said. "She would have died within hours if she hadn't been buried first."

"Ricin," Simon repeated loud enough for the others to hear. Bailey and Tucker stopped searching and came to join him as Lucas knelt and retrieved something from the sidewalk near the victim. It looked like a small business card.

"Still don't know how it was delivered, though," the coroner went on.

"Search her system for nanobots," Simon suggested.

"Nanobots?"

"Yeah, Lucas recognized the puncture marks and ran a search," Simon said. "We think that may be the source. Some could still be in her body."

"They are probably biodegradable," Lucas noted.

"So maybe there's nothing, but look," Simon said.

"Okay," the coroner agreed.

"We just found another one," Simon said.

"Shit," the coroner replied. "Just when I was hoping to head home for a break."

"You've got an hour or two but heads up," Simon said and hung up. He heard a familiar buzz and turned to see three media drones bearing the logos of the local news affiliates circling toward them. "Fuck. Press is here."

Bailey jumped into action, extending his arm palm out and marching toward the drones. "No media past the perimeter." He waved at several uniformed officers lingering nearby and sipping coffee from styrofoam cups bearing the café's logo. "Keep them outta here!"

The uniforms scrambled to respond as Simon heard questions being fired off from the drones. "Detectives, is it true the city may have a serial killer?" "Is it true this victim is tied to another body found in a cemetery early this morning? The public has a right to know."

"No comment," the uniforms said in unison and used their bodies to block the drones, though everyone knew it would have little effect.

Tucker motioned to the crime-scene team leader. "Get a tarp over that body."

"At least they don't trample any evidence," the crime-scene tech muttered as he signaled his crew.

"Are we officially calling this a serial killer now?" Simon wondered.

"No," Bailey said. "Not 'til there's more evidence of a connection."

Simon grunted. He felt the same. The designation "serial killer" elevated cases to a whole different level, often drawing federal interest and press. This one wasn't there yet. "Need us to guard the scene?"

"Do *not* go in there," Lucas said, imitating Ace Ventura.

"No, we got this," Tucker said. "You two keep working witnesses."

"Alrighty then," Lucas said.

"You and Ace check in regularly," Bailey said. "Find us that connection."

"On it," Lucas said as he followed Simon back to the car.

As they settled into their seats, Simon shot Lucas a curious look. "What did you find?"

"The business card for a place called Pack-N-Ship up north in the old Italian district."

Simon adjusted his seatbelt and started the ignition. "Let's check it out. It's the only lead we've got."

GIANNI'S PACK-N-SHIP was at the corner of Gillis and Missouri, just north of downtown, in one of Kansas City's oldest neighbourhoods, one once dominated by Italian immigrants, including a very active and dangerous group of mobsters like John Lazia. Although the mob was long gone, descendants remained and owned and operated many of the businesses in a several-block radius of what was now called the Columbus Park Neighbourhood.

Simon parked the Interceptor at the curve in front of a row of linked brick businesses, the middle of which bore the Pack-N-Ship logo on a sign over the door, and Lucas followed him as they went inside, where an older man in his fifties wearing a well-worn apron was stacking boxes in front of a UPS Dropbox. The room smelled of dust mixed with industrial cleaners and stale cardboard.

"May I help you?" he asked.

Lucas badged him. "Are you the owner?"

"Stanley Gianni, yes."

Simon nodded. "We're here investigating a case, and a business card for your establishment turned up at a crime scene earlier today."

Gianni frowned. "We run a legitimate business. This is not that kind of neighbourhood." He shot them a proud look before adding softly, "Anymore."

"We're not accusing you," Simon said, "but we wondered if you could tell us what kind of items you've shipped lately."

"We ship all kinds of things," Gianni said, relaxing slightly as he absentmindedly fluffed back a tuft of grey hair at his temple. "Half of which we never see or identify because they're brought in already packaged and ready to go."

"You both send and receive?" Lucas asked, motioning to a row of locked, numbered post office-style boxes lining a wall.

"Of course," Gianni said. "All your shipping needs."

"So this might be something one of your customers received," Lucas said.

"And what's that?"

"Nanobots or nanotech," Simon said.

Gianni shook his head. "I've seen nothing like that."

"No return addresses or shipping labels from a nano company, perhaps?" Simon asked.

Gianni's brow furrowed. "Honestly, we handle so many packages, I don't usually pay much attention. We sort them into boxes and get on with it."

"Okay, well," Simon said, setting a business card with the official KCPD logo on it along with his name and phone number on the counter, "perhaps if you think of anything, you could give us a call?"

Gianni shrugged. "I doubt it, but I'll call if I do."

Simon smiled. "Thanks."

He headed for the car again, Lucas following. "That was most unhelpful," Lucas observed.

"We knew it might be, but something could come up," Simon said.

"Anyone could have dropped that card," Lucas replied.

"Yep, but it's one of the only leads we've got."

THE SECOND VICTIM'S name was Al Johnson, Jr., and although Bailey and Tucker had already questioned the young man's parents and given the notification, Simon wanted to ask them a few questions, so he and Lucas headed there on the way to Simon's favourite local haunt, the City Diner on Grand Avenue, for a meal.

"Never heard of it," Al Johnson, Sr. said when Simon asked if he knew the Pak-N-Ship.

His wife shook her head vehemently. "Does this have something to do with what happened to our baby?" she asked through sniffles.

"We are not sure," Lucas said honestly.

"But we're following every lead we can," Simon added.

"Who would have done this?" Tamika Johnson asked, tears flowing again. "He was a good boy."

"We'll do everything we can to find them," Simon said. He asked a few more questions about Al Jr.'s activities that might involve the shipping store. Neither parent had any clue if he might have come upon it. Then they asked about Tracy Ramirez.

"I think she was in Junior's class, but I don't know if they were friends," Al Sr. said.

"Did he have a yearbook?" Simon asked.

"Yes," the father replied, brow furrowing in puzzlement.

"Can we borrow it?" Simon asked.

Al Sr. shrugged. "I'll have to check his room. You think it will help?"

Simon nodded. "It might give us an idea if they knew each other, or at least some people or activities they had in common."

Tamika sniffled and stood. "I know right where it is. I'll be right back." And she hurried down the hall.

Five minutes later, they gave their condolences again and left, yearbook in hand, headed for the City Diner. Simon ate his usual 2x2x2 breakfast fare, while Lucas, who didn't need to eat, flipped through Al Johnson, Jr.'s yearbook as they discussed the case.

"Why do we not call this a serial killer?" Lucas wondered. The android had never worked an official homicide case and had never been around a serial case.

"Serial killers are rare, but more than that, they tend to bring national attention from both the press and law enforcement," Simon said. "The only thing connecting these victims so far is the MO. Until we are sure there's a firm connection, we don't want that attention. It can be a real circus."

"The circus is the only fun you can buy that is good for you," Lucas said.

"Yeah, this one's less fun and less good," Simon replied. "The last thing we want is the press spreading unfounded rumours that scare the public."

"Not my circus, not my monkeys." Lucas smiled.

"Exactly."

"So many freaks and not enough circuses!" Lucas replied.

Simon chuckled. "Now that one I agree with as well. So let's get back to catching a freak before he starts a circus."

"Robotics club," Lucas said, suddenly serious.

"Robotics club?"

"At East High School."

"What about it?" Simon asked.

"Apparently, both Al Johnson, Jr. and Tracy Ramirez liked robots."

"They were both members?" Simon said, realizing. "Let's go to school."

"THEY WERE part of it for a little while, until I kicked them out," said Jackson Fale, the robotics team supervisor and East High's popular science teacher, when Simon and Lucas asked him about Al Jr. and Tracy in his classroom an hour later. The classroom itself was surprisingly clean, though the odour of human sweat and cheap perfumes and colognes permeated everything, like most high schools.

"You kicked them out?" Lucas asked. "Why?"

"They were a couple of bullies and not near the intellectual level of the others," Fale said as he moved around the room, setting up tables for his next class. "I have no use for people picking on each other. We're a team, and we act like it, or you leave."

"Who were they bullying?" Simon asked.

"A couple of the others, what you might have called 'nerds' in our day," Fale explained.

"How did they bully them?" Lucas asked.

"Teasing, taunting, harassing—pick your word," Fale said. "They also spread rumours on social media that encouraged others to do the same. Made those boys miserable."

"We need their names," Simon insisted.

"Why? They're the victims," Fale said, looking away as he slammed a toolset down on the last table to match the others.

"They've been through enough." He marched back across the room toward his desk, Lucas and Simon following.

"Al Jr. and Tracy were victims too," Simon snapped. "Of murder."

Fale winced, his shoulders drooping as he sank into the chair behind his desk. "It's terrible. I heard she was buried alive, too. Just awful."

"What kind of robots do they build?" Lucas asked.

"All kinds," Fale said. "Some are workers who use tools for various tasks, from building to cleaning. Others are attempts at humanoid forms, even speech. Some are fighters."

"Fighters?" Simon repeated it as a question.

Fale shrugged. "They like to have little fights to see whose robot is superior."

"You encourage this?" Lucas asked, his brow furrowing.

"No," Fale said. "They do it off-hours, but there's nothing in the rules that says they can't build robots that fight each other. And sometimes they have other functions of a more approved nature as well."

"Is that why Al and Tracy teased the boys? Their fighter lost?" Lucas asked.

Fale shook his head. "Those boys weren't into fighters. Al and Tracy definitely were. They did, supposedly, have their fighting robot tear up one of the boy's projects after hours, but no one could prove it. Yet another form of torture."

"Bullying by proxy," Simon said. "You do anything with nanobots in here?"

"We talk about them," the teacher said. "All kinds of androids, cyborgs, AI, and robots in all their forms. But no, that's tech that's far beyond our budget and abilities. We don't have a sterile lab to work in either."

"Any of the students have connections to nanobots?" Simon asked.

Fale frowned. "One or two may have fathers who dabble in tech. Not sure what they do. I think it's top secret. But nanobots were mentioned a few times."

"This is the boys who were victims?" Lucas asked.

Fale hesitated, but both detectives' eyes locked on his until he sighed. "One of them."

"Names, please. We have to talk to them," Simon insisted.

Fale sighed again and wrote them on a sheet of paper, sliding it across his desk.

"We'll go easy, I promise," Simon said.

THE FIRST TWO boys were in class and sufficiently upset about what had happened to their classmates that Simon believed them when they swore they knew nothing about who might have wanted to harm them. They admitted not liking them but seemed genuinely horrified by what had happened. The third, however, had called in sick, and when he wasn't at home, a neighbour in the next apartment over directed them to a video arcade down the street on the corner. There, they found Alec Garrett playing *Guitar Hero* vigorously with a friend.

They'd been told he was seventeen and a senior, but he didn't look a day over thirteen or fourteen. He was short for his age and clearly had no sense of style in how he dressed or groomed. He was dancing around and flailing at a guitar solo as they approached.

Simon badged him. "Alec Garrett, we need to talk."

"I'm busy," Alex said, not even looking at them.

"He's on a roll," his friend said. "Come back later."

"We're the police," Simon said. "We need to talk. Now."

The boys went on with their mock-n-roll, ignoring him. So Simon stepped forward toward the wall and pulled the plug, killing the machine with a sudden flash of lights and whine as the sound effects and music faded.

"God damn it! That was our best score ever! What the fuck?" Alec said, whirling toward Simon, who merely badged him again.

"What? I didn't do anything," the youth insisted.

"Then you won't mind if we talk," Simon said, grabbing him by the arm and dragging him back toward a food area around the corner.

"Hey!" Simon heard Alec's friend call out, but when he turned back, he saw Lucas had blocked him and was warning him off.

Simon pulled Alec around the corner and shoved him into a booth. "Sit!" Simon stood beside him to keep him from escaping as Lucas came to join them.

"What the fuck do you want?" Alec demanded.

"You to tone it down and have some respect, first of all," Simon said.

"You just ruined the game of my life!"

"It's just a game," Simon said. "You'll have another one. We're here about Al Johnson, Jr. and Tracy Ramirez."

"What about them? They're dead," Alec snapped.

"Exactly," Simon said. "So, what do you know about it?"

Alec scoffed a moment until the seriousness of the inquiry sunk in, then he waffled. "I—I don't know anything. Just heard they were dead."

"Apparently, you were real broken up about it," Simon observed.

"Hey. They were bullies. Not my friends," Alec said. "I'm sorry they're dead, I guess, but I didn't like them."

"Which makes you the perfect suspect," Simon said.

"Wait! You think I killed them? I didn't kill anyone!"

"Who did?" Simon asked.

"I just told you I don't know anything!" Alec was staring at Lucas, and then suddenly, his eyes widened with realization. "Hey, are you that android cop?"

"Lucas George," Lucas said.

"Oh, man! Wait 'til Gus hears about this! He'll be so mad he left!" Alec said, clearly referring to the friend Lucas had warned off. "Say something roboty, okay?"

"He's not a robot," Simon said.

"Android, robot—same thing," Alec replied, and then said to Lucas, "How many languages do you speak?"

"I am fluent in six million forms of communication, and can readily . . ." Lucas said, quoting *Star Wars* in his best imitation of C-3PO, a pretty good one.

"Splendid!"Alec cut him off. "We've been without an interpreter since our master got angry with the last protocol droid and disintegrated him!"

"Disintegrated?" Lucas replied. The android frequently fell into conversations like this with Simon's daughter, Emma.

Alec giggled. "Awesome! A real live droid! So cool!"

"You knew the victims from your robot club?" Simon asked, hoping to cut off any more robot-quote exchanges.

"Barely," Alec said, annoyed at the interruption of his fun again. "I don't know why they were even there. They clearly didn't know much or have any respect for robots. They were all about fighting them and destroying them."

"And you didn't like that?" Simon asked.

"A lot of us didn't, but we didn't *kill* them." He glared at Simon. "They were mean to lots of people."

"Any of those people the type who might have wanted to get back at them?" Simon asked.

"I don't know," Alec said. "Kids fight and they get back at each other. No one said anything to me."

"Okay, tell us about the nanobots," Simon said.

"My dad's company makes them," Alec replied. "He's the one you should ask."

"He has never brought any home to show you?" Lucas asked.

"Well, you can't see them with the naked eye, you know. You'd need a microscope."

"So you don't know anything?" Simon's words dripped skepticism.

"I've seen them," Alex admitted. "Been to the lab, too. They're cool. He knows I like robots and stuff and wanted me to see, but I've never touched them or worked with them. They're expensive. Not toys. What's any of this have to do with Tracy or Al, Jr.?"

"Ever heard of ricin?" Simon asked.

"The poison?" Alec said, then gasped with realization. "They were poisoned?" He looked back and forth between Simon and Lucas, then his eyes widened. "Wait! Poisoned with nanobots? Is that what you're saying?"

"We did not say that," Lucas said.

"Then why are you asking me about it?" Alec retorted.

"Just questions," Simon said.

Alec scoffed. "Hey, I'm seventeen, not stupid. You wouldn't be asking if it wasn't related. You said you came to ask about their murders."

"We never said anything about murder," Lucas said.

"Look! I didn't kill them! And no, I don't know anything about poison either. I'm just a kid! If you want to know about nanobots, talk to my dad," Alex said, then stiffened, staring at them. "That's all I've got."

Simon stared back a moment, but it seemed clear the kid had nothing more to tell. "We may be back."

"I didn't like those jerks, okay? But I am not a killer," Alec said. "I've said everything I know."

Simon believed him and headed for the door, Lucas following as they heard from behind them, "I can't believe I just met an actual living, breathing robot!"

"WHAT DO YOU THINK?" Lucas asked as they returned to the Interceptor.

"I think he likes robots a lot," Simon said. "But I don't think it was him."

The radio beeped.

"All units, shots fired at 518 Emanuel Cleaver II Boulevard, active shooter," a dispatcher called.

Simon picked up the handheld from the charger under the dash and clicked transmit. "706 responding." Simultaneously, he pushed the ignition button and shifted to drive, pushing the accelerator as he guided the car away from the curb and into traffic.

Beside him, Lucas flipped on the lights and siren. In ten minutes, they turned left off Locust and pulled to a stop beside Tucker, Bailey, and several black and whites surrounded by uniformed officers who were holstering their weapons. Neighbours and other onlookers were crowding across the street, where uniforms were running interference and rolling out yellow crime-scene tape as traffic hummed by loudly on nearby streets, their main thoroughfare cut off by the emergency vehicles.

"Three victims, one perp in custody, one survivor," Bailey said as Simon and Lucas joined them. "A security guard interrupted a robbery at gunpoint of two residents and opened fire."

"One resident, one robber, and the security guard are dead," Tucker added.

"Shit," Simon said.

A uniform hurried around the black and whites and curved toward them. "The survivor's name is Ted Garrett," she said, looking back and forth among the four detectives. "Who's working it?"

"Did you say Ted Garrett?" Simon asked, then turned to Lucas. "Isn't that the name of Alec's father?"

"Yeah, Ted Garrett," the uniform confirmed.

Lucas nodded. "That is what he said."

"We just talked to his kid about the murders," Simon said to Bailey and Tucker.

Tucker shrugged. "You take the initial interview, then, while we sort this out."

Simon and Lucas made their way through the commotion and past where yellow tarps covered three bodies to find Ted Garrett, the sole survivor, leaning against a Cadillac, his expensive three-piece suit as dishevelled as his hair. Mid-forties, he looked shocked and confused.

"Mister Garrett?" Lucas asked as Simon badged him then clipped the badge onto his belt. "Can you tell us what happened?"

"There were two men with guns waiting for us when we came out onto the drive," Garrett said.

"Did you recognize either of the men?" Lucas asked.

Garrett shook his head.

"Did they say what they wanted?" Simon asked.

"They were upset about a shipment from my business that went missing in route," Garrett said. "We've been working overtime to replace it."

"Did you report it to the shippers?" Lucas asked.

"Someone at the office was supposed to be working on that," Garrett replied.

"This was a shipment of nanobots?" Simon asked.

Garrett's brow furrowed, and his eyes darted away from Simon's gaze. "Yes, how did you know that?"

"We just spoke with your son about another matter," Simon said.

Garrett's eyebrows drew together as he fumbled at his pockets for his cell phone. "Alec? Is he okay?"

"Two of his classmates were murdered," Simon said.

"Oh, yes, my wife saw it on the news," Garrett said. "Just terrible. What does that have to do with Alec or nanobots?"

"They were all three members of the robots club at school," Lucas explained, "so we talked about robots a bit." Garrett seemed to noticeably relax at the explanation.

"So you saw the two men, and they confronted you about their shipment," Simon said. "What happened next?"

"They pointed their guns at us and were threatening us when that guard from across the street saw and came running over, calling out, and drawing his weapon," Garrett said. "Then they just started firing. Next thing I know, the guard, one of the men, and my neighbour, Paul, were dead."

They took him through the timeline, Lucas recording the entire interview with his internal systems for evidence, then asked for a few more details before Tucker and Bailey came to confirm they'd landed the case. After Simon and Lucas filled them in on the interview, Lucas internally emailing the recording to their phones, they left the homicide detectives with the victim and headed back to their car.

"What now?" Lucas asked.

"I want to check out Garrett's office and talk to a few employees about the mission shipment," Simon said as he settled into the driver's seat and fiddled with his seatbelt. "He was pretty dodgy the moment I mentioned nanobots."

"I thought you just startled him because of Alec," Lucas said.

"Possibly, but I have a hunch there was more to it," Simon replied.

At Garrett Robotics' corporate office just south of Crown Center, they were directed to Dave Ainsworth, Vice President of Distribution and Logistics.

"Actually, there were two," Ainsworth replied when they asked him about the shipment.

"Two missing shipments?" Simon asked.

"Yeah." Ainsworth nodded. "Another one went missing yesterday from the same batch."

"A batch you were working overtime to replace?" Lucas asked.

"Why, yes," Ainsworth said.

"Are there any serial numbers or other markings on the nanobots we could use to identify them?" Simon asked.

"Well, you'd need a microscope to see them, but they do have serial numbers," Ainsworth said. "I can print you a list."

They'd finished interviewing Ainsworth and were on their way back to the car when Simon's phone rang. It was the coroner again. Simon put the phone on speaker as they moved across the parking garage.

"We found part of a nanobot in Al Johnson's system," he said. "If there were any in Tracy Ramirez, they had dissolved already."

"Were you able to look close enough at it to find a serial number?" Simon asked.

"Just a partial my assistant wrote down," the coroner said, and read it off while Simon quickly checked the list Ainsworth had given them.

"Holy shit," Simon said, pointing to a row of numbers as Lucas looked on. "Thanks, Doc."

Simon hung up and was about to call Bailey when the phone rang again.

"Hello?"

"Detective, this is Stanley Gianni at Pak-N-Ship," a familiar voice said.

"What can I do for you, Mister Gianni?" Simon asked.

"A package came in overnight that got damaged in transit, so I had to take a look," Gianni said. "I was about to call the customer and do a little repair when I noticed a label on the contents that said 'nanotech."

"Who's the recipient?" Simon asked.

"A TGI Inc.," Gianni said. "I was about to phone them."

"Don't," Simon said. "We'll be right over."

"WHAT ARE YOU DOING? I'm the victim!" Ted Garrett demanded as Simon tightened the cuffs and Lucas recited his Miranda rights.

Lucas finished with, "Do you understand these rights as I have explained them to you?" and Simon announced, "You're under arrest."

"For being attacked in my own driveway?" Garrett replied.

"For the murder of Al Johnson, Jr. and Tracy Ramirez," Lucas said matter-of-factly as he led Garrett, hands behind his back, across the driveway toward the waiting Interceptor. There were still several emergency vehicles parked about, and a crime-scene unit was hard at work processing the site, but the tarps and bodies were gone, and the onlookers had started to disperse.

"What?" Garrett demanded.

"Using Pak-N-Ship to mail the packages to yourself was clever, but you screwed up with that phone number," Simon explained. "If the second package hadn't arrived damaged and revealed the contents, we might never have caught on, but the serial number matched the nanobot found in Al Johnson, Jr. by the coroner."

"The only missing piece is why," Lucas added as they stopped beside the Interceptor and he reached around Garrett to open the back door.

"I don't know what you're talking about," Garrett insisted defiantly.

"TGI Inc. was easily traced back to one of your companies, and you did a crappy job disguising your voice on the voicemail message, but it was the handwriting on the labels and the serial numbers inside that really did you in," Simon said, then added, "Our handwriting expert will match it in an hour or less."

"And there is the ricin powder we just found in your garage," Lucas added.

"I have rodents and snakes I need to get rid of," Garrett protested.

"Kind of overkill, don't you think? Most people use rat poison for that, " Simon replied. "What happened? Did they bully Alec?"

"Those bastards tried to cancel my son! They deserved what they got," Garrett spat.

"So, you decided to divert a couple of shipments and use your expertise for a special kind of revenge," Simon said, nodding. "Why bury Tracy but not Al?"

"There wasn't time," Garrett said. "I was interrupted."

"Well, I'm sure your son will consider losing his father a fair trade for revenge, don't you?" Simon said as he pushed Garrett's head down and forced him onto the car's back seat, then slammed the door behind him.

"We should call Bailey and Tucker," Lucas observed.

"We will," Simon agreed. "Just let me enjoy it a bit longer while we book him."

"I do everything professionally, I do nothing for fun," Lucas fired off—another movie quote—as he walked around the car to the passenger side.

"I don't recognize that one," Simon admitted as they climbed inside.

"*Under a Cherry Moon*," Lucas said. "People tend to enjoy what they're really good at," he added, another unfamiliar quote.

"I don't know that one either," Simon admitted. "But that I agree with."

"*Sweet November*," Lucas said.

"Are you ever gonna get tired of quoting movies?" Simon asked as he slid his seatbelt over his shoulder and clicked it into place.

Lucas smiled. "So many movies, so little time."

"How about just running out?" Simon suggested and started the engine.

"Because sometimes even if you know how something's gonna end, that doesn't mean you still can't enjoy the ride," Lucas said.

"Okay, enough already," Simon said as he slipped the car into reverse and slowly backed out into the street. "I'm serious. You're ruining this for me."

"Oh, I will usually enjoy my own thoughtfulness," Lucas said, then added with a big smile, "*Serendipity*."

"Shut the fuck up," Simon replied. "Every action movie ever."

"You say that one yourself all the time," Lucas said. "It is your catchphrase."

"I do not have a catchphrase," Simon said, and knew they'd still be arguing when they got to the station.

RIVER OF ICE

By David D. Levine

Airlock doors don't slam, but Lai Meifen gave it her best effort. Gritting her teeth, she pushed against the obstinate hydraulics until the hatch shut with a thud she could feel even through her suit's heavy polycarbon-fibre gloves. She couldn't hear it, not in this thin excuse for an atmosphere, but it would have to do.

Even at a distance of a billion kilometres, Lanfen—Meifen's fraternal twin sister—could still make her furious. This time, it was a cheery little email announcing that she had been promoted to team lead in the exobiology department and promising more exciting news to follow very soon. Meifen had sent a polite reply of congratulations, then immediately suited up and charged out the door.

She would show Lanfen. She would show them all!

Meifen paused, closed her eyes, and breathed through her nose to calm herself. She was on Enceladus—*she* was the one who was on Enceladus, not Lanfen!—and running off angry could get her killed. Once her heart rate had slowed, she opened her eyes, checked that the hatch was properly sealed, then turned to take in the view.

Saturn dominated the scene, looming like a gigantic glowing dome on the horizon. Fifty times as wide as a full moon, it was horizontally banded in a hundred subtle shades of butterscotch, yellow, and brown, roiling with storms bigger than Earth. The rings, alas, were below the horizon and always would be—Saturn never moved in Enceladus's sky, the moon being tidally locked.

The International Space Agency had denied Meifen's request to rotate the lander so that Saturn would be the first thing they saw on each EVA. But, one by one, she had gently persuaded her three crewmates to join in a small rebellion. Dr. Seung, the stern Korean commander, had been the most difficult, but eventually, Meifen had managed to convince the commander that it had been her own idea in the first place. The four of them had simply lifted and turned the lander—it had been easy in the moon's minuscule gravity, had taken less than an hour, and the ISA had been powerless to prevent it. Meifen smiled at the memory.

Her smile widened as she reminded herself again that it was *she* who was beholding this view with her own eyes, not Lanfen— the elder, the taller, the smarter, the prettier sister. This time, for once, Meifen had won out. And she would win out again, definitively, when she found proof of extraterrestrial life.

She shook her head, tried to put old rivalries and anger aside, and set off toward Silverstein Ridge. The bright white ice was not slick beneath her feet; at these temperatures, water ice behaved more like rock. It vibrated faintly with the constant distant thunder of Enceladus's cryovolcanoes, like an engine running somewhere far below.

Walking on Enceladus was more like skipping underwater and

remarkably difficult. The tiny moon's gravity was only a hundredth of Earth's, barely more than a downward drift; too forceful a step could easily send you tumbling helplessly until you impacted some icy scarp. For this reason, their suits were the toughest ever built, layered polycarbon fibre with synthetic diamond faceplates, and sported gyroscopes and attitude jets. Nonetheless, despite all her training, Meifen had been a mass of bruises until she'd learned the knack.

Meifen's destination for this EVA was a new feature that had just appeared on the far side of Silverstein Ridge in the latest imagery from the orbiter. As seen from above, it looked like a river —a snaking curve, brighter than the surrounding terrain, flowing down a valley from the cryovolcano called Kowal Peak. But it couldn't be a river of water, not at a hundred below zero Celsius.

Not *liquid* water, anyway.

As she loped across the landscape, Meifen's thoughts returned to her sister. She could not deny that Lanfen was more than quali- fied to head up an exobiology team; in fact, Lanfen would certainly have risen even higher in the bureaucracy by now if she hadn't been so focused on her deep-ocean extremophile research project. She had been certain it would give her the edge in selec- tion for the Enceladus mission—and she had nearly been right.

It was probably inevitable that the twins had both become exobiologists, with their astrophysicist mother and biochemist father both so enthusiastic about their fields. It was equally inevitable that they had turned out so competitive—Mother always said that she had felt the two of them jockeying to be born first. Lanfen had won that race, but Meifen had beaten her to Enceladus; perhaps that would finally even the score.

And perhaps Meifen's victory had even done Lanfen a favour. After her project collapsed and she lost the competition for Enceladus, Lanfen had thrown herself into more collaborative projects; that surely must have helped in gaining this new position.

Meifen paused to sip some water—cold though it was outside her suit, bounding across Enceladus's surface was hot and sweaty work—and mark a new vent on her map. Dr. Lufkin, the stolid, babushka-like Russian geologist, was insistent that any significant changes in the terrain be properly recorded, and this vent was certainly significant: a jet of steam several metres wide, bursting from a crack in the ice and hurtling skyward at hundreds of metres per second, freezing to snow as it rose. Even from a hundred metres away, she could feel the thunder through her boots. Perhaps someday, it would grow into an enormous cryovolcano like Mount Hurst, whose geyser-topped peak was the second-largest feature on the horizon after Saturn itself.

Much of the water in this jet would escape Enceladus's gravity to add to Saturn's E ring, while the heaviest, saltiest particles would fall back to the surface. Those particles—frozen drops of water from the salty ocean forty kilometres beneath her feet—were the thing she, the mission's exobiologist, had come to Enceladus to study. But though she'd collected and inspected snow of every type, age, and temperature, she had failed to find incontrovertible evidence of life. Organic molecules, yes; dissolved minerals that might be life precursors, yes; but nothing with any structure. If any life swam in Enceladus's subsurface ocean, the violence of the geysers destroyed all evidence of it.

But the river of ice on Kowal Peak, she hoped, might be different. Meifen checked her map, took a breath, and loped off toward it.

The craggy terrain as she approached the peak reminded Meifen of the last vacation she and Lanfen had taken together, on Kaua'i, together with Lanfen's husband, Zhou Sheng. The tension between the sisters had been fierce then—both had made it to the finals for astronaut selection—and Sheng, along with the sisters' parents, had insisted that they take a break to do something together.

And, indeed, there had been a certain amount of togetherness...

The ground rose swiftly, becoming twisted and jumbled, covered with a loose scree of ice crystals. She deployed the climbing claws on her boots, but even with their help, she often slipped and stumbled, only the sudden hissing shove of the attitude jets at her shoulders keeping her upright. Sometimes, she had to jump across chasms tens of metres wide, but after months of EVAs, she was confident in her abilities and her suit. She continued to climb, drawing closer and closer to the shimmering geyser that rose like a gigantic white tree from the cryovolcano's summit. The ice rumbled beneath her boots and gloves.

Soon, she found herself on Silverstein Ridge, comparing the view with her map. And there it was, flowing down Yule Valley toward Cooper Crater: the river of ice she'd spotted on the satellite view, gleaming smooth and white against the jagged terrain around it. She bounded off toward it.

It was the pressure that was her greatest enemy, she thought. The pressure of forty kilometres of ice on the ocean below forced liquid water up through cracks to the surface, where it met near-vacuum and flashed to steam, destroying any evidence of life.

The same sort of pressure—from her sister, her parents, from society at large—had forced her, too, into space. And had destroyed so much.

With a skipping, bobbling step, she brought herself to a halt on the surface of the ice river. She was no geologist—that was Dr. Lufkin's job—but the instruments in her suit and her cross-training let her identify at a general level what she was seeing. The river was, as she had suspected from the satellite imagery, much warmer and hence softer than the rocky stuff around it; it was behaving like lava, flowing downhill at a comparatively rapid pace. But the gravity here was so low that it piled up on itself as it flowed, forming heaps and ridges like frozen waves. Even Meifen, who knew she had no aesthetic sense whatsoever, had to admit that it was beautiful.

She took several photographs, then set off uphill. What she was seeking was most likely to be found at the river's source—the newest, warmest part of the flow.

It had been while climbing Mount Wai'ale'ale on Kaua'i that she and Sheng had begun flirting. She hadn't even meant it at first; she felt nothing for the man. But when he had appeared to respond, that response had triggered an impulse in her. A greedy, nasty, competitive impulse.

She should probably not have followed through.

The source of the ice river came suddenly: an enormous crested dome of smooth, gleaming ice, and beyond it, nothing but stony grey. In places, the dome was completely transparent; in others, a froth of glittering, crystalline white; it had the appearance of a breaking wave. Through her boots, she could feel a low, intermittent creak as the mass of water slowly pressed its way to the surface, freezing as it came.

This was exactly what she had been searching and hoping for: a slow seep, ice from the ocean below that had *not* been vaporized and catapulted into space. From her toolkit, she brought out drills and scrapers and sample containers.

The work was difficult, the positions into which she was forced to contort herself uncomfortable. But she persevered, gathering samples from high and low and deep and shallow until the beep of her air supply's monitor forced her to gather her equipment and head back to the lander.

She was happy but exhausted and stumbled frequently. At one point, she misjudged a leap over a gap she had cleared with no difficulty on the outward journey and wound up scrabbling on the chasm's edge for interminable seconds before clawing her way to safety. She lay on her stomach, gasping, for some minutes, until she was calm enough to continue.

She would have to be more careful. It would be horrible to die now when she was so close to victory. She had worked too hard, sacrificed too much, made too many difficult choices, to fail now.

Although she had to admit that the choices that had secured her position on the Enceladus mission had barely been hers at all. It had been Sheng who had responded to her subtle overtures, Sheng who had come to her tent in the middle of the night.

And it had been Lanfen's choice to smash her own equipment in a jealous rage when she'd found out, destroying years of her own work.

Lanfen had told the ISA that the data had been lost due to a lab accident. Bad enough that her project had collapsed; even worse if the agency had reason to doubt her emotional stability. For obvious reasons, neither Sheng nor Meifen had been inclined to reveal the truth. But, in the end, the deception had done Lanfen no good; Meifen had been selected instead.

The sisters had barely spoken since. Lanfen had not even come to the launch, to their parents' puzzled disappointment.

Back at the lander, Meifen fidgeted impatiently as the airlock cycled, listening to her suit creak as air pressure returned. She began doffing the suit as soon as she possibly could, her breath fogging the air and the cold metal of her neck ring burning her fingers, and left the helmet bouncing lazily on the EVA prep room floor.

Dr. O'Neill, the disgustingly perky Irish engineer, tried to interrupt Meifen as she rushed to the science bay. "There's a priority transmission coming in from Earth," she said as Meifen rushed past.

"I'll be there in a minute," Meifen replied, not slowing. She took the ladder in one jump, the precious sample container clutched to her chest.

Her fingers trembled, and not just from the cold, as she thawed and prepared the first sample and slipped it into the microscope. She held her breath as the image came up on the screen.

And took in more air in an excited gasp as the view swam into focus.

Curved, transparent forms drifted in the water, the salty Enceladan water from forty kilometres below the surface. One resembled an amoeba with a tail. Another looked more like a paramecium, only arrowhead-shaped. Structures were visible within, resembling vacuoles and organelles.

They were unmoving, clearly quite dead. They were in bad shape—exploded by decompression, torn by ice crystals that had frozen and thawed. But there was no question that they were life forms, possibly even multicellular. And they were definitely no Earth species.

Extraterrestrial life! She was the first human being to ever behold extraterrestrial life! Her place in history was assured!

A sudden happy shriek from the wardroom two levels above was the only thing that could have broken her spell of exhilarated wonder. "Dr. Lai!" called the commander, his voice full of surprise and delight. "Get up here right now! You don't want to miss this!"

"Coming!" she called, barely able to contain her own excitement. She couldn't wait to share her news with the rest of the crew . . . and the anticipation of her sister's reaction was even more delicious.

She leaped up from the science bay to the engineering deck in one jump. A second jump took her to the wardroom, where her three crewmates were gathered around the big wall display.

And on that display . . .

Fabulous creatures.

Golden-skinned they were, and large-eyed . . . nocturnal, perhaps, or evolved for a lower level of sunlight than Earth's. Tall and slim, with gill-like structures pulsing on the sides of their heads. Tool-using hands. The rest was obscured by clothing, colourful and diaphanous.

The camera pulled back, revealing the big press room at ISA headquarters in Mumbai. The head of the ISA was there on the stage with the aliens, and the president of the Asian Union, and . . .

. . . and her sister.

LAI LANFEN, read the text beneath her grinning face. XENO-BIOLOGY LEAD, FIRST CONTACT TEAM.

Meifen's knees buckled, but it was three long seconds before her body hit the deck.

I HID IN THE BATHROOM WHEN THE ALIENS ARRIVED

By Lisa Foiles

Time: Present Day

Universe: Three to the Left and Two Straight Down

Planet: Tycho, Galaxy K4-Q88P

Weather: Balmy

We had one alien encounter. It was embarrassing how much this dude looked like the stereotypical movie alien. Tall, slender, leathery skin. Deep green. A space suit filled out by arms and legs. And holy cow, a HUGE noggin. Big ol' head. He looked like a cake pop. A babysitter once traumatized me with *Mars Attacks!* when I was a kid, so not gonna lie, I was pretty apprehensive about this guy. The only unexpected feature was his lack of eyes. He didn't "see" in the way we do . . . he sensed things . . . ? I'm still not sure.

My apprehensions subsided because . . . he was kind. The linguists attempted to communicate, but it wasn't happening. Yet, the alien continued to visit. His ship would arrive on our planet, he'd step out, look back and forth as if to scan the area, and then just sort of . . . co-exist with us. We would—I say *we*, but I mean *they*, as in all the smart people on Tycho, who don't include me— attempt to offer him all sorts of things, including food, and he would reject them all. I remember they played Beethoven for him at one point. (I would've chosen Beyoncé, but it's all good.) I stayed far away from the alien and just kept baking.

Oh. Yeah. I'm a baker. I'll get to that.

The final visit from the alien was last year. He looked . . . ill. I don't even know how to explain it because frankly, he looked pretty ill to begin with (in my opinion). His green faded to grey. He seemed weak. He stayed with us for two days before he died. His body was on the ground, motionless. I guess our doctors were able to confirm his expiration. I mean, did he even have a heart to stop beating? These are the types of questions I would *think*, but never *say*, because I'd end up sounding like a toddler who wandered into a UN meeting. "Georgia is also a *country*?" is something I would probably ask in that scenario.

Anyway.

The scientists dissected our alien friend because they're scientists, and that's kinda their thing. After months of experimentation, they discovered something incredible: we could access the brain's information. Just a little at a time. I was never allowed inside the building, so I don't know how they did this, but it's how we learned about the Sludge. The Sludge is a green mucus-like substance extracted from Tycho's core, which can be used as both a clean, viable energy source *and* as artificial intelligence. It consists of . . . nucleus-like . . . micro-organisms . . .

Okay, stop. This is where we're going to have problems.

I don't know. I don't know how or why it works. I don't know *any* of this science-y stuff. Whenever this crap is talked about in my presence—which is ALL THE TIME—my brain rejects the information and curls up into a ball to protect itself. My brain is a possum. In fact, I'm the only person from Tycho who doesn't have the slightest grasp of anything we're actually doing.

Or, I guess, I *was* the only person.

And nobody on Tycho is doing anything now.

All I know is that it became clear that this alien brain could teach us a lot. If this one tiny peek led us to the Sludge, think of the infinite secrets that could be unlocked.

All right. Time to make like cloud storage and back up.

I'VE BEEN LIVING on the planet Tycho in Galaxy K4-Q88P, and I shouldn't have.

With the invention of a new fast travel system, Earthlings have explored space like a kid armpit-deep in a cereal box in search of a decoder ring. We're hittin' every nook and cranny. Several planets have been recognized as Earth-like, so colonization has begun, with the most successful so far being Tycho. Obviously, you need really effing smart and cool and good-looking people to be part of these ventures. Not morons. I cannot stress this enough. You do not want morons in charge of interplanetary travel and space colonization.

My older siblings were both selected for the Tycho expedition. Cole is . . . dammit, I have to use past tense now.

Cole *was* a Sergeant Major in the US Marine Corps and Amelia *was* a space-systems mechanical engineer. (No clue what those job titles meant.) They both spoke twelve languages or some absurd number like that, which is helpful when you're stationed in a remote corner of space with the most diverse group of intellectuals imaginable.

As you could guess, I was not the most impressive of my parents' three kids.

But I had a plan.

After five years, Tycho became . . . almost normal. Like, a normal place to live. Like Denver or some shit. Houses. Buildings. Farms. Indoor plumbing. Wi-Fi. They were starting to expand from their utopian "everybody share!" way of living and considering adopting the idea of currency exchanged for goods and services.

That's where I came in. I could never match the IQ scores or physical skills of my brother and sister, but dammit, I could bake. After begging, pleading, and just the right amount of strategic blackmailing that only a little sister is capable of, I convinced my siblings to get me to the planet. They put their careers at stake and fudged my documents to make me appear . . . smart. On paper. Instead of a 25-year-old basic Hallmark Channel-loving, Taylor Swift-listening, frappuccino-drinking white chick who flunked out of culinary school and ran her bakery into the ground after six months.

But that's neither here nor there.

I was accepted as a crew member on the next trip to Tycho to introduce outer space to sugar, fat, and a hell of a lot of sprinkles. This was a new start for me. No one knew me. As long as I held my idiot cards close to my chest and kept people in frosting, no one would suspect that I wasn't qualified to be there. Hey, Mom and Dad! Try telling your neighbours your youngest is the "odd" kid who "struggles" when she runs a SPACE BAKERY.

It was all working out as planned. Until . . .

Okay. I guess it's time.

It was a Tuesday. Everything had gone eerily quiet. Moments earlier, the world above me was deafening with the sounds of guns, explosions, and hysterical shouting. Now, nothing.

I waited for what felt like a lifetime curled up beside a toilet in an underground bathroom stall. I didn't have the training of everyone else on the planet—so, yeah, when the aliens attacked, I hid.

With trembling hands, I opened the stall.

I shoved through the rubble with my scrawny arms to reach the surface. I squinted from the light as I took in the scene.

Obliteration. No building stood. Bodies lay motionless beside their small companion robots. A few fires flickered in the breeze.

My town was gone. The aliens had destroyed it and left.

I was too shocked to cry. I searched for my brother and sister. My instinct was to shout their names, but I knew they hadn't survived. No one had. No one *could* have.

I kept searching. If my underground bathroom was unharmed, maybe other basements contained survivors!

I found our main laboratory—or, at least, the area where it used to be. There was so much Sludge seeping into the ground, as if yearning to return to where it was extracted. That building had stored every canister: years of meticulous collection, wasted.

Then I saw it: the Preservation Orb that once contained the brain of our late alien friend. It was cracked open and empty. I'm a ripe dunce compared to everyone else who lived on Tycho, and even I knew *that* was why this all happened. They had vengefully returned for their own.

Another hour passed before I found Cole and Amelia. Lifeless. I wept beside their bodies.

Dusk approached. Fear began to overtake me. I had to find food, water, shelter—I had to protect myself from the creatures that lurked on the planet. I needed to reach the neighbouring town of Ūnus.

I grabbed Cole's Blasty (the nickname I gave to the guns), but it felt clunky in my untrained hands. I'd surely shoot myself in the face while trying to find the trigger. I wished at that moment I hadn't turned down the firearm lessons Cole offered. And ignored all the times Amelia suggested I study maps of the planet. They'd wanted me to finally apply myself, but my lazy ass didn't listen.

I was screwed. I was the last person who should've been left alive.

The only way I was going to get to Ūnus was with one of those *stupid robots*.

I saw the remains of my bakery as I headed to the Robotics building. All the fruits, berries, plants—everything I had stored in Porbs was destroyed.

Oh, "Porbs" was my nickname for Preservation Orbs. I like to give borderline disrespectful nicknames to scientific marvels. I *so* wish they would've been cubes.

Anyway, Porbs are transparent spheres made of . . . poly . . . polycarbonate? Is that a word? . . . which preserve perishables for months, even years, using . . . Look, I'm just going to refer to things I don't understand as Advanced Science Stuff, or "ASS."

. . .

Hmm.

Too late, we're committed now.

Porbs work using ASS. End of story. I'm bored talking about it.

Finally, I saw one: a Sludge canister. I ran to it like a golden retriever to a mailman. This shit was a commodity. Everything ran on Sludge. I pulled the small yellow canister out from under a cement block. It only had a little over a fourth of Sludge left (maybe nine ounces), but that was enough to power a Prius for ten years. Most household appliances needed mere teaspoons of it to run for an eternity. Like, had it not been demolished, my blender would've outlived me tenfold. I'm telling you, there is no liquid more intense than this stuff.

Well, maybe Mountain Dew.

"Motherf—UGH! Why?" I screamed as I sifted through what was left of Robotics, the former centre of many things ASS-related.

Every robot was destroyed. I just needed *one*.

***

I FORGOT I have to explain everything. Okay, quickly:

Once they discovered the Sludge could learn and manifest itself as AI, it needed a host. The engineers shit their pants with glee when tasked to create a Sludge-powered robot body. They went through many iterations of what they called "shells" until they developed the perfect one for the Sludge to embody. Then we had hundreds of these little helpful shits hanging around, being productive and making me look bad. Officially, the shell was an "Inhabitation Chassis for the All-purpose Responsive Utility Sidekick," or . . . ICARUS!

Which I was like, "Wow, *thaaat's* a stretch, guys." In my best Chandler Bing voice. Like, could there *be* a more pretentious moniker? Some engineer really wanted to sound like he invented something cooler than Irritating and Temptingly-Kickable Little

Know-It-All Robots. Or ITKLKIAR. Not quite the same ring, I agree.

Naturally, I gave them a nickname for their nickname. I call them Ickys.

RECIPE FOR AN ICKY:
  1 Canister of Sludge
  1 Inhabitation Chassis
  1 Memory Card

I NEVER WANTED an Icky of my own. An Icky would discover I didn't belong on the planet. They would surely see it as their duty to alert my superiors that I should be sent back to Earth for my own health and safety.

Screw that. I was never going back. There was nothing left for me there.

But now, there was nothing left on Tycho either.

I found the Robotics basement. The roof had caved in, but one storage room was unharmed. Inside were mostly boxes of paperwork—but propped in a dark corner was an Icky. It looked radically different than any other I'd seen, but it was intact. That's what mattered.

I picked up the three-foot-tall robot. Its chest read:

(V1) ICARUS

"A Version 1 Icky?" I said. "What archaic treasure will I find next? A phone with buttons?"

I checked its memory card slot. Still a card inside. With the

Sludge's learning ability combined with the memories on the card, in theory, this robot would already be intelligent; we wouldn't be starting from scratch, thank God. I'd hate to have to explain how the universe works or what happened with the *Game of Thrones* finale.

"Please work," I muttered, inserting the Sludge canister.

The robot jolted and twitched. Lights blinked. Circuits sparked.

It screamed in a high-pitched female voice, then ran head-first into the wall.

I looked down at her collapsed body.

"DID YOU KNOW?" she yelled. "Deep sleep helps relieve anxiety! I am completely STRESS FREE!"

She bounced to her feet and started screaming again.

"Okay, um, stop," I begged. (Always hated talking to these things.)

"Anxiety and excessive stress can lead to hair loss!"

"You don't have hair," I replied. It was true. Her head was the size and general appearance of a toaster. If I was drunk enough, I'd probably shove bread in there.

"DID YOU KNOW? The average human head has about 100,000 hairs with a similar number of—" *glitchglitchglitch* "HAIR! What is it good for? Absolutely nothing!"

I debated whether to reason with it or remove the canister and see how far I could punt it into the nearest crater.

"So. Hi, first of all. I'm Saryn—"

"Like the nerve gas?"

"Um, nope—"

"DID YOU KNOW? Sarin was developed in 1938 Germany as a pesticide—"

I snapped my fingers. "Focus. Look at me. Over here."

Its bobbly head swung toward me. We locked eyes.

I inhaled deeply. "I don't know how much you remember about Tycho, where you live, and the people who made you, but . . . something has happened. There's been a devastating—"

"*APPLESAUCE!*"

"Do you . . . need applesauce?"

"No . . . I am unable to consume human food."

She hung her head and looked really sad.

"Great. Anyway, aliens have destroyed our town, and I need your help to reach the neighbouring settlement of Ūnus so I can, you know, not die."

"Oooooooh! Tragedy is an event! Events are log opportunities. Log #156."

Beep.

"No, cancel, I don't want to log anything."

"Logging is super important! It allows you to record events for historical purposes AND helps you sort out your personal thoughts, feelings, and EMOTIONS!"

She began dancing, until something sparked in her neck, and she started screaming again.

"Look, I'm not interested in pouring my heart out to a skinny can of wires with an oversized head, I'm interested in *survival*. CAN YOU STOP SCREAMING, FOR THE LOVE OF—"

She stopped. She looked stoically to the horizon.

"Ūnus is that way!"

A propeller unfolded from her back like an ironing board. The blades spun and lifted her little body into the air. She looked like a drone that had accidentally flown too low and picked up some scrap metal.

I followed her to the edge of town. Our sun star began to sink. Tycho sunsets are stunning. I never got used to them.

But the one thing I did get used to was living in that town, with my brother and sister, and my bakery. And now it was gone.

I glanced behind me one last time.

TYCHO WAS a temperate planet with minimal humidity. It never got above 87° F, nor below 55°. Real estate developers were eyeing this place as the new California. I mean, Elon Musk's kid, X Æ A-Xii, was still in diapers, and they'd already built him a mansion here. God, rich babies get everything.

So, even though I was starving and walking through empty, desert-like terrain, it wasn't absolutely miserable.

My new Icky companion kept offering me bugs to eat that she assured me were safe for human consumption, but that was a big rock-hard pass from me.

We walked. And walked. And walked. Finally, we sat in the sand to rest.

Distant howls unnerved me. Even though there were very few deadly creatures on Tycho, I still ensured my Blasty was within reach.

"Can I sit by you?" the Icky asked.

"No," I replied.

"But I want to learn everything about you cheese curds are made from fresh pasteurized milk in the process of *LIVE* from New York, it's *SATURDAY NIGHT* I think you're fascinating."

"Are you okay?"

"No one is okay! Ha ha ha ha ha ha ha ha."

Then she chased a bug.

Fantastic. I was in space wilderness with a faulty VI Icky.

Vicky.

Yeah. I'd call her Vicky.

I WOKE ABRUPTLY to frigid water being dumped on my face.

"GOOD MORNING YOU NEED TO HYDRATE!" Vicky screamed.

I stood up, gasping.

Vicky held a small metal cup. "I found a stream while you were going HONK SHOO HONK SHOO and gathered water in my foot!"

She slid the cup back over the wires on her foot.

"None of this was helpful, Vicky."

Her head tilted. "What did you say?"

"I named you Vicky."

"My name is Number 3."

"Number 3? What are you, a *Stranger Things* character? You're Vicky now."

She wrapped her arms around my leg and squeezed tightly.

"I . . . love . . . it . . . so . . . much."

I shook her off after an awkward moment. "Don't—don't get—please don't touch me."

She gasped. "You're a baker!"

Dammit. That effing Sludge. I couldn't have this blabbermouth bot learning more about me. My brother and sister wouldn't be in Ūnus to vouch for me. I couldn't have people questioning why I was approved for a Tycho mission over more qualified candidates.

"Forget it, let's go."

We found a forest. I remember the hunters talking about venturing here for food, but I never cared to explore the area myself. Not one for walking. Or the outdoors. Or tiny robots that scream things like—

"*TREEEEEEEEEEEEEEES!*"

"Yes. I see them."

"Visiting a new location is a discovery! Discoveries are log opportunities. Log #156."

Beep.

"Cancel log."

She hovered beside me as I looked for berries. I'd cooked with berries from this planet, so I knew which ones were edible. There had to be some around. Though, focusing on anything was a struggle.

"What invaluable service do you provide to your fellow citizens using your baking skills?" Vicky asked.

"I . . . make people happy. Sweets give you endorphins. Endorphins take everyone's mind off work. I mean, what good is ASS if you're not happy?"

A convincing answer, ruined by the ending.

"*Endorphins* sounds like *dolphins*! Maybe that's why dolphins are so happy!"

I think it'll slide.

"What will you do once we reach Ūnus?" she continued.

"Tell them what happened, then eat a hamburger."

"What makes you think Ūnus is still standing when Duo was annihilated?"

She asked it innocently, but it plunged into me like a bread knife. I'd been trying not to think about that possibility.

"Because . . . we were the town with their alien buddy's brain."

Vicky began hopping from rock to stump to rock, and so on.

"What's a buddy?" she asked.

"Like . . . a friend. Like a close friend."

"Saryn is Vicky's buddy! Saryn is Vicky's good buddy."

I rolled my eyes.

"You seem grumpy! You could be suffering from dehydration, hypoglycemia, and starvation! Might I suggest that we locate *APPLESAUCE!*"

"No applesauce."

We heard rustling nearby.

"OH OH OH!" Vicky shrieked. "I know what that is I know what that is I know what that is I know what that—"

I kicked her. Gently, of course.,

"—is, it's a *meleagris coturnix*. A forest-dwelling creature said to most resemble a cross between Earth's quail and turkey."

"Oh yeah, I call those Quarkeys."

"HA HA HA HA HA HA HA HA—"

"Stop. It's not that funny."

"I like your silly words," she said.

More rustling.

I shushed Vicky. I motioned for her to get down. She actually obeyed. I crawled behind a large fallen tree, sat, and waited.

"Can I sit by you?" Vicky whispered.

"No!"

Soon, a Quarkey waddled out from a bush.

I put my finger on my Blasty's trigger, hands shaking. I was so hungry I could barely control my movements. Plus, I'd never shot anything before.

I applied pressure . . .

"IF YOU SHOOT IT IN THE HEAD, YOU WILL PRESERVE THE MOST AMOUNT OF MEAT!"

Startled, I shot the gun. It blasted a hole through a boulder, and the Quarkey fled.

"Are you for real?" I yelled. "Vicky! You just scared away my only hope for food!"

"DID YOU KNOW? *Meleagris coturnix* are plentiful in this region—"

"Yeah, and they're all twelve miles away by now!" I exhaled with frustration.

"You are experiencing heightened emotions! Heightened emotions are log opportunities. Log #156."

Beep.

"No! CANCEL! You are UNHELPFUL. You are ANNOYING. You are WORTHLESS. All of the other robots are BRILLIANT and AMAZING, yet I get stuck with YOU."

Vicky backed away from me fearfully.

"I'm—I'm sorry, I just—Cole and Amelia are dead. They're dead. I'm never going to see them again," I vented through tears. "I'm alone. I'm scared. I'm so hungry. And . . . everything that everyone in Duo worked for is gone."

Vicky remained motionless.

"We had the brain of an alien that was teaching us things— things that could change everyone's lives! Look at the Sludge! Look at what it can do! Sludge can't survive in Earth's atmosphere, but what if the brain could've taught us how to solve that? Imagine everything powered by Sludge instead of fossil fuels and electricity and and and—"

I regained composure.

"And I was part of that," I said proudly. "I was *part* of something."

I paused.

"Sort of," I continued. "Was I? Was I part of it? Did I help at all?

I don't—let's just—maybe it's better if . . . we don't talk. You just go . . . and I'll follow you."

Vicky, without hesitation, walked.

THREE DAYS PASSED. I lived on berries since my further attempts to kill Quarkeys failed. I literally couldn't shoot to save my life.

Finally, we saw Ūnus. With renewed energy, we sprinted toward the city.

But it was empty.

Ūnus, with its shiny buildings, cozy neighbourhoods, and massive spaceport, was a ghost town. Parts of it were destroyed from a battle, but it looked like everyone just . . . left.

I fought a panic attack.

My only hope was to get to the spaceport and pray an escape capsule remained.

THE PORT WAS PROBABLY five miles away, but to me, it was light-years. I was weak. And sad. Even if I did reach a capsule before I collapsed into a depressed puddle of goo, how the hell would I pilot one? I was just an idiot. That had become abundantly clear.

Vicky and I entered an abandoned neighbourhood. No vehicles to borrow. They'd clearly all been vused to reach the port.

We found a house for the night—it felt like a normal, midwestern house, like my old one in Nebraska.

Nebraska. Wow. To think, if I survived, I'd be downgraded from Tycho to Nebraska.

I opened the refrigerator and . . . *CLUNK.* Vicky stuck to the door.

"You're magnetic?" I asked.

"I guess so," replied her muffled voice.

I started laughing. I couldn't help it. Maybe I was delirious, but it was so damn funny. It took me twenty minutes to free her, using a cutting board for leverage.

Thankfully, the house was stocked with food. There was even a Porb containing a tomato plant. I ate until I resembled an inflated pool toy, then I made a mug cake. Even if it was a half-assed attempt, I had to bake one last thing on Tycho.

I took my mug cake to the living room and Vicky, still timid, followed me. We both stopped and eyed the biggest, fluffiest couch I'd ever seen.

"You should probably jump on that," I suggested.

Vicky squealed with joy. I smiled as the little bot hop-hop-hopped.

Afterward, we sat on opposite sides of the couch.

"Vicky," I asked, "do you have one hundred fifty-five previous logs?"

"That's what my memory card is for! Memories!" she said, excited to talk to me again. "'Memory, all alone in the moonlight . . .' DID YOU KNOW? *Cats* was an award-winning musical by Andrew Lloyd Webber—"

"Vicky, play Log #1."

She did.

"Hi, this is Brian in Tycho Robotics, testing the log system for ICARUS: Version 1. Testing, testing . . . my colleagues and I finally have all three of

these little guys up and running. My Number 3 here is struggling a bit more than 1 and 2, but we're still tweaking, aren't we, little one? High-five! . . . Or dance, that works too."

Beep.

———

"VICKY, PLAY LOG #155."

She did.

———

"BRIAN here with the FINAL log for VI ICARUS, #3. This piece of shit has destroyed the lab for the last time. I don't know what happened, but this one is completely malfunctional—"

"DID YOU KNOW? Mayonnaise is—"

"Shut up! You are completely worthless! You've made me look like an idiot! They might demote me because of you! You started a fire! You destroyed an entire shelf of Sludge canisters! Goodbye forever, Number 3. I hate you. Rust in peace."

Beep.

———

I STARED AT HER. She stared at me.

"Rust in peace is a pun!" she said.

My eyes welled up. "Do you wants to sit by me?" I asked.

"Okay!"

She plopped down beside me, and we peacefully watched the sunset through the window.

Until we saw an unmistakable silhouette.

An alien walked down the street, scanning each house. He held a massive weapon. He would see my lifeform, in whatever way he "saw."

"Vicky. We have to run," I said intensely.

We crawled through the kitchen toward the back door. I opened it and ran.

With pure adrenalin, I sprinted to the forest's edge. Maybe among the woodland lifeforms, I'd be less noticeable.

I hid behind a tree, breathing heavily.

"Vicky?"

She was gone.

My heart pounded. Did the alien get her?

I should've made a break for the spaceport. But I didn't. I returned to the house.

I crept inside and whispered, "Vicky?"

"I'm magnetic!" said a muffled voice by the fridge.

I pulled, and pulled, and pulled, and finally freed her.

When I stood up, the alien was right in front of me.

I froze. Vicky hid behind my leg. The alien scanned the room but acted like he didn't see me. Or maybe it wasn't acting. He *couldn't* see me.

After a few moments, he left the house.

It all made sense. I didn't survive the attack on Duo because I hid like a coward in a bathroom. I was spared because the aliens didn't see me. For some reason, these bastards that killed my family couldn't recognize me as a lifeform.

Rage bubbled up inside me.

I ran into the street.

"Hey!" I yelled. "You can't see me, but I can sure as shit see you."

The sound caught his attention. We squared up on the street like an old western.

He approached me. Quickly.

I grabbed my Blasty and aimed. I shot twice and missed. He walked faster.

"In this scenario, you should *avoid* shooting him in the head!" Vicky advised.

"I'm aware!" I said frantically.

He aimed his weapon at me. I shrieked and fired.

The beam blasted a hole through his chest, and he collapsed. Guess they did have hearts to stop beating after all.

"You just murdered an extraterrestrial! Murdering extraterrestrials is a—"

"Log opportunity," I interrupted, panting heavily. "Maybe later."

Vicky and I retrieved the Porb from the house, ditched the tomato plant, and put the alien's head inside. (After I asked Vicky to saw it off his body, of course. Ick.)

With the Porb tightly locked, we headed to the spaceport. More aliens were bound to show up once this asshole didn't return home.

The port was like an airplane terminal—clean and welcoming. A wall exhibit with a sign reading THE GREATEST ACHIEVE-MENTS IN TYCHO HISTORY greeted newcomers with shelves displaying photographs, gadgets, etc. You know. ASS stuff.

"YEEEE! There's one escape capsule left!"

Vicky was right. I pushed a green button to open it.

It was small—the size of a Smartcar. We jumped inside and entered our coordinates into the computer.

"CAPSULE REQUIRES [8 OZ.] SLUDGE TO REACH [EARTH]. INSERT CANISTER NOW."

We hopped back out and searched the building. The storage room containing the Sludge canisters was locked.

I grunted in frustration. What was I supposed to do? Go back into town and hope I found Sludge somewhere? Search the eight thousand desks in the building for keys?

We returned empty-handed to the capsule. I sighed with defeat.

"I have Sludge!"

Vicky turned around and shook her hips while pointing to her back.

She did, indeed, have [8 oz.] of Sludge.

Oh, no.

I looked at the capsule. I looked at Vicky. Sludge couldn't survive on Earth. Even if Vicky came with me, she would be instantly defunct once she entered the atmosphere. She only worked on Tycho, and what good was it to leave her there, all alone?

I knelt down. "Vicky, I'm sorry I yelled at you. I'm so sorry. You aren't worthless. You're anything but. If I make it home, it's only because you saved me."

She tilted that little head of hers. "It's because I'm your good buddy, right?"

"Yeah," I said, smiling through the tears. "You're my good buddy."

And with that, I removed the Sludge canister.

Her little body toppled from the weight of her big toaster head. She collapsed.

I inserted the canister into the escape capsule.

I sat inside, strapped myself in, and the door closed.

"LAUNCH IN THIRTY . . . TWENTY-NINE . . . TWENTY-EIGHT . . ."

"Wait!"

"TWENTY-SEVEN . . . TWENTY-SIX . . ."

I frantically unstrapped myself and opened the door.

I swept Vicky's body up and ran to the big wall exhibit.

Shoving some kind of Sonic Screwdriver-looking bullshit off the central shelf, I replaced it with Vicky—the *real* greatest achievement in Tycho history.

"SEVEN . . . SIX . . . FIVE . . .

"FOUR . . .

"THREE . . .

"TWO . . ."

DID I make it back to the capsule?

Yes. And now I'm here, sitting in a tin can, very Bowie-like. This thing claims to be headed for Earth, and I'm too dumb to know otherwise. But it's okay that I'm dumb—because I'm bringing home someone a lot smarter than me, aren't I, Mr. Big Alien Head? Yes, you're so ugly, yes, you are!

You know, Vicky, we aren't so worthless after all. Maybe one day, I'll see you again. I'll put this memory card back in your toaster head, and you'll be so super excited that I finally . . . what was it? Recorded events for historical purposes and sorted out my thoughts, feelings, and EMOTIONS! Ha. Miss you, good buddy.

End log.

A tin wind-up drummer marched jerkily in its red uniform along the broad, flat surface of the Thangdu Temple balustrade as Orville waved a handful of the mechanical soldiers and cried out to buyers in the crowd. Above the restless flow of the market, the high, white cliffs of Khangchengyao sparkled in the clear morning air.

"Orville!" A face Orville knew jostled through the press. The wiry man grinned a greeting, his thinning hair tied back in an untidy braid, his sun-browned face a nest of wrinkles. "May the seven Gods smile upon you." He spoke Bhutanese.

Orville nodded and put a hand on the marching drummer before it toppled from the temple wall. "Paldun. Your family is well?" A dig. Unless things had changed in the last year or two, Paldun wouldn't know.

"I'm glad to see you. *Tensung.*"

Orville's neck flashed, hot. Tensung, the name his parents had given him, was the name of a troublemaker. He'd given it up twenty years ago—more—and now was only known by the name the British had given him. "How did you find me?"

"You come here every month to sell imperialist bric-a-brac." Paldun gave him a look that said nothing happened in Thangdu he wasn't aware of. "I understand it falls off the train every week in Gangtok. Free for the taking, if you're quick."

Orville let the clattering drummer die in his hand and slipped it into the British jacket he wore over his bakhu. "What do you want?"

"I have work for you."

"And if I don't want work?"

"Then you're no patriot." Paldun nudged him and nodded along the street. "Besides, you'll want this work."

There was no dodging this. Paldun knew every crime Orville had ever committed and wouldn't hesitate to use that knowledge to coerce him. He'd done it before. Orville followed him, worming through the crowd to the main road to Gangtok, a narrow lane lined with shops. The buildings ended, and they came to a forest that dropped away to a wide, brown river a thousand metres below. The late winter wind cut more sharply as Paldun led him up a winding path through steeply terraced tea plantations.

"We need a guide," Paldun said once they were away from listening ears.

We meant the revolution. *Guide* made no sense, though. Paldun and those he worked with knew every inch of these mountains, every hiding hole, every ambush.

"Someone who speaks English. Knows the local languages. Someone with light fingers."

"Revolution is for young men," Orville objected.

"Revolution is for every Sikkimese," Paldun corrected him. "Everyone who wants to see our Chogyal returned from exile."

Four years, the Chogyal had been gone. The British had sworn to occupy only the southern part of the country, but this was a blatant lie. A land dispute between the Chogyal and the neighbouring Nepalese was the pretext to bring the colonizers—and their troops—north, to "settle the claim." They never left.

"Once the paths are passable, the British are sending an agent up from the south. He's bringing plans for steam turbines, cannons, and black powder to Colonel Digby in Lachen."

"Lachen? Whatever for?"

"The British plan to build a munitions factory there once the rail extension is complete."

"That's insane." But the British had no idea of their own limits, so they dreamed up astounding engineering, defying logic. And . . . a munitions factory. To solidify their local dominance. "What? The British want unrestricted trade with countries to the north? Nepal? It's hardly worth it."

Paldun tilted his head. "They've heard of another country."

Orville pulled back. "Other than Nepal or Bhutan?"

"Shangri."

Orville peered at Paldun. "It doesn't exist." But he remembered stories at his mother's knee. Orville's mother was born in a village far up in the mountains, beyond Lachen, and she'd believed such things.

Paldun gave the hint of a shrug.

"You know every valley," Orville argued. "All the borders."

"Not every valley. That area's enormous. Difficult."

"All right, there are places anybody would be crazy to go." Too steep. Too remote.

"You're a trader. You'd know better than anyone," Paldun said. "Jewels in improbable markets. From where? Those little villages?" he scoffed. "Fabulously tanned furs have shown up, Orville.

Thicker and softer than anything we have. Medicines no one can explain."

Yes. Every once in a long while, there was a rumour of some breathtaking raw gem, fine yak wool, or unbelievably warm down. But . . . Shangri? No. Shangri was a land of magic, a land said to perch at the top of a hanging valley, accessible only by no more than a gossamer ladder, a land that touched the realms of the Gods.

Men had died searching for it. "It doesn't exist."

Paldun lifted a shoulder. "Whether it does or not, the British think it does. Once they have cannons and rifles in Lachen, our homeland will never be ours again."

Orville let out a long breath. "I can be a guide. I don't want to be your thief. I'm already on British lists. One more arrest, and I'll never see Phuntsog again." Or his lousy brother, but that was another matter.

"This has to be subtle. One man. Contact the courier, become his guide, and steal the plans quietly before you reach Chungthang. Don't alert him. Bring them here, *without* Colonel Digby's troops on your tail. I'll take the plans across the border to the Chogyal."

"So the Chogyal—so his allies can build the factory."

Paldun regarded him from beneath lowered brows. *Exactly.*

Orville felt his head shaking slowly back and forth. So.

"Or, a small voice can speak to a policeman. And you can still find yourself in a British jail."

Orville's gaze snapped up to Paldun's face.

Paldun looked over the landscape, signalling an end to their meeting. "How is your father?"

"Why?"

"We don't want your work to go unrewarded. Phuntsog still loves the joy plant?"

You know he does, you bastard.

"I will have a kilo of opium for you when the work is done."

GANGTOK.

When the steam whistle blew, all heads turned. Orville had a good position along the railing, watching for any man who looked as though he might be a Briton working for the Sikkim Munitions Company.

Today was his day.

The man was older than Orville expected—older than himself—one of only a half-dozen foreigners to disembark. He carried a small case and, with some difficulty, dragged a portmanteau.

Orville shoved his way out of the station to the street where half a dozen carts waited, his own among them, and watched the First-Class doors for his man, pouncing as soon as he emerged. "Sir? Carry your bag, Sir? I am a very good porter, and I have a cart."

The Englishman eyed the other porters springing forward. "And what do you charge?"

"One rupee to the hotel, Sir, and I am very strong. I also speak English superbly." He ducked his head in a quick bow.

"Very well." The man grimaced, as if with pain, as he reached into a pocket inside his coat. He deposited two British coins in Orville's hand. "Take me to the hotel."

"Very good, Sir." Orville strapped the portmanteau to his back with a headband and led the way to his donkey cart.

The businessman followed, but as he allowed Orville to hand

him up to the plank seat on the front of the cart, Orville wondered if this man had the strength to make the journey to Lachen.

"I am also an excellent guide, Sir," Orville said, loading his luggage and coming around to drive. "I know the roads in this area, and I speak all the local languages. Should you wish to visit historical and cultural places in our beautiful country, I can give you a very good price."

"How much would you charge to take me to Lachen?"

Yes. This was the one Paldun had told him to find. "Good price. Five rupees a day, five days." A low rumble echoed distantly from across the valley, and Orville almost had to smile at his good fortune. He pointed. "Sir."

The man looked where Orville indicated. On a distant peak, a cloud of snow descended into the valley with terrifying power.

"Avalanches, Sir. Very dangerous. They come with fine weather, warm weather in the spring. I can take you by safe paths."

The man lifted his brows, impressed. "Very well, then. I'll hire you to take me to Lachen."

Though the weather had been pleasant all day, rolling white clouds turned dark with threatened rain before they arrived at Tumlong, and there was no hotel in the state's unofficial capital. Orville asked in the street, and a family gave him and Leopold a room in their own home and a meal at their table. Orville thought the price reasonable, given the black looks Leopold drew. Orville left his cart at the Tumlong stable and carried the luggage—except for the small case, which Leopold carried—up the switchback streets.

At dinner, shouting filtered up from the centre of the town, dampening the already awkward—translated—dinner conversation. The father rose from the table and bolted the door, exchanging uncomfortable glances with the uncle, and the sons looked down at their bowls. When the women had cleared the last of the dishes, the father hustled Orville and Leopold up to a cramped attic furnished with a single bed and a table with a pitcher and basin. The father brought Orville blankets, closed the shutters, and advised him to douse the candle as soon as they could.

The night was chill, but the cold rain did not diminish the chanting and angry shouts in the streets below.

"What are they saying?" Leopold asked, sorting his portmanteau. Though the older man had managed the first day's journey without complaint, Orville thought he'd seen signs of pain: a pinched jaw, an occasional grunt. The bureaucrat had assured him he could march all day, but Orville wondered how his charge would manage once they left the cart and donkey behind.

"They are cheering the Chogyal, Sir." Orville laid blankets on the floor for his bed. All day, he'd managed to steer the conversation away from politics, and didn't want to start now.

"It doesn't sound like cheering," Leopold said. "In any case, I thought your former king was truant. Exiled to Bhutan."

"The Chogyal's brother is in Tumlong, Sir."

"Ah. And does this brother have pretensions to rule?"

"No, Sir."

Leopold settled into his bed, resting the candle on the floor between them. "Orville, I've served this colony most of my life. I am not unaware of people's sentiments toward the British."

"Yes, Sir."

"I am assuming this royal brother, consciously or not, raises the people's hopes that the Chogyal will return and the British will withdraw. But I hope you and others of your countrymen are aware we want only to establish strong trade that benefits both parties."

"Yes, Sir."

"Now, your professional opinion as guide." Leopold tucked the case under his blankets, next to the wall. "Do you expect insurrectionists to be a problem on our journey?"

"Oh, no, Sir." Paldun wanted the plans stolen quietly, without tipping Leopold off. "I will explain to any ruffians we meet that you are simply brokering good commerce."

Leopold nodded thoughtfully and doused the candle.

Orville listened in the dark. The protesters' voices drew closer. *Down with Britain. Down with colonial rule.* The Sikkimese had long controlled the lucrative trade with Nepal and Bhutan, but the British brought competition and opium. Orville sympathized with the rebels. Too many in the south had been caught in that net of addictions.

The mob moved on, and the chants receded. Orville closed his eyes. He would stick to the plan.

"Orville." Leopold's voice was quiet in the dark.

The unexpected whisper roused him. "Sir?"

For a long moment, only the rain on the roof was audible. "Have you ever heard of . . . a country called Shangri?"

Shangri. He remembered Paldun's words in Thangdu. *"They've heard of another country . . ."*

"Orville?"

"Yes, Sir. It is a place in my culture's religion." *Paradise.*

The rain drummed.

"Tell me. What your religion teaches you."

Orville considered this, unsure what words would best please his client. "It is the gateway to the heavens of the seven Gods."

The pause this time was shorter. "A place of miracles? A place one goes to be healed?"

Magic. "Yes, Sir, so we are taught. But it is not a place that exists in this world."

"No?"

"No, Sir."

Leopold shifted on his mattress. "Are there not things that come in trade from the north, beyond Lachen? Fantastical jewels, thick, soft furs? Healing potions?" Leopold hesitated. "Amulets that grant access to Heaven?" His words became a murmur. "Regardless of how a life is lived."

Death tokens. Myth. "Maybe from Nepal? Or Bhutan?"

Leopold was quiet for some time, and then, as it had many times over the day, the coughing took him.

The suffering in the older man's eyes. Leopold's ailment— whatever it was—was not a passing one. "Sir?" Orville knew he should not ask, but . . . "Are you ill, Sir?"

Beneath the beating of the rain, a rustling from the bed suggested to Orville that the man had lain back. "All of us . . . pass on, Orville. Some sooner than others. Sooner than . . ." his voice broke off. "Good night, Orville. And I pray your seven Gods watch over you."

WHERE THE PATH left the trees, Orville lowered his burden to the ground and surveyed the road ahead. Above the trail, a long ramp of snow rose to heights hidden by the angle of the slope. Across the broad valley falling away to his right, summit after summit stretched north in an undulating line, white with winter's farewell gifts. Below their cliffy crests, paths cleared naked of trees by avalanches broke the forest into vertical slashes. But it was the snowy flanks between the forests and peaks he scanned.

Yes. There, and there. There. Faint lines indicated cracks where the snow had released, and trails of fresh ice debris marked several of the chutes. Small sluffs, loosened by spring warmth and rain. He peered up and down the valley. Odd. A weak layer of crystals had formed at the bottom of the snowpack early last winter, during an unusual period of warm winds. The heavy spring snows should have triggered big slab avalanches, but he saw none.

Yet.

Leopold crunched up the snow behind him, leaning on his walking stick. "Ah. Good," he panted. "That last hill was a long one." He set his case on the snow and sat on it, wiping his forehead and grimacing, the spasm recalling pain Orville had seen so often in Phuntsog's eyes. He looked away. He could not afford to like this old man.

Orville had not yet done anything to provoke British fury. Had not yet stolen the plans. The theft wasn't as easy as Paldun seemed to think.

And, two days ago, he'd made a serious error. He'd chosen a river crossing on a snow bridge too rotted by the spring thaw to support Leopold's greater weight. The bureaucrat had fallen in, soaked to the waist in frigid water, and Orville had reached out his arm, pulled him from the water. Given him dry clothes—his own —and built a fire.

Now . . . he felt different.

Could Orville betray this man? For a bitter insurrectionist such as Paldun? Not that such a fine moral point would make a difference to Paldun's willingness to have Orville arrested.

But as the days passed, the more he thought about the plans, about the Chogyal's scheme to manufacture weapons, the more he wondered if an escalation of war was the best way forward. Not that it was his choice to make, but could the Sikkimese win such a war when endless foreign soldiers could materialize on every train?

Too, Orville needed to wait for the right opportunity, not take too great a risk, delay until the last moment so as not to arouse suspicion. If Orville needed to boldly slip the case from Leopold's bed as he slept, he could, but only as a final recourse.

The older man scrutinized the indentation in the snow across the pitch before them. "You said we could make Chungthang by mid-afternoon? Perhaps even Lachen by nightfall?"

"With an early start and a good pace, Sir."

"We certainly had an early start."

"Yes, Sir. But I think we must take a small deviation."

"Deviation? I say. Why?"

Orville nodded to the sun-filled path before them. "This slope has not yet slid. Wind last night, and fresh snow above. It is afternoon, and the temperature is rising."

Leopold scanned the pristine path. "It's not that far. Then we're in the trees again."

"Yes, Sir. But our footsteps could free the slide." Orville nodded down the hill. "We should stay in the forest. Cross the gulley down there and climb back to the path."

"Rather steep, that."

Orville turned and fixed his eye on his client to reinforce his point. "Yes, Sir."

"Add an hour to the trip."

"Very likely, Sir." At the pace they were going. "But we can stay tonight in Chungthang. The villagers are friendly." Friendly to Sikkimese, at least. It would take Orville some work to charm them into hosting an Englishman. "We can reach Lachen tomorrow." Another night to give Orville an opportunity to abscond with the contents of Leopold's case.

"All right, then. But what about him?" Leopold nodded past Orville, up the path.

Orville swung around. Emerging from the forest at the far side of the avalanche chute hurried a Sikkimese peasant, lightly burdened, casting apprehensive glances up the slope as he darted toward them.

"Fool," Orville muttered, holding his breath and watching the slope.

Yet the man crossed the entire slide path in safety.

He only noticed Orville and his companion when he was almost upon them. "Oh!" he said, pulling himself up short at the edge of the trees.

"Friend." Orville addressed him in Sikkimese. "What hurries you that you risk your life?"

The man, draped in furs and leathers that hung open from the warmth of the day, spoke in a rapid voice, his eyes round. "There's a *magiel* in Lachen. A *magiel*, friend. From Shangri."

"A magiel?" Orville stared at him.

"I'm going to Tumlong. The Chogyal's brother has to know about this before the—" For the first time, the peasant seemed to see the Englishman, listening intently.

"There's no such thing as a magiel," Orville sputtered. "No such thing as magic. Or Shangri."

"Are you bound for the British outpost at Lachen?" the peasant said, eyeing Leopold as if gauging how much the foreigner could understand of their conversation. "You'll see him. He's there."

Orville squinted at him, trying to read why the man would jest with a complete stranger. Or if he was completely deranged.

The peasant pushed past them. "I have to go."

Orville watched the man hurry down the path through the trees, still trying to figure out what on earth that exchange had meant.

Leopold stood. "Shall we?" He dusted the snow from his case and nodded toward the path across the slope.

Orville hoisted his burden. It was going to be tricky punching or cutting holes in the untrodden snow below the path.

"No." Leopold again gestured to the tracks on the slide path.

"Sir—"

"I don't speak your language, Orville, but I have quick ears. I heard the word, *Shangri*. And *British*, and *Lachen*." He held his walking stick out toward the path. "Your countryman used this path. If it is safe enough for him, it is safe enough for me."

Where did this old man find the drive to fulfill his mission, even as death haunted him? Was he stupid? Stubborn? . . . Honourable?

Orville hesitated. Every sense told him not to step onto the slide path.

"Orville." A hardness had come into his patron's eye. A hardness Orville had seen before, in factory overseers and soldiers. British.

Hot violence flashed through Orville. *No. Not honourable. An ugly colonial master*, regardless of his previous magnanimity.

Orville choked back the tremors in his hands and clenched his jaw into a stiff smile. If he wanted the plans, he had to stay with Leopold. Besides, if Orville didn't attend him, the man would surely lose himself in Chungthang, or be beaten for an Englishman, or die of exposure on one of the maze of trails leading to or from the village. And Orville would lose the chance to rob him.

Orville stepped onto the path. The theft would have to take place in Lachen, then.

THE BRITISH OUTPOST in Lachen crouched in the gloom of near-night. The single-story stone house, the size of any ten peasant huts, stood with its outbuildings above a narrow canyon, five miles beyond the village proper, on a promontory overlooking the little-used trail to Nepal. Candlelight seeped through windows shuttered against the cold. Orville rapped at the door, then stood back.

A peasant answered in due course and showed them into a spacious entryway with stone flagging, local tapestries, and two framed photographs of the village.

"Leopold?" An older man of military stature with a generous moustache strode down the corridor, reaching out a hand in greeting. "Good God, it didn't take you long to get here. Roads passable, then, eh?"

"John. Good to see you again." Leopold shifted his walking stick and took the offered palm.

"My wife and I were just sitting down. I'll have Chakdor set another place and show your man where to put your things. He can get a bite in the kitchen."

The servant, Chakdor, helped Leopold from his coat, and—miracle—Leopold handed his case to Orville.

THE ROOM the British colonel had given Leopold was the size of the apartment Orville shared with Phuntsog and his brother. It was appointed with rich carpets and tapestries and framed photographs of the Sikkimese mountains and villages. Orville nodded to Chakdor, who left the candle and departed, and lowered the portmanteau to the floor. There was a good-sized bed with a fur coverlet, a desk and chair, and a nightstand with a basin.

Orville opened the case. The documents were there. Drawings. Materials lists. Detailed instructions. Orville's fingers hesitated, touching them. What would Leopold's superiors do to him?

The door clicked.

Orville shoved the documents into the inside pocket of his coat and turned, composing his face.

Chakdor stood, framed against the dim hallway, a water jug in hand, his mouth open in surprise. "Friend . . ." Chakdor whispered in Sikkimese. A warning tone.

He'd seen.

Piss! Orville strode to the door and, pulling the servant in, closed it.

The man was small but wiry. A struggle would make noise, its outcome uncertain. Then Orville would be on the run, the mission botched.

Orville pressed his back to the door. Chakdor stared at him, clutching the water jug to his stomach.

What could he say? Yes, many Sikkimese hated the British, but not all. Some had gained in status, wealth, prospects.

Orville shoved his hand in his trousers pocket. He carried a mittful of paper money, Leopold's payment, some tips. He pulled it out and offered it to the man. "It's all I have. Don't tell your master."

The servant stared at the money as if it were a cobra. His eyes snapped up to fasten on Orville's.

"No one saw you come in. You don't know I took these. I'll be gone before morning." Orville's breath became shorter, and sweat soaked his armpits.

Chakdor seemed to recover himself. His gaze flicked about the room.

What would he do? Orville's mouth dried. He had to risk it. "The British are building a munitions factory. Guns. War. Lachen will be overrun. People killed."

Chakdor's doubtful gaze returned to him.

"The Chogyal. I have to bring the plans to him. Proof the British have no intention of peaceful trade with Nepal. They plan to invade, and Sikkim will be the battleground." Orville waved the money, his arm shaking.

Chakdor looked at Orville's fist. He carefully set the water jug on the table, then stepped forward and took the money, slipping it under his bakhu. He cast his eyes down and brushed past Orville, opening the door.

Colonel Digby's voice called out down the corridor. "Chakdor! Drat it, where are you? Call that Gangtok guide!"

Chakdor turned, his face pale, and locked eyes with Orville.

Orville's breath came hard. He nodded and followed the man from the room.

———

CHAKDOR SLUNK OFF to the kitchen as Colonel Digby and Leopold stood in the entryway, their coats on. Orville hurried down the corridor, ducking his head as he came, hoping the profile of his jacket didn't bulge where the documents hid. "Sir, I have not yet unpacked your luggage."

"Don't worry about that, Orville," Leopold said, an intensity shining in his eyes. "All that can come later."

Carrying a candle lantern, Digby led them into the star-splashed night. Snow filling the valley gleamed, pale and ghostly, as they crunched on an icy path around the back of the house to the outbuildings. One, larger than the others, looked much like the barracks Orville had seen in other British outposts. A small but likely well-trained troop to keep the locals from stringing up the colonizers.

Digby produced a ring of jangling keys and opened a steel padlock on the door of a smaller hut. He lifted the candle lantern, and each of them ducked, one at a time, inside.

The hovel was a wooden storage shed, lined with shelves of horse tack and wagon parts, murky in the dim light of the candle lantern, and it stank with human waste. A straw pallet had been thrown on the stony floor, and an ancient man in a woollen blanket huddled there, squinting up at them from a halo of fluffy white hair, his hands manacled. The water jug on the floor beside him was empty, and the chamber pot, full.

But . . . the old man's skin.

It blurred in the light of the candle lantern. Shimmered.

Like the old myths. A blow thumped once in Orville's chest. Orville's mother's stories, at his bedside long ago, of the ancient Gods.

A magiel. From . . . Shangri.

And—*chained*.

Piss. Even if this were no revered being of myth, to *shackle a man like a dog*—

"Well." Digby stood aside and held the candle lantern above the old man's face. "Now. What do you think of that?"

Orville could not look away. His blood pounded in his ears.

Leopold stared down at the man. "What . . . what is it?"

Not it! He!

"We don't know." Digby set the lantern on a shelf. "He speaks, but no language anyone knows."

"Not even your man, there? Or the locals?"

Digby shook his head. He looked at Orville. "But you say your man is good with languages?"

Gaze still fastened to the stranger, Orville lowered himself to his knees before him, his breath coming hard. He unstrapped his waterskin and held it out to the . . . man. "Magiel," he whispered, distrustful of his own eyes.

The . . . *magiel*—if that's what he was—took the water from him and drank thirstily, emptying the skin. He wiped his lips, gratitude in his eyes. "Thank you," he said—or, Orville thought he said—in a language that danced at the back of Orville's memory.

"Thank . . . you?" Orville repeated, badly.

The magiel tilted his head, hope dawning on his face. He spoke rapidly.

Orville held up both hands, still unable to look away from the man's glimmering skin. *Slow down.* What was the word? "S . . . low."

"I'll be damned." Leopold, behind him.

The magiel reached out a tentative hand toward Orville, questioning.

Orville stiffened but did not object, and the man touched him. He stared intently at Orville for a long moment.

And, something . . .

Everything was the same, yet *something* was different.

"My name is Roane." The magiel spoke slowly but clearly.

A ball of fear plunged through Orville's gut. *He understood.* What had the man done to him?

"Is this Aadi?" the magiel asked.

Aadi . . .

Yes, Orville remembered his mother telling him. The small northern valley where she was born ninety years ago had been called Aadi. Was it his mother who'd spoken this language? If so, it must have been when he was very small. He had no memory, and yet . . .

But the magiel's touch. Something had shifted. "What . . ." Orville stumbled through the language, uncertain, speaking by instinct. "How do—I know—your words?"

The magiel shook his head, peering at him. "My magic shifts time," he said. "I found this speech in you. Sometime in your past or your future, you learned these words."

Magic . . .

No. Orville drew back.

"Well? What does he say, man?" Digby asked impatiently.

"Magic," Orville breathed. It wasn't possible.

"Magic," Leopold, behind him, murmured just as softly.

"What? What are you talking about?" Digby demanded. "Have this man tell us why we can't see him properly, why his skin doesn't stay still."

A magiel's skin shifts in time. Time is his magic.

Orville pulled himself back from the impossible man. Not magic. It couldn't—

The magiel slid up onto his knees. "Friend. Help me."

Orville shook his head. His pulse thumped. There was nothing he could do.

"I ran from Shangri. There's been a coup, a thousand battles, and magiels' freedoms are curtailed. I didn't think I could escape with the snow softening, but I did. But—" He stared fearfully around the storage hut. "This land of Aadi is worse. Far worse. Let me out of these chains, I beg of you. Let me go home."

"What does the man say?" Digby demanded. "More than just the word, *magic,* I say. Nonsense, that."

Orville stood, stepping away from the magiel. "He says he's hungry. It's cold in here."

"Well, I'm not putting a fire in here," Digby said. "Burn the place down." He stamped his feet. "But the bugger's right. It's cold. Let's go in and finish that dinner, eh, Leopold? I'll send Chakdor out later with more blankets."

"And food," Orville said, forcing the words through tight jaws.

Digby stared at him. "Yes, food and water." He took up the lantern and led the way out. "Your man," he said to Leopold, "is rather ill-mannered."

Orville had a quiet supper in the kitchen, oblivious to the outpost's few servants bustling about the day's final chores.

One of them, not Chakdor, showed him to a small room with a straw pallet on the floor and a supply of warm blankets. Good. A solitary room suited his purposes. But before he could settle, a tap came at his door, and Leopold slipped inside.

Orville's mouth dried. *The documents.*

Leopold sat on the floor at Orville's side and set the candle between them. "You must help me."

Not—the documents?

"That man. He's from Shangri."

Orville blinked. He breathed.

"You saw him. He looks different from us. That fellow on the trail, he said they'd caught a man from Shangri. He said that, didn't he?"

Leopold had pieced it together.

"That's what Digby said," Leopold pressed. "They found him trespassing and caught him, but there's something different about him. And tonight, when you spoke to him. He said *Shangri*."

Orville grappled for an answer.

"Magic, Orville."

Orville shifted onto one elbow, careful of the documents under his clothing.

But Leopold seemed not to notice. "The stories are true. Furs. Jewels. Magic potions."

"Sir . . ."

"I told Digby. His wife had never heard the stories, but his clerk had. We discussed it at supper." Leopold gripped Orville's wrist. "And the amulets. The ones that grant one access to Heaven. To *anyone*, Orville, not just the pious."

"What can I . . ." The words of a servant came from Orville's mouth. "What can I do, Sir?"

"You know I'm dying."

". . . yes, Sir."

"It's a cancer, a tumour. In my lungs. Doctors can do nothing."

Like Phuntsog.

"But this man, this shaman, he can help me. He can cure me."

No. Such cures were a lie. As opium was a lie.

Leopold spoke faster. "And I can pay him. I have money, Orville, not a lot, but enough. I can give him a better life. A house in Gangtok." Leopold's grip on his wrist grew firmer. "But you have to help me, now. You can speak to him. Get the cure for me. Or, failing that, the amulet. Before everyone discovers what he can do. Before he's overwhelmed." By men richer than Leopold.

Had Leopold discussed this with Digby, too? Perhaps not—not if he wished to keep the medicines to himself.

"In the morning," Leopold went on. "First thing. I'll make an excuse to John. Get access to the shaman. Will you do it?"

In the morning.

"Good God, man, I'll pay you, too!"

"Yes, Sir." Sweat chilled Orville's neck, and his tongue tasted like sand. "In the morning."

TIME TICKED BY. The house grew still.

Leopold knew. He believed. Even if Digby didn't believe in magic, Leopold's words might be passionate enough to persuade the colonel to direct British troops away from invading Nepal to seeking out Shangri. Jewels. Furs. Elixirs.

Riches. Digby would become a Peer of the Empire. Shangri, a baby bird beneath the tramp of invaders' boots.

The theft of the plans would only delay the factory, not stop it. The Chogyal would use the plans, or the Bhutanese would, claiming to do so on his behalf. Build an army, with rifles. With Sikkim as the bloody battlefield.

IN THE DARK OF THE SERVANTS' quarters, Orville reached a hand out to the lump on the pallet, touching the man's wrist. When he didn't move, Orville gave him a small shake.

"Aii!" Chakdor squealed, waking.

"*Shh!*"

Chakdor stilled, and his gaze darted about the room in the dark, then back to him. "What?" he whispered.

"Do you know who your master has? Chained in the shed?"

A pair of eyes gleamed from deeper in the room. They'd woken another servant.

Chakdor's lips clamped closed. He nodded.

"I need the keys. I looked for them but couldn't find them."

Chakdor's eyes, black in the darkness, fastened on his. Calculated.

"The plans I stole. For the munitions factory. It won't be enough. The foreigner I brought here told your master about Shangri. They'll just build another factory and invade anyway. Invade *Shangri*."

Chakdor took in a sharp breath.

"The old man in the shed is proof Shangri exists. And he's the only one who knows the way. He could be forced to lead an army there."

Chakdor slipped from his covers. "I'll get you the keys. Food and water."

ROANE'S VOICE was warm with surprise and gratitude as Orville fumbled with his manacles in the dark of his cell. "I did not think you would come."

Orville's fingers were slippery with sweat as the keys, one after the other, refused to find the keyhole. "We're not gone yet."

The old man waited patiently until, with a jangle, the manacles fell away.

Orville breathed. "You go. I must . . . return keys." He peered out of the door. "Luck. Find . . . your way. Home."

The magiel, surprisingly spry, gripped his arm. "And to you. Friend."

As Orville stepped into the night, the sound of feet scuffling in snow whispered from beyond the central house. A lamp swung out, and a voice—Digby's—shouted, "There he is!"

Leopold blundered into sight. "Thief! He's stolen the plans for the factory!"

Roane was wallowing up the snowy hill. His way led into the mountains, but Orville had to get past these British and down through the village, take the plans to Paldun. As fast as he could, he punched steps toward the far corner of the outpost house.

Someone—Digby—shouted orders. A figure hastened to the barracks.

Another struggled from the house—the clerk? A handful of servants followed apathetically behind.

Orville ran, sometimes on top of hard snow, other times poking through to soft crystals beneath. His progress was nightmarishly slow, but his pursuers were no faster.

He reached the far corner of the house. Beyond this, the cliff plunged to the Nepal road in the canyon below. The way past the house to the outpost's approach was narrow and blocked by another foreigner.

Piss. The others were rounding the house behind him.

Orville cast a glance up the hill. The magiel was struggling but had already covered a fair piece of ground.

Nothing for it. He ran uphill.

A shot rang out. *Piss!*

Panting, his heart in his ears, Orville struggled through the snow. Roane was far ahead of him, a distant figure approaching a straggle of trees.

Another shot.

Orville had to get out of range. But the soldiers behind him didn't need to fight the snow. They could stand still and aim.

The slope eased and the snow became firmer, and he pushed himself to cover ground.

Another shot—close—and he chanced a glance over his shoulder.

Chakdor struggled with a sniper.

He reached the trees. Roane's footprints. The way became steeper but easier. He forced his legs to pump.

A shot.

He turned.

Chakdor lay in the snow.

Roane was waiting, breathing deeply, behind an outcropping of rock as Orville caught up. They'd made good distance, but the soldiers now swarmed the area around the outpost, forming ranks. Someone directed them. Digby. And . . . by his side. Leopold.

Orville put a hand on Roane's arm. "We cannot . . . let them . . . find Shangri."

Roane's gaze darted to his. "Their barbarian ways."

"Their guns."

Roane bit his lip. "Then we must surrender. Not show the way."

The plans secreted in Orville's clothing. He'd be executed. "They will pry the way from you."

"Then I must die," the magiel whispered. "Here."

"I could hold them off. Lead a chase." Bury the plans in the snow? The Chogyal would have to get his weapons from someone else. "You can get home."

Roane shook his head. "Tracks."

There had to be some way. "You can't . . . do magic?"

Roane glanced sidelong at him with a sad smile. "My magic is small. Bring a branch from withered to seedling. Age my skin to look older." He gestured at the troops assembling below. "I cannot delay an army. I can do nothing at a distance. No erasing of memory."

Orville sank to the snow, and the softness shifted, caving under his weight.

The slope.

Steep, and laden.

Time.

"Roane . . . the heat. Tomorrow's sun on snow. Is that small enough magic? Can you . . . bring it . . . here? Now?"

Roane looked up sharply. "Perhaps." He nodded. "Better to try, than wait."

THEY MOVED to the top of the avalanche chute above the canyon, and Roane crouched, his hands spread on the snow.

Nothing.

Below, the soldiers' column and its two leaders crawled above the canyon onto the open space denuded of trees.

Roane moved to another place in the unstable upper reaches of the slope and placed his hands again on the snow.

The column stretched across the chute below. Defenceless. Exposed.

Roane moved again, repeated the ritual.

The column switch-backed. Climbed the pitch.

Again and again, Roane performed his magic, until he'd cast his spell nine times across the snow. He walked gingerly above the line of charms to the centre of the chute. Orville waited well above him.

The column trudged steadily up the mountainside.

Roane positioned his hands and completed a final spell. He lifted his head. "It's all I can do."

Orville let out a long breath. They needed a trigger. He cast about. Perhaps a rock of sufficient size to hurl against the surface, or . . .

Roane climbed up, his weight shifting.

A crack ran out across the surface of the snow. Roane's face blanched. *Too soon.*

With a small thrum, the slab shifted. Gave way.

Roane's feet slid from beneath him. With a cry, he fell forward toward Orville, arms outstretched.

His hand—

Roane slid away with the surface, oh, so slowly.

Orville scrambled back onto higher ground.

Then Roane was tumbling into the snow, disappearing into quickening chunks and cloud.

Orville crawled upward, snow disappearing beneath his feet as he climbed. Behind him, the thrum vibrated into a gathering thunder.

He climbed, climbed, to the rock band, up a narrow defile to the top, then collapsed onto the shelf. He watched.

The cloud below bloomed to immense proportions, a grandfather of avalanches, lunging majestically down the mountainside, widening the existing shaft.

Roane. Drowned and crushed within it.

For an eternity, the blast boomed, its echo reverberating across the valley. Then the rumble died away, and only silence and stars filled the dark.

Below, there was no sign of an army. Of Leopold or Digby. Of Roane.

But the British outpost remained, a speck to the side of the devastation, perched on its promontory. A handful of figures milled beside it.

The only road to Chungthang—to Gangtok—was still guarded. Orville would not pass without being captured. Tortured. Not just for the factory plans but for the way to Shangri. And soon, the British would bring more soldiers up from the south.

But if Orville did not attempt to pass the outpost, they would not look for him. Or Roane. They had perished, had they not?

And, the British would not search for Shangri, not for an unsubstantiated myth. Not without pressure from Leopold or Digby.

Shangri would remain as it always had been. Tale. Legend.

<hr>

Tale. Legend.

Orville slogged on through swirling snow. Three days past, he'd run out of food.

Shangri was not real.

Roane was not real.

Magic was not real.

Only this never-ending procession of valleys, each higher than the last, was real. He would die here. Was dying.

And . . . was that so bad? Maybe this was his payment, punishment for all those petty crimes.

Phuntsog would not get his opium. Maybe that was a blessing. Maybe Orville's brother would begin to take responsibility, take care of their father. Or maybe Orville's final choice, to put one foot in front of the other in this futile attempt to stay alive, was just his final betrayal. Betrayal of the Chogyal, of the revolution, of Roane. And now his father. For what? For a last chance to—maybe—survive.

If Orville died here, the plans for the factory would be lost with him. A war—with *Nepal*—would be averted, for a few months. Perhaps long enough for the Chogyal to come out of exile. Raise an army.

Or, with no weapons, perhaps negotiate a peace.

Orville topped a ridge and stopped to breathe, take in the next, higher, valley.

There.

At the end of a wide, trackless sweep, beneath an immense cliff, a village. Beside it, the thin line of a rope ladder, climbing to the brim.

THE CAT AND THE MERRYTHOUGHT

By Matthew Hughes

"Where does it all come from?" Oldo asked.

"I have no idea," Baldemar said. He was squatting down and reaching into the demon-magicked valise, as he did whenever he needed fresh funds, and scooping out handfuls of coins and gems. Mostly, the jewels were single specimens, but occasionally his hand encountered worked pieces: necklaces, bracelets, pendants, and once only, a diamond-and-ruby-encrusted crown that must have belonged to a king.

Oldo could not see the valise. The interplanar entity had made it so that it was visible—and touchable, for that matter—only to Baldemar. It was a reward for the former wizard's henchman's having relieved the demon of a tedious obligation, and the reward included the seaside house in the city of Golathreon to which Baldemar had retired. His old friend and supervisor Oldo was now a welcome, permanent guest.

"Does it matter?" he asked Oldo, bringing out a handful of

gold ducats and an emerald the size of a double-yolk egg, the items becoming visible to the older man the moment they left the bag. "The stuff is always there. I emptied the bag once, just to see, and a little while later, it was full again."

"I was just wondering," Oldo said. "Curiosity."

Baldemar transferred the wealth to a stout leather carryall. He shrugged as a cascade of coins clinked into the satchel. "The world is ancient. There must be fortunes on top of fortunes in shipwrecks at the bottom of the sea, forgotten tombs of long-dead kings, buried hoards that no one ever came back for. The demon says, 'Come,' and it comes."

He took up a heavy gold coin and studied it. It featured a face and a circular frieze of letters in some alphabet Baldemar had never seen. The portrait was of a heavy-faced man with a full beard, wearing a helmet that looked more ornamental than useful. "I consider them a lesson in the truth that nothing lasts: not wealth, not power, not glory, so we might as well enjoy the moment before it goes fleeting on its way."

"Are you becoming poetical in your retirement?" Oldo said.

Baldemar dropped the coming into the satchel. "I hope not. I've no evidence the time-weary world is crying out for another poet."

He hefted the carryall and made for the door. Oldo followed. They would take the loot up to the city's treasury, where the duke's groat counters would weigh and assess its value, then count out the equivalent in staters and silver pennies. Part of the funds would go toward acquiring a larger boat than Baldemar's old skiff so that they could both fish from comfortable seats. Fishing had become Baldemar's true retirement pastime, and Oldo was developing a taste for the pursuit.

As they made their way up the hill to the duke's bastide, Oldo brought up the subject again. "Let me have one of those old coins," he said. "There's a necromancer who sets up a booth in the marketplace once a week or so. He might be able to tell us something about its origins."

"If you need to scratch the itch," Baldemar said. Digging in the satchel, he came up with a worn disk of silver half the size of his palm. It showed the figure of a long-gowned woman standing in an archway. Words made of unreadable characters could be made out circling the coin. The obverse showed a jowly man's double-chinned head wearing a headdress that looked like ram's horns that came down past his ears.

"Could be a talisman or a medal," Oldo said, examining it. "Maybe some brave hero was buried with it and deserves to be remembered."

"We don't often get what we deserve in this life," Baldemar said. "For which most of us ought to be grateful."

AFTER THEY HAD PAID off the man with a boat to sell and arranged for it to be brought round to the little wharf at the end of the street where Baldemar's house stood, they went back home to store the rest of the proceeds from the demon's pelf in a strongbox beneath the stairs. They were greeted as they entered by the cat Baldemar had inherited—perhaps temporarily, perhaps for good—from the old woman who had lived a few doors away and who had turned out to be more than an old woman.

She was the retired goddess of those who flee injustice, Fresscatria, who had come to rescue Baldemar and Oldo from two of Thelerion's old enemies. But she had been captured by the pair of wizards, who planned to drain her of her *mana*. Still, all had worked out well, and now Fresscatria was enjoying an extended stay with Aumbraj the Erudite, an academic thaumaturge. Baldemar had volunteered to look after her cat.

The feline was oversized but svelte, coal-black but with a few touches of grey. She purred and rubbed herself against Oldo's ankles, having taken a cat's inexplicable preference to the older man, despite the fact that it was Baldemar who fed her daily and rubbed her glossy black neck occasionally, an intimacy that the animal tolerated for a few moments.

"She wants feeding," Oldo said.

"Then we'll need to go fishing," Baldemar said.

The conversation was repeated almost every day, but sitting in a boat in companionable silence, with their lines in the water a few dozen ore-strokes offshore, was not an onerous duty. Baldemar, after a more than usually contentious career as a henchman, was content to pass whole weeks without feeling his heartbeat quicken.

They took their gear and went out to the skiff. Starting tomorrow, they would fish from the larger boat. Before he closed the door, Oldo told the cat, "We'll be back with your supper." The animal regarded him for a moment, then seemed to nod in acquiescence. As they walked down to the wharf, he said, "Sometimes I think that cat could talk if she wanted to."

Baldemar laughed. "Like the boy in the joke about the burned griddle cakes?"

"Well, her former owner was a retired goddess," Oldo said. "The cat could be a transmogrified priestess."

"We have seen stranger things," Baldemar said. "But sometimes, a cat is just a cat."

THE NECROMANCER SET up his tent in Vashmir Square at the end of every week, when punters had their pay in their purses and, by evening, had spent some of their earnings on ale and wine. Oldo timed his visit for the afternoon, when there would not be a line waiting outside the tent flap. He found the necromancer sitting on a folding stool out in the afternoon sun, reading a leather-bound book. He was a thin-visaged man, clean-shaven except for a spot between chin and lips, dressed theatrically in a long, black robe decorated with stars, crescents, and stylized lightning bolts. He even wore the traditional conical hat, tall and with its point folded over, adorned with the same symbols. A sign hung from one of the tent poles declared him to be Nachecko the Perspicacious.

Nachecko looked up as Oldo approached, set the book down, and rose. He spoke in a sonorous tone, "Would you know the secrets of the dead, the location of things buried in far-gone times, the meanings of omens and signs?"

"I've got something I want you to look at," Oldo said, "and tell me what you can."

The man swept back the flap of the tent and gestured for Oldo to enter. "I shall tell you matters of great dread, mysteries none other can plumb, ancient deeds terrible and dire—"

"Bottle it," Oldo said, entering and sitting on a stool before a small table set on an old carpet whose geometric designs were faded and wan. "I spent more than thirty years as chief of security to a thaumaturge of the Red School."

It was sufficient explanation for the ghost-raiser. "Fair enough," he said, and named his fee. Oldo opened his purse and paid out the silver. Nachecko let the tent flap swing closed and took a seat across the table from Oldo. "What have you brought?"

Oldo had wrapped the silver disk in a soft cloth. Now he uncovered it and laid it between them. "This."

Nachecko leaned over the table to peer at the silver without touching it. His hat threatened to fall off, so he removed it and stood it upright on the rug beside him. His brows knitted. "Where did you get that?" he said.

"I'm not telling you," Oldo said. "You're the . . . necromancer." He had almost said "ghost-wrangler," a term Nachecko's kind disliked.

"You didn't steal it from your Red School wizard?"

"He's dead. Why do you ask that?"

Nachecko cocked his head sideways and looked at the disk, as if a new angle of view might reveal something. "It has an odour of . . . Well, let's just say it is no ordinary coin."

"I was thinking a medal," Oldo said, "or maybe a talisman."

The necromancer tilted his head a different way. "You could be right."

"I've brought it to you to find out."

The man regarded him for a moment, then said, "Why?"

Oldo shrugged, rubbed a calloused hand over his close-shaven pate. "Curiosity, I suppose."

Nachecko's brows rose. "With some objects, curiosity is not advised. Remember the cat."

"The cat is fine," Oldo said, reaching for the silver. "But if you don't want the fee . . ."

"It's not about the fee," the ghost-raiser said. "Now you've got *me* curious. Let's see what we can see."

From under the table, he brought up a small, square box, its every surface carved with figures in relief: men and women in antique costumes, beasts both real and fanciful, and the usual complement of astronomical signs.

"Since you're not a complete noncomp," he said, "I'll skip the pitter-patter." He undid a latch on the front of the box and lifted its hinged lid.

Oldo craned his neck to look. An amorphous grey substance filled the container, but when the necromancer said, "Ghost, arise," the greyness spiralled up and took on the general shape of a long-haired man standing beside the table. The figure was dressed in a floor-length robe, both man and garment rather diaphanous and with a tendency to waver around the edges.

"My predecessor," said the ghost-raiser to Oldo. "You don't see the hat because I kept it for myself."

Oldo shivered as he felt a chill emanate from the phantom and knew from experience that here was the preserved *kra* of a once-living person. His former employer, Thelerion the (self-described) Incomparable, used to keep a couple to guard certain doorways in his manse.

The necromancer indicated the silver disk on the table. "Ghost, examine this and tell me what you can."

The *kra* bent to look. A ripple shot through its fog-like substance. It sprang back, and a look of horror distorted its nebulous features, the mouth falling open to a depth that would have been anatomically impossible in flesh. A thin shriek filled the tent, then the ghost fled back to its box, dwindling rapidly until it was again just a puffball of mist within. A small hand emerged from the greyness, grasped the latch, and pulled the lid shut.

"Well," said the necromancer, "that was unusual."

"Wasn't it?" said Oldo. "Now I'm even more curious."

The other man looked from one side to another, then back to the silver. "I'm still curious, but . . ." He gestured with both hands. "Consider: what is there that can frighten a ghost?"

Oldo weighed the question. He was thinking that the old medal, or whatever it was, might be worth more than its weight in silver. If it was valuable, he could deliver a boon to Baldemar, who was putting him up for free. "Let's find out."

"It could be dangerous," said the ghostman.

"I'll double your fee."

"He said he would need to make preparations," Oldo told Baldemar, back at the house. "He'll come here when he is set up."

Baldemar was at the kitchen counter, cleaning the day's catch, a fat bumbler. The cat was sitting on the floor nearby, her tail twitching in anticipation. He put the fish's liver in a bowl and set it down where the feline could get it. The cat managed to purr loudly while eating.

"What would frighten a ghost?" he said.

"I told him a demon was involved. No details, of course. He said that could explain it."

Baldemar gave a small grunt. "Let me see it again."

Oldo brought out the cloth-wrapped object and laid it on the counter. Baldemar studied it, flipping it over to examine both images. "Could be a goddess," he said, "and a king or emperor on the other side. It would help if we could read the script."

He peered at the silver again. Oldo noticed that the room was silent. He looked down at the cat. She had ceased purring and was ignoring the half-eaten fish liver. Now she was looking up at the counter, and her ears were laid back flat against her black-furred skull. Oldo heard a hiss.

"Not *her* goddess, then," he said.

"Let me know when the ghost-wrangler is coming," Baldemar said. "I think I'll sit in."

"Now you're curious, too?" Oldo said.

Baldemar went back to scraping scales off the bumbler. "Feels that way."

Nachecko arrived carrying a large, square travelling case but without his distinctive robe and hat. "Can't walk about dressed like that," he said as Oldo answered the door. "Half the people want to ask me about their dead kinfolk—for free, no less—while the other half throw stones and make signs against the evil eye."

"Every profession has its drawbacks," Oldo said. "You should try henchmanning for a narcissistic wizard."

"No, I shouldn't," the necromancer said. "Nobody should."

Baldemar came into the foyer. "Come through to the grand parlour," he said and led the way across to the double doors. Oldo looked about for the cat, which usually came to vet anyone who had the temerity to enter her territory, but she was nowhere to be seen.

"Do you need anything?" Baldemar said when they were in the room that neither he nor Oldo frequented, preferring to spend their together time in the kitchen.

Nachecko looked around. "Can we clear off that table? I have to set up my apparatus."

The table was covered in bric-a-brac that had come with the house, based, Oldo assumed, on a demon's sense of sophisticated décor. He and Baldemar gathered up the figurines, miniature vases, engraved copper plates, and indefinable oddities that covered the tabletop and piled them on the plush seat of an over-stuffed armchair.

The necromancer opened his case and brought out a bundle of rods. He tugged at and manipulated them, revealing that they were jointed and connected at several points, until he had contrived a free-standing network that supported a multi-sided cavity at the top. Into this, he inserted a semitransparent blue globe, after first wiping it carefully with a cloth of pure white silk. Finally, he set beneath it a disk of what looked to be gold, as wide as a palm and the height of a finger's width. He adjusted the circle's position, a little this way, a little that, while peering at the blue orb.

Finally satisfied, he said, "That looks good."

"What's it for?" Oldo said.

Nachecko assumed a knowledgeable air. "You probably think a necromancer's only line of business is summoning ghosts and compelling them to answer questions."

Baldemar said, "Isn't it?"

"That's the bread-and-cheese level of the craft. 'Ghost-wrangling.' I'll bet you've used that one yourselves." Neither Oldo nor Baldemar made a response. The necromancer eyed them both with suspicion, then went on, "But we of the upper echelons of the profession can lace up our boots in other ways."

"And we're about to see one of those alternate lacings?" Oldo said.

"You are." Nachecko flourished a hand toward the apparatus. "Given the right circumstances, this device can summon from the Underworld the *ba* of a deceased person."

Baldemar issued a skeptical grunt. Oldo was more willing to be convinced. He knew what everyone knew: that every person had two essences, a *ba* and a *ka*. During life, the former accumulated all the evil that its possessor performed, while the latter gathered the good. After death, the *kra*—a spiritual hinge that connected the two "souls"—set them loose. The *ba* went to the Underworld, and the *ka* to the Overworld, one to dwell in eternal misery and the other in perpetual bliss.

Kras usually evaporated, although some lingered at the site of a particularly memorable death. And some were captured by those who knew how to set spiritual nets for them.

Why the demiurge had established these conditions, no one knew. He had created Phenomenality and set it running, then went off to do other unimaginable things without bothering to inform any of his creation's denizens of the whys and wherefores.

"Behold," said Nacheko. He rested his palms upon the blue globe and spoke, in an undertone, several syllables. When he lifted his hands away, the glass began to glow, brighter and brighter, until it flashed in a moment of harsh actinic glare. When the spots that had appeared before Oldo's eyes faded, he saw that the orb was now clear as crystal; it showed a harsh landscape, as seen from high above, of bare rock and grit, stirred by a scouring wind that whistled and moaned. The perspective shifted as the view enlarged, as if they were descending. Now huddled shapes, widely scattered, could be seen: ragged figures, each hunched in solitary misery, clothed in scraps of tattered fabric that fluttered in the constant gale that whistled and moaned.

"The Underworld," Nachecko said.

Baldemar leaned in for a closer look. "It is," he said. "I've been there." When that won him a sharp glance from the necromancer, he added, "I led an unusual life."

Nachecko recovered his aplomb. "If we have an object, the right kind of object, that is closely associated with one who formerly lived, it is possible to make a connection with the deceased's *ba*. If the connection is strong enough, the remnant can be forced to respond."

"Forced?" Oldo said. "How can what those poor wights are going through be made worse?"

"There are ways," the necromancer said. He rubbed his hands together. "Now, let us see if your silver piece has the power I think it has."

The disk was in Oldo's pouch, wrapped in its silken cloth. He brought it out, and when instructed to do so, placed it on the gold circle beneath the apparatus. Nachecko studied it for a moment, then nodded to himself.

"Yes, indeed. I think so."

He placed his hands on the top of the globe again and began to hum. The sound was tuneless, atonal, and gradually it blended with the sound of the wind. Now Nachecko removed one hand from the globe and touched his fingertips to the silver disk. The scene in the clear orb began to shift, as if seen from a pair of eyes flying across the desolate landscape. The ground sped by faster and faster, the huddled figures blurring as the velocity increased.

Then the speed slowed. The viewpoint slid down an invisible incline toward the murky horizon, passing over *bas* hunched against the wind, until one heap of fluttering rags became the sole focus. The image of the hunched shape, seen from the rear, grew until it filled the globe. It grew further, and now it was just the back of a head wrapped in coarse cloth.

The viewpoint circled the head until the three observers were looking into the haggard face of a man. He seemed to be of advanced age, with deep seams graven into the cheeks and around the mouth and eyes and grey stubble sprouted on the chin. The rheumy eyes stared sightlessly ahead, all vision concentrated on inner despair and regret.

Then the eyes blinked and focused.

"He sees us," Nachecko said. "Now, we can begin."

"Who is he?" Baldemar said. "Or I should say, 'was' he?"

"Someone with a close connection to your medal," the necromancer said. "He either wore it or made it, would be my guess. Let's find out."

He lifted his hand from the globe, reached into his case, and brought out a metal tube about the length of a forearm and the thickness of a wrist. He did something to one end and out of the other shot an intense beam of light. This he aimed at the face filling the globe.

The *ba* flinched and tried to turn away, and the dry-lipped mouth uttered a moan of pain.

"They can't close their eyes," Nachecko commented, "nor look away from the desolation of the Underworld. It's a little added misery, and it's usually enough."

He extinguished the beam and said, "*Ba*, are you ready to answer questions?"

Another moan was the only answer. Nachecko reestablished the light, drawing a shriek from the *ba*. "Answer, and I'll take it away," the necromancer said.

"I will answer," said the *ba*.

Nachecko cut the light. He reached for the silver disk and held it where the weeping eyes could see it. "What do you know of this?"

The face's gaze centred on the metal, and a new species of sadness transformed its features. "Ah," the *ba* said, "I used to make things of beauty, things of power."

"So, you made this?"

"I did."

Nachecko turned to Baldemar and Oldo with an expression

that invited them to admit that he knew his art, then he went back to the *ba*. "Tell us about it."

The *ba* began to speak in a sepulchral voice. "I was a master silversmith in the City of Ambit. I made many a piece of supernal beauty and many that were transferred into objects of great power by the rulers of the city."

"Tell us of these rulers."

The tale continued. There were five archmages, each a thaumaturge of surpassing strength. They governed by whim and caprice, oppressing the citizenry, turning an ancient city into a playground for their strange appetites. One of them, Margrippe the Dominance, liked to fill his manse with young women of great beauty, though they were no longer beautiful once he was finished with them.

Margrippe's desire was piqued by the daughter of a priestess. Her name was Brythe, and she was beyond beauty, with golden eyes and hair as black as midnight. He summoned her. When she felt the irresistible tug, she cried out to her mother. Her mother, in turn, threw herself at the feet of the goddess and begged her to intervene.

But Margrippe's spell had woven itself deep into the fibres of Brythe's being. To have vitiated its power would have left the maiden an empty shell. So, the goddess did what she could: she transformed the victim into a new form, one to which the spell's elements could not cohere.

Nachecko asked the question that was on everyone's mind. "What new form?"

"It was the talk of the city, that Margrippe had been gainsaid," the *ba* said. "He rampaged and caused destruction, demanding that the goddess's temple be razed. The other wizards of the ruling cabal, alarmed that their sway could be opposed, joined with him, and together they drove the goddess out of Ambit. The trans-formed maiden went with her."

The priestesses went with their patron, and so did the trans-formed young woman.

"But that was not enough for Margrippe the Dominance," said the former silversmith. "He got the others to help him enslave an imp from the Seventh Plane and force it to keep an eye on the young woman. If ever she came out from the goddess's protection, the imp would know and would tell him."

Baldemar and Oldo looked at each other again. "Ask the *ba*," Baldemar said, "was it the goddess named Fresscatria?"

Nachecko did, and it was.

"And was the young woman transformed into a cat?"

She was.

"Oh, my," said Oldo. "We may have a problem."

The *ba* continued its tale. Margrippe had ordered him to make what they ironically called in those days a "merrythought"—a charm that could hold a magical action until it was triggered by some specific event.

"Was it in the form of a silver disk?" Nachecko asked.

It was, with an image of Margrippe on one side and the young woman on the other.

Baldemar was looking thoughtful. "What are you thinking?" Oldo asked.

Baldemar asked the necromancer, "How long ago did all this happen?"

Time meant nothing to the *ba,* but the remnant knew that it had lived during the Twenty-Second Aeon.

Oldo was consulting his own memory. "Ambit was a city at the centre of what is now the wasteland of Barran. A cabal of thaumaturges, led by one called Majestrum, destroyed it at the end of the Twenty-Second Aeon."

"Thousands of years ago," Baldemar said.

"Thousands and thousands," said Oldo.

"Well, then. We may not have a problem after all."

They paid the ghost-wrangler his fee. Oldo said, "I don't suppose you'd take the merrythought as sufficient payment."

"Not a chance," said Nachecko. He packed up his equipment and let the *ba* return to its misery, there being nothing else one could do for a remnant of the Second Plane.

"I think," Oldo said, after he was gone, "I'll throw the thing into the sea."

Baldemar rested a hand on the older man's shoulder. "Probably for the best," he said.

THEY WERE PREPARING the evening meal when the cat appeared from wherever she had been self-sequestered and wrapped herself around Oldo's ankles, purring loudly.

"All is forgiven, then," Baldemar said.

Oldo picked her up and held her to his chest, then at arm's length to study her. "Do you think? Could it be her?" he asked Baldemar.

"I prefer not to think about old magics," was the answer. "Except for what comes out of the demon's satchel, I want no more to do with the 'scintillating realm.'"

Oldo caught the reference. It had been one of Thelerion's gaudy descriptions of the life he and his fellow thaumaturges led. "Remember," he said, "when we were henchmen, and sometimes we felt as if we were just playing pieces on someone else's great board?"

"Sometimes?" Baldemar said. "It was a rare day when—"

"It's just that I'm getting that feeling again."

"Ah," said Baldemar. "Then we'll keep a watchful eye."

———

THE FOLLOWING DAY, the boatman brought the new craft to the wharf. Summoned to see it, Baldemar and Oldo made a final inspection before paying the last instalment. It was a single-masted sloop, sporting an afterdeck with a tiller to control the rudder and a closed cabin below. The living space was a master-piece of efficiency of design, with bunks that folded down from the walls and endless cupboards, drawers, and cubbyholes to store gear and provisions.

"But you don't know how to sail," Oldo said when they were back on the afterdeck. It was moving up and down as swells came in off the sea and the wind picked up.

"Every dock along the river has its company of idlers with nothing to do but watch the marine traffic and tell lies to each other about their exploits on the briny," Baldemar said. "I will hire one of those old codwallopers to teach me the ropes."

"Was that a pun?" Oldo said.

"Not an intentional one," Baldemar said. "Look at all those pulleys and things."

So, they would not be sailing out into the Sundering Sea today, and Oldo's desire to throw the silver medal into its depths would not be realized, unless they rowed out in the skiff. But the sea was getting into one of its temperamental moods, arguing with a stiff and rain-filled north wind over who was in charge. It was not a good argument for two dabblers in a small, flat-bottomed boat to get involved in.

They tied up the sloop, fore and aft, and made sure that the stuffed leather bags hanging from its sides were set to protect its strakes from the wharf timbers. Then they went home to wait out the storm.

The cat welcomed Oldo, ignored Baldemar, but allowed the latter to feed her. Afterward, she sat in a window embrasure, licking her paws and watching the rain-swept street. Her tail flicked without cease.

Nachecko had told them the transformed woman's name. Oldo stood a few paces from the cat and said, "Brythe?"

The tail stopped moving.

"Are you Brythe?"

The cat looked back over her shoulder at him, but her face was as unreadable as any feline's. After a moment, she blinked and returned to surveilling the rain bursting on the cobblestones.

The merrythought had been put away in a drawer. Oldo got it out and examined it. Could there be an imp in there? Or worse, could there have been an imp that had now fled to wherever Margrippe had ended up, assuming he was not long since turned to dust? Before it was dismissed, the *ba* had said the thaumaturge had translated himself to another Plane.

Baldemar said, "If he went to the Overworld, he ended up with all the other unwanted migrants on a barren little island near the south pole. The *kas* of the Fourth Plane resent intrusions by obstreperous wizards."

Baldemar did not ascribe much credence to what they had heard during the necromancer's session. "*Bas* are not reliable informants. They are the parts of us that lie and deceive and believe self-aggrandizing fictions about ourselves. They carry all that mendacity with them down into the Underworld."

"Hmm," Oldo had said. "But still, a watchful eye."

"What could it hurt?" Baldemar said.

———

THE CAT usually slept in the kitchen on a wool blanket, folded several times and laid behind the stove. The hours following the necromancer's session did not make for a usual night. Oldo, who had become a light sleeper as his age advanced, was awakened by a scratching at his chamber door and a yowl such as he had never heard from the feline.

He got up, wrapped himself in a robe, and opened the door to find the cat already halfway down the hall, pausing briefly to look back at him before tripping down the stairs to the ground floor. He followed her toward the kitchen, whose door was ajar, though only wide enough to have permitted a cat to slip through. A wavering, eerie light, pale as a spring wine, shone through the gap. The cat was sitting just outside the spill of illumination, her tail twitching metronomically. She looked at him again, then returned her gaze to whatever she could see in the kitchen.

Oldo advanced carefully, listening for any sounds of movement or presence. He heard nothing. He took hold of the door's handle and slowly drew the portal open. The glow grew brighter, and he could see that it came from around the edges of a closed drawer in the dresser that held the dishware and cutlery.

Oldo stood and watched to see if anything would occur. Nothing did, but he startled as the cat yowled from down beside his feet.

"All right," he said, "I'll take a look."

She followed him into the room as he crossed to the drawer and pulled it open. The silver disk, which had been wrapped in its silk, now lay uncovered. He could scarcely make out the features of the head engraved on its surface, so bright was the light that emanated from the merrythought.

"Oh, ho," Oldo said.

He had not heard Baldemar come downstairs behind him and jumped again as his friend said, "I was thinking we might put it back inside the demon's satchel, to contain it."

"Too late now," said Oldo.

"We'll see," Baldemar said. He crossed the room and reached for the object but had barely lifted it out of the drawer before he swore and tossed it away. It went skittering across the stone-flagged floor. He shook his hand then looked at his palm.

"Burned?" Oldo said.

"No. It was more like deep cold. The bones in my fingers ached." He reached for a kitchen towel hanging from a bar by the sink. "I'll try this."

But he did not get the chance. The glow emanating from the disk now cohered into a column of light rising straight up from the floor, brighter and full of swirling shapes that mutated from one amorphous form into another.

"Time to go, I think," Baldemar said, cocking his head toward the door. But as Oldo turned to follow the suggestion, the door slammed closed. This time it was the cat that reacted in shock, yowling and scratching at the wood. Baldemar was there in a moment, yanking on the handle, but though the door had no lock on it, it refused to open.

Oldo came and added his strength, but the resistance was complete.

"Uh, oh," said Baldemar.

Oldo followed his gaze. The pillar of light was now brighter than ever, and the shapeless forms within its column were ceasing their aimless motions. A human figure was emerging from the chaos, corpulent and clad in antique garb, and with a circlet around its brow from which depended two golden horns.

"Margrippe," Oldo whispered.

"Just so," Baldemar agreed.

The cat hissed, its spine arched, hair standing straight up, ears flat and teeth bared. It backed up until its twitching tail was against the closed door.

The man in the light was becoming clearer now, details of heavy features and sumptuous attire settling into place. The blank stare of the eyes gave way to a piercing gaze that swept around the kitchen, lingering for but moments on the two men, until it fixed upon the cat.

Margrippe took his first inward breath, held it for a moment, then spoke in a tongue that meant nothing to Oldo and Baldemar. But the spell had an effect on the cat. She froze, one paw still extended to claw at the closed door. Now a tendril of light emanated from the pillar, snaking through the air until it touched the black fur. Then it coiled and entwined around her until she was completely immersed in the pale glow.

The ancient thaumaturge spoke again. The light surrounding the animal seemed to grow somehow denser, as if it were congealing into another kind of substance. For a long moment, nothing happened. Then the cat began to grow, and as she grew, she changed. The limbs lengthened, the tail shrank back into the body, the hips and shoulders widened, and the head changed shape profoundly.

The light around the transforming body winked out. And now

there was no cat. There was a woman on hands and knees, naked except for a fall of black hair that reached the floor. She pushed herself back onto her haunches and looked behind her, as if to confirm that her tail was gone completely. She turned green eyes on Oldo and Baldemar, and her brief nod made it clear that she recognized them.

Then she rose and looked at the man still enclosed by the pillar of light. Her eyes narrowed, and her jaw set firm. She opened her mouth, but all that emerged was a hiss. Then she appeared to take thought for a moment, and when she opened her mouth again, out came words—but again in a tongue neither man could make sense out of.

Margrippe smiled. A cold smile. A smile of triumph. He said something that had the sound of a long-prepared phrase.

Then he stepped out of the column and onto the stone floor, his flesh solid, his garments fluttering as he moved. The woman raised a hand in seeming warning as he took a second step toward her, his smile still in place.

And then the smile became less certain. Now it was Margrippe's turn to freeze. He raised the hand that had directed the beam of light at the cat and turned it over to look at the palm. He brought up the other hand and studied it. The mask of triumph had become a picture of first confusion, then a dreadful, dawning realization.

He turned back toward the column of light. But Oldo stepped forward and kicked the merrythought across the floor. The thaumaturge turned his head toward him, and Oldo saw the mouth turn down at the corners, in a frown that continued to deepen until it became as stretched out of shape as the grimace on a trage-dian's masquerade.

"Ho, ho," said Baldemar. "They always overreach, don't they?

What's it been, twenty thousand years in another Plane? Thirty? Time enough for his enslaved imp to plot its revenge."

Oldo didn't get to answer. The woman moved, crossed the floor in three quick steps, raised both hands, clasped them together, and brought them down on Margrippe's head. The horned head-dress split apart and crumbled. Then, from the top down, like a cake decoration made of spun sugar, the thaumaturge broke apart, his pieces tumbling to the floor, where they burst into flakes and powder.

In a moment, he was no more than a heap of desiccated flesh and loose fibres.

The woman said something in her unknown language, but Oldo could guess the meaning from the tone and circumstances.

"That's you settled and sorted," he translated.

The door opened easily when Baldemar pulled on it. "I'll get her a robe from the closet in the foyer," he said.

Oldo looked at Brythe now and realized that though she had been a young woman when Fresscatria transformed her, the goddess had not been able to keep the millennia entirely at bay. He saw some streaks of grey in the fall of black hair and a few lines and creases around the eyes and lips.

He also saw that she was smiling at him. He smiled back. He touched his chest and said, "Oldo," then pointed to Baldemar as his friend came into the room and named him as well.

Her quick nod told him that she already knew who they were. She let Baldemar slip the robe over her shoulders, put her arms through the sleeves, and belted it closed. Then she touched herself and said, very carefully, as if not sure of the effort's outcome, "Brythe."

"Brythe," Oldo said. He performed the formal gesture appropriate to a first encounter. "How do you do?"

Baldemar did the same, but she gave him only a passing glance and a brief thank-you smile before turning again to Oldo. She beckoned him to approach her, and when he did, she put her arms around him and nuzzled his neck, much as she had done when she had been a cat.

She even purred a little.

"Well," said Baldemar, "this ought to be interesting."

Oldo did not reply. He was otherwise engaged.

ANAMNESIS IN RUINS

By Heli Kennedy

My sister had promised to write me. A week had gone by, and no message came.

It wasn't like her. Özge never broke promises. She had also never been away from home this long. Something was wrong. I could feel it. If Ma was being honest, she'd admit to feeling the same way. But she and Father were too stubborn to admit anything. They went about their business like nothing had changed. I didn't press them about Özge. Ma's shaking had gotten worse, and I had already caused too much pain.

I needed to fix it. Take matters into my own hands.

Özge said she might go to the city. Where, exactly? I had no idea. But if I was there, I just *knew* I could find her. Something inside would direct me to her, like a compass. It had to. We had lived together our whole lives. Surely, we had a connection. Not by magic. That wouldn't be real or trustworthy. No, our connection was by blood.

I snuck out of the house at dawn. Walking in the damp air, I wished my sister would appear, so I could go back home and curl up in my woollen blanket. I sniffed the wind, trying to pick up her scent like a dog. All I smelled were cowpies. Eventually, I reached the edge of the village. Here, the caravan collected city-bound goods and passengers. It was too early for the carts. No one was there, except for a very wrinkled woman on a log, clutching prayer beads.

"How much is it to the city?" I asked, hoping my handful of copper was enough.

"They charge four pecks," said the old woman.

I felt a jolt of excitement. I could afford that.

"What's it like, the city?" I asked. I suddenly felt close to her, like she was my grandmother, about to pass on wisdom to me.

"Never gone, never goin'," she said. "I just watch. And know what? In eighty years, it's all the same. Same people goin' here, goin' there. Doin' this, doin' that."

"Maybe you've seen my sister—tall, long black braid, blue coat?"

"Oh, shiny copper buttons?"

That was Özge. She bought the coat a month ago. It was beautiful and fashionable, but our parents said it was too flashy.

"Did she say anything before she left?" I asked, desperation creeping in.

"No. 'Cause she didn't get on no caravan," the old woman said, glaring at the dirt as she remembered. "Actually, in all these years, she's the only one that did somethin' *different*."

"Different? How?"

"She shuffled around here for some time, then went in the stones." The woman waved toward steeples of jagged rock down the road.

I broke into a cold sweat. Özge went into the ruins? Why? She knew well that people who walked in there never came back out. They were *devoured* by the stones. Anyone that returned went mad. Sure, in my fourteen years, I hadn't seen anyone go in or come out of the ruins. Or seen anyone who went mad from them. But Ma told us about it, over and over. I knew they were evil. I could feel it, even from this distance.

"You sure she went in there?" I asked.

"Fine, don't believe an old woman!" she snapped. "Ask the drivers when they come. They'll know if a girl was on the carts."

So, I did. The drivers said no one from the village had gone to the city in weeks. Only cabbage and goats. My stomach dropped; the woman could be right about my sister. I walked to the toppled mountains of rock. A faint footpath led into them.

"Özge?" I shouted, my voice weak.

No response.

If Özge had gone in there, my trip to the city would be pointless.

My hands began to sweat. Going to town alone had been a scary prospect. Now, that seemed like a child's game. In the dim light, the stones looked like hunched people and towering giants, ready to mob and crush me the moment I set foot in their home. I thought of Ma's warning; if I went in, I could be lost to the curse. But I already felt cursed. My only sister, and friend, was gone. If I never saw her again, I would be lost anyway.

Inhaling deeply, I flung my bag over my shoulder and paced into the ruins. They were larger than I expected. Limestone both rose above me in jumbled heaps, all that remained of toppled towers, and sunk below me in deep pits. Despite the occasional standing wall or fractured pillar, it was hard to tell what I was walking through. An old temple? Palace? Crypts? Once, I'd asked

Father what the ruins had been and why they were cursed. He told me it didn't matter. All that mattered was that I stayed out of them. I could never tell him I'd done this. He'd tan my hide.

Walking, I kept my eyes wide open, on high alert for a magical beast or the shimmer of a dark enchantment, ready to ensnare me. But I only saw crumbling stone. There was no beast or spell to be found. I didn't *feel* cursed. Maybe Ma and Father had been wrong. I kicked a rock in defiance. *Take that, ruins!* I thought.

I called out for Özge. Each time I shouted, the echo of my own voice answered. If my sister was hiding in here, she didn't want me to know. Or she was . . . no, I couldn't think about that. I might jinx my chances of finding her.

I kept on until the path ended at a colossal pile of oddly shaped stones. One shard held the faint trace of a large carved eye. Next to it was a narrow opening. Peering in, I saw light at the end of a crude tunnel that I could fit through. Özge could have fit too.

Turning to the side, I squeezed through and found myself in a large clearing walled in by heaps of stone. The sight before me was mesmerizing: I was in an old square enclosed by collapsed buildings and carpeted with strange weeds. I'd never seen anything like them. There were black stalks with small gold flowers, bright-blue grasses, and corkscrewed magenta shrubs. In the centre of the space, rising out of the blanket of colour, was the bottom half of an enormous stone dog, sitting at attention. The statue's upper torso and head were missing, but its four legs were distinct.

Nestled between the paws, I found a pile of ash and charcoal—remnants of a campfire. Next to it, gleaming silver weeds had been flattened. Someone had slept here in the past week. I ran my hand over the plants, hoping my skin would sense my sister's presence.

My palm grazed a small hard lump. I dug my fingers into the shrub and pulled out a copper button—it was from Özge's jacket.

"Özge?" I shouted.

Nothing.

"Özge!"

Still nothing . . .

"No!" croaked a brittle voice in return.

I froze. The voice spoke my language, but it was not human. It had a metallic drone to it, like a metal spoon dragging on an iron pot. *This must be it—the curse*, I thought.

"No!" droned the voice again. "No!"

"Show yourself," I choked, worried I was going mad.

"No!"

My eyes shot to one side of the courtyard. It was coming from a wall.

"No!"

Cautiously, I paced toward it. Nothing was there. Just lifeless stone.

"No, what?" I said.

"No!"

It was coming from a crack. Squinting into the fissure, I spotted something. I blew into the opening. The thing buzzed in reply. I poked a long blade of grass into the hole—out darted an irritated fly the size of my palm. I jumped back, shielding myself with my bag. It didn't move. It just rolled its bulbous emerald eyes, assessing me. I sighed in relief; I wasn't cursed, just haunted by an insect. A golden sucker, as long and sharp as a sewing needle, slid in and out of its head.

I realized I'd seen this thing before. Özge had shown me one in a book. It was an *anamnee fly*. They were rare and could sleep for years, sometimes centuries. But no matter how long they were dormant, they held recent memories of whomever they fed on. Blood memories. Wild magic. If Özge had slept here, the fly might have fed on her. It might have answers about where she had gone. To reveal the memory it was holding, I had to get it to talk.

"Do you . . . speak?" I asked awkwardly.

"No!" it droned.

"Well, clearly you do. Was my sister, Özge, here?"

The anamnee fluttered its iridescent lavender wings.

"Was . . . she . . . here?" I shot at the fly.

Its dumb eyes rolled around.

"Özge? Özge?" I shouted at it, hoping her name would trigger it to open up.

Instead, it rubbed its hairy legs together.

It was pointless. Only a skilled magus could coax recollections out of an anamnee, and our village didn't have one. The Elders forbid it. Our general store sold potions for things like tending to rashes, controlling livestock, and growing a man's horn. The Elders claimed that was all we needed. A magus would just bring trouble. "They divide villages, seed chaos, create inequality," they said. Up until this point, I had believed them; the thought of a dark magus sprinkling seeds around that made us turn on each other terrified me. But that was before I needed one. And before I had gone in the ruins. Maybe the elders were like Ma, insisting the curse was real without going to see for herself. They refused a magus but never tried one.

The city had a school for magi, but I didn't have enough to get there *and* pay for one. I'd have to rely on the village, which had only one option, if you could even call it that. I dumped my provisions out of my travel sack and swiftly scooped up the anamnee fly. Trying not to crush it in my bag, I headed for the only person I knew who had some knowledge of magic: stupid Caul.

AT CAUL'S DOOR, I hesitated. Was getting him involved wise? I didn't like the big oaf, and just being associated with him could mean trouble.

He'd been punished for using spells to pull pranks. Where he had learned his magic, I didn't know. They didn't teach it in our school. Yet somehow, he performed an illusion that tricked the village drunk into drinking piss. For that, the Elders threw him in the stocks for a day. But that didn't stop Caul. He gave the most popular girl in school a bracelet that made her body turn blue. He said it was a mistake but refused to reveal the true intentions of his charm. To top it off, he had no idea how to get rid of the colour. This landed him in the stocks for *three* days. He was released only after he swore he'd stop doing magic. I figured he was lying and thought he should be locked up for good.

The last thing I wanted to do was beg him to use his ill-gotten abilities again. He probably didn't even know how to get an anamnee to talk. If he did, he'd probably mess it up and land me in the stocks with him.

But the stocks would be nothing compared to losing Özge.

I knocked on his door.

"You?" he blurted, confused. We had barely exchanged ten words our whole lives.

"I need magic," I blurted back.

"I don't do magic," he said loudly, in case anyone was listening.

"We all know you do."

"I do *not*."

"Fine," I said, lowering my voice, "then I need some of the magic you *don't do*."

"Go to the general store. Buy a potion for your cow there."

"It's not for a cow," I said through gritted teeth.

"What's it for?"

I quickly showed him what was in the sack.

"Is that . . . ?" he asked, frowning.

I nodded.

He grabbed my jacket, hauled me into the house, and slammed the door.

"What's a farm girl doing with one of those?" he asked.

It was a good question, and I didn't have a good lie. "Reee-search," I said.

"On an anamnee?" Caul raised his eyebrows.

"I'm . . . interested in magic." The words felt wrong coming out of my mouth. They couldn't have been further from the truth, and Caul could tell. I hated magic. It got me into this mess in the first place.

"If this is a trap . . ."

"I swear it's not. I need to make it talk."

He eyed me for a moment. "Why?"

I searched for an excuse. "It knows something . . . about someone I know. Something . . . I need to know."

"Is that a riddle?" Caul scoffed. "Guess we've all got our secrets in *this* village."

"Here," I said, shoving my change purse at him. "Just give me a spell, or potion, or something, so I can leave."

He poked at the copper in the purse. "With this piddly amount? No, you can't leave with my product. Too dangerous. We're doing it here. Together."

"Dangerous?" I managed, feeling heat rise across the back of my neck. "Gods, am I going to go to prison for this?"

He sighed. "Relax. What we're doing isn't illegal. The Elders would *like* it to be. But they don't write laws, and they can't ban wild magic. That's impossible. Sure, they might punish us for playing with it. *If they find out.* But we won't let that happen, will we?"

I shook my head.

He walked off into his house, forcing me to follow. I realized he was going to hear what the anamnee had to say. He might hear something about Özge. If word about my sister got around, our family might not be able to live in the village anymore.

"You sure I can't take the spell or potion-thing home to get the confession?" I asked.

"One: confession's the wrong word," Caul corrected, leading me into his cellar. "What you need is for it to *share memories folded deeply within its mind.* Two: you know how rare these flies are? I'm sure only two people in the whole city have seen one, never mind *heard* one. Angering the Elders is worth it."

At the back of the cellar, he slid a large wine barrel aside to reveal a doorway and stepped through. I stopped at the threshold, hit by an odd stench. Was he boiling rotten onions in vinegar?

"I know, impressive," gloated Caul, noticing how carefully I stepped into the room. "Welcome to my brewing lab."

It was packed to the ceiling with glass tubes, boxes, and large jars. I looked closer to see they were filled with moulds, moving liquids, and shimmering dust. The floor was slick with spills. Scorch marks streaked the wall. Stained rags were flung everywhere. *Ugh, what a sty.* Along one wall, he had dozens of tiny ornate bottles. I read the fancy writing on them: *Aeria, Amora, Audax . . .*

Caul pulled out a wire cage. "Put the fly in here."

I shook the bag over the tiny prison—the anamnee dropped out. Caul slammed the door shut. The fly scrambled to a corner of its cell.

"Where'd you find it, again?" he asked.

"Our fields," I lied.

He poked the insect with his finger. "Thing's got no body weight," he muttered to himself. "Madeleira might kill it." He saw the blank look on my face. "A spell-fortified wine that makes people spill guts they didn't know they had."

"We're getting it *drunk*?" I said, worried. "I don't want any . . . disasters, okay?"

Caul's face soured. "I'll have you know, sharp-tongue, I've come a long way from the blue bracelet." He uncorked a wine bottle, then grabbed a tall glass vial and dropped a tiny gold flower in it. The bloom looked like the ones I saw in the ruins.

"Where did you get that?" I asked.

"A supplier. See? Magic can be pretty too," he said, showing me a box filled with them. "But it's expensive as hell. These are hard to find and essential for Verbosia potions." He poured a bright-yellow liquid from the vial into the wine and shook the bottle. Scrutinizing the anamnee, he filled a small bottle cap with the drink and set it in front of the insect.

"Brace yourself. I have no idea what this thing's 'talking' will be like," he said.

We got in close and waited. After ten minutes, I began to worry I was wasting time.

"I don't understand," huffed Caul. "If I leave wine out, it attracts *dozens* of flies."

"Wine is full of sugar," I answered. Then, it became clear. "This fly doesn't feed on sugar. It feeds on blood."

"Look, a budding magus," Caul said with a chuckle. "Go on, put a few drops in." He handed me a small blade. I didn't take it. "Well, *I'm* not going to do it. I can't have you knowing my clientele. Magus-customer confidentiality."

I took the blade, made a shallow cut in my finger, and squeezed a few drops into the cap. The anamnee perked up, then stopped.

"Put more," urged Caul.

I sliced another finger and added more blood. The fly approached it. Its golden proboscis slid out of its head, probed the wine, then retracted. I added more droplets until the anamnee went to the cap and sucked it dry. For a minute or two, nothing happened. Then, its wings vibrated.

"No!" the insect buzzed.

Caul's jaw dropped.

"It's been saying that since I found it," I told him, unimpressed.

The fly began to hum, low and rich, like it was singing to itself.

"A drinking song? Was it doing that when you found it?" he jested.

Its hairy body began to glow like an ember. The humming got louder and louder until it filled the room. The melody ran up and down, from deep and flat to high and piercing. Each note wrapped around us, like swaddling.

A second later, I couldn't move. My eyes were glued to the insect as it performed. My head filled with its song. We were the anamnee's captive audience.

Suddenly, my vision went dark.

FOOL, you believed them, droned the fly. I didn't hear the words through my ears; they hung in my head like a thought.

The image of white stone buildings formed around me, as though one of the Gods painted them into existence before my eyes. I noticed the buildings were moving—no, *I* was moving. I was running through a town under the midday sun, but I couldn't feel the ground beneath my feet. I couldn't feel my body at all. I ran past a bustling, tented market, where smoke billowed from round ovens. But I couldn't smell anything or freely turn my head to look around. All I could see was the wide road I was barreling toward.

I realized I was a passenger in someone else's head. Was it Özge's? Had she been running from something or someone?

As I sprinted, I realized this town was ten times larger than my village. I raced past temples with giant columns and elaborately carved fountains spurting water. Weaving through curving alleys, I dodged women in long robes with hair tied up in cloths. I zigzagged away from men in fine belts and scarves. Their clothing was ornate, cumbersome, *ancient*.

Scrambling up a steep, narrow street, I burst through a door into a cramped workshop. It was filled with neatly arranged jars, bottles, and vials. Herbs and fungi filled bowls. It reminded me of Caul's crude lab. Rifling through drawers, I jammed papers, bottles, and clothes into a sack. I noticed my hands were wide, the skin thick—they were masculine. Not Özge's.

I heard the slap of wood behind me.

My head swung around to see two men in gambesons standing in the doorway.

Trying to run—the words were metallic, like the anamnee's voice, but they came from one of the guards.

We don't let conjurers poison our town, the other guard said in the fly's scratchy tone.

I'm a healer. I heal people—this time, the anamnee's voice vibrated from inside me, though I hadn't meant to say anything. *I am permitted to be here. I was invited*—

Ignoring me, the guards grabbed my arms and hauled me out of the workshop.

Please, you don't understand—you don't understand! I'm trying to help, "my" voice pled.

Again, I was ignored. Paving stones streaked past my eyes as I was dragged through the streets. Suddenly, I hit a hard curved surface. The hands released me. I pushed myself up and looked around to see a large square. Above me loomed the head of a giant stone dog. Around me, a circle of townsfolk formed. I tried to shield myself against their spit and screams. Scrambling backward, I pressed my back against the statue's large paws and realized: *I'm in the ruins, long before they crumbled. This is where Özge slept hundreds of years later.*

One of the guards grabbed my hair and yanked my head back, forcing it onto the stone paw. The other approached with a sword.

You don't belong here, the guard said, raising his blade.

Wait—you don't understand, I begged.

He sliced through the air, toward my head—

No! my metallic voice cried out.

Everything went black.

I THREW my arms up to shield my head. The blow never came. Opening my eyes, I saw Caul sitting in his lab, covering his head, too. He had also seen it. Slowly, he realized the memory was over and lowered his hands.

"The man was a magus, like me," he said quietly. "Where was that memory from?"

"No idea," I lied. "But it was old. At least a thousand years."

"Lucky for me, magic's mostly legal, now," Caul said.

"Mostly. But it'll probably be another thousand years before the Elders stop throwing you in the stocks," I said, only partly joking.

Caul grumbled under his breath, clearly unamused.

I got up and stumbled. My stomach felt loose. My head swam. I looked at the fly—it was motionless but still glowing deep crimson.

"Hope that was worth it for you, because I feel like shit," I said.

"Completely worth it," replied Caul.

It hadn't been for me. If anything, it was a rude reminder of my situation. And I still didn't know where my sister was. I needed to continue my search. I went to collect the fly—

"Özge? Özge?" it cried.

Then, it hummed *again*.

I WAS PLUNGED into pitch blackness. I could hear the creaking of wooden floors beneath me. A door swung open to a sky filled with stars. Soon, I was rustling through grass toward an inky forest. I slinked between trees, heading for a dim green glow—it was a tiny fire the colour of spring leaves. A figure was hunched over it, holding a bowl of simmering liquid.

Oh, Gods. I was in my *own* memory. I'd been stupid to put my blood in the wine. I didn't want Caul to see this. And *I* didn't want to see this. Not again. I tried to thrash around and yell to break the vision. It was useless. For a second time, I was a captive passenger.

Seeing my sister made my heart sink. I watched as she crumbled something into the bowl, which made the liquid pop with sparks. She whispered to the mixture—it glowed indigo, and the fire snuffed out. She poured the contents of the bowl into a tiny bottle and corked it.

Unseen, I followed her back to the house and into our parents' room. They were in a deep sleep and didn't stir as Özge dripped the liquid into Ma's ear.

Everything went dark.

Next, I found myself in our bedroom, digging through Özge's bag like a dirty rat scrounging for scraps. I found the small bottle of indigo liquid and made my way through the house to Father's workshop. I watched for a moment while he sanded a walking stick. He looked tired. Then, I tossed a boulder into his pond.

Father, my metallic voice buzzed. *This was in Özge's things. I saw her make it.*

I put it on the table and darted out of the room.

Darkness fell.

My vision bled in again. I was at our table. Özge sat beside me, sipping a bowl of Ma's spiced stew. Father was on his third cup of wine. He drained it. Ma gave him a disapproving squint. Then, he placed the tiny indigo bottle on the table.

Özge stared at it in shock. Finally, she said, *You went through my things, Pa?*

Explain, Father demanded.

I made it for Ma. Though Özge's words came through the anamnee's voice, I could still hear her—always soft, yet certain.

Wh-what? Father said, confused.

To stop her shaking.

Father's scowl deepened. *You've been giving her this?*

He looked at Ma, who was just as confused.

Yes, Özge said. *And it's working. For her and many people outside this village.*

At this point, I crumpled inside. I couldn't look Özge in the eye. I'd taken the bottle, thinking it was poison. I didn't know it was medicine for Ma. *This goes against nature,* Father said as he raised the bottle. *You will stop.*

Özge balled her hands into fists. *You want me to stop helping her because you don't understand something?*

You're the one that doesn't understand. Magic has warped you, made you entitled. You're reckless. With yourself, and your mother.

Özge shook her head. *I can't watch her crumble just to obey you.*

You won't have to, Father said as he rose. *I want you out. This doesn't belong in my house.*

Father and Özge glared at one another, each chewing a corner of their mouth. Gods, they could be so alike yet so different.

Özge broke the strange silence. *Ma?*

Ma looked down and shook her head as she held back tears.

You can go now, or I can bring this to the Elders, Father stated.

Then, he collected the dishes and started washing up, like it was a normal evening. My sister sat at the table a while before going to our room. I followed to find her packing a satchel.

Özge, where will you go?—the anamnee's metallic voice vibrated from within me.

I don't know. The city, maybe, she mumbled. *Somewhere that wants my help.*

It hit me like a sack of stones: she was really leaving. I couldn't be the only one at home with Father and Ma. Who would I talk to? Who would keep my secrets? Who would tell me how things worked?

Don't go, I said. *Just tell them you're sorry and you'll never do it again.*

Can't, she said.

Why?

Because he's right—I don't belong here.

Then, I'm going with you.

You're too young, Özge said. *Don't worry. I'll send you a letter.*

Pitch black fell over my vision again.

———

THE IMAGE of the ruins crystalized next. My buzzing voice called out for Özge as I walked through mountains of stone. Eventually, I reached the square with the broken dog statue and coloured weeds. I found the old campfire and my sister's button and teased out the anamnee fly.

Özge? Özge? I shouted at the insect just before capturing it.

Darkness.

———

WAKING FROM THE MEMORY, I lurched forward and gagged. Nearby, I could hear Caul vomiting. Bile rose in my mouth and splattered on the floor. Wiping it from my lips, I sat up to see him burning a hole through me with his eyes.

"Your own sister," he said.

"I didn't know—I thought she was doing something bad," I said, my throat getting tight. "But I'm trying to get her back."

"By going in the ruins. You didn't tell me about that. I could be cursed by association."

"You won't. They're just stones. There is no curse."

"There is," Caul insisted. "But it's not magic. The curse is this village. Did anyone see you go in?"

"Uh, an old woman at the caravan stop."

"It's only a matter of time until everyone knows. You have to leave here—for good."

"What? No! If anyone finds out, I'll just explain the ruins."

"Like your sister explained that potion to your Pa?"

I tried to imagine convincing Father there was no curse and found I couldn't.

"When people find out you went in there, they'll blame you for everything," said Caul. "Dead crops, sick babies—you'll be the reason why. And if misfortune runs too high, who knows what they'll do . . ."

I could tell what Caul was thinking because I was thinking it too: the man dragged to the dog statue. Though it was ancient history, it didn't feel that far away.

AFTER NIGHTFALL, I packed up the anamnee fly and crept out of Caul's house, careful not to be seen. With nowhere else to go, I stumbled through the dark stones to the old square. I lit a fire on top of the ashes under the statue and lay down on the silver shrubs. I thought of my woollen blanket at home, but it brought me no comfort.

The night lasted forever. When morning finally came, I looked at the anamnee and considered crushing it. I couldn't. It held the last memory of my sister. If I killed that, I'd be no different than anyone in the village. I put the fly back where I found it. The insect scuttled into its hole. If it was going to sleep for another thousand years, I hoped whoever found it next would see the memories and know Özge was good.

I left the ruins to continue my search for her.

ANGEL & MONICA

By Helen Dale

AUTHOR'S NOTE: Kingdom of the Wicked *represented a change of genre for me. I had an established reputation as a writer of literary fiction and political commentary and no plans to venture into the realm of speculative fiction. Once I realized that's what I was doing, however, I sought to combine the worldbuilding and plotting of genre with the careful character development of literary fiction, which meant I wrote a lot. And as is often the case, some of what I'd written had to go. Even after the editorial process,* Kingdom of the Wicked *turned into a two-book series (Book I: Rules; Book II: Order) with a third book left on the cutting-room floor.*

Much of what my editor removed was surplus to requirements— self-indulgent, meandering, or irrelevant—but some of it wasn't, and I agonized over its loss. The section below was meant to be the second chapter of Book I and provides Linnaeus's backstory. Andreius Linnaeus is Yeshua Ben Yusuf's (Jesus of Nazareth's) defence counsel, and Yeshua Ben Yusuf is up on terrorism charges. Kingdom of the Wicked *retells the Canonical Gospels as though they took place in a*

Roman Empire that has seen an industrial revolution and now bestrides Europe, North Africa, and the Middle East as the world's first industrial superpower.

I've written elsewhere about the extent to which industrialization depends on the abolition of chattel slavery, which means my proto-modern Romans must go through the same process as Britain did in the late eighteenth and early nineteenth centuries. The story told here, of Angel and Monica, Linnaeus's parents, was an unremarkable one in Roman times. Slaves could not marry, and if a master or mistress wanted to marry one, the slave had to be freed first, a process known as manumission. Because Romans did not enslave based on race, this practice was both commoner and far less fraught than the arrangements familiar to us from slavery in the antebellum South. Nonetheless, apart from a few intellectuals (mainly Stoics), Romans did not question the existence of slavery.

To that end, I had to depict a practice widespread in the Roman world against a changed background, one where there is now intense public debate around the morality of chattel slavery and disquiet about the brutal and entitled behaviour of slaveowners. Imagine, then, this story taking place in an ancient Mediterranean civilization about to do what the United Kingdom did in 1807: abolish the slave trade throughout its vast Empire.

At dawn, Angelus "Angel" Linnaeus supervised the barge loading outside his mill gate, bolts of fabric in different colours, swatches and samples, yarn and thread. He had cause to swear at one of his weavers for getting in the lighterman's way; he chased the lad back into the mill, where he yelled for the supervisor. *Supposed to be teaching him a trade, not letting him dance about on the water.* She hauled the boy off by the ear. Angel collected a heavy canvas bag—clothes and paperwork, mainly—from the mill office, turned out the gas lamp on his desk, reminded his clerk that he had full authority for the four days, strode out along the path, and stepped nimbly into the cabin with the master.

THE MASTER—BEARDED, Greek, and wary—looked at the mill owner; the latter was one of the new class of Romans who'd moved to the Padan Plain and the Adriatic coast from Rome and Umbria. Lean as a crow, dark, curly, and fierce, the young man ran his mill like his people's generals ran the legions.

"A business deal?" the master asked.

"If it goes to plan, yes," the mill owner said, not looking at him and declining to introduce himself. "I've got the product, the Senator's got the coasters."

The master smiled; the mill owner was in a rough linen shirt and heavy cotton trousers, like a barbarian. His hands were stuffed in his pockets.

"A Senator? I hope you've got some good clothes so you can dine."

The mill owner grumbled at this. "Went and bought some, yes, out of necessity."

The master smiled again, guiding the barge down the canal. *They either piss it away like water, these Romans, or they're as tight as a fish's arse.*

ANGEL HAD BEEN FORCED into town to buy two new tunics (*probably sold the cotton cloth in them myself*) and a long stole. He'd even run to a haircut and a fine solid-gold band, which fitted around his forehead. He drew the line at a toga—no one in his family had ever worn one, and he wasn't about to start now. That was for higher-ups, not for the likes of him. After he came home from the store, he'd dressed in one set of the new clothes, looked in the mirror, and admired the effect. He looked good; the gold set off his black curls well. *About time you got yourself a woman, Angel. You'd be in demand, now.*

If all went well, there'd be a joint venture with Senator Flaccus from Angón with his ships and a big fat profit at the end of things. He smiled at the thought; he was pretty sure this one was in the bag, and four days as a guest at the Senator's harbourside resi-dence (*How many houses does the fucker own?*) promised to be an entertaining diversion. He sat on a bolt of cloth and admired the sun on the water and the fields, houses, and a rival mill as they slid by.

Senator Lucius Flaccus—fat, balding, but somehow impres-sive—was seated on his private pier in the sunshine enjoying a glass of wine, waiting as the barge glided in. A big cheese in the *Parti Optimates*, he was well dressed—thankfully, not in a toga, but in a rich, dark, ankle-length gown—and if he objected to Angel's appearance, he gave no sign. He stood up and extended his hand.

"Good to meet you at last, Angel. You're quite the success story —my wife's very anxious to make your acquaintance."

"I hope I don't disappoint her, Senator."

They retired to Flaccus's shipping offices and haggled for a good four hours, nailing down the terms of the deal while lightermen unloaded the barge. Angel was surprised the Senator didn't want to inspect his samples; had the boot been on the other foot, he'd have gone over the contents of that barge with a fine-tooth comb. Instead, the Senator paid for its contents in crisp notes. Angel pocketed the money with some care; he preferred to pay by cheque.

"Consider it a little water to prime the pump," the Senator said.

Angel enjoyed the deal-cutting; he was born to bargain and was good at it.

An obsequious man Flaccus identified as his lawyer joined them, gradually reducing the transaction to writing. After Angel was satisfied it was a true and correct record of their agreement, they both signed it. The lawyer gave each of them a carbon copy.

"And now, after all that hard work," said Flaccus, "we play."

Angel followed the portly Senator to his carriage, and they made their way to his residence, all sweeping colonnades and manicured lawns and topiary and mosaic and parquetry floors. When they arrived, Flaccus pointed at two women in brown tunics waiting by the double-door and then waved his hand in Angel's direction.

"Take my guest to the baths. We dine this evening."

They inclined their heads. "Yes, *Domine.*"

Angel flinched when he heard the form of address, and then remembered Flaccus's politics. *He keeps slaves. Should have realized that.*

The older of the two—he noticed she had flecks of grey at the temples—picked up his bag, while the younger one took his hand, intertwining her fingers with his. He felt an instant sexual frisson: she was stunning. He suspected the two were mother and daughter. The older woman had the same high cheekbones and green almond eyes as the younger. Her hair was swept up in a functional bun, while the younger woman's hung loose over her shoulders and down her back, black and glossy.

"What's your name?"

"I am Monica," she said, smiling at him.

He enjoyed being scrubbed, oiled, and massaged without taking what was apparently on offer. He was floating on his back at one point, admiring the glittering mosaic ceiling, when Monica swam up beside him and slid her hand across his chest. He corrected himself—upright now, while treading water—and took her wrists, crossing her hands in front of her breasts.

"You don't have to do that. If I want you, I will ask, and I will pay you."

She nodded, looking down.

———

"WE'VE FITTED the exterior up for the new electric light," Flaccus was saying, "but inside, we prefer to stick to the old ways."

Large braziers lit the smaller of his two banqueting halls, the one they were using. In the middle of the hall stood Flaccus's new "toy," as he called it. A model of the solar system, it was powered by a paddlewheel turned by a water fountain and moved before the diners' eyes. Angel had seen a simpler one before—his mill worked on a similar principle, on a larger scale and steam-powered—but there was no doubt that the Senator's mechanical acquisition was a thing of great beauty.

"It's quite old, fifty years or so," Flaccus was saying. "The chap who sold it to me hitched it to the water supply; otherwise, you have to wind it up. I never get tired of looking at it."

"This is the clever part," Angel said, pointing at the interlocking set of gears. "This is what's making us rich."

Flaccus had invited half-a-dozen wealthy neighbours to make the acquaintance of the thrusting young industrialist from upriver, and they were now at the pleasantly squiffy stage. Angel found himself fielding questions about everything from construction to power to labour, all of them interested after his discussion of the Senator's astronomical machine. He struggled to keep a grip on sobriety: Flaccus's glasses were of the large, flat, decorative type and seemed to hold about half a bottle each. Angel was a quick and greedy drinker when he got the chance; this time, he was careful to keep stuffing himself with food as he went along. The experience of reclining to dine was very pleasant, and Flaccus had gone to town with the food and wine. Angel's modest house up the *decumanus* from the mill did not run to a dining hall, and in any case, there was little point: he spent most of his time in his office, dozing in an alcove behind his desk, immune to the clack of looms and the dull thump of machinery.

The Senator's wife was most pleased to meet him, as he'd said she would be. "Angel, Lucius keeps telling me how men like you are making the Empire rich."

"Well, men like your husband are making the Empire bigger; we're always getting more places we can sell things. Onwards and upwards."

Monica had changed into a simple cream robe, twisting her hair into a loose braid. It hung down her back. She served them, along with the woman Angel now knew for certain to be her mother (he'd asked Flaccus) and a young man.

With several glasses of wine coursing through his veins, he was finding it much harder to resist her charms. Flaccus—although Angel could not see him smirking in the flickering light—found this amusing.

"You like her, don't you?"

"Yes, I do." The wine was also making him truthful.

"I'll have her dance for us."

The young man reappeared with a pair of drums—one large,

one small—and sat on the floor; Monica's mother stood to one side with a cithara, although she sang for the most part—high, intense, even ecstatic. Angel had seen performances like this before, at the theatre in the presence of hundreds or thousands of others, but never in such an intimate setting. Monica started with one hand open behind her head and one hand open in front of her face, her elbows pointing out. Her dance was traditional and skilful: she did not strip off or approach any of Flaccus's diners individually. She did not need to. Her movements were erotic without any further assistance. One of his lifelong memories would be of her sleek figure whirling and twisting behind Flaccus's marvellous machine, its planets rotating one way while she spun the other.

When she finished, her fingers pointing at the floor, her head thrown back, Angel could not speak. He rolled onto his stomach and clasped his hands around the back of his head, looking down. The sexual vision he had in his mind's eye was intoxicating.

Flaccus smiled and snapped his fingers, attracting Monica's attention, and then pointed to Angel's couch. The movement was so sudden he was caught unawares.

"Take her for the night. She's yours."

She moved across the room, sitting—although, he noted, not reclining—beside him. He propped himself up on one elbow and handed her his cup. She curled both hands around it and drank, then handed it back, smiling at him. He reached out to touch her cheek; she was slippery with sweat. The casual way Flaccus had dispensed her made the hair on the back of his neck stand up. Angel smiled at her with what he hoped was real warmth and handed her a chicken leg. She ate it, licking her fingers.

Flaccus found this vastly entertaining. "Despite the rumours, Angel, most slave-owners do not underfeed their slaves. That's just

Populares propaganda. She would not look like she does if we starved her." The rest of the diners joined their host in chortling at his discomfort.

Angel handed her his cup again. He turned to face Flaccus. "I don't like slavery, Senator."

Flaccus grinned at this. "How many ten-year-olds have you got employed in that mill of yours, Angel?"

Angel pursed his lips. There were a few.

"You lot and your Stoic friends are going to win the slavery argument sooner rather than later, after all the dreadful slave insurrections we've had. Enjoy the institution while you still can. Use her. I do."

Flaccus's wife had a sour expression on her face.

Monica intertwined her fingers with his again and led him to his guest room. He tugged her toward him and closed the door, kissing her with all the gentleness he could muster.

"I want you, Monica. Do you want me?"

"Let me give it willingly, *mi domine* Angelus. He just takes it." Deftly, she undid the tie behind her neck and dropped the cream robe at her feet.

He kissed her again, this time passionately. "Not *domine*, Monica. Just Angel. I am Angel."

She lay on her back and used her hands to draw her knees up and apart, waiting for him to mount her. He undressed, standing at the foot of the bed, watching her eyes fix on him. He shook his head, making a point of lying beside her, curling one arm around her head and stroking her cheek and hair. She turned to face him, smiling, her face shiny with tears now.

He coiled his lean brown arms around her and wriggled onto his back, pulling her on top of him. "I'll treat you like a free woman, Monica."

She leaned forward, over him, her hair framing his face.

———

THE NEXT NIGHT, there came a single knock on his door. He put down the book he was reading and went to answer it, perplexed at the interruption; he'd been about to turn out the gas lamp beside his bed.

Monica stood on the threshold, dressed in a short blue tunic calculated to show off her long brown legs, her eyes made up with kohl. "*Domine* Flaccus did not send for me."

"And you want to be with me, Monica?"

"Very much, *mi domine*."

She looked down; he put his fingers under her chin, lifted her face, and gazed at her. She smiled. He drew her into his arms, once again taking care to be gentle with her.

"If Dominus Flaccus is angry with me for coming to you, will you speak for me?"

He closed the door behind her. "Of course. If I didn't know better, I'd think he's trying to get rid of you."

"*Domina* hates me. Once she cut off all my hair."

Angel laughed, pulling her hips into his. "Maybe he *is* trying to get rid of you. If she divorces him, he'll have to repay her dowry and any profit he made from the *commixtio* in the proportions it went in. He may lose his property qualification for the Senate."

"You're very clever, *mi domine*."

———

ON THE THIRD day of his visit, after she'd voluntarily come to him again—and after he'd made several trips to the household shrine, burning incense and asking the *Lares* and the ancestors for their permission—he went to Flaccus.

"How much do you want for Monica?"

Flaccus laughed. "You're very lucky my wife isn't fond of her, Angel, otherwise she wouldn't be for sale."

Despite the fact that the transaction made him feel queasy, he negotiated for her with all his considerable skill, something that Flaccus found even more amusing than his conflicted restraint on the first evening.

"I got her two abortions; didn't want her to lose her figure," he said at one point. "You should get her medically examined if you want offspring."

Angel resisted the temptation to kiss his teeth and curl his lip. "I'll do that."

Flaccus stood up and extended his hand. "As always, a pleasure to do business with you."

Angel did not reveal his intentions to Monica as she collected her clothes and few personal possessions from the slaves' quarters and hugged her mother.

"He's a good man. He will look after you," her mother said.

"He's gentle with me."

Angel stood in the doorway, this time dressed casually. His hands were in his pockets. He'd left the gold band around his head; Monica told him it made him look good.

"It's a bit flash," he said.

"You're a bit flash."

EARLY ON THE day of his scheduled return home, Angel took Monica into Angón's Forum and went into the vaulted *Basiliké*

Stoà. He spoke to a minor public official behind the front counter, paid money over, and collected some paperwork. He sat down to fill it out. Monica propped her chin in her hands, watching him write. He took out her bill of sale and began copying information across into the blank spaces on the form.

"What are you doing, *Domine*?"

"Shh. Let me finish here, and I'll explain."

One of the public employees walked toward them. "The magistrate will see you in half an hour."

Angel nodded and kept writing. Monica rested one hand on his thigh. He smiled at this. Eventually, he collated all the documents, rolled them up, and bound them with a length of dark pink tape. He stood up and held her hand to his chest.

"I am going to manumit you," he said. "I can't make you stay after that, but I would like you to stay with me. If Flaccus hasn't hurt you too much, I would also like you to bear my children."

She began to cry, and he folded her into his arms, rocking back and forth. "Thank you, *Domine*."

"You can only call me that for a little bit longer, Monica."

Even though Flaccus was helping him get very rich (instead of just rich), had the Senator materialized before him at that moment, Angel would have laid him out.

The magistrate—grey-haired, florid, and harried—sat on a raised dais behind a vast bench littered with stamps, papers, and several empty inkwells. A tub of wax with a spoon perched upright in it hung above a candle. Rome's eagle and the letters SPQR were carved into the stone behind him.

Monica gazed up at the ceiling: it was decorated with maritime imagery. A mosaic telling the story of the Municipality of Angón was set into the walls: ships and fishermen featured heavily. She could not identify the language the labels were written in. She pointed it out to Angel. "What's that?"

"It's Greek. Angón was once mainly a Greek city."

Angel handed the magistrate his paperwork. The latter read it through, scribbled something on a sheet of paper, and rummaged under his desk for something—his head disappeared momentarily —and found it, handing Angel a decorative staff and a printed card.

"That's the correct form of words."

He pointed to a spot on the floor and told Monica to stand there. Angel took his place opposite her. "Angelus Caius Linnaeus, do you manumit Monica, of the Isle of Sardinia, before me and all the Gods and Goddesses? Do you discharge her from all services or demand of service to be hereafter made either by you or any other person by, from, or under you?"

Angel read the words on the piece of paper, holding it up in front of his eyes. "I, Angelus Caius Linnaeus, do so manumit Monica, of the Isle of Sardinia, before you, Magistrate, and all the Gods and Goddesses. I do so discharge her from all services or demand of service to be hereafter made either by me or any other person by, from, or under me."

"Touch her with the staff."

Angel reached out and touched the top of her head.

The magistrate signed and stamped the paperwork in front of him, spooned some of the hot wax onto the top document, and then removed the ring from his little finger. He pushed it into the wax. "Given under my sign and seal, Magistrate of the Civitas of Angón, this day the Ides of May, in the year seven hundred and twenty-eight *ab urbe condita*. Monica Linnaea, you are free."

Angel exchanged the staff and printed slip for Monica's paperwork. The magistrate smiled at her as her erstwhile owner took her hand and pulled her close to him. "Good fortune for both of you."

———

MONICA'S PRESENCE inspired Angel to renovate the little house on the *decumanus* and to abandon sleeping in the mill office; in her turn, she decorated both places with Sardi talismans against the Evil Eye. Her husband was rich; people could look envy on him without even thinking, and this had to be warded off. He learned to work and sleep under a forest of blue and white glass, dangling mirrors, and bronze statuettes. For some reason, she seemed to think these things were best when hanging from the ceiling or above the door. Angel's clerk sometimes smiled at her collection, but Angel did not care. He was besotted with his wife, and if she wanted shrines and talismans, she could have what she wanted.

Monica was illiterate for the most part, which annoyed him. It turned out she knew her letters and how to write her name and was a little better than that with arithmetic, but not much more. She was young enough for Flaccus to have educated her, even if only at the most basic level. Instead, he'd had her taught to dance and sing, which—to be fair—she often did for Angel. He found it arousing, and she liked to please him.

Angel hired a tutor and then sent her to adult education classes organized by the local office of the *Parti Populares*. She learned fast, which he also liked: she had a good head for figures and in time developed a genuine appreciation for the theatre. "Sometimes it's nice to watch other people do the performing," he'd say.

"We go to the provinces and make them send their children to school for five years, but don't do it in Italy," he complained to the district organizer who ran the classes.

The organizer shrugged and made his usual attempt to interest Angel in joining the *Populares* and running for office—he'd satisfied the property qualification for the Senate after his second joint venture with Flaccus, under one of the new limited liability agreements. They'd made quite a few investors very rich as well as lining their own pockets. Angel now owned several mills and most of the town. "If it upsets you, perhaps you should try to do something concrete about it," the organizer said. "Your story is a compelling one. It would do well for some people in our country to hear it."

"I won't humiliate Monica like that," he said. "It's her story, not mine."

"I take it the business with Flaccus is too profitable to jeopardize, then?"

Angel was nothing if not honest. "That, too."

He waited until Monica was twenty before he fathered children on her, listening to the *medica* in Angón. "You need to wait until she's stopped being a child herself," the woman said. "Enjoy the beauty of each other's bodies for a few years."

First, she bore him a daughter, who was named Monica for her mother but always called Moniculla by her parents. Next was a boy to take over the mills, which pleased Angel no end; he became Corinnus Angelus, after Angel's father and Angel himself. Finally, there was another boy, one who inherited his mother's almond eyes and straight black hair.

"He'll have to have a Sardi name," Angel said. "He looks like you."

Monica ran through her small stock of Sardi boys' names,

finally settling on Andreius. "My mother's brother, from before we were sold to the slaver in Rome."

Angel gazed at the bundle in her arms and chucked his fingers under the baby's chin. "He looks like a clever one. Maybe we'll have someone clever in the family."

"I thought you just wanted to buy me," she said. "Not free me and marry me and let me choose my children's names."

He slid his hand along the line of her jaw and under her ear, shaking his head and blinking the way he always did when lost for words.

ROOT MOTHER

By Adria Laycraft

Naois peered through the downpour and called once more for her niece. The rain made a hushed roar that drowned her voice, but she'd be damned if she'd let the girl elude another day of chores.

Naois swung her pot off the heat of the flame and scooped up her shawl from the wooden bench, watching for any sign of the girl as she wrapped her shoulders. Rain sizzled on the fire, dripping through the opening in the roof that released wood smoke into a charcoal sky. With another huff, Naois struck out into the wild weather.

Despite her frustration with Annwn, Naois thrilled at the wildness of the storm, the clean air away from the hearth, the bit of freedom from all that needed doing. How sweet it would be if she were Root Mother, as much a leader as her brother the Druid, favoured by the Fae and free of daily manual labour.

Alas, she had neither sign nor Sight and was instead burdened with the care of her late sister's child, though her brother had wriggled his way into the role of Druid with only minor Sight. He liked to say everyone had the Sight, that those blind were only blocked by evil. Did he realize how he insulted her?

He should be cautious. Fate could be a harsh mistress.

Annwn was not with the other girls where they stitched clothing in a circle, nor was she in the lodge spying on the elders. She was not by the midden, or annoying the weavers, or gathering clay by the creek.

Wet through now, Naois shivered. Annwn had a wild way about her. . . would she dare go to the grove? It was the only place left to look.

The woods were dark and darker, shadows looming out from under the deepest trees. The way soon opened into meadow, and the sacred grove stood beyond at the bottom of a ridge. Shadow obscured the grove, a dark smudge on the green, and the circled trees bowed toward the central oak, its proud canopy reaching high and wide. Branches met overhead to create shelter for those who dared go within.

Naois crossed the meadow to the grove, careful to keep her feet outside the sacred place while her gaze searched within. Annwn had a knack for being unseen. She could be in that shadow, or behind that bit of brush, only to appear when you least expected her.

A Root Mother would know where Annwn was. She would stare into the mists and proclaim her inner visions, and Annwn would be found and put back to work.

Upon the ridge above Naois grew a beautiful rowan tree, heavy with clumps of red berries. The red caught her eye like a sign, and there below sat Annwn. She had her back to the trunk and her face turned up to the branches above, mouth agape.

Naois sighed. "She looks like the village idiot," she muttered to the rain. She gathered her skirts and climbed to the tree. As she drew closer, Naois saw that Annwn wore something on her face, covering her left eye. Naois flashed a warding sign with her fingers, then took a deep breath to shout, "Annwn!"

Annwn rolled her head to the side without lifting it from the tree trunk. Her bare eye opened and blinked a few times. Naois felt a flash of resentment, realizing the girl sat, comfortable, within the shelter of the tree while she stood soaked to the bone. Annwn's calm response—no flinch of surprise, no hunch of guilt—did nothing to improve Naois's mood.

"What are you doing? Come away."

Annwn had a gaze as disconcerting as any Root Mother's. She looked back up into the laden branches and seemed to be speaking, but Naois couldn't make out the words. They were directed to the tree, in any case, not at her.

Naois checked the woods around them. Rowan trees drew Fae, and every tree had its power, its tales, its rules. Only fallen rowan branches could be gathered, and Naois always wondered if that was because something *other* lived within the tree.

"Come away!"

Annwn's head turned once again. "Why?"

"Now, Annwn, or you will suffer the end of my wooden spoon. I have mutton stewing, and you have chores to do. I've had enough of your shirking."

Annwn shifted and stood, her face disappearing behind the heavily laden branches and her smock blending so perfectly with the trunk that for a moment, all Naois could see was the child's feet—as if they no longer had a body. She hitched a hard lungful of wet air. The feet moved, and Annwn ducked up from under the hanging branches.

The thing over her eye was a leather patch with a hole cut in the middle for a stone. Taken with her odd ways and her disconcerting stare, it made the child look as wild as any witch. A thought steeped in possibilities took root.

"What are you wearing on your eye, child?"

"Nothing, it's only a stone," she said, pulling it off and hiding it within her sleeve.

"Let me see it."

Annwn frowned at her. "It's mine. I made it."

Naois knew what she must do. "Then answer to the Druid," she said, keeping her tone as pleasant as possible. "He surely will want to see this."

Naois herded a reluctant Annwn through the sodden village. They entered the Druid's cottage. He looked up from his herbs and bones, his eyes widening slightly when he saw his sister and niece.

She gave the girl a shove forward. "Show him." Annwn flashed a sullen look, and Naois frowned right back at her in warning.

"What do you have to show me, child?"

Fear replaced the insolence in Annwn's face. The Druid was their clan leader and had the power to banish anyone who angered him, especially a young orphan who didn't do her share of the daily work. Annwn extended her arm and opened her hand.

A child's mess of deerskin and fine threads sat in the centre of her palm, the ties dangling. Annwn had cut a hole just smaller than the smoky-clear stone in the leather patch, then stitched a filament net to hold it there. Once secured about her head, Annwn could gaze through the stone.

The Druid inspected her creation, his lined face unresponsive. "A see-stone."

Naois grew impatient. "Yes, and she spoke with a tree."

Donal's attention turned on her. "In the grove?"

"No, no. The rowan that grows on the ridge above the grove, where we gather fallen branches for Beltane."

"And what did she say?"

Naois waved him off. "I could not hear, Donal. The rain is as loud as a hundred voices."

"Druid, Clan Leader, or Protector of the Grove," he reminded her. His imperious tone was like a fan on the flame of her anger. Naois shoved the girl aside and came close to her brother.

"We have not had a Root Mother for five seasons now," she said in a hushed tone. Naois leaned in and spoke so low her words became like the hiss of rain on the fire. "We could make her so."

She leaned back. Donal's face showed little emotion, but she knew him well enough to see the thought was being considered. He gathered his white robe around him and took up a heavy cloak against the rain.

"Bring her."

Naois had to force Annwn along, back through the wet, to the ancient circle of trees. At the edge, Naois stopped, but she gave Annwn a push over the boundary. Annwn's face was lost deep in her hood, her head bowed.

"Put it on, child," Donal said. Even his deep voice could barely be heard in the rushing downpour. Naois shifted, anxious. Her plan depended on this moment.

Donal tugged off Annwn's hood. The girl reluctantly lifted the see-stone to her eye and tied it on. She raised her face to the great central oak.

Annwn cried out and fell back, warding her face with her arms. She scrambled out of the grove, twisting to find her feet, and ran, heading toward the low ridge and the same rowan tree Naois had found her under.

Naois tried to catch her as she passed, but the child was too quick. She turned back to her brother. "She saw something. This is a sign. The clan would accept her as Root Mother."

He stared at the central oak with new guardedness. "She saw *something*," he agreed. "But the right sign would be to feel at home in the grove. She does not."

"We can make it so."

Donal's sharp gaze pinned her. "You said that before. What are you suggesting?"

"Do the oak-root ritual but let me give her a little something beforehand. It would render her more relaxed and open to the grove."

"You would do that to our sister's child?"

Naois wanted to shake him into sense, but he stood out of reach within the grove.

"Being Root Mother would give her a life of being cared for," she said. *Like you*, she wanted to add, but bitterness wouldn't help her argument.

Donal stroked his beard, a good sign he was considering her suggestion. She pressed on.

"There are many tales of creating a Root Mother in times of need. The right potion would . . . lessen her fear."

"You mean the herbs would numb her mind. What sort of Root Mother would that make?"

"We would guide her, of course," Naois reasoned. "You and I have many wise ideas of how to lead the clan."

Now Donal stared at her, cold-eyed and thin-lipped. "You know better than anyone that I almost died in that ceremony. If you are wrong, the ritual could kill her."

Naois shivered. She might anger her sister's ghost. "I kept you alive," she said, wanting recognition for that. "I can keep her alive, too." Something had to change. She couldn't bear to go back to her endless life of drudgery, alone in her hut, ignored by the others. With the Root Mother living under her roof, they would all scramble to be her friend. "The villagers pester you for a Root Mother. Would you just let this chance go, then? There is something magical about her. Why can not we use it?"

He pressed his lips together. "I will only do it with her consent. I must know what she saw. Bring her back."

Naois trudged through the rain once more, her feet sodden and cold. The girl was under the rowan, sobbing against the tree's trunk, the see-stone clenched in one hand. Naois hesitated. Rowans were trees of protection.

A glance back showed Donal waiting in the oak grove. This was her opportunity to take control of her miserable life. If Annwn became Root Mother, Naois would never need to tend her own fire or cook her own food. It would be done for her by those seeking her favour. She would have a better place in the community and be shown the respect she deserved.

New determination sent her under the branches to pry away the girl's arms from the tree. Naois gripped tight to ensure she would not run.

"Druid Donal asks you to return," she said. "You must listen."

Annwn's face reddened. "Why would you do this?"

"I am helping you. If you become our new Root Mother, I'm bringing luck to our village," Naois said.

"No," Annwn said. "You only seek power over others."

"Well, perhaps you won't abandon me with all the work of the day next time," Naois snarled. "The Druid will see you now."

Naois shoved her along, and Annwn's face grew dark with anger. Naois set her own mouth in a stubborn line to match.

Annwn stopped many steps away from the outer oaks. "What

did you see, child?" Donal's deep voice held the force of command, making Annwn flinch.

Annwn pinched her mouth tight, then relented. "I am hers," she said, waving back at the ridge. "The old one in the grove is scary. He has no need of me."

Donal looked at Naois and questioned the child further without looking away from his sister. "You saw a man in the grove?"

"Not in the grove, in the tree. The great middle one."

Naois's heart surged. She tipped her head at her brother. "You are our Root Mother," she told Annwn. "How can you deny your responsibility?"

The girl flashed wild eyes. "Your thoughts are nothing but greed."

Naois ground her teeth. "Take care," she warned the girl, wagging a finger at her.

Donal pulled Naois away, ordering Annwn to wait.

"What have you decided, Brother?" Naois asked, confident.

"We cannot do this thing."

Naois could only shake her head in disappointment. "And those babies that died? What of them? What of the stunted crops and the stillborn lambs? What of the fever that has taken so many from us, our own sister among them? Druid, your village is in need, and it is up to you to ensure we have a Root Mother. She must take on her proper duties!"

Donal stared off into the rain and did not speak for a long time. When he did, she could sense his misgivings. "We must conduct the ritual in secret. And you will be sure to give her something to calm her, but not too much."

Naois gave him a quick nod. "How will the clan accept her without witnessing the ceremony?"

He gave her a grim look, and for the first time, Naois saw the true Druid in her little brother's face. "We will repeat it again later for all the clan to see . . . if Annwn survives."

<hr>

"STOP FIDGETING. Everything has to be just right." Naois stared at Annwn, wishing she could have been the one blessed with Sight, the one to lead the clan with as much right as the Druid. Naois reached out to stroke Annwn's cheek, but the girl pulled away.

"The ritual will fail," Annwn mumbled, the potion already taking effect. "The Oaken King will strike you down if you force me on him."

The slap cut the air and stung Naois's hand. Annwn straightened her head and cautiously touched her reddened cheek.

"Your parents might still live if we had a Root Mother," Naois said with cold reason. "All the babes we've lost these many moons, and the withering grain, and the harsh frost, it's because we don't have a Root Mother working with the Druid. You have the wild Sight; you show signs of being the one we need. All would be fine if you accepted this burden willingly."

Annwn hung her head.

"I only seek the best for our people, girl. You could make everything well again."

Annwn lifted her head, her gaze unfocused. "All right," she slurred. "For our clan, for the people. I will try . . . for them."

Naois handed her the see-stone, and they slipped out of the village to find Donal at the grove. Twilight made colours die and shadows merge. Drifting showers wet the forest, broken by starlit sky.

Donal led Annwn on into the deeper shadows of the grove.

Naois waited at its edge. Darkness ate at her. She pictured what he must be doing within. She wished she could wait in her cottage for the ritual to be over, but she could not be seen as anything less than essential.

First, he would lay out offerings of brambleberry and mead. A sage bundle smoked—she could smell it. Soon he would pray to the Oaken King. When the sound of his chanting voice rose, she relaxed. It would all be over soon. Once Annwn drank the dark, mystical liquid that Donal had prepared from the roots of the Great Oak, the ritual would be done.

Shadows shifted. A lady stood at her side.

Dressed in soft wrappings, she was tall and slim, terrible and lovely. Every move the woman made, even the turn of her head, was beauty and grace and dread.

For all her desire to have the Sight, when the lady's gaze met her own, Naois felt only terror.

"She is mine, not the Oaken King's."

Panic numbed her, and Naois's brain refused to make sense of the words. "Donal," she cried. "Help me!"

The chanting ceased, and he emerged from the shadows.

"What is it? Why do you shout?"

The lady no longer stood there, but Naois heard her voice as if she spoke by her ear. "Beware the cost if you seek to harm a child of mine."

Then the forest was still, the wind gone, and the gods silent once more.

"Did you hear that? Did you see her?"

"Who?" Donal stared at her, confused, and Naois lost faith in her own sanity. She shook so hard she didn't know if she could get the words out.

"The lady. I think she was Fae."

Donal looked all around, his face eager.

Naois's heart failed her. "Maybe this is all wrong," she said. "Perhaps we should stop."

"By the gods, no," Donal said. "We are blessed with a Fae presence. We will proceed. Besides, you have reminded me of the need to share these responsibilities I bear."

"She warned me, Donal. She told me to let Annwn be."

Donal growled. "You drove me to this. You and every villager demanding I do something."

He turned away.

"Don't leave me here," Naois gasped, reaching for his sleeve.

Donal shook his arm free. "If you are seeing the Fae, it will be no better for you in there."

"I don't care. Please don't leave me alone."

He only turned and went within, the shadows swallowing him but for the faint wisp of his white robe. Gathering her fears and weighing them one against the another, Naois chose and stepped within, forcing her feet forward, desperate to stay as close to her druid brother as possible.

Donal bent over Annwn, his hands pressed to her head, and began whispering the words of his chants once again. Naois stared at the Great Oak behind him, terrified of what might lie within.

The air condensed with moisture and magic, and a weight pressed at her like a heavy stone. Her breath grew short. The wind picked up, tossing the great branches towering over them.

Then, a great stag stepped out of the tree. He became man, still bearing the huge rack of antlered glory, then beast, then tree again.

Naois took one step back.

Donal, triggered by some knowing, stopped chanting and

turned, only to fall to his knees and press his face into the damp earth.

Naois stepped back once again.

The great stag turned his gaze on her. Man, tall and mighty, and yet beast, and yet tree, he looked right into her heart.

Naois cried out wordlessly and fell to her knees, burying her face in her arms.

His antlers touched the sky. "It is true. The child attunes to the Lady Rowan." His voice moved within her chest and within her mind. His voice became everything and nothing. "In your greed, you do more harm than good."

Naois peered over her shawl to see him change from tree to stag, to man, to beast once again. Her mind grappled with reason.

An arm like a thick branch gestured at the oak-root potion. "Why don't you try it for yourself?"

Naois could only shake her head. She knew the risks of the ritual. That drink could kill her.

"Yet, you would force another?"

"I only strive for the sake of our clan . . ." she began, eager to defend herself, but her words faltered to silence.

She became nothing.

"What have you done? Bring her back!" Donal cried.

Naois watched her brother. She heard words but did not understand their meaning.

"Why should I?" the great voice questioned. It came from without and within, new and old, perfect and terrible.

"We are only trying to save our clan. The harvest fails, fevers beset us, babes die. I have brought you sacrifice, done all you have asked, and still, we are cursed. Why?"

The great stag stomped one front hoof, chest heaving with anger, and Donal quieted. Then he no longer knelt there in the grass, either. Naois knew this but didn't know. Understood, but could attach no meaning, no emotion, to it.

"What have you done to them?" Annwn asked, and Naois didn't even care to wonder who the girl might be referring to.

"Nothing too horrid, I promise."

"But we need a Root Mother. I am supposed to do this. And it's unthinkable to leave them like . . . that."

"It is not for you to decide."

Annwn climbed to her feet and lifted her chin. "Take me instead, if you will, Great One, and I promise to serve the people."

"No, child, you belong to the Lady. I will not take that away from either of you."

"Then how can I help my people?"

Stag became man became tree, always shifting, merging. "By being the true you."

Annwn stared at Naois. Naois felt a twinge, a faint remembering. "What of my parents? They died because we had no Root Mother."

"Lives come and go, child. It is the way of things," the forest god said.

"We humans treasure each life," she countered.

Then she knelt in one swift movement, lifted the bowl to her mouth, and drank.

"No!"

The grove shook with the protest, and the trees that circled them stirred in a great wind.

Naois found awareness again.

The girl fell to the ground, writhing. Both hands clawed at her throat. Her muscles went into spasm, her face blackened, her eyes rolled back in her head. A woman's scream echoed from the ridge.

Naois tried to move. A weight held her, great roots running

deep, power that was old and slow and unfathomable. Her arms reached high but could not grasp. Power wound through her, yet anchored her, a prisoner. And that power was not hers to use.

Donal was there too, within the tree, like her. Dread shrank her gut, fear coursing ever higher as she struggled to move, speak, breathe.

The great beast that was also a man reached for the girl and drew her up, wrapping his arms around her and swallowing her into his tree-trunk body.

Naois pleaded within her mind, begged for another chance to walk the earth, to feel the rain on her skin, to taste the air. Did the tree god hear her? Did It care? The rain had cleared, and the moon climbed high now, lighting the grove in a way sunshine never could.

The great tree shifted again, opening and changing, and Annwn came tumbling out. She gasped, tears pouring down her face, and made for the ridge, for her Lady.

The black potion Donal had prepared as the ceremonial drug coursed now through the sapwood of the great tree.

"Here," came the offer once again. Naois shied from the liquid. The reality of her situation brought Naois's fear to new heights. Panic clawed her, spiralling in waves of terror. But she still turned away from the offer. The drink would kill her. She could not be made to take this on. She was too old, no one special. She had enough to do already.

The girl stood on the ridge, framed by moonlight, gazing upwards into the rowan's branches. Naois heard Annwn's whispers as the wind in leaves, a bargaining of sorts, but could form no words of her own. Annwn trailed fingers through hanging branches, then slipped within and hugged the rowan trunk.

"Let me do this." Annwn's request rang clear. The Lady opened her arms and set her free, each move like a dance of branches in a summer breeze.

Annwn approached the grove once more. Entering the grove, she came before the Horned God and paid her respects, offering a cluster of bright-red rowan berries that was graciously accepted. She took out the see-stone and tied it around her head. Then Annwn searched out Naois, reached in, and pulled her free.

Naois fell to her knees in the wet grass, sucking air as if drowning, the half-empty bowl of black liquid before her, tilted, where Annwn had dropped it. Naois flung it away, spilling the contents, closing her eyes to shield them.

Annwn slipped behind her, placing something like rope on her head, and Naois thought the foolish girl was trying to bind her. It got stuck, though, and Naois opened her eyes to fight back just as she felt the cool stone settle against her eye. Annwn whispered one word.

"*See.*"

And she did. A great twisting ran through Naois, tearing at her, opening her mind, as she gazed through the see-stone upon a world hidden to the everyday eye. Fae stood at each tree in the grove, and sprites danced amongst tiny night blooms. Strange horned beings drifted in and out of shadow, dancing on cloven hoof. Upon the ridge, the Lady Rowan stood with arms crossed.

Naois stared at the murky colours ebbing around Donal, each layer edged with black and marred by jagged slices. Unable to stop herself, she looked to the Great Oak holding him. Power flowed up the thick trunk and radiated outwards. Each of the surrounding oaks also surged with bright energy that pulsed up and out, joining overhead in a spiral of magic.

Annwn moved into her field of view. The girl glowed like a sun-dappled lake on a perfect day, rainbow lines dancing around her where tiny sprites played. She pulsed with a hazy green light from within that seemed to nurture all she touched.

"Be worthy of it," Annwn said. Naois could only stare at her in uncomprehending wonder.

Annwn turned back to the Great Oak and reached for Donal, but the Great Tree withheld him. "He is mine as much as you are hers, and he has some education to complete."

Annwn nodded her understanding, bowed deeply, then ran back to the Lady Rowan. As Naois watched, her blood raced, her mind spun, and new understanding dawned. Now the voices rang clear, easy to understand. "Come, my sweet. You have helped your people as you wished to do." The Lady Rowan also bowed deep to the Oaken King, then folded Annwn into her heartwood.

Naois struggled, overwhelmed. "Donal," she weakly protested. The girl was gone from normal sight, yet Naois could see her within the rowan. Just as the Great Oak held her brother within.

"Our Druid is needed . . ." she began, but she heard herself differently now. Her head hung low. "I'm sorry." Her mind continued to unfold, and she sensed the great fight for balance between Light and Dark, the endless dance, the cycles of loss and gain, and the weight of her great responsibility in the infinite struggle. As Donal lay trapped within the confines of the Oaken King, undergoing some process she wondered if he would survive, Naois understood there was no going back, no unseeing what had been seen and understood, and no denying what had been done.

The Great Tree stirred. The stag stared down at her.

"Behold, your wish is granted . . . Root Mother."

THE COOL SEQUESTERED VALE OF LIFE

By Edward Savio

Arcing north of Spaceport, the hills climb untamed and untrampled, strangely left off the routes of both beings and beasts. Below are valleys with thick forests that no beaver or axe has ever taken a bite out of. And within these woods, dark glens hide where the trees bend in on themselves, creating a canopy that blocks out all but a trickle of the noonday rays. Along the floor, streams of water run and pool and get absorbed without ever having reflected a single glint of sunlight.

Ancient outcroppings camouflage moss-covered cottages dotting the slopes that sit in judgment of the valley below. These dwellings keep secrets they have never revealed and can never reveal as they are all abandoned—the chimneys crumbling, the siding warped, the roofs concave and near collapse. The owners of these bungalows and shanties, fashioned out of the remnants of starships and containers mixed with local materials, are long gone. Did they flee? Were they murdered? The stories that have escaped from this place have told of this and many other outcomes. My first question, of course, was, *How did these tales spring up from a portion of fertile soil where no one lives, and no one has ever lived, for as long as anyone in these parts can remember?*

It is an even greater mystery because this stretch of land is the most precious on this world, green and moist. Many brave foreigners, for we all are aliens on this orbiting sphere, have attempted to exist in this seeming paradise—hardy individuals of many races and worlds. The poor and the exiled. The hopeful and the hopeless.

They have all come, they have all tried it, and they have all departed as quickly as the rest.

It is not, I am assured, because of anything that can be seen or touched, nor anything that is whispered from the trees in the deepest portion of the night.

It is something imagined.

That is what I thought when I first showed up on the surface of this alternately beautiful and accursed place. Perhaps the strangest thing about this forgotten waystation in this corridor of the galaxy is that the entire population resides on a plot of land that is thirsty for water, barren except for the constructed temples to commerce and shelter and power generation, while not too far in the distance, not a mirage, but real and reachable, is that verdant land rising out of the sterile desolation.

In the open spaces beyond the protection of Spaceport, one could die by merely walking in the heat of the midday sun. So why is it upon this most hellish patch of a hellish dwarf planet that everyone lives?

There is a road—really just tracks in the cracked dirt—that runs straight from Spaceport to the foot of the mountains. I am told that once, a trail wound its way from the valleys into the high hills, hugging the edges of cliffs, leading to those abandoned homesteads. But a great long time ago, everyone ceased to use it, and the path has been blown over by the winds on the flats and grown over by the vegetation in the hills.

They say the viridescent peaks and valleys are not good for the imagination. Or rather, perhaps, they are too good for it. Within a mile of that place, no one has restful dreams at night.

And despite all of this, the stories and the warnings and the refusal of almost anyone to assist me, it was my job, it was the reason I was here, to go up into that mountain and find a way to extract its useful contents.

The Collective needs its raw material, and better to lift it from a wasteland than a less depressed, more pristine world. The proximity of this rock to several wealthier planets made it a prime candidate for plundering, for it is costly to move anything through space, and the more millions of miles away, the more immoderate it becomes. Gearing up for the trek, I was told I was a fool, and I will admit that I was both curious and concerned by what I had heard. But my options were limited as going back empty-handed would be ruinous for me, and going back without even trying would be worse than that.

Not just my own but a dozen hundred lives depended on my succeeding.

It would be easy to dismiss what I had been told as the superstitions of the ignorant and ill-informed. The quality of settler that would come to a rock like this was not as high or high-minded as those closer to the centre or on any one of the more elegant worlds hiding in the night sky.

I had the feeling, speaking to the locals, that most found themselves here purely by accident. They had been going somewhere else or coming from somewhere else and had gotten bogged down here, always meaning to continue on but for some reason not being able to. And yet, there was no desperate push to leave, and the residents seemed complacent and unmotivated.

The narrative they gave of the lush mountain seemed like tales recited to children to keep them in their beds at night. But then I entered the dark tangle of trees and vines, climbed the hillocks, traversed the almost impassable path, and at the end of it, I ceased to dismiss their words as easily as I had at desert level.

It was early in the morning when I first rode out from Spaceport. The low sun was freckled by one of the larger moons. I had finally hired a person willing to escort me. There is always someone desperate enough to take any risk for a price, but it took longer than expected to find someone so lacking. She said her name was Atu Par, but she had no identification to prove that. Given any other alternative at all, I would not have gone with her to a street fair, never mind the last place anyone wanted to go on this forsaken rock, because I had the distinct feeling I might be in danger. Not from the stories of evil told about the mountain, but from her, slight as she was. I feared she might rob me of my belongings and my life: take the one and leave the other and return to Spaceport, where there would be another addition to the deadly legend of this organic anomaly.

I grew even more suspect once I found her company so agreeable and charming on the way out.

If she had been rude or threatening, I might have been more at ease. But her agreeableness was not the only troublesome part. It is odd to go from bright, blinding sunlight into heavily canopied forest in the blink of an eye. I have travelled to many peculiar places and seen many unusual things, but the trees here grew too thickly, their trunks too angled and curvaceous to be sustainable. And there was a silence, deep and suffocating, as we travelled the switch-backing path, forced to turn this way and that by the pattern and denseness of the forest.

It was this lack of sound that disturbed me most. No birds calling or animals rustling or insects buzzing or chirping or clicking. Life needs life to survive. I was sure that if I had deigned to stop and turn over a spade full of dirt, I would find no crawling creatures beneath the surface.

When the vehicle could go no further, we continued on foot. The ground was soft with the unburned and uncleared decay of hundreds of years. It felt spongy, almost as if I were standing on a balloon cloaked in needles and leaves.

I struggled to keep up with Atu, constrained by the weight of my equipment. "Why did you really agree to take me?"

She seemed surprised by the question and laughed. "Because you asked. And because no one else wants to come up here with me."

Let me be clear. I had not been foolish enough to take this journey with this diminutive, somewhat grimy, yet striking woman with piercing violet eyes without first asking around about her. Generally speaking, I was told, she was someone who talked a lot without saying much, would disappear from time to time, and seemed to have a supreme fascination with the green valleys and hills we were now walking. "Mostly harmless," "somewhat insane" were the two descriptors most often attached to Atu Par. But as I said, I had little choice.

"You don't seem to be afraid," I said, "about the stories?"

"Plenty of people have come here at one time or another, and almost all of them have made it back."

There was no wind, even though the treetops swayed and tagged each other. At this time of day, beyond these woods, the breeze was picking up, scouring across the desert, the heat baking the ground. But here was a cool, sequestered vale of life. A vale under a veil, lacking diversity but teeming with copies of the few organisms it contained.

"So, the legends are true, at least partly."

"People hacking off parts of their bodies because they believe something evil has invaded them? People being swallowed whole by the land? Torn apart by the trees?"

I nodded, although nothing in the accounts I heard or my considerable tailspins of conjecture had risen to this rank of horror.

"Who's to say? People either come back, or they don't. There is no in-between. No one to relate the story. So people make them up."

She fitted herself in a crevice in the crag and climbed, her hand reaching down for mine as I neared the top. I noticed some subtle change in the tilt of the trunks at this level, the shapes of the branches less abnormal than those below but still unnatural.

"You come hoping to find something," she said, daring not to look back until she was far past a stretch of boulders on the high ground.

"I do."

"Something you can take back that's precious enough to make it worth the effort. But what if there is nothing so valuable?"

"Then I am ruined. Many people have risked much to bring me to this place."

I told her of the distorted satellite images. Few known elements could throw off the lenses in such a way. It was speculated that a strange metal ore rested beneath the surface, a compound that was plentiful in the aggregate but rare in proximity to inhabited worlds.

Deep in the hollows, I took my first samples. I had tested my equipment outside the protection of the settlement and was obliged to double-check my findings—the gathered specimens had been wholly unconventional. When I picked up the dirt, the heat within it lingered persistently in my palm. It was devoid of life, as I had expected, but it was conversely rich in nutrients—albumins, mucoproteins, and globulins.

"What do you hope to find here?" I asked.

"Oh, I have already found it."

"So, you . . . like to come up here?"

She pondered the question, pursing her lips and narrowing her eyes. "I would say I am drawn to it."

"That is what they remarked about you back in Spaceport."

"What other remarks did they make about me?" The edge with which she spoke made clear she had heard the unkind chatter.

"'Harmless, mostly. Crazy, somewhat.'"

"'Insane' is what they call me."

I kept my eyes lowered to the mossy trampoline we were traversing.

"I am not offended. You see, I try to tell them things they don't want to hear, and they think it is my brain that is the problem when really it is their blindness and faulty memories."

Having no direct response, it was a moment before I spoke. "You are not exactly what I expected."

"I am sorry to have disappointed you, but there is still a ways to go, so your assumptions may yet turn out to be correct."

I crouched down and took a few more samples from deeper beneath the spongy soil.

"It's growing," she said as I sealed the last container.

"What is?"

"The mountain, the valleys, the forest. They're all expanding."

There was liquid water beneath the skin of the planet, slightly saline, perhaps fed by the streams that disappeared in the forest, but there were no large surface bodies of water on the surface, no molten core, no earthquakes to alter the land.

"How do you know this?"

"I have been measuring it."

She led me to the first unnatural thing I had seen in the forest —a pipe of iron covered in moss halfway up its length, the exposed portion a screaming, bright orange. I suddenly felt queer about the lack of sound and shadows. Unnerved and disoriented, I had no idea which direction we were travelling besides generally up.

"This is a marker I placed at the edge of the green on the desert floor." Anticipating my next question, she continued, "I was part of a survey team doing something not all that different than you—looking for valuables to steal to make our settlement more habitable."

"How long ago was this?" We were more than a mile in from the sunbaked flats.

And this is where she became evasively loquacious. I could not get any satisfaction from her despite the volume of words in her meandering torrent, and I wondered if what she was saying was part of the "mostly harmless" or the "somewhat insane."

"These trees have to be hundreds of years old," I pointed out.

"I do not claim to know how many seasons they have seen. But they were not here when I drove this stake into the ground."

Atu Par was like me, a being of the same descent. I had met some from other worlds who looked different and survived longer, but we did not live nearly as long as the trees.

It was within this rambling tirade that she revealed how she had come to this mostly desolate world. It was a tale of heartache and misery. A sister, a mother, a brother—influential and powerful citizens of a planet well known to everyone in this sector of the galaxy. The father had been murdered, the mother and the brother had been blamed, and the sister took her own life when she could not endure the fallout from the affair. Atu Par, too, could no longer bear the hushed slanders of her own people. Even before this tragedy played out, her life was lonely and remote. And so, she fled that house of ruin, left behind her home, her city, her planet, escaping with nothing but what she could carry.

On the way to somewhere else, she found herself bogged down here.

The most shocking element of this ... recitation ... was that I well knew this particular story. It offered the intrigue, violence, and pathos of a great dramatic tragedy. But it was no play. These events occurred exactly as she described them. The names. The places. All intact. Her name.

This was a backwater place, and I wondered if she had been able to pass off this history as her own because the locals did not know any better.

I felt an odd reluctance to confront her about the lie. "I'm sorry," I said.

We had reached a crest. I could see across the divide the tumbled stone, the rusted and crumbling metal that had once been containers for whatever supplies had originally been lugged to this planet.

She shook her head. "No need to apologize. I am the only one of my family to have made it out alive."

"No, I'm sorry because the story you told, I know it, and—"

"You have heard of the plight of my family?" She was genuinely surprised. Pleased, even.

"Everyone in this part of the galaxy has heard of the plight of this family. It was a scandal that threatened a linchpin society of the Collective."

She nodded. "I guess it is difficult to recognize the renown of one's own family if you are within it. When I left, it was only a local matter."

Uncomfortable, I took a measure of her, the rumours whispered in Spaceport screaming in my ears. "I wish to return." I was conscious of our isolation.

"Turn back now? We are nearly there."

"I will come back another time with someone else."

"No one else is going to bring you here."

"Then I will return alone." I spun around, trying to get my bearings in the dark woodland climbing on either side of me. Distracted by the audacity of her dishonesty, I had spent my attention on her spinning of the yarn and not on where I was going or from where I had come.

"Complete your task, and I will take you back."

"No. You are a deceiver, and I feel I can no longer trust you."

"I have told no untruth."

"I do not pretend to understand why you have fabricated this elaborate perjury, but I would have trusted you more if you had told me you were a murderer."

In the truest indication of her madness, she was bewildered and wounded by my words. "You are a cruel being."

I grabbed her by the shoulders and shook her. "That story, that family, that horrific tragedy, took place five centuries ago, and you and I are not the kind that would make it past three-quarters of two."

Truth can sometimes damage a feeble brain. And there is no telling what kind of vandalism my naked veracity had done to Atu Par. She gave a violent start, stumbling back and sitting hard on an outcropping of stone. "If you came here to hurt me, you have done it."

I was speechless.

She got to her feet and ambled up the steepening grade.

"Where are you going?"

"To where I have always been headed. You can follow me, or you can try to pick your way back and hope you make it out alive."

I ran after her as she disappeared over a ridge. Out of breath, my chest heaving, I tugged the back of her jacket to halt her march forward.

The air was not thinner here. In fact, it was thick with oxygen, too much so, and I felt lightheaded because of it. I slowed my breathing, taking shallower breaths.

"I want to go back to Spaceport now!"

She looked down at my hand grabbing her jacket. "Your threats are idle. Harm me, and you will never find your way."

"I make no threat. In truth, I believe you are more a danger to me than I am to you."

She chuckled at this, then turned serious. "What you seek is not much farther."

She trudged off. Reluctantly, I followed.

Coming over another crest a few moments later, I saw a most ridiculous sight—a black curvature of terrain that was brittle and cracked. The moss near the edges appeared charred. And no tree sprang up from this colorless expanse. Before me lay an exposed vein of the most precious material in the universe. A scarce and crucial ingredient that has allowed us to move between distant star systems. A substance that fetches a hundred lifetimes of income for a mere portion of what was in front of me. So large was this deposit that I feared its discovery could upend the economics of the Collective.

Atu Par watched me as I surveyed the glassy black field, my mouth agape, my eyes not once blinking.

"You see it, then?"

Before I could manage a nod, she turned away and wrapped her arms tightly around her body. She began speaking and gesturing to phantoms, telling the air, "I miss you," "I love you."

It was only because of this lunacy that I was able to lure my attention away from the riches at my feet. Atu Par gave herself one last embrace, turning her face as if she were resting it against someone's chest.

But even her freakish behaviour could not long distract me from my ruminations.

As I said, moving any item through space is prohibitively expensive. If there is any way to beg or borrow or steal a resource from a nearby moon or asteroid or passing comet, it makes far more economic sense. But this amount of—I don't want to say what it is for fear that someone might try to cheat me out of my claim—changed the equation.

My ransom would be erased. My long journey through the oblivion of space would come to an end.

I could afford to take this barren waste of a planet and transform it into a paradise, buy the freedom of my clan, and create a home for us. Spaceport could be revamped—larger intake pads, new transport, cargo, and mining facilities, better living quarters. The cost was minuscule, a fraction of the worth I could see, never mind what might be hiding below this black plane.

When Atu Par turned back to me, her eyes were red, set off eerily against her violet irises. Tears streaked down her grimy, stunning face. "You found what you were looking for, yes?"

"Yes."

"Is it everything you thought it would be?"

"No."

She tilted her head, her eyes narrowing as she viewed me. "No?"

"It is everything I dreamed it could be."

And then, a wide smile spread across her face.

She gazed up at a sky we couldn't see. The luminosity of our shadowless realm was dimming. My anger at her became malleable, cooling quickly, and in its stead, another kind of heat was rising as she stood close to me. And just like that, I reconnected to the charming and engaging person I had met on the short journey out to this curious, uncommon place.

"We should not stay here as long as we would like to," she said. "That is the test we must pass every time."

We made our way quickly down and up the slopes, trekking over the hillocks and into the valleys and around groves of eccentric trees, and as we travelled farther from that ultimate summit, a stubborn sadness took hold in me. I began to doubt what my eyes had seen. Several times, the desire struck me to turn back, but the fading light prevented me from foolishness.

We made it back to the vehicle in a tenth of the time it took to get up to that highest point. The tires spun and gouged deeply into the moss and needles.

As we pulled away, I glanced back to find our transport had left a hollow where it had sat waiting for us. By a trick of the fading day, the depression seemed to rise back up the more separation we put between us.

As twilight rested on the horizon, we exited the forest on a heading straight for Spaceport, riding the distance in a satisfied silence of warmth and possibility. Only once was the quiet broken, when she reached out and took hold of my hand and said, "Can I tell you a secret?"

I waited for her to reveal some personal truth.

She waited for my anticipation to build. "It could always be like this."

ONCE WE WERE SAFELY inside the perimeter of Spaceport, Atu Par inquired as to where I was quartered. I gave her the location of my temporary lodgings, and she mentioned it was not far from hers.

I asked her if she wanted to have dinner.

"Not tonight. I am tired and drained. And I think I should leave you with your thoughts for the evening. If you still want to take a meal with me tomorrow or the next day or the one after that, go to the main market and ask for me by name. They will tell you where you can find me if I am to be found."

"I'm sorry," I said.

"For what?"

"What I said was unkind, and I—" I searched for a mannered way to navigate the matter. "—I did not mean to dismiss whatever misery befell your family."

"I am soothed after I go up to see them," she said. "They are happy for me. And that brings me comfort."

A twinge of uneasiness crept into my chest, but it was short-lived.

"Maybe I will see you," I said.

She grinned. "Maybe you will."

As I lay in bed, working over in my mind the logistical challenges of bringing that most precious cargo to market, I could not help but ponder Atu Par hugging the air, embracing the phantoms of her kin.

It was rude and unkind of me to attempt to dispel her delusions. Who knew what misfortune her true past contained?

She was mostly harmless, somewhat insane.

I have taken crazy lovers before. They are some of the best lovers I have ever had. But like that green mountain, you should not stay so very long in their presence. And so, I thought I might visit with Atu Par, but only briefly, in another night or two.

I finally fell asleep.

MY EYES SHOT OPEN. I did not know where I was. Or how long I had been dozing.

I realized, in that brief envelope between slumber and consciousness, that something was terribly wrong. I could glimpse it out of the corner of my eye, yet every time I tried to see it fully, it receded.

I dressed quickly, my body feeling as if all the bugs missing from the forest were within me, scratching to crawl out, and the birds that weren't on the branches were instead whistling their mocking tunes inside my head.

I went looking for her.

"Are you going to make it an even dozen?"

"What?" I turned toward the man who had spoken.

"Are you planning to go up that mountain with her again? Have I not warned you? We are not sponges. That place is a deluge, and unless taken in small measures, it will drown you."

"I have only been up there once."

"By my count, it is eleven, but the days here all run together, so it could be a hundred."

I stared at the man, dumbfounded and dumb.

"What is it you see up there?" He was eager, almost conspiratorial in his wish to know.

"Where can I find Atu Par?"

"The illusion of your desires will consume you," he cautioned before directing me to her location.

In my mind, I replayed our excursion into the green, only this time I saw a blossoming number of versions of each and every moment—like a love letter to an old flame that you write and rewrite and rewrite and eventually throw away.

At the summit, she found her family. I found the greatest treasure anyone has ever known.

I felt drawn to go back there. To prove it was not a mirage, not a hallucination. And while twisting and turning down alleyways searching for Atu Par, I realized I had made this march many times before. A handful? A hundred?

I felt another pull, just as strong, in the opposite direction, twin desires tearing at me, slanting me into a wall. I stood immobile for a moment. Then, mustering my resolve, I turned and compelled myself to run.

I did not collect my things; I did not go back to my room. I headed straight for the landing bay.

"Can I tell you a secret?" she said. "It could always be like this."

I stared at the three getting off the transport. No one else was waiting to leave.

"Can I tell you a secret?" Her eyes were bright, and she was smiling as if she was about to give me a gift. "Nothing ever changes around here. Nothing."

That is what she said during the ninth iteration, proving to be a lie and a truth all at once.

There is an ancient ditty about a place where you can hire

temporary shelter. I cannot remember the melody, but the last line has entered into universal consciousness:

You can check out any time you'd like. But you can never leave.

It did not matter how much it cost, it did not matter that I would be ruined, it did not matter that I had no way to repay my debt, and no idea how I would save those I was responsible for—I needed to get off this world, out of Spaceport, and away from that verdant outgrowth.

Strapped into my seat, waiting to be ferried up to the passing long-hauler, I thought any second someone would put an end to my escape, drag me out, and force me to stay—because there were no other people or creatures of any kind onboard this shuttle save for me.

But I was leaving. If I had to take control of this craft myself, I was going. I would rather die in the cold vacuum of space, floating for eternity, than remain one more minute on this strange, accursed rock.

I doubt very much if Atu Par consciously lied to me, whether in the beginning or at the end. It is this place that is the lie. I know for certain her story was not the mostly harmless talk of the somewhat insane. Because something terrible resides in those hills and valleys.

It has no name. That does not make it any less dreadful.

At last, the shuttle broke with the surface and rose into the bluish-violet sky that progressively grew darker until it was inky black. Once I was beyond the reach of that thing below, I could begin to unspool the tangled memories. As the docking procedure began, its slow, methodical process stretching on, I peered down toward the green splotch on the sandy-coloured marble. My blindness had been removed, and gazing from this vantage point, I saw what I was really looking at: not a forest or a vale or an oasis, but an emerging embryo of a colossus, growing, spreading, devouring the nutrients around it.

What was it?

What would it become?

I would be dead a thousand years before anyone might know for certain.

Yet, if I could recount my tale to someone with the means and ability, they might be convinced to bring an armada of ships and destroy this monstrous thing.

But who would believe me? Who would waste their credits on such a fantastic story? A threat no one else seems to see, and none here now would be around to worry about—except maybe those trapped on the surface in their unrelenting, timeless loops. A threat some distant generation—if we managed to endure that long—would have to confront.

As for me, the veil has been removed. And though I have escaped, I am not nearly free.

Because from that day, forever would that menace in the green haunt my dreams.

THE LOST CIPHER OF DR. JOHN DEE

By Lisa Kessler

The stifling scent of mould stung my nostrils as I descended the stairs into the dank basement. This was not how I had pictured this day ending, but to be fair, in my line of work, surprises were the norm.

"Watch your step. There's a tricky one down here someplace, but it's probably nothing for a young man like you. I should fix it, I suppose." Abigail Cousins let out a heavy sigh. "You know, Agent Bale, I was surprised when you contacted me. I wasn't sure the FBI would be interested in this book." She continued babbling over the groaning and creaking of the stairs as we made our way into the darkness.

I wasn't in the FBI, but it was easier to flash a badge and pretend than to explain I was the head of Department 13, a top-secret branch of the US government charged with protecting Americans from paranormal threats. We were one of the best-kept secrets in Washington, DC, and I planned to keep it that way.

When we reached the cracked concrete floor, she stretched her gnarled fingers to grab a dusty chain hanging from the low ceiling. She gave it a tug, and dim light flooded the basement. Her silver hair was up in a tidy bun that contrasted with her rumpled housedress and stained apron.

"Almost there." She glanced over her shoulder and waved her hand for me to follow, flashing a shockingly white smile of perfectly straight veneers. "It's in this old trunk back here."

Dust and cobwebs covered everything, including the forty-watt bulb swinging from the ceiling. It cast us in a washed-out yellowed hue, alternating between illumination and long shadows as I scanned the grubby, cluttered area.

I couldn't find a single sign that she'd touched anything down here in a very long time: no footprints or disturbed grime.

Something was off. "Have you had this trunk long?"

She looked back at me, and although deep wrinkles lined her face, I caught a spark of power in her eyes before she could hide it from view. Magic. A less experienced agent might've dismissed it in the poor lighting, but I was far from inexperienced, and I trusted my intuition as much as I did the protective adder-stone amulet in my pocket.

"It's been in my family for generations." She kept walking, leading me deeper into the basement. "Didn't you read about it in the paper?"

Her story about an ancient cipher written by Dr. John Dee, Elizabethan astrologer to kings and queens, being discovered in a long-forgotten trunk had run in the *World Globe* gossip paper recently. Most of the stories they printed were pure fiction, but occasionally my department uncovered nuggets of truth hidden in the pages. We had two full-time agents dedicated to reading and researching a few of the more niche "news" sources from around the world to keep our finger on the pulse of magical relics that might be surfacing.

"What led you to open the trunk after all this time?" I followed her to the westernmost corner of the basement, past dented, dusty file cabinets, piles of extension cords, and rusted tools. Each step seemed to bring me closer to another dead end.

There was no way the fabled lost cipher of Dr. Dee, the sixteenth-century Elizabethan spiritualist and mathematician, was hidden in the basement of a rundown farmhouse outside of Lawrence, Kansas.

But I needed to be certain. The lost cipher held the key to unlocking the Enochian language of the angelic realm. Because the doctor's books potentially documented the path to bringing about the apocalypse, the missing cipher was a high-priority item for my department to lock in the relics vault.

Abigail Cousin's laughter was almost a cackle. "Dreams. So many dreams keeping me up at night. The book called to me. If I told the world, a new guardian would come for it. My family could be free of the burden."

I rubbed my forehead. This was getting me nowhere.

She reached the corner and gripped the latch of an oversized travel trunk. The lid screeched, echoing through the stale, dank basement. "Come over here and see."

The hair at the back of my neck prickled. She was baiting me into a trap. "Why don't you just show me the book with the cipher?"

"Oh, it's very heavy." She peered back at me, suddenly looking decades older than the spry woman who had led me down the stairs.

"Why don't you tell me why I'm really down here?" I slipped

my hand inside the pocket of my slacks and grasped the smooth adder stone, relieved I'd decided to bring it along.

The black stone had been favoured by the druids for protection from magic. The natural hole in the centre of the rock collected the enchantments instead of allowing the magic to penetrate the person grasping it. My gun was still in my shoulder holster, but in this instance, my gut told me it wouldn't be much help anyway.

Abigail turned around slowly to face me. "You're a smart one." Her eyes flashed a bright violet in the swinging light. Definitely not human, not completely.

I tightened my grip on the stone. "Who are you?"

"Rude," she spat. "This is *my* house." She pointed a crooked finger up at me. "I bet you're not even with the FBI."

I raised a brow. "If you don't have the cipher, then I'll save us both some time and get out of here."

"Yes. Leave!" She balled her hands into fists and blurted out a Gaelic incantation. My Gaelic was rusty, so I couldn't place if it was Scottish or Irish, but the way her eyes glowed made her intent clear. The adder stone heated in my grasp, burning my fingers. I dropped it as I whispered my counterspell of protection.

She looked back up at me, confusion pinching her wrinkled brows. "Who *are* you?"

Now that I was certain I wasn't really standing with a human grandmother, revealing my agency wasn't so risky. We both had secrets to protect. "I'm a federal agent from Department 13." I tightened my jaw. "Do you really know where the cipher is hidden?"

She stumbled back. "You have magic."

I bent to retrieve the adder stone and met her eyes. "It appears I'm not the only one." I studied her, piecing together her perfect veneers, her small stature, and her glowing eyes. "Are you . . . a changeling?"

The last time I'd come in contact with a fae trapped in the human world, it had been a leprechaun. I hadn't seen an actual changeling since I'd first joined the department in 1963 after the Kennedy assassination. Before the industrial revolution, it was more common for the fae to walk on our side of the veil, swapping their infants with human infants. These days, changelings were rare.

Her eyes narrowed, but she didn't confirm my suspicion.

I put the adder stone back in my pocket. "Why did you share your story in that paper? Who are you looking for?"

She crossed her arms and sighed. "I'm tired, and I want to go home. My real home."

I raised a brow. "What's the cipher got to do with interdimensional travel?"

"Nothing." She lifted her gaze to my face. "But I swore an oath to protect it. I can't leave until I find someone who can take on that burden. That's why I talked to the reporters."

I shook my head and let out a frustrated breath. "So, this basement was some kind of test?"

"Yes." She nodded.

I crossed my arms, tipping my head to the box in the corner. "What's in the trunk?"

She mimicked my stance, which only further revealed the fae blood in her veins. "Devil's Breath powder."

My eyebrows shot up. The CIA used to use the white powder as a truth serum. It left its victims in a compliant, trance-like state. "How did you get . . . ?"

"That doesn't matter now. I've seen your magic." Her eyes

sparkled. "I believe you might be the one we've been waiting for. You could be a worthy guardian."

"We?"

She nodded. "My last descendant."

The air sizzled and sparked around us as her form gradually changed from a decrepit elderly woman into a younger version, with tawny brown hair and a black suit like mine. Her smile was like pure sunshine radiating across the basement wasteland.

My jaded knees almost wobbled. I straightened my jacket. "Let's get out of here."

She followed me up the stairs and through the small kitchen, and out to my rental car. The high-pitched buzzing of the cicadas popped and sizzled like surging power lines as I disengaged the car's locks and got behind the wheel. She settled into the passenger seat, my first time seeing her in the sunlight. Her smooth skin glowed, a sharp contrast to the crone who had met me at the worn screen door of the faded pink house. She had delicately precise features. Only her pert nose was still recognizable from her earlier form.

She turned my way. "Is there a problem?"

Her voice had lost the crackly drawl too.

I searched her eyes. "Am I looking at your true form now, or is this glamour?"

Her lips curved at the corners. "I'm not your first encounter with the fae."

"No." I shook my head. "So, which is it? Have you been pretending to be elderly, or is this your mask?"

She tilted her head slightly. "I have never been elderly by human standards. I was raised as Abigail Cousins, and when I came of age, I vanished before I could be accused of witchcraft." She clicked her tongue. "Now you owe *me* answers."

I chuckled, but I shook it off. Fae magic was insidious. You could become enthralled without ever noticing. It was a slippery slope. I cleared my throat. "I don't recall agreeing to answer questions."

She shrugged. "I believe humans call it being polite."

I chewed on the inside of my cheek to keep from smiling. She was funny. "Okay. Ask your question."

There was that bright smile again. "Tell me about Department 13."

I shook my head. "I've told you all you need to know. We protect Americans from paranormal threats."

"Fine." She smirked, shaking her head. "Then I get another question."

What could it hurt? I started the engine and drove down the dirt drive toward the street. "All right."

"Why do you care what happens to people you don't even know?"

I stopped at the end of her driveway. "I'm not sure. I guess I got it from my father. I looked up to him, and when he died, I wanted justice."

She nodded slowly. "A magical justice the police couldn't give you?"

"That'll cost you another answer to my next question."

Her laughter was like the melody from a wind chime. "Agreed."

"How did you find the cipher?"

"It was entrusted to my husband." She pointed to the right. "This way."

I followed her directions and glanced over at her. "You were married?"

Her lips curved into a wistful smile. "Lifetimes ago."

"And you've been keeping the cipher hidden all this time?"

"Of course." She looked out the passenger window. "We were told the power of the angels could be wielded by speaking their language."

I tightened my grip on the wheel. I'd had my share of run-ins with angelic beings. They were powerful and seemed to suffer from an inability to relate to mortals or mortality in general. "Does your descendant know I'm here? Is he fae too?"

"You're tenacious." She rolled her eyes. "He's human. My great-great-grandson." She stared out the window, her voice softening, becoming distant. "My family has been protecting the book since it arrived on this continent in the 1800s."

She pointed out the final turn, and I frowned. "This is a graveyard."

"Yes." She nodded as we drove into the Oak Hill Cemetery. "The perfect place to hide a valuable book."

I parked alongside the grass, got out of the car, and sucked in a deep breath, grateful I didn't have the ability to hear the cries of the dead like a few of our agents. Scanning the headstones, I saw that many were from the 1800s. Old cemeteries unleashed an almost unbearable burden on psychic mediums.

Abigail stopped, frowning as she checked the area. "He's usually here by now. Maybe he's already in the tomb."

She started walking again, faster, leaving me in a state of confusion.

I scanned the cemetery for any sign of life, but we were the only movement, and the only sound was Abigail's footsteps on the road. Could her grandson be . . . a ghost?

I hurried after her and caught her arm. "Wait."

Her eyes dropped to my hand and back up to my face.

I released her. "Is this person . . . alive?"

"Of course, he is." She let out an exasperated sigh. "How long have you been in this world, Agent Bale?"

This wasn't information I usually shared with anyone outside the department, but Abigail wasn't an ordinary citizen. "Almost one hundred years now."

Her gaze slid up from my shoes to my face. "I've never met a human with glamour before."

I shook my head. "Not that kind of magic."

After I joined Department 13 in 1963, I rose through the ranks quickly. Directors of our secret division had access to an herbal mixture that combined the Balm of Gilead with water collected from the Fountain of Youth. It healed our wounds and kept our bodies from aging. I hadn't changed since the 1960s, and I wouldn't again until I retired from the department.

She studied me for a moment and finally shook her head. "I've been here since this fledgling country started. I was Margaret back then. I came to Kansas with my husband, John P. Usher, and Dr. Dee's cipher. We came here after Lincoln was assassinated. We've been protecting it ever since."

The hair on the back of my neck tingled at the mention of Lincoln. Recently there had been novelizations about Lincoln slaying vampires and the like, and while the world looked at it as satire, there were nuggets of truth in the story that no one would believe.

Lincoln and his wife had forged a connection to the spiritualism of the time. Mary Todd Lincoln's curiosity about the occult led her husband to discover some of the first powerful relics to be housed in the Department 13 underground vault.

But other than Poe's story of "The Fall of the House of Usher," the name Usher didn't ring any bells with me.

We rounded the corner, and a foreboding crypt came into

view. "USHER" was carved into the stone between two polished marble columns. Locked doors with iron bars blocked the entrance to the massive facade that seemed to open into the side of a grassy knoll.

I glanced around the cemetery and frowned. "I don't see any other hills around here."

"That's why John picked this spot. He wanted to be sure the only way to access the tomb would be with a key."

My curiosity was piqued. I crossed to the tomb and peered through the dusty glass. I could make out a plaque for John P. Usher, entombed in 1889. There were more Ushers laid to rest with their founder, all the way up to 1957 that I could see.

But no sign of Dr. Dee's missing cipher.

I stepped back, inspecting the ornate carvings in the stones at the tops of the columns. Algae had dyed the surface to a faded green colour, but the engravings were still fairly distinct even after more than a century of weather. The trim bore a traditional grapevine, signifying Jesus as the vine and his followers as the branches, but at the top of the right column, I noticed an anomaly in the trim. I went to that side for a closer look, and my pulse quickened.

It was the *Monas Hieroglyphica*, the esoteric symbol designed by Dr. John Dee to represent the unity of the cosmos. The crescent shape at the top represented the moon, and it intersected with the circle in the center symbolizing the sun. Below the circle, a cross joined the sun with the elements and the base of fire. There was no mistaking the unique engraving. And here it was, far from England, in a cemetery in Kansas.

I looked over at Abigail. "Do you have a way to contact your grandson?"

"There he is." Abigail pointed.

I turned around to find an elderly man with a cane approaching us. His gait was slow, but the cane hit the rough pavement in a steady rhythm. He had pure white hair, and his complexion seemed ashen.

He reached into his jacket and withdrew a gun. "I got no desire to pull this trigger. Leave her alone."

I put my hands up, but I didn't walk away. "I just want to talk."

As long as he didn't shoot me in the head, I wouldn't die, but it would hurt like hell until I could use my healing herbs to close the wound. I'd rather avoid getting shot altogether.

Besides, this was one of my favourite black suits.

"Walter, this is Agent Bale." Abigail took a step in his direction. "He saw the article. I think he's the one we've been hoping for. He can protect the book."

Walter didn't lower his gun, but the barrel shook, the weight beginning to tax his muscles. Behind his wire-rimmed glasses, his eyes narrowed as he studied me. "What's in it for you?"

I crossed my arms. "It's my calling. I lock up items that could be dangerous if they fell into the wrong hands."

"Put the gun away, Walter." Abigail looked at me and back to the armed man. "Trust me, Agent Bale is our best chance to keep the cipher out of human hands."

Walter holstered his gun. After smoothing back whisps of silver hair from his forehead, he came a little closer. He eyed Abigail. "How can you be so sure?"

Abigail gestured to me. "He has strong magic, and his job is to defend humanity from paranormal threats."

Walter stopped in front of me. "Is this true?"

I nodded. "I'm the lead agent with one of the most secret departments of the government. We protect Americans from relics that could harm humanity. My agency saw the article about the missing cipher, and I came to retrieve it and lock it in the underground vault in Washington, DC."

Walter raised his chin. "Do you have any proof?"

I handed him a business card. He took it, flipping it over before he chuckled and lifted his gaze. "This is a blank card with your name and phone number. I'm going to need more than this."

I took out my phone, scrolling through my contacts. Usually, we went to great lengths to be sure no one knew who we worked for. Trying to prove the department's existence was a new exercise. Which staff member would be the most believable to vouch for me? My finger hovered over Kingsley Pratt. The Brit was our shamanic computer programmer. He had the ability to weave spirit magic into his coding that supercharged our searches.

He was also sarcastic and a high-functioning alcoholic. He might be jaded enough that Walter would believe me. I pressed Kingsley's name.

He answered right away. "Did you find it, sir?"

"Not exactly." I looked at Walter. "But I think I just met someone who has seen it. I need you to explain who we are and what we do." I put the phone on speaker and held it out toward Walter. "This is Kingsley. He's our programmer at Department 13."

Walter's silver brows popped up. He looked skeptical, but he leaned in and said, "Hello?"

I had the volume up so loud we could all hear Kingsley's clipped British accent. "This is Kingsley Pratt, Agent and Shamanic Programmer for Department 13. To whom am I speaking?"

"This is Walter Usher the Third." He stared at me. "I'm not sure how this proves anything."

"I agree," King answered. "Agent Bale must be desperate to choose *me* to validate his mission."

Walter's lips twitched as he bit back a smile. I crossed my arms, trying to keep my body language from exposing the rush of hope. I'd chosen the right person to call.

Walter cleared his throat. "Maybe you can confirm what your department does, exactly."

"We protect Americans from paranormal threats," King said without hesitation.

Walter pointed to a stone bench near the entrance to the Usher tomb, and we walked over so he could sit down. "Funny, you don't sound American to me, Mr. Pratt."

Kingsley chuckled on the other end of the line. "I wasn't born here, but more years ago than I care to count, I fell in love with an American woman and earned my citizenship."

Walter mulled over the information. "Tell me about this vault you have."

I half expected King to ask me for clearance to discuss it, but he surprised me. "We have a high-security subterranean vault that holds dangerous and valuable metaphysical relics and artifacts. We monitor and inventory the items to be sure they remain locked up and hidden from humanity."

Walter handed the phone back to me. I quickly ended the conversation and slipped my cell back into my pocket.

Abigail went to the bench and sat beside Walter. "This could be the chance we've both been hoping for."

He met her eyes. "Or this is the moment I become the Usher who made it possible for someone to bring about Armageddon."

She patted his knee. "Agent Bale is the one we've been waiting for. I can feel it."

Walter searched her eyes and tightened his grip on his cane. He pushed up to his feet and approached me. "I'm ready to release this burden."

He took out an old skeleton key, but he didn't move toward the tomb. "This key has been handed down since my great-great-grandfather John P. Usher took his eternal rest." He lifted his gaze to my face. "I suppose I should give you the story so you understand the importance of keeping this book hidden."

"That would be helpful." I nodded. "I can add it to the inventory sheet so that a hundred years from now, no one will be tempted to release the contents."

Walter glanced at Abigail. "Do you want to tell him how the book got to America?"

"All right." She looked over at the tomb with a sad smile. "John was the love of my life." She turned my way. "After spending ninety-three years as Margaret, I used my magic to still my heart and allowed her to fade from mortal memory."

Walter came to her side and took her hand as he focused on me. "We were hoping to find a way to entrust the book to someone worthy, so my great-great-grandmother wouldn't have to watch another generation fade away."

I looked at Abigail. "How did this responsibility fall to you and your husband?"

She stared into the distance. "My sweet John and Abraham Lincoln practised law together in Indiana. We followed the Lincolns to Washington, DC, and he made John his Secretary of the Interior. We were entrusted with many secrets, but none more dire than Dr. Dee's cipher. It held the key to the Enochian language." Her gaze snapped to my face. "If humans learned to recite the magic incantations of the angels, they could unleash . . ."

". . . the end of days," I finished.

She nodded slowly. "Mary Todd Lincoln worked with a psychic from England named Charles L. Colchester. He was the one who brought the president the cipher and asked him to protect it. Apparently, his family had received a few manuscripts from Dr. John Dee as payment for defending him in a legal dispute in 1580. It wasn't discovered among the family library until the 1800s, but by then, Aleister Crowley had already begun dabbling into Enochian magic, and Colchester was desperate to keep the cipher from him."

She took the key from Walter and led us to the doors of the tomb. "Lincoln entrusted John with the relic and asked him to lock it away someplace no one would ever look. It needed to be far from Washington, DC, and under watch. John resigned from his position in the cabinet, and we took the train to Kansas. As he grew old, we started constructing this tomb." She glanced my way, but there was no twinkle of magic in her blue eyes, only sadness and regret. "We entombed the book in my place, where we knew I'd never lay."

I focused on Abigail. "If you've been here for centuries, why go back to Summerland now?

"It was my idea." Walter cleared his throat. "I'm the last of the Usher family line, and I've got a slow-growin' cancer. I thought if we could find someone to take the book, then Abigail could go home. We could say our goodbyes at our own choosing instead of letting death decide."

"I kept my word to John." Abigail tucked her hair behind her ear. "I've watched over all the generations of Ushers to be certain they protected the cipher, but Walter is the last of my family line. I have no desire to stay in this world alone. I want to go home."

"Department 13 was made for this kind of burden. We can keep the book locked up." I turned to Abigail. "Can I see it?"

"Yes." That magical spark flashed in her eyes again. She slid the key into the lock, and it disengaged with a clunk. She grasped the right side of the door, and the hinges squealed as she opened the crypt.

I followed them inside, and Walter let out a lung-rattling cough, shaking his head. "Sorry. The smell of the mildew chokes me every time we come in here."

Abigail ran her fingers over John Usher's name on the plaque and sighed. "I still miss him." She glanced at me over her shoulder. "You know, Colchester had a premonition and warned Lincoln a few days before he visited Ford's Theatre. Can you imagine how different the world might be now if Lincoln had finished his presidency?"

"I try not to play the 'what if' game." I broke eye contact, scanning the other plaques in the crypt. "Here and now is all I can control."

And sometimes, even that seemed like an impossible dream.

She knelt in front of the plaque that read Margaret Usher and ran her finger along the edges, whispering her magic incantation. The faceplate loosened, and she removed it. Instead of a coffin or an urn, there was a small wooden box. She took it out and handed it to me, then reached for the marble plaque.

Walter tapped his cane on the floor, breaking the eerie quiet that had descended over us. "Quiet as a tomb is pretty damned silent, right?" His laughter was soft and wheezy, but it echoed through the crypt chamber. "Follow me. We can open it back here."

I carried the box, leaving Abigail to replace the plaque at the empty memorial spot for Margaret Usher. Walter led me into an alcove. The ceiling was lower here, forcing me to hunch over slightly to keep from hitting my head. I studied the wooden box. I didn't think to bring a crowbar with me.

Walter spun the box around and pointed to a latch. "It opens over here."

I raised a brow and unlatched the box. Inside was a leather-bound booklet with thick, yellowed pages. A *Monas Hieroglyphica* symbol was carved into the oil-stained cover. I lifted the book out of the box and opened the cover. The old English ink was faded on the edges, but I was looking at Dr. John Dee's nearly five-hundred-year-old handwriting.

A smile tugged at my lips. This was my favourite part of the job. Finding priceless relics and artifacts and preserving them made all the days I had to fight demons or secret societies worth the effort. These were the moments I felt closest to my calling, like devoting my life to this work was worthwhile.

I closed the book and turned around. "I have a case in the back of the car. I'll have my office send the private jet for me, so there's no chance of anyone intercepting the cipher."

Walter nodded. "Thank you."

We stepped out of the Usher crypt, and Abigail handed the key back to Walter.

He locked it and dropped the key into his pocket. His voice wobbled as he lifted his gaze. "I guess that's it, then."

Abigail's form shimmered until she was once again the elderly woman I'd met at the house earlier. She opened her arms to Walter.

They embraced, and she whispered something in Gaelic.

He straightened and shook his head. "No, no magic."

The crevasses in her lined forehead deepened with worry. "It's better this way. You won't be sad if you have no memory of me."

"No." He took both of her hands in his. "I wouldn't give up these memories for anything, Grandmama. Don't take them from me."

A tear slid down her cheek. "You are my most treasured gift."

I turned away from them, staring down at the book. Abigail had stayed in this world for lifetimes because her husband had given his word to protect and hide this book. That was a love I would never understand. There was a pang in my chest and a bitterness burned through my gut.

The thrill of finding the artifact had been quickly overshadowed by the all-too-familiar emptiness that haunted me. I had no loved ones to remember me, no legacy to leave behind when I left this plane.

But because of my work, the rest of the world would continue. I took solace in that as I walked to my rental car.

"Agent Bale, wait."

I turned around to find Abigail, but she was alone. I frowned. "Where's Walter?"

"He's going back to his car." She pointed in the opposite direction. "But I needed to tell you thank you."

"I'm just doing my job." Aching to change the subject, I asked, "Can I give you a lift? Where is your portal to Summerland?"

She held up an amber-coloured stone that sparkled in the sunlight. "Right here." She closed her fingers around the stone with a smile. Her form shimmered, and she was back to her younger form in the black suit. "This is my gateway. I had planned to use it after I lost John, but he asked me to stay and keep protecting the book, so I stowed the gateway stone in the crypt beside the box." She studied the light coming through the amber. "I will miss this world, but I'm eager to go home." She searched my eyes. "I recognize the emptiness in your soul." She pressed her lips together. "You sacrifice too much for your country."

I rolled my shoulders back and shook my head. "If not me, then who?"

"I've been in this world for hundreds of years. You don't have to be alone." She reached out to squeeze my forearm. "Love changes everything." Before I could respond, she opened her hand and whispered a Gaelic incantation over the stone. The air crackled around her and a fog formed. "Take care, Agent Bale."

She stepped through, and the mists gradually dissipated.

I was alone again. It was better this way. I put the book under my arm and texted my office to send a jet before crossing the road to the rental. Inside the car, I stared at the centuries-old tome on the passenger seat. The ability to translate the magic of angelic beings was sitting right next to me. I could open those pages and bring about the beginning of the end.

There was no one to stop me, and I wouldn't have anyone to mourn. It would be simple, and I could finally rest. The temptation of the dark thoughts weighed on me.

I forced my eyes up and started the car. I might not have a significant other or children, and my parents were long gone from this world, but I'd never surrender to the dark, selfish urges.

As I drove out of the cemetery, a smile tugged at my lips. I'd still sacrifice my life if I had to in order to protect my country and its citizens from paranormal destruction. The thought of missing out on the cherry blossoms in DC, or the holiday decorations at Rockefeller Center, or the snowflakes fluttering down onto the Statue of Liberty, or a sunset over the Pacific Ocean from the Santa Monica pier made my gut twist with grief.

They were all worth fighting for.

The cemetery disappeared in my rearview mirror, and I focused on the empty road ahead.

She was right.

Love did change everything.

MESSAGE FOUND IN A VARIABLE TEMPORALITY APPLIANCE

By Ira Nayman

BREAKFAST
powdered eggs
burnt toast
fruit juice (never a fruit I like)
coffee

LUNCH
baloney sandwich
bag of chips
fruit (never a fruit I like)
flat soda
coffee

DINNER
burnt meat
chewy spaghetti with thin sauce OR lumpy mashed potatoes
brown salad with oil-and-vinegar dressing

fruit pie (never a fruit I like)

flat soda

coffee

one can of beer (domestic)

Given this menu, is it any wonder I rebelled?

"What the hell is this?"

"Ah, is dat a trick question?"

"No, this is not a ferking trick question! What the ferking hell is this?"

"Aah . . . Ah would say it is a . . . piece of . . . *papier*?"

The short black man who wore a business suit despite the heat of the construction site—not to mention the fact that his bulging muscles made the fabric look like it was the subject of a stress test it was in imminent danger of failing—had all of the men's attention. He was, indeed, angrily waving a sheet of paper—an oversized yellow Post-it note with blue lines down one side that had been unevenly torn on the top . . . or the bottom—it was hard for even the men who were closest to him to tell . . . waving it as if the force he was using could somehow wipe the offensiveness off of it.

His name was Sam MacDougall because the universe has a ridiculous sense of humour. He was the construction foreman because the universe's sense of humour had made him tough and angry.

"You know, Levesque," MacDougall shouted, "if it was possible to fire somebody from this crew, your smart mouth would get your legs of indeterminate intelligence taking you home before your dumb brain knew what was happening!"

Antonin Levesque, a man of average height and sandy hair who was mainly distinguished by a tattoo of a fleur-de-lis under his left eye (which people often mistook for a teardrop because they worried that looking at it long enough to properly make it out would give offence), considered whether this was an insult, and, if so, to which of his body parts.

"Hey, Chief," called Jackson Tootoo, who, with his golden-brown skin, tight cheekbones, and jet-black hair, would have won the Best-Looking Crewman three weeks running if that was actually a thing on construction sites, "what's on the paper?"

MacDougall knew that Tootoo's use of the word "Chief" was not in recognition of the fact that he was the boss, that Tootoo called everybody Chief, as a way of pre-empting them from calling him Chief. He decided to overlook the (somewhat tenuously) implied disrespect for the time being in order to focus. "$1,000 or the deal is off," MacDougall read. "What the ferking . . . ferk does that mean?"

"Is dat a trick question?" Levesque asked. He pronounced it *kes-tyahn*. He was just brought up that way.

MacDougall gave him a look that asked, *Why aren't you dead from the sheer force of my will?* Out loud, he said, "What? Deal?"

The fifteen men on the work crew who were standing in the half-built reception area of the Sisters of Mersey Hospital managed to find fifteen different areas of intense interest in the walls around them or the girders above them.

"Come on!" MacDougall screamed. "Out with it! What are you bastards up to?"

When it became apparent that none of the bastards would be coming out with what they were up to, MacDougall began one of the deep-breathing exercises he had learned in his week at that ashram. When he felt calm enough, he said, "Okay. This is what we're going to do. I have been authorized to put a lock on the variable temporality refrigerator—"

A great moan rose up among the multitude (if fifteen can constitute a multitude). "What if I need my grape-infused tonic water?" yelled Volga Glockenspiel, a mountain of a man with a baby's face. He had a look that only David Lynch could love . . . or even imagine.

MacDougall shouted them down. "I didn't want to do it! But this project is too important for any of you to screw around with it. As of 2100 hours site time, the variable temporality fridge will be locked. It will only be opened for meals. If anybody needs to get anything out of it between meals, they will have to talk to me. Any questions? I don't give a shit. It's been a long, hard day, and we have plenty more where it came from. I'm going to get some rest— I suggest the rest of you do the same."

———

THAT EVENING, site time, three shadowy figures met in the area where the gift shop was taking shape.

"De plan, *c'est fini*."

"No, it isn't. I sent a note to our contact on the outside letting her know that we agree to her terms, and we will be going ahead with the plan."

"'Ow . . . ?"

"I managed to get it into the fridge before that bastard MacDougall put a lock on it."

"No, I mean 'ow do you know dat son of a *couchon* MacDougall won't find de note?"

"I hid it behind some asparagus. *Nobody* who isn't looking for it will find it!"

"I'm sorry."

"Don't worry about it, Chief."

"If it wasn't for me, that bastard MacDougall wouldn't have found the message."

"Like I said: don't worry about it."

"There was a problem with the rivets on the second floor. I had to stay to deal with it."

"Wasn't your fault."

"I couldn't get to the fridge on time. I couldn't get the message."

"It's a complication, but it doesn't have to derail the plan."

"'Ow can it not derail de plan?"

"If the lock had a key, we would have to find out where Mac kept the key, then figure out a way to get it away from him. Complicated. But it's a dial lock. So, all we have to do is figure out the combination."

"And 'ow should we do zat?"

"Weeeeell . . . I don't suppose either of you has any safe-cracking experience . . . do you?"

"I had to crack a safe once while playing a spy game called *Smiley's Revenge.*"

"Great! How did you do?"

"I . . . that was the level I stopped playing the game."

"What about you, Chief?"

"What? You zhink all Quebecois are criminals, den? Is dat what you zhink? *Maudits anglais!*"

"Okay, okay—I was just asking. That being the case, we'll just have to . . . improvise."

"Improvise?"

"Yeah. We'll work in shifts while everybody else is sleeping, trying different combinations until we hit the right one."

"Trying different combina—*sacre merde!* Dat's crazy!"

"We've got nine and a half days before the package is due to arrive. Plenty of time . . ."

THE SISTERS OF MERSEY HOSPITAL was planned to be a five-story facility taking up a city block at the corner of College and Jarvis; it was meant to be a bleeding-edge research hospital dealing primarily with diseases of the spleen. Sensing the urgency of the cause, Toronto Mayor Mike Myers applied to the Time Agency for a Temporal Anomaly Permit for the site. The TAP would allow time to move differently on the construction site than it did outside: the building would take six months to erect, but it would only seem to take a day to anybody off the site.

Around the site was a thin translucent wall. To anybody inside the wall, people on the other side appeared to be moving slower than a high school calculus exam. To anybody outside the wall, the activity inside looked like a tornado without sharks. The wall was equipped with a Bunuel Filter that caused anybody who approached it to feel that breaching it wasn't worthwhile and to turn away from it. (Nobody from the construction company could get near enough to place any identification on the barrier, so Teperman signs were nailed to nearby power poles.) This was necessary because the Time Agency had allotted a specific amount of time to the project, and people or objects crossing the barrier would upset their calculations. And the Time Agency was very proud of its calculations.

There were only three points of contact between the two time zones: the materials bin, the waste bin, and the fridge, each of which backed onto the barrier between time passages. The materials bin, the size of two dumpsters and almost as visually appealing, was necessary for girders, beams, gas for the machinery, and other building materials to be transported to the site. Because of the time difference, the city had to issue a special permit to restrict traffic for several blocks of Carlton to allow a steady stream of trucks to haul stuff to and from the site. The fridge, the size of a dumpster on its side and almost as visually appealing (it being possibly the only fridge in the city without a single magnet, Post-it note, or other adornments), was replenished daily for the culinary needs of the construction crew; this had to be done roughly every eighty seconds, outside world time. The necessity for and functioning of the waste bin should be obvious.

The men lived in tents on the site; this allowed them to move away from the most active parts of the site on any given day. Powered by generators within the barrier, stadium lights around the perimeter of the site simulated a twenty-four-hour day/night cycle. There was no contact with the outside world; workers were welcome to bring electronic devices, but they had to be pre-loaded with games, movies, or—ahem—other diversions. Members of the crew who attempted to call somebody on the outside world received the message: "Don't bother. Even if you could, you would sound like a chipmunk on acid!" Members of the crew who attempted to access Web pages would get the endless donut of death. In the third month of production, some of the crew members had a contest to see who could stare at the endless donut of death longest; the winner was not somebody relevant to this story, so he will not be named.

As it happened, it took the conspirators eight days to find the correct combination to the lock; with eleven hours, fourteen minutes, and twenty-seven seconds to spare, it was hardly dramatic.

"Y'see, people get anime all wrong," MacDougall, sitting on a folding chair in his tent, was saying. "Wrong, wrong, wrong, wrong, wrong. It isn't all frilly underwear and tentacles—anime has weight. It has depth. It's serious ferking art, man!"

"I know exactly what you mean," agreed Tootoo, standing by the flap to the tent, although he thought *Ghost in the Shell* was a form of pasta and *Dragonball Z* was a sex toy. Opera was his preferred method of escape; something about the *sturm*, not to mention the *drang*, resonated with his Indigenous soul.

"Take the classic *Mobile Suit Gundam*. It—"

"Would you like another beer, Chief?" Tootoo offered a can to his boss.

"Yeah. Yeah. Oh, yeah," MacDougall agreed. As he eagerly opened the beverage, he muttered, "How'd you get so much beer?"

Tootoo explained, for the fourth time, that some of the men (only three for more than a week, but if the boss was under the mistaken impression that it had been seven or eight over a couple of nights, who was Tootoo to correct him?) had saved their beer to give him to show their appreciation for the great work he was doing keeping the project on schedule. The first time he said this, MacDougall responded, "Are you shitting me? The men think I'm a hardass asshat—if even one doesn't hate me by the time this job is over, I will have failed as foreman. I—wait, where are you going with that? I didn't say I wouldn't take your damn beer! I just said you better come up with a better excuse for giving it to me!" This time, his response was to purr, "Yeah, I'm pretty great, aren't I?"

Tootoo looked nervously out the flap of the tent. The other conspirators would have slunk past it on their way to the fridge long ago, site time, but he was saddled with a paranoia of Shake-spearean proportions.

MacDougall was past noticing. "Let me explain why *Katsugeki Touken Ranbu* is better than *The Animaniacs* ..."

Meanwhile, on another part of the site, Glockenspiel was saying, "Why do you even want to see the fridge?"

Matthew Frewer, a tall, skinny man who twitched like a squirrel, said, "No reason. No reason. That's okay, friend. Only, I just want a couple of minutes with the fridge. Just a couple of minutes. No problem. No problem."

"You . . . can't even get in it," Glockenspiel protested. "It's locked."

"Oh, locks, *phhffft!*" Frewer scoffed. "Not a problem for me, mate. I got skills, doncha know." He touched a finger to his nose.

Glockenspiel was trying hard not to panic. "But . . . but . . . but what do you want from the fridge, anyway?"

"Today's food should have been delivered by now," Frewer informed him. "I . . . I . . . I wanna coupla beers. You know. To take the edge off. To help me to sleep. Just a coupla beers."

"Can you, umm, wait a few minutes?"

"What's it to you?" Frewer's jumpiness was often mistaken for belligerence, which tended to make people miss his *actual* belligerence. "I mean, I mean, I mean, what are you even—"

Before Frewer had an opportunity to finish the thought, Levesque appeared from around the half-finished building wall that obscured the fridge. "Did I 'ear somebody ask for *une bière*?" he asked, dangling three bottles in front of his colleague.

"Don't mind if I do, friend. Don't mind if I do," Frewer enthused, grabbing the bottles out of Levesque's hand. He turned to go back to his tent, frowned for a moment, and, turning back, wondered, "How did you get these?"

"You are not de only one wid skills," Levesque said with a grin.

Nodding, Frewer touched a finger to his nose. At least, he tried to touch a finger to his nose; instead, he hit himself in the face with a bottle. He jumped a foot into the air. Then, he scurried off.

"The package arrive yet?" Glockenspiel asked in a nervous whisper.

"*Non*," Levesque curtly replied.

"It's late," the big man sulked.

"Negotiating time differentials—eet is not an exact science. Prepare your moose call—de package will be here, *mon ami*. It will be here soon!"

As he watched the small man disappear behind the partly finished wall, Glockenspiel played with his lips in anticipation of making the sound that would signal to Tootoo that the package had been successfully delivered. Moose were not native to Toronto; in fact, it is unlikely that there were any within a hundred kilometres of the major metropolitan area. Part of the plan was hoping that MacDougall would be so drunk that he wouldn't notice.

Levesque approached the fridge with reverence and slowly opened it. His eyes widened. "Oh, you beauty!" he exclaimed. "Tonight, we feast!"

WHEN THE BARRIER came down with a slight buzz and the distinct smell of strawberries and Gordie Howe's sweat three months, a week, and two days later (site time), the men cheered. Some were disappointed that their wives, husbands, lovers or other signifi-cants hadn't come to celebrate their return after such a long absence; they didn't fully appreciate that to their significant others, they had been gone for less time than if they had been on benders . . . or having affairs.

"Well, hello, boys." A woman's voice stopped the workers from dispersing. The woman who belonged to the voice was petite, with long black hair in a tight bun; she had heavy black makeup around her brown eyes, with a tight black zigzag from her left eye to under the lobe of her heavily pierced left ear. Although it was November, the woman was wearing a white and black striped body stocking and a pink tutu. "I'm looking for Volga Glockenspiel. Would he happen to be around?"

Glockenspiel walked up to the woman, who seemed to disappear into his voluminous shadow. "Well, hello," he crooned, no longer sad that his wife and seven children had not appeared. "And who might you be?"

The woman smiled prettily. "Volga Glockenspiel?"

"Yes, that's my—" Before he could finish his sentence, the woman had spun him around and put a cuff on his left hand. Where the handcuffs had come from, none of the onlookers could say.

"Volga Glockenspiel, you're under arrest for crimes against time." The woman's demureness had been replaced by a stern librarian thang. Under other, less public circumstances, that might have worked for Volga. Unfortunately, these were not other circumstances.

He spun around, handcuffs dangling from one wrist, and roared, "Who the hell are you?"

"Anita Alcaraz-Bientot," the woman calmly informed him. "Time Agency agent." From out of nowhere, she produced a card on which the image of an hourglass flanked on either side by Earth could be seen. To the left of the symbol were the woman's name and some contact information. Just as quickly as it appeared, the card disappeared; a smarter man might have realized that there was more to her tutu than met the eye.

"Hey!" Glockenspiel protested. "I was reading that!"

"Were you?" Agent Alcaraz-Bientot wryly asked. "Were you really? That would be a first."

Although some of the men had peeled off to go back to their lives, many stood in a semi-circle around the pair, including the other conspirators. Glockenspiel didn't want to admit that he hadn't been reading the woman's ID in front of the other men, but he wasn't quick enough to come up with a reasonable retort, so he did what men in his situation have done since time immemorial: he changed the subject: "What are you arresting me for? I've done nothing wrong!"

Agent Alcaraz-Bientot smiled; explaining the crime and naming the culprit was the part of the job she enjoyed the most. "Are you familiar with the Law of the Conservation of Time/Energy?" she asked.

Glockenspiel was offended. "Do I look like I know about the ferking Law of the Consummation of—"

"Conservation of Time/Energy," Agent Alcaraz-Bientot corrected him.

"Lady," he roared, "I know from riveting steel girders into place and hooking up electric and sewage systems. If you—"

Agent Alcaraz-Bientot held up a perfectly manicured hand. "They never do," she sighed. "But we live in hope. Let me ask you a different question: you know you lived the past six and a half months in a bubble where time moved differently than it does for the rest of the world. Right? Right. *Where do you think that extra time came from?*"

Glockenspiel looked at the other men, who suddenly found

their own pieces of street life to be fascinated by. "Umm, I never really—"

"I'm sure you didn't," Agent Alcaraz-Bientot said in a voice so patronizing it shrivelled men's . . . men. Let's leave it at men. "So, let me explain it to you. Time can neither be created nor destroyed; it can only be moved from one universe to another. The extra six months you were given in the Time Bubble—yes, that is a term of art in my profession—came from another universe. Ordinarily—"

"Lady, I don't need no science lesson," Glockenspiel sneered.

Agent Alcaraz-Bientot had to bite back on rolling her eyes. "Nonetheless. Ordinarily, the Time Agency arranges to have extra time taken from a universe where it wouldn't be missed: one without life. As we did in this case. Only—"

"So, what's the problem?" Glockenspiel asked his coworkers more than the woman he loomed over. Most of them nodded in agreement, although one or two of the smarter ones sombrely expected something bad to happen—soon—and were slowly backing away from the centre of attention.

"So, the problem," the loomee calmly responded, "is that, against the strict provisions of your contract with Teperman Construction, you arranged to have something brought into the Time Bubble that hadn't been allowed for in the Time Agency's calculations. That meant additional time had to be taken from somewhere."

"Couldn't it have been taken from the universe without life?" John Manatee shouted from the middle of the crowd.

Agent Alcaraz-Bientot looked the group of sweaty, tired men who just wanted to get back to their lives over to see who had asked the question, but she couldn't identify him. So, she turned her gaze back to the loomer in front of her and explained, "It's your bad luck that that universe didn't have much time left after accounting for all of the time needed for the construction project. You used up what little was left. Heat death. Kaput. Still, your little stunt required more. So, it took it from the universe next door to the one that we were using, a universe where Earth was populated. Much like this one, in fact. That was bad. Very bad."

"'Ow much time was taken?" a voice from the back of the crowd asked.

Agent Alcaraz-Bientot didn't even bother to look for the source, replying, "Three seconds."

"Three seconds?" Glockenspiel shouted incredulously. "Three whole seconds? What difference could three seconds possibly make?"

"Well . . ." Agent Alcaraz-Bientot considered. "Three missing seconds from a person's life are enough time for one driver to not notice somebody switching into the lane in front of them, causing a multi-car pileup on a freeway. Three seconds of distraction are enough for a doctor to miss internal bleeding, causing a patient to die on an operating table. Three seconds is enough time not to pick up the fastball that is coming straight for your head. All in all, we have accounted for seventy-nine thousand, three hundred twenty-seven deaths caused by your meddling with things you clearly do not understand."

"Eighty . . . thousand deaths?"

"Probably, once the fatally wounded succumb to their injuries," Agent Alcaraz-Bientot genially agreed. "I hope the pizza was worth it!"

"How did you know it was Volga?" the best-looking man in the group asked.

"Who wants to know?" Agent Alcaraz-Bientot responded.

"A concerned citizen," the man, probably Indigenous, sneered.

Agent Alcaraz-Bientot considered him for a moment. Then, with a shrug, she answered, as a black dot appeared in the air above and behind her and started to grow. "The transfer was organized by notes left in the variable temporality refrigerator. Your accomplice on the outside was happy to supply us with them. We noticed that the person who wrote the notes dotted his eyes with little skulls and crossbones. We approached friends and relatives for samples of writing for each of the men on the site—it was time-consuming, but time is obviously not a problem for us. There was only one person whose handwriting matched that of the negotiation notes. Honestly, are you going to make me say it?"

"But ... but ... but ..."

The black dot stopped growing at about the size of a person-hole cover, and a small metal ball with translucent wings flew out of it. The device (which has a name, you know) fleebled and quarflobbled.

"Ah," Agent Alcaraz-Bientot said. "Our ride is here."

Glockenspiel goggled at the device (aren't you even the least bit curious about its name?). "*That* is gonna take us somewhere?"

"No, TAMI is not going to take us anywhere," Agent Alcaraz-Bientot stated. (Okay, now you know what the device's name is, but it sure looks like an acronym. Do you want to know what the—?) "The Time Amplifying Mechanism, Indeed opens up the Time Tube, but it can't force anybody to go through it." (Okay, now you know.)

Glockenspiel refocused his goggling at the black circle hovering over the sidewalk. "*That* is gonna take us somewhere?"

"Time Agency headquarters," Agent Alcaraz-Bientot informed him, "where you will be tried for your crimes."

"I'm not going anywhere in that!" Glockenspiel bellowed.

"Oh, don't be like that." Agent Alcaraz-Bientot waved away his concern. "It's not unlike being born, only at the end of it you won't be covered in placenta and feces."

"Lady, if you think I'm going anywhere with you . . ." Glockenspiel spread his legs and held out his fists in a boxer's stance.

The urge to roll her eyes was too great for Agent Alcaraz-Bientot to resist, but at least she made it quick. "Nobody respects the badge," she muttered. "Why does nobody ever respect the badge?"

TAMI squawkerbled. "Fair point," Agent Alcaraz-Bientot agreed.

"Can we make this quick? I have to . . ." Glockenspiel started, but petered out as Agent Alcaraz-Bientot got *en pointe* on her elegant ballet slippers and started to twirl around him. "What. The. Hell?"

If they had listened carefully, the construction workers would have been able to hear the Love and Rockets song "Haunted While the Minutes Drag" playing on a calliope. The scent of popcorn wafted over the smell of car exhaust from the nearby intersection.

When Agent Alcaraz-Bientot had made one orbit around the construction worker, he doubled over as if punched, with an audible, "Oomph!" The men watching would have sworn that the Time Agency agent hadn't laid so much as a pinkie on him; when they thought about it afterwards, this creeped them out all the more.

Agent Alcaraz-Bientot danced around Glockenspiel again. This time, when she appeared in front of him, his head snapped back with an audible crack. Some of the construction workers blanched; others turned away. Glockenspiel fell on his back.

Shimmying in place, Agent Alcaraz-Bientot asked, "Ready to come in, now?"

"Oh," Glockenspiel, getting unsteadily on all fours, gasped. "I … I'm only just … only just … starting!"

"So am I," Agent Alcaraz-Bientot assured him. Just as she started twirling around him for a third time, he collapsed into unconsciousness, blood dribbling out of his nose. Agent Alcaraz-Bientot went into final position, then bent over and poked the prone man in the stomach.

TAMI fleopolled and qventched.

"Yeah, well, you're not the one who has to deal with it if he's only faking being unconscious, are you?" Agent Alcaraz-Bientot groused. When she was satisfied Volga was really out, she grabbed him under the shoulders and hauled him toward the black circle. "You couldn't have made the Time Tube closer to the ground?" she groused anew.

TAMI qwueflobbled. Best I don't translate that.

Alternately grunting and moaning, Agent Alcaraz-Bientot pulled Glockenspiel up to the black circle and shoved him into it. Then, TAMI flew into it. Then, Agent Alcaraz-Bientot climbed into it. But before she dropped out of sight, she turned and said, "Remember, people: don't mess with time travel!"

TAMI fwoplollied.

As the black circle started to smallen, Agent Alcaraz-Bientot could be heard saying, "No, I'm not going to tell them to stay away from drugs. I'm not some ferking public service ann—"

Then, as quickly as it appeared, the black dot vanished.

***

ALTHOUGH IT'S BEEN many years (normal, non-time adjusted years), I still feel bad about what happened to old Glockie. Bad. Hunh. Okay, that might be overstating the case a little. Yes, using the fridge to get something better to eat was a group effort, and it certainly wasn't his idea. But, I mean, dotting your "i"s with a skull and crossbones—who does that? It's not a very smart thing to do. Almost like he was asking to be arrested, really.

Realizing that maybe Toronto was going to be too hot for me for a while, I moved back to Montreal. I—what? You thought I was —really? Oh, sure, the Indian had a way with words and definite leadership potential, but that was a very specialized kind of intelligence, not the kind to pull something like this off.

I know what it is—you're confused by the accent. You would prefer it if ah talk like dis, wiff an outrrrageous Frrrench accent, *non*? No. I speak that way so that anglophones underestimate me. Pretty effective, wouldn't you say?

And it really is a shame that all those people in some other universe had to die. But I have to say, despite being cold and soggy, the pizza was delicious.

SALVAGE

By Carrie Vaughn

"You two ready?" I ask.

"Yes, ma'am," Gert says with forced brightness, and Rally nods quickly, a shake of motion behind her helmet's face-plate. She's nervous, but she always seems to be a little nervous, so I'm not too worried.

We wait in *Iris*'s airlock for the air to hiss out around us. It's a dangerous, thrilling sensation. I can almost feel air rushing over the fabric of my suit, hear a bit of wind through the helmet, until I can't hear anything. Then comes the eerie moment when we open the door to the unknown.

I know the captain isn't supposed to take part in these operations. I'm supposed to stay on the bridge, safe and sound, and not expose myself to unnecessary risk. Stick around to take the blame if something goes horribly wrong. But if I think that much risk is involved in boarding the *Radigund,* I wouldn't send any of my people aboard. We'd do an automated sensor sweep, mark the site for salvage, and let someone with more personnel and big guns do the work. *Radigund* is dead in space. No life signs, no energy readings, nothing. We have no reason to believe anything is there.

So we board, to better investigate and make a full report. Recover bodies if any are there to recover. *Radigund* is—was—a small survey ship, like us, plying the edges of known spaceways, tracking routes and charting what we find. Trade Guild diverted our mission to look for her. It took us a month to find her, she'd drifted so far off course.

Using the mechanical override, we force open *Radigund's* hatch into the opposite airlock. I enter first, Gert and Rally follow, slipping soundlessly behind me. It's dark. My lamp, panning across the space before me, disorients rather than illuminates. I have to piece together a flash of wall, the viewport on the opposite hatch, a warning label above a control panel.

Gert closes the hatch behind us.

Sealed in the other airlock now, we have to pull off an access panel and open the interior hatch manually. *Radigund* has no power. No air, either, which gives a clue as to what happened. The door grinds open, gears stiff. I can't wait to get my hands on the log and the black box to learn what happened. Assuming we can get enough power to the computer to download anything. No power also means no artificial gravity. We float through, pushing ourselves along the corridor walls.

"God, I hate this," Rally says, her voice thin over the comm. "I feel like something's going to jump out at us."

Gert chuckles. "You've been watching too many films."

We continue on to the bridge. Nothing unusual so far, besides the lack of power. The lack of life.

A second channel on my comm clicks on. It's Matthews, from *Iris's* bridge. "Captain, I've finished the second hull survey. Not so much as a pinhole."

Hull breach could have shut down the ship in a hurry. That had been my first thought. Matthews closes that possibility.

"Thank you," I say. Voices murmur in the background. The whole crew is on the *Iris* bridge, watching our progress on our suit cameras and monitors. Like it's one of Rally's films.

"What was that!" Rally says suddenly, and we all swing around, bumping against the walls and each other.

Her light shines on a blanket floating halfway through the hatchway leading to crew quarters.

"You really are losing it," Gert says unkindly.

"Focus, you two," I say. I'm beginning to regret my decision to bring these two in particular. But Rally knows the computers; Gert knows the power system. And they mix like oil and water.

They're good people. Good crew. But sometimes, I'm tempted to lock them in a room together and watch the fireworks.

Our progress is slow, slower than I like. Because of the shadows, I think. Rally's monsters hiding in them. Venting, tubing, ladders, open hatches, all of them are shadows, foreshortened and flickering in our helmet lamps. We're hesitating, holding back. Expecting an unnamable thing that we don't want to find. My breathing grows loud, sealed with it against my ears as I am. A ship shouldn't be so quiet.

Gert's hand clutches my shoulder, hard enough to feel through my suit's padding, but I've seen what he's seen in the same moment. Breath and heart both stop, no doubt prompting spikes in biometric readouts on *Iris* that stop hearts among the crew there. Rally stifles a whimper.

It's a face glaring out from a doorway, all teeth and eyes, arms reaching.

We freeze, and all three helmet lamps focus on it.

It's a photograph, printed large and hung on the door. A

person in a blue Trade Guild uniform. Male. He's grinning, throwing his hands up to guard against the camera, to prevent this picture from even happening. But it's all in good fun. Someone has drawn a party hat on the man's head and a garland of flowers around his neck and written in large, enthusiastic letters, *Happy Birthday, Captain.* I could guess the joke behind it: the Captain had declared he didn't want a party for his birthday. No celebration, just another day. And someone on the crew had taken revenge. *Radigund* must have been that kind of ship, where the crew could play a small joke on the captain, and he wouldn't mind.

Frost curls the edges of the paper.

"Geez," Gert breathes.

We climb the ladder to the bridge, following the circles of our flashlights. We find bodies there. Navigator, pilot, comm officer. Captain. Even frozen and dead, rimed with frost, I recognize my counterpart from the picture. There ought to be six more, somewhere on the ship. Crew cabins, engineering, and medical are where I expect to find them.

Captain and pilot are strapped to their seats, stiff arms raised a few inches above armrests. Weightlessness had set in before the freezing cold. The other two are curled up near the floor. All are wearing oxygen masks. They knew this was coming, that something was wrong. An open plate on the deck, cabling exposed, shows an attempt at repairs.

Ice crystals frost hair and skin and open eyes. They're all in their twenties and thirties, our age. Far too young to be so still. I don't know them. Didn't go to the Academy with any of them. But I might have. Close to home.

But there are bodies. I'm almost relieved. How much stranger, to come aboard and find nothing. To wonder if they all stepped out of the airlock twenty light years back, with no explanation.

Sweat trickles down the back of my neck. My heart rate still feels too fast, but *Iris* hasn't said anything about it yet. The air inside my suit smells too much like me.

"Matthews," I say to my own comm officer. "Is this coming through?"

"Yes, ma'am," he says softly.

"Gert, start on the power. See if we can get the computers up. I want to see the log."

Rally's bulky glove touches Gert's padded shoulder. He can't possibly feel the contact. "Can I help?"

He glances at her awkwardly, sideways, through the helmet plate. "Yeah. We're going to take those panels off."

I work on retrieving the black box. The battery-driven recorder is stored in a protected safe in the back of the bridge. *Iris* has one just like it. I find it, pull it out, send it back through the airlock to *Iris* so Matthews and Clancy can look at it. Gert and Rally are still working. Over the comm, I can hear them arguing the whole time.

"We shouldn't let the captain wander off by herself," Rally says. As if I can't hear.

"She's fine. What do you expect is going to happen?"

"That's just it, I don't know. But this is weird. What happened here?"

Four frozen sets of eyes are staring at her. She has every right to be uncomfortable. Gert hides his own discomfort by mocking hers.

"You're paranoid."

"It's always the captain who dies first in these stories. Know why? Because it leaves everyone else feeling directionless, guilty, grief-stricken—"

"Rally! Please! Are you going to help me with this or not?"

A few moments of quiet, then, "There's nothing wrong with these circuits. I think the problem's in engineering."

A long pause, then Gert's gruff admission. "Okay. We'll check there. Captain?"

"I'll meet you," I say.

We find the engineer floating before his station, bundled in a suit. He'd survived the freeze but asphyxiated when his suit oxygen ran out. He'd been working on the engine right up to the end.

I touch both Gert and Rally, patting the fabric of their suits. "You two work. I'm going to check for the rest of them."

I find them in crew quarters as I thought I would. We'll have to make recordings. ID, photos. Then we'll jettison them into the next star. Traditional burial in space. There'd never be a question about what happened to them.

I'm almost back to engineering when Gert and Rally start in again. But it's different this time.

"Rally, don't start. Not in your suit. Do you know what a pain in the ass—"

Rally sniffs. Tears thicken her voice. "I can't help it. I keep thinking—what if it was us? It could have been us."

"No, it couldn't. *Iris* is a good ship, this wouldn't happen. Captain wouldn't let it happen."

His earnestness surprises me. I'd have expected more mocking. I approach cautiously—as cautiously as I can, in a suit, bouncing against walls to control my momentum.

Rally and Gert are helmet to helmet, faces pressed as close together as they can, holding each other's arms. I can see their profiles in the halo of their helmet lamps. Gert is talking, Rally nods.

"You going to be okay?" Gert says.

"Yeah. Sorry. I just let it get to me. I'm okay now. I'm okay."

"Good. I need your help. I need you."

They gaze at each other. I back away and leave them alone. Head to the airlock, where Horace comes aboard to help me with the bodies.

WE'VE BEEN HERE two days, working in shifts, when Gert reports.

"I can't get power online, Captain. Not with what we have here. She's cooked."

That was always a possibility, and we have a plan for this. We mark the *Radigund's* position, place a beacon tagging Trade Guild property, though I doubt any other ship looking for salvage will find it. A cruiser with the power to tow the ship will have to retrieve it. Unless Trade Guild decides to junk her and let her float out here, a dead shell, forever.

We undock and leave, taking a course to the nearest star system for the burial. *Radigund* is a dark hulk in space. Her stories, the thousand little mundane events that happen every day aboard any ship, are her own. Gone, now.

Matthews heads the briefing around the galley table. Scenes like this play out thousands of times on hundreds of ships. A thousand little events. Gert and Rally are sitting next to each other, and I can't remember that ever happening before. They're side by side, shoulders brushing, on the bench attached to the wall.

"Engine failure due to a corruption in the fuel cell line," he says. "There was a cascading failure in all systems after that. They were working on getting the engine back online when power to life support cut off. It was the compression system. Air pressure went fast." Air pressure went, temperature dropped, and the portable oxygen only lasted so long.

"Clancy, take a look at our fuel lines. Just in case," I say. "Thank you, all of you. Your professionalism has helped make a difficult situation go smoothly and is noted." Commendations go into the log, into personnel files, and they all know it. Maybe it'll help.

I start to walk out, to give them the space to vent or complain or laugh or cry without their captain looking on. Rally reaches out when I walk past her and takes my hand. A quick, warm squeeze and a smile of comfort. It's enough to make my own eyes sting.

I squeeze her hand back and continue out of the galley.

CASEY'S EMPIRE

By Nancy Kress

AUTHOR'S NOTE: Writers are often fond of writing stories in which writers are the protagonists—usually sympathetic protagonists. Several recent short stories and at least one major fantasy trilogy come immediately to mind. There is something distinctly self-indulgent about this, but writers fall prey to self-indulgence at least as much as the rest of the population (editors might say, "More.") "Casey's Empire," then, is a double self-indulgence: the fortunes of not only a writer but of a science fiction writer.

The business of writers is to tell lies, and the business of science fiction writers is to tell large lies. Large lies can be seductive. It has always seemed to me that one could easily come to prefer them to the truth.

But it costs. It always costs.

This is the story of Jerry Casey, who lost a galactic empire. Oho, you sneer to yourself—one of those. You know, of course, from your vast reading, what a trivial and hackneyed idea a galactic empire is—even now. You know, of course, from your vast reading, about the convoluted, melodramatic machinations by which a hero loses an empire, and what that feels like. Go suck an egg; you wouldn't know a galactic empire if you tripped over it, which Casey did. Tripped over it and lost it. You think you know how that feels? You don't know. Unless it has happened to you, you don't know. You can't ever know.

He was born in the 1950s in Montana, but he didn't let it bother him. To his child's eyes, the big, lonely, empty plains were within the sound of the sea, within a hard day's climb of the Himalayas, within touch of the hibiscus-smelling rain forest. He walked on desert sands or ancient glaciers or the bottom of the Mariana Trench. At night, the wide sky was impossibly full of stars, and he named them all and walked on their spangle-coloured planets. Part of it, of course, was his reading, which he did so constantly that he failed the fifth grade. But not all of it. There was something else, something extra, something his own. His parents were puzzled but tolerant. They bought a new car every three years, new drapes every five, and saved up for yearly vacations in Las Vegas. Older people—he was a late, only child. Kind, decent, stupid people. Casey loved them.

His high school years were no more hellish than anyone else's; his college years were an anonymous marathon of beer blasts, rock concerts, and overdue term papers; his decision to enter graduate school was complicated by his adviser's doubt that any graduate school would enter him. But enrolment was falling, programs were being cut if too few live bodies registered for thesis seminar, and Casey found himself a teaching fellow in a small, undistin guished college that was part of a large, undistinguished state university system in the Northeast. He also found himself scorned. Politely, judiciously, even indulgently—he was in the Humanities, and indulgence was encouraged—but scorned is scorned.

"What's your area?" asked Paul Rizzo, the stocky, bearded teaching fellow with whom Casey shared an office. Rizzo was wearing a plaid flannel shirt, jeans, and Frye boots. All the male teaching fellows, Casey had noticed, wore plaid flannel shirts, jeans, and Frye boots. So did some of the females. Casey wore a sports jacket.

"Area?"

"For your thesis."

"I'm doing the option—the creative-writing thesis. A novel."

"A novel?"

"Yeah, you know," Casey said, "a fiction narrative over 40,000 words. You've heard of them."

Rizzo's eyes narrowed. "Have you started this, uh, novel?"

"Yes."

Rizzo seemed surprised. He stopped in the middle of changing his plaid flannel shirt for a football jersey, arms suspended in midair. Twice a week, he scrimmaged to keep in shape, playing on a team limited to grad students and captained by a third-year fellow in the biology department who had his own grant from the federal government.

"What's it about?"

Casey smiled. "In twenty-five words or less?"

"All right, then, what's it like? Who would you say your writing was closest to, if you had to name an influence, a mentor? Barth? Hemingway? Dickens? Faulkner?"

Casey took a deep breath. "Burroughs."

"*Naked Lunch*?"

"No, not William."

"Then who—"

"Edgar."

"Edgar Burroughs? You write . . ."

"Yes. Yes, I do."

Rizzo finished sliding into his football jersey and picked up his helmet, rubbing a finger over a jagged nick. Then he smiled. Politely, judiciously.

"Well, *chacun à sa gout*, right?"

"*Son gout*," Casey said.

"My thesis is on Keats. The psycho-sexual relation of the 'Hyperion' fragment of his later work. You probably don't like Keats, though?"

"Why not?"

"If you write that . . . do you like Keats?"

Casey picked up Rizzo's football shoe and fingered the cleats. He tried each one in turn, pressing lightly with the end of his index finger. They were all dull. Rizzo waited. Indulgently.

"Well, I'll tell you, Paul. I really think Keats is some kind of poet. Not too commercial, you know, but a strong sensory receiver, quick on the end line. Some kind of poet. But overall, I guess I have to go with Edgar Guest. Enjambment-wise, that is."

Rizzo turned maroon. Casey smiled. Politely, judiciously, indulgently.

"WHO YOU GOT FOR FROSH COMP?"

"Some flake in a striped sports jacket. Young. He talked about semicolons."

"Must be the new guy. Casey."

Casey, the new guy, ducked behind the grey bulk of the candy-and-pastries vending machine. The styrofoam cup he was carrying sloshed coffee onto his striped sports jacket. The student on the other side of the vendor kicked it.

"Took my quarter again!"

"Here, have half my Babe Ruth."

"Eff-ing machine. Any frat files on his assignments?"

"Not yet. He's new."

"Just my luck."

"It'll be all right. The new ones don't like to flunk anybody. Just go to class. The new ones take attendance."

"He wants us to write a paper for Friday."

"Get Sue to do it. She's an English major."

"Yeah. Jesus—semicolons!"

"Yeah."

He got used to teaching freshmen. He made a truce with Rizzo. What he couldn't get used to or make a truce with, what led him to discover why a university was a bad place to write, was the faculty.

His professors spoke blithely of Shakespeare's "minor plays," Shaw's "failed efforts," Dickens's "unsuccessful pieces." Stories that Casey, stretched out on a flat rock under the blank Montana sky, had thrilled to and wondered at and anguished over, were assigned grades like so many frosh comp papers. B+ to Somerset Maugham and Jane Austen. B- to C.S. Lewis and Timon of Athens. His own half-finished stories, Casey figured, the stories sweated and bled and wept over in the eighty-three-dollars-a-month hole above a barbershop, were about an H-. On a good day.

His thesis adviser was a Dreiser man. If you are a Dreiser man,

Casey learned, if you champion Dreiser and the American realists for twenty-five years (including six articles in *PMLA*), if you dissect and evaluate and explore Dreiser, you can be Dreiser. You know what he wrote in the margins of his books, how he wore his hair and who cut it. You have his/your position in belles-lettres to defend, and you fight for it ferociously. When a prestigious Eastern university has a sudden unfortunate death among its existing faculty and so needs to acquire another American realist, you throw your hat into the academic ring and play politics with dead candidates. You win, and jolly well you should. Dreiser is a definite A. And then so, of course, are you.

Casey walked. He walked on village streets at noon, over snowy athletic fields before dawn, in night woods where one clumsy step could break his unwary neck. While he walked, he agonized. He agonized because he was not Tolstoy or Shakespeare or even Maugham. He agonized because he was honest enough to know that he never would be Tolstoy or Shakespeare or Maugham, complimented himself on being "at least" that honest with himself, and agonized that his self-compliments showed a lack of artistic passion. When he wasn't walking and agonizing, he wrote. It was all H-. When he wasn't writing, he read Dreiser. It was a definite A.

"BUT I HAD my adviser's approval for the thesis before I began!" Casey said. He tried to sound indignant rather than desperate and knew he failed. "Both Dr. Jensen and Dr. Schorer signed the approval form!"

"I know that," said Dr. Stine, Chairman of the Graduate Committee. He sat behind his book-cluttered desk in his book-lined office and looked distressed. Beyond the open window, three students, exhilarated by the spring, were tossing a blue frisbee; occasionally, it hit the building with a soft clunk muffled by budding ivy.

"They both knew my novel was going to be s—"

"I know that, too, Mr. Casey." The chairman's distress was genuine. Casey didn't care. "We are not narrow in our academic outlook, Mr. Casey. There is room for many different types of writing in our creative thesis option. The graduate committee is perfectly aware that a lot of exciting research is being carried out right now in your field and that there is much literary merit in selected examples of sci-fi."

Casey winced. Dr. Stine didn't notice. The frisbee hit the wall.

"We're also aware that PhDs are being granted by very prestigious universities for scholarly work in sci-fi. But both the writing and the research ends that are worthy of serious attention concern the best sci-fi, the work concerned with social insight and human verities. Hawthorne's 'truth of the human heart, you know,'" the chairman said, and smiled, obviously pleased with this reference. The frisbee hit the wall.

"Your novel, on the other hand, is just—just adventure. Escapist improbabilities. You must see—'galactic empire'!"

"It's a realistic interpretation of a possible technological—"

"Precisely. Technological, not humane. You don't deal with psychological or social themes at all. When your protagonist meets those aliens in the blue UFO—blue—I'm sorry, Mr. Casey. It's not that your novel is badly written. In fact, it shows some commercial promise; it's colourful and fast-paced. But it doesn't measure up to the standards of serious fiction. And serious literature is what a thesis-novel acceptable to the English department must at least try to be."

"It could very well happen just the way I—"

"I'm sorry, Mr. Casey. I wish you would believe that."

Casey did believe it. He uttered a short expletive that he hoped made the chairman even sorrier and left the book-lined office just as the frisbee missed the wall altogether and sailed through the window, a miniature blue UFO.

HE RESIGNED FROM THE UNIVERSITY, regretted it as pretentiously self-indulgent, and stayed resigned. To fill his time, he wrote, waited on tables at a local pizzeria, brooded over his rejection slips, and walked. The walking, he figured, was the best thing he did. He could walk for hours, could walk all night. After a while, he no longer needed to look down at his own feet in even the darkest, most unfamiliar woods; his feet developed such sure sensing of the dead twigs and leaf-covered rabbit holes that he never stumbled. He could walk looking upward at the stars, which, in some way, he couldn't say just exactly how, had betrayed him. He could walk on desert sands, on ancient glaciers, on the bottom of the Mariana Trench. His walking was a definite A.

"HEY, CASEY!"

"Hello, Rizzo. What'll you have?"

"What do you want, Darlene?"

"Oh, I don't know—pepperoni, for sure. Mushrooms, green pepper, onions. And anchovies, if they're fresh. Are the anchovies fresh?"

"Are the anchovies fresh?" Rizzo asked Casey.

"No," Casey said.

"Well, then, no anchovies. Okay, Darl?"

"Are they good frozen anchovies?" Rizzo asked Casey.

"No," Casey said.

"So, what are you doing now?" Rizzo said, and added hastily, without glancing around the pizzeria, "What are you going to do? I mean your, uh, plans?"

"Bring you a pizza without anchovies," Casey said, saw that he was being a bastard again, and tried harder. "Guess what, Rizzo? I sold one."

Rizzo wrinkled his beefy forehead. "One what?"

"One story. I sold one."

"You did? Hey, that's great! Is it . . . is it one of those—"

"Yes. Yes, it is."

"Well, that's still great! Do you mind if I ask you what you got for it? No, never mind. None of my business."

"It wasn't much."

"I hear that market pays less. Comparatively."

"Generally, yes. There are exceptions."

"Of course—there always are. Speaking of exceptions, do you mind if I brag a little? I got a job. A real, tenure-track, full-time job. Starting as assistant professor."

"Congratulations. Where is it?"

"Lunell College. It's a small liberal arts college in Mass-achusetts. I really lucked out, you know what the market is, nobody wants humanities people. Only technology-gadget guys, computer specialists and all. But this is a bona fide good deal. Guess what the salary is."

"I couldn't."

"Go ahead, guess."

"I couldn't."

Rizzo told him. Casey smiled and underlined "no anchovies" on his order pad, thick and black. Twice. The pencil broke.

"I really did luck out," Rizzo said. "They just happened to need a Keats man."

He had not forgotten his childhood nomenclature for the stars, but now he learned everyone else's. This was easy because there seemed to be fewer stars than there had been in Montana. He wrote out a list of the more mellifluous ones, set the list to the melody of a sixteenth-century English madrigal, and chanted it while he walked:

Regulus Fomalhaut Betelguese
Ri-i-gel,
Arcturus Polaris Cano-o-pus
AL-TAIR.

The chant stayed in his head while he tried to write about galactic empires and interstellar battles; since he couldn't get the tune out, he learned to ignore it. After a while, he found it rather soothing and came to depend upon it while he sweated and thrashed and fought, motionless at his Salvation Army desk.

The actual presence of real stars was less soothing. Nightly, he glared upwards, weather permitting, with real anger, while summer dew soaked his sneakers and a crick developed at the back of his neck. He didn't try to understand his anger; it was more satisfying to revel in it. They had let him down, Regulus Fomalhaut Betelguese Ri-i-gel. They had all let him down. They had not delivered, somehow, what had been promised, promised to the

Montana kids playing on the big flat rock in the middle of prosperous insignificance: Marty Hillek and Carl Nielsen and Billy DeTine and Jerry Casey, playing UFO and Sirian Invaders and Would-You-Go? They had deceived. They were not what he thought them. They had refused to let him go, as they had let Marty Hillek and Carl Nielsen and Billy DeTine go, but they had also refused to satisfy him. They were heartless, they were cold, they were shallow, and he himself was probably crazy to stand here thinking of them as anything but ongoing nuclear fusions. "'Many thynges doth infect the ayre, as the influence of sondry sterres,'" he quoted aloud, enormously pleased to have remembered the quote from Renaissance Lit. He only quoted aloud when in deserted areas, however; his angry craziness demanded privacy to be fully wallowed in. It was a lover's quarrel.

⸻

"Jerry! Happy birthday, dear!"

"Thanks, Mom."

"So, how does it feel to be twenty-six, son?"

"Oh, I don't know, Dad. Not too different from twenty-five."

"Your presents are in the mail, dear. I'm sorry they didn't get East by your birthday, but I just couldn't get to town to the post office; the car was acting up, and your father couldn't figure out if it was the starter or that little black thing that goes from the—"

"Now, Mary, we don't need to tell him all that long-distance."

"Guess not. How's everything going, dear?"

"Fine, just fine."

"Did you sell any more—"

"No. No, I haven't. It takes time, you know, Mom."

Fourteen hundred miles away, his father cleared his throat.

Jerry held the receiver a little away from his ear and closed his eyes, waiting.

"Speaking of selling, son, I happened to talk to John Nielsen yesterday, and he still needs someone to help him and Carl at the Grain & Feed. Now I'm not pressuring you, you know that. Whatever you want to do is fine with your mother and me. That's what we've always said, and we mean it. But I just promised John I'd pass along the information to you, so I am."

"Okay," Casey said. "The information is passed." He could see his father holding the phone—the upstairs extension, it would be—lightly in his big hand, still wearing his Stetson with his boots and plaid flannel shirt.

"Just so's you know, son."

"I know," Casey said. There was a pause.

"Are you still seeing that girl, dear, that you wrote us about? The kindergarten teacher? Kara Phillips?"

"Yes. No. A little."

"I have an idea! Why don't you bring her with you when you come home for Christmas? You know, we'd just love to have her!"

"Now, Mary, don't push," Casey's father said.

"I wasn't pushing, Calvin Casey! All I said was that we'd love to have Jerry's friend stay with us over Christmas if he'd like to bring her. She could have the spare room, it was just freshly papered, it'd be no trouble at all."

"Thanks, Mom. Maybe I'll ask her."

"Of course, it's up to you. Write us when your presents arrive, so I know they fit, and tell us if Kara is coming for Christmas."

"Assistant manager," his father said. "Did I mention that it's assistant manager?"

"Well, bye, dear. Happy birthday!"

"Good starting salary, son."

"Love you," Casey's mother said.

"Love you, too," Casey said, and hung up the receiver carefully, with no sound.

———

HE QUIT THE PIZZERIA. One night in October, he had waited on the Chairman of the Graduate Committee, Dr. Stine. The man had been so tactful, so diplomatic in chatting with Casey without once mentioning Casey's failed novel-thesis, Casey's inexpert self-haircut ($4.70 at the barber, and that without sideburns), Casey's tomato-and-mozzarella smeared apron, that Casey had been unable to stand it. He smiled at the chairman, said yes, fall was beautiful in this part of the country, said yes, it was interesting that the papers always reported an increase in UFO sightings in the fall, said no, he didn't think there was anything in it. Then he went into the kitchen and stuffed his apron into the pizza oven, where it turned the exact colour of flabby, frozen anchovies.

He found a job as part-time grounds man for an old, beautiful, tree-shaded cemetery. He wrote all morning and raked leaves all afternoon, avoiding funerals in progress. The metal rake prongs caught repeatedly at the bases of tombstones and then twanged back, a sound as monotonous and hypnotic as a pendulum. Some-times, he returned late at night and walked through the cemetery. The darkness was rich and velvety; it was the quick flashes of headlights beyond the iron gates that seemed like ghosts. He read the oldest of the tombstones with a penlight, stooping to trace the letters with his finger when age had made them illegible:

ELIZABETH ANN CARMODY

1851-1862

Eleven years old, he thought. At eleven years old, he had been playing Would-You-Go? on the big flat rock on the plains. *Eleven years old.*

JAMES ALLEN ROBERTS

1789-1812

DULCE ET DECORUM EST PRO PATRIA MORI

Ha, snorted Casey, child of draft-card burnings and ping-pong detente.

CECILIA HARDWICK SMITH

1884-1879

BEYOND THIS NARROW VALE OF EARTH

WHERE BRIGHT CELESTIAL AGES ROLL

THE COUNTLESS STARS OF HEAVEN'S REALM

GUIDE AND LIGHT THE WAND'RING SOUL

Ha again, Casey told the stars, the lover's quarrel having solidified into the cynical half-banter of an accepted marriage. *So go ahead, guide and light. Send down knowledge. Send down enlightenment. Send down a publisher. Go ahead, I'm waiting, I'm a wandering soul, as duly specified, I'm ready. H- has arisen. Go ahead.*

Clouds started to roll in from the west.

"AND SHE SAID to tell you that it would be no trouble at all, you could have the spare bed in the spare room, and they'd love to have you."

Kara raised herself on one elbow in Casey's rumpled, un-spare bed. The neon barber pole just outside Casey's window striped her breasts with revolving red and blue.

"I don't think it's fair of you to change the subject in the middle of a discussion just because you're losing."

"I was losing?"

"You know you were. And then you just drop in this invitation to your parents' house for Christmas, and that really puts me at an emotional disadvantage, Jer. It's not fighting fair."

"So report me to the Geneva Convention."

"There you go, getting nasty again, de-railing the argument just because you haven't got a valid viewpoint that will stand up to close scrutiny."

"I haven't got a valid viewpoint that will stand up to close scrutiny? And what is it you've got, an airtight case?"

"I didn't say that. I said—"

"More like a braintight case."

"—that not being able to prove that a thing exists isn't the same as being able to prove that it doesn't exist, and—"

"Absolutely impervious to the osmosis of facts."

"—just because the Navy doesn't choose to admit that a UFO—"

"Last month, it was transactional analysis."

"That was different! If you'd just have an open mind—"

"With enough holes to fit the airtight case in?"

"That's enough!" Kara shouted. She bolted upright in bed and clutched Casey's grubby sheet around her. "You're so superior, aren't you, with your clever little wisecracks about my intelligence! Just because you've never seen one, they don't exist, right? If Jerry Casey, great unpublished novelist, hasn't personally seen and touched and goddamn tasted a UFO, then there's no such thing. Of course not! No matter that hundreds of sightings have been reported, no matter that a respected witness right here in town saw a ship streaking over the woods, no matter that there doesn't —if Jerry Casey didn't see it, it doesn't exist, because Jerry Casey is the great fictional expert on spaceships and galactic empires! If Jerry Casey, with three unpublished novels and the enormous authority of his sacred pile of rejection sl—"

Casey hit her. It wasn't a hard slap, he didn't know he was going to do it until he had, and instantly he regretted it more than he had ever regretted anything else in his life. Kara put her hand to her red cheek and turned away from him, the sheet twisting itself around her small striped breasts. Tears filled her eyes but did not fall. Casey put out one hand to touch her shoulder, but he couldn't make the hand quite connect, and it hung there, suspended between them, useless.

"Kara . . . oh, God, Kara, I'm sorry."

She didn't answer. The sheet humped up over her thin legs. Something broke in Casey, something so light and delicate he hadn't known himself that it was there or what he would say when it wasn't.

"Kara, listen, I'm sorry I hit you, so fucking sorry I don't know how to say it. But, Kara, you don't know, you can't know, I've wanted there to be something out there since I was a kid, wanted it more desperately than anything else in my whole fucking life. I used to stand out there on the plains and squeeze my eyes shut and will them to be out there, to come down to me, because I was one of them. I knew it, so they had to know it, too. I made up whole stories, epics, about how I got left here by mistake and adopted by my parents, but they'd come back for me eventually. It was so real I could taste it, Kara, could shiver with it down to my bones, my marrow. It was like a religion, or an insanity. And I still would like to believe, would give fucking anything to believe, but I can't. The evidence against it is just too strong. Do you know what the odds are that intelligent life would behave like . . . so I started to convince myself that the stories were just made up. I started to make them up, to write them down. Kara, it's not 'superiority,' it's not wisecracks, it's . . . Kara, do you see what I'm talking about? Can you understand what I'm trying to mean? Kara?"

She didn't answer. After a while, he touched her. She put her head on his shoulder. He wiped her tears. She let him. He stroked her hair and apologized all over again. She said it was all right, looking pensive and thoughtful. He pulled the blanket protectively up to her chin. She lay still in his arms. He kissed her. She smiled. A few days later, she called and said they should have a long talk. He never saw her again.

PAUL RIZZO WAS GETTING MARRIED, and he wrote to invite Casey to the wedding. His bride was a fellow faculty member at Lunell College—an assistant professor, Rizzo wrote, underlining the words twice. She was also "the only child of a wealthy shoe-polish entrepreneur." Casey tried to figure out how you got really wealthy from shoe polish, couldn't, and knew that this proved nothing. He wouldn't have known how to become really wealthy if the process were detailed for him in heroic couplets. For all he knew, shoe polish was a rewarding and fulfilling way to make money enough to freshly wallpaper all the spare rooms in Montana. For all he knew, shoes and the right polish were what his life had been missing all along, the yin and yang of his universe's deficiencies. For all he knew.

With his letter, Rizzo had enclosed a picture of his fiancée, cut from the local newspaper that had announced their engagement.

She looked pretty, if a little blurry. The invitation was embossed with blue-and-white doves swooping around a quotation from Keats.

Tramping along over the hard Montana snows on Christmas night, Casey tried to picture the wedding. There would be champagne, and sexy-coy toasts, and good food. There would be women—bridesmaids in silky dresses, Lunell professors with good minds, college-student relatives giggly and flushed with wine. The wedding was in April, over Easter recess, so the bridesmaids and professors and gigglers would have on spring dresses, light and bare. They would smell of flowery perfumes. They would dance on strappy, high-heeled sandals. They would talk to Casey on the dance floor, at the bar, on the church steps. And they would all ask him, eventually, what it was that he "did." Or tried to do. Or was supposed to be doing.

Somewhere near the barns, a cow lowed. Casey tramped up to his old flat rock, knocked the snow off it, and sat down. Overhead, the stars blazed. He willed himself to concentrate on the stars, to forget the depressing mechanics of attending Rizzo's wedding, the self-kept scoresheets. He just wouldn't think about it. Above him glittered Thekala, aka Aldebaran, aka The Red Terror. To the south and east shone Rigel, Sirius, Betelguese, Pollux, Procyon. The Orion Nebula, spawn-ground of new stars. They used to pretend it was alive, like a queen bee. Only the southwest looked subdued, empty of all but the faint stars of Cetus. The sky there was a soft, even black, lustrous with reflected light, like . . .

Like shoe polish.

IN JANUARY, the ground froze so hard that no graves could be dug. People continued to die anyway, and their caskets were stacked, carefully labelled, in a brick vault to await a thaw. Casey was laid off. Nothing else seemed to be opening up in the cemetery line. So he took a job as a part-time janitor in a high school, nightly scrubbing anatomical impossibilities off lavatory walls with industrial-strength cleanser. He wrote.

In February, it snowed fifty-two inches, a century's record. During the entire month, the sky remained cloudy; if the stars had all simultaneously winked out, their light spent like so many weary philanderers, Casey wouldn't have known it. He caught the flu and spent six days in bed, feverishly watching the barber pole revolve against the grey snow. He wrote.

In March, Dr. James Randall Stine, Chairman of the Graduate Committee and a widower for two years, announced his engagement to Miss Kara Phillips, a kindergarten teacher in the local public schools. Casey's father called to just pass on the information that Marty Hillek's father was looking around for someone with business sense to help him run the Holiday Inn. He wrote.

In April, a week before Rizzo's wedding, Casey's third attempt at a novel sold to a major publisher. It was about a galactic empire.

HE LEAPED through the dark April woods, the letter in his hand, the ground inches below his feet. He was Pan with scriptorial pipes, Orpheus with graphic lyre, Caesar of the literary spaceways. He was the godchild of intergalactic muses. He was the first person in the universe to publish a novel. He was the Pied Piper with hordes at his singing back, Circe with spells to drive men mad. He was drunk, but only partly on California champagne.

Running wildly through springtime smells unseen in the darkness, he held the letter before him and a little to one side, like a spear, brandishing it upward.

"See! See!" he called up between the trees, drunkenly flaunting his own theatricality. "See! See what I did about you! Look! Look!"

The stars glittered.

Casey stopped running and stood panting beneath a sugar maple, holding his side. He was Shakespeare, he was Tolstoy, he was Dreiser, he was a definite A. He could walk on spangle-coloured planets forever, just as soon as his stomach lay still.

The stars glittered.

Across the sky, the branches of the sugar maple slanted like bars. Gemini sliced in half, Dubhe divided from Merak. Through the bars, the Milky Way looked broken, fitful, about to sever and recede even more, and it was already so far away, so high . . . so high . . . they were all so high . . . For a dizzy second, Casey put his hand on the tree trunk, searching for a foothold. But the second passed, and he stood on the ground, half-trampled fern shoots under his worn boots.

The stars glittered.

Okay, so the universe doesn't notice, hardly an original observation, Casey ol' boy, got to do better than that. What'd you expect—a supernova? No romantic despair; cosmic self-pity strictly forbidden in moments of drunken triumph, on pain of triviality. No brooding, no self-indulgent self-incrimination. "A man's reach should exceed . . ." so you've got a hell of a reach, kudos to you, ol' Jer, good to have a hell of a reach. Supposed to have a hell of a reach. Reach for a star a star is born born to boogie . . . oh, hell. I am not Prufrock, nor was meant to be—

Meant to be what?

Abruptly, he saw that he was not alone. Under the sugar maple, at the edge of the wide circle of branches, stood a child. A skinny, grubby boy, eleven years old, gazing upward. Casey lurched forward, but the boy ignored him. Motionless except for his eyes, he was conquering distant, spangle-coloured planets, and in his shining look, Casey saw, there was no longing; no one longs for what he already possesses. He was still, complete, but as Casey grabbed wildly to throttle the unbearable wholeness in the rapt face that he knew perfectly well was not there, the champagne heaved, and he threw up into the trampled fern shoots. When he could finally wipe his mouth on his shirttail, the boy was gone.

The stars glittered.

Casey stumbled back through the woods. In one small clearing, he smelled lilacs, barely budded but sweet in the dark, and he turned his head away. Somewhere, he lost the path. Scratched by brambles, scuffing the decay of last year's leaves, he thrashed forward until the moon rose. It was easier, then, to walk, but the moonlit pattern of dark branches on the white letter made him squeeze his eyes shut, and it was thus that he tripped over the spaceship.

It wasn't really, of course. The ship itself was a hundred feet away, dully black in the moonlight, circled with birch branches that had been pushed aside by its landing and had snapped back. Casey, sprawled on the ground over a foot-long, log-shaped . . . whatever it was, could almost feel the crack of those returning birch limbs on his back and shoulders. He reached under himself to feel the Whatever; it was—hard and smooth, faintly vibrating. Unlike the boy, it did not vanish.

Unsuspected additional champagne churned in his stomach.

The ship was small; it could hardly be more than some sort of shuttle. Curved into flowing lines and embraced by budding trees, it looked weirdly beautiful in the night woods, weirdly right. Moonlight slid off the black surface, a deep, rich black the colour of loam. Leaves and ferns grew right up to where the ship rested on the forest floor. There was no burned patch, no sign that the ship had not always been there, would not always be there, a part of the ferns and birches, surrounded by the usual night rustlings and scamperings. An owl hooted.

Under Casey's belly, the Whatever began to hum.

He rolled off it and scrambled to his feet. A section of the ship slid upward, sending a shaft of blue light over the ground. Slowly, a ramp descended until it met the dead leaves, which sighed softly.

Casey closed his eyes. He was drunk, he told himself. He was drunk, he was emotionally exhausted, he was hallucinating in some bizarre, wish-fulfillment fantasy. He was insane, he was schizophrenic, he was dead. He was a grown man with a more-or-less job, aging parents, and his own copy of the ten-volume Oxford English Dictionary. He was afraid, but not of the ship.

When he opened his eyes, it was still there. The "door" was still open. Nothing was visible inside except the bright blue light. The log-shaped Whatever rose into the air as high as Casey's chest and floated toward the ship. Ten feet away, it stopped, floated back to Casey's chest, then again toward the ship. When Casey didn't follow, it repeated the whole sequence. Casey took one step forward.

He was on the flat rock under the twilight sky. "Would You Go?" they asked each other, sprawled on concave stomachs. "Nah," said Marty Hillek—too dangerous. "Chicken!" said Carl Nielsen, "chicken!" "I'd go," said Billy DeTine, "I wouldn't care, I'm not afraid, I'd go." "Me too," whispered little Jerry Casey, youngest of the lot. "Me too." "What if you never got back?" said Marty Hillek, and no one said anything.

"The probability," lectured the professor to Astronomy 101, "of intelligent life visiting Earth covertly is very small. Even if we generously suppose a fifty-fifty chance of life developing on any planet within a twenty-five-light-year radius of Earth, the next calculation would—"

"You don't know," insisted Kara Stine, née Phillips. "Nobody really knows."

Casey took another step forward. Wet leaves squished under his boot. The letter rustled in his hand:

Dear Mr. Casey:

We are happy to inform you that our editorial staff is very impressed with your book, and that we are interested in publishing it. First, however, it is necessary . . .

The Whatever floated back to Casey a third time. It was humming more loudly now, and in the humming, Casey heard a soft urgency.

Moonlight shone on the letter, crumpled where his fist had tightened, fouled at one corner with vomited champagne.

"Would You Go?" asked Marty Hillek and Carl Nielsen and Billy DeTine. "What if you never got back?" Nights on the cemetery tombs: Regulus Fomalhaut Betelguese Ri-i-gel. Days at his desk, struggling with stars on the head of a pin. "If Jerry Casey, great unpublished novelist, hasn't personally seen one . . ." "Me too," whispered little Jerry Casey. *We are happy to inform you . . .* "What are you doing now? I mean your, uh, plans?" "Me too. Oh, me too." *Happy to inform you . . .* "Escapist improbabilities, Mr. Casey. You must see . . . 'galactic empire'!" *Happy to inform you . . .*

Casey, battlefield for two warring empires, hiccupped in anguish.

Carefully, as if he might break, he took three steps backward. Then three more.

The Whatever followed him, then reversed direction and floated towards the ship, but only once. It floated inside, and the curved section of hull lowered slowly. The ship started to rise, slowly at first, then more rapidly. For a moment, the dark hull stood poised above the birches, blotting out the stars. Then it blurred and was gone. The birch branches snapped back. Something small and furry scuttled away through the leaves, startled by the sudden sharp sobbing that went on and on, the unchecked tearless sobbing of an eleven-year-old boy.

YOU KNOW THE REST. All but Casey's name, which is not Casey. You can read in any standard reference work about the first official UN contact with the Beta Hydrans, fifteen years ago last May. You can read the pages and pages of testimony from the Des Moines dentist and the Portuguese fisherman and the Australian housewife who visited the Beta Hydran spacecraft during their reconnaissance landings. You can read about the shifts of global power and the scientific boons and the interstellar promises of good faith and speedy return by the Beta Hydrans, who were not part of a galactic empire and who seemed bewildered by the entire concept. You can't not read it; it's everywhere.

You can look up Casey, too, in the reference works, and read about how he became the most famous "name" in SF before he was forty-five. You can look up his awards, his honorary this-and-thats, his movie credits, the alimony he pays both wives, his bout with alcoholism. If your mind runs that way, you can look up his biographies—written, all, by impoverished PhDs weary of Keats—

which will analyze for you all the early environmental influences on Casey's writing. You can look up the academic critics, also impoverished PhDs, who have concerned themselves with Casey's novels. They find in all of them, except the first, a "lost, human yearning, a quality almost mythic in the scope of its cosmic root-lessness" (Glasser, Richard J., "Rockets and Wanderjahr: Another Look at SF." *PMLA*, 122 (1992), 48-76). You can look it all up, or could if you knew Casey's name. You'd recognize it, even if you don't read "that space stuff."

But what you don't know, can't look up, is the loss of Casey's galactic empire. What it was, what it meant, how it felt. You don't know. Unless it has happened to you, you don't know. You can't ever know.

I REMEMBER PARIS

By James Alan Gardner

We've all heard one version of the story. Zeus hosted a banquet but didn't invite Eris, the Goddess of Discord. Eris showed up anyway and threw a golden apple inscribed TO THE FAIREST into the gathering. Hera, Athena, and Aphrodite each claimed to deserve the apple. Zeus was too wily to judge among the goddesses himself, so he appointed Prince Paris of Troy to pick which was the most beautiful. All three goddesses offered Paris bribes...

But here we stop. Fate isn't fixed. Small things can produce big changes, especially when gods are involved.

In the best-known version of history, Zeus moved quickly to pass on the burden of judging. He tossed the golden apple to Hermes. "Take this to Prince Paris, as fast as the wind." The apple reached Paris in a heartbeat.

The prince was a virile young man, so whose bribe did he choose? Aphrodite's, of course. She offered him the love of the world's most beautiful woman. Naturally, young Paris leaped at the chance.

But in another version of the tale, Zeus acted with less haste. When the goddesses began to argue, Zeus rose from his throne and glared as if to say, *Must we, really? Do you have to fall for such an obvious trick?* But none of the goddesses backed down. In annoyance, Zeus handed Hermes the apple but said, "No need to rush."

So, Hermes took his time . . . and for gods, whole years pass like minutes. By the time Hermes reached Prince Paris in Troy, the prince had aged two decades and was not so thoroughly ruled by his loins. He still found Aphrodite's offer tempting, but after sober deliberation, Paris chose Hera's bribe instead. She had promised to make Paris king of all Europe and Asia . . . and a man in his forties wants status and power more than he wants a mere roll in the hay.

In the world that ensued, poets sing of the great Parisian empire: a realm which united half the world, both for better and for worse. But the saga of that empire would last a hundred days in the telling; let us not take the time. Tonight, we will share a briefer tale, one as true as the others.

In this final version, Zeus got morosely to his feet when he heard the goddesses start to bicker. After long, weary moments, he trudged across the Olympian feast-hall to where Hermes awaited. "Take your time," Zeus said to his messenger. "Maybe the goddesses will eventually let this go."

Obediently, Hermes dawdled en route. He sported with dryads, satyrs, and centaurs. By the time he gave Paris the apple, the prince had passed his sixtieth year.

As in the other versions, the three goddesses sent messengers to offer Paris bribes. The prince smiled fondly when Aphrodite tempted him with visions of an ardent young beauty, but the woman merely reminded him of his granddaughters. Nor was Paris at all tempted by Hera's offer of ruling all of Eurasia. While the prince retained ambitions, they were not for ruthless conquest.

Instead, he took the bribe from the goddess Athena: the gift of never-failing wisdom. Athena also offered skill in war, and the prince said, "Sure, why not?" No point in turning down presents—that wouldn't be wise. Paris had no hunger for battle, but perhaps "skill in war" included the knowledge of how to soothe sore knees and aching feet.

THE WORLD WAS OLDER NOW. Its greatest heroes, Trojan and Greek, had aged just like Paris.

In this version of history, the Trojan War never happened. Those who might have been enemies met as friends instead. Greek Achilles and Trojan Troilus, for example, got together every year to drink wine and hunt boar. At night around the campfire, the two felt sorry for themselves; shouldn't two such peerless warriors be slaying monsters instead of mere dumb animals? But they never found a single magical beast who needed killing. Earlier heroes—Heracles, Theseus, and many others—had dispatched every epic horror years before.

Meanwhile, on the island of Ithaca, clever Odysseus grew bored of idling time in his gilded palace. He bequeathed his crown to his son, then set sail with his wife, Penelope, to explore the world and raise a legend or two. Aeneas of Troy did the same. When they crossed each other's paths, they traded stories, bragged about their children, then set off wandering again.

In Sparta, King Menelaus, married to Helen, treated her badly until she walked out. Menelaus announced to anybody who'd listen he didn't care that she was gone; Helen was old and definitely not beautiful anymore. Menelaus wouldn't take her back, even if she came crawling. Then he took up with slaves and concubines, as one does.

In Troy, Athena's gifts had made Paris feel no different. Was he wise? Not that he noticed. But Paris continued to help his brother, King Hector, rule Troy, and the city was blessed with peace and prosperity.

Even so, Paris knew this golden age wouldn't last. When he'd given Athena the apple, he'd offended two other goddesses. Hera was famous for being vindictive, and Aphrodite, Goddess of Passion, was not apt to be a good-tempered loser.

Paris wondered what the goddesses would do. At first, he worried they'd rile Greece into a full-scale invasion of Troy. But that wasn't likely. Greece was a jumble of city-states, Sparta, Athens, Corinth, Thebes, squabbling among themselves. The Greeks would never form a united front unless someone from Troy did something foolish.

So, what else could the goddesses do? Paris thought the question over. And after he thought, he planned.

A BEAST SLOUCHED OUT of the sea in front of the walls of Troy. The beast had three heads: a lion, an eagle, and a crimson dragon. Its body resembled a rhino, and its tail a cobra. Its back was covered with razor-sharp quills, standing straight and tall and fierce.

Within seconds, the beast had murdered a group of fishermen who were on the beach patching their boats. Some of the victims were pierced with quills; others died of cobra venom; others were trampled to death. Then, the dragon head of the beast gave a roar and opened its mouth. Flames shot forth and set the fishermen's boats on fire.

Atop the city's ramparts, a sentry raised his bugle and blew a warning. Guards drew their bows and rained arrows down on the beast, but none could penetrate its hide. Other guards readied their spears; others boiled cauldrons of oil; but all of them feared the beast would easily shrug off every attack.

Paris and Hector stood on the city wall above the beach. They could see the terrible beast devouring the men it had just slaughtered. Hector sighed. "You were right, my brother. I'd hoped you were mistaken."

Paris said, "I'd hoped the same. Those men are dead because of me."

"No," King Hector said, "because of Aphrodite and Hera. Also because of Zeus, who forced you to judge that ridiculous contest. Any dunce could see what Eris was trying to do."

"The gods are not what they were," Paris replied. "Zeus, Hera, all of them. Their wits are slow and they're set in their ways. They're all just rolling downhill now, like stones."

King Hector looked at his brother in surprise. He'd never before considered that gods might age and fade. But Hector knew his brother was wise; perhaps Paris was right, and the Time of the Gods was waning.

Down on the beach, the beast gave a hideous cry: the roar of a lion, the scream of an eagle, the hiss of a dragon combined. The beast stomped one last time on the devoured fishermen's remains, then turned toward Troy. Its thunderous feet pounded the sand as it headed for the walls.

"It's time," Hector said. He donned his helmet, then went down the stairs that led to the beach.

Paris put on his own helmet and waved a signal to the bugler. As Paris hurried away, the bugle blared out a clarion call to glorious battle.

The gates of Troy flew open, and every hero in the world came charging forth.

ACHILLES AND AJAX, Glaucus and Memnon . . . in another reality, they'd fought on different sides, but now they were here as allies. Paris had asked if they'd come to protect his beloved city of Troy. They'd said yes as soon as he mentioned, "A monster might show up and try to kill me."

A monster? Was there truly a monster left in the world? The warriors had scraped the rust off their armour and sharpened their aging weapons. One last surviving monster! There might never be another. One last chance to fight and live or die as legends!

They fought on the beach before the walls of Troy, with boats still burning on the sand. Using swords and spears, cunning and strength, they assaulted the beast with decades of pent-up zeal. For many, a whisper of foresight told them this was the end of an age. In future, combat would lose all sense of splendour. It would become the business of soldiers, not warriors—pragmatic, bloody slaughter. But for now, these fighters were heroes facing a monster: a nightmare that damned well needed slaying.

They attacked it with joy. Together. One last time.

Many died . . . even the great Achilles, pierced with a poisoned quill that struck his heel. But in the end, the monster perished, as everyone knew it must. Paris and the other survivors marched back into Troy to heal their wounds, mourn their dead, and celebrate their triumph.

THAT NIGHT, under a sky that was milky with stars, Paris sat on the beach with Odysseus. They passed a wineskin back and forth as they leaned their aching bodies against the dead beast's carcass.

Odysseus slapped the monster's flank. "What do you think?" he asked. "Another child from Echidna?"

Paris nodded. Echidna was famed as the Mother of Monsters. She'd birthed the chimera, the hydra, the sphinx, and dozens more.

"Might there be more on the way?" Odysseus asked.

"No," Paris said, surprised at his own certainty. "Echidna was already past her time. I think Hera, the Goddess of Childbirth, helped her squeeze out one monster more, but now it's over. Echidna's womb is truly barren."

"That sounds like Athena's wisdom talking," Odysseus said.

"Do you think so?"

Odysseus nodded. "I've been Athena's golden boy for ages. It takes one to know one." He swigged deeply from the wineskin. "So, what are your plans now? If Echidna has finished, Hera and Aphrodite won't find another monster to send against you."

"I still have to leave," Paris said. "People died because I was here. And this pack of heroes will soon go home—they've had their victory moment in the sun. If they stick around, they'll only start picking fights with each other, and Hector will kick them out."

"I can believe that," Odysseus agreed. "So, where will you go?"

"I have no idea. Even without any monsters left, Hera and

Aphrodite will try again. A plague, perhaps. A swarm of rats. I'll have to go on the run."

Odysseus handed Paris the wineskin. "I've got a ship."

THEY DEPARTED TWO DAYS LATER: Odysseus at the helm and Penelope charting the course. "My husband's a terrible navigator," Penelope told Paris. "If we had to rely on him, it would take us years to get anywhere."

But with Penelope handling the maps, they'd never get lost. She let Paris choose where to go . . . and after discussing the world's many wonders, he decided to head for Egypt. "The pyramids and the sphinx really are amazing," Odysseus told him. "And there's quite a pleasant Greek community in Rhakotis at the mouth of the Nile. You never know who you'll run into."

They ran into Helen.

DESPITE WHAT HER HUSBAND CLAIMED, Helen was still quite handsome at sixty. Then again, Helen's beauty had never been purely physical. Many women have clear complexions, expressive eyes, and well-built figures, but a woman needs more to deserve being called "the most beautiful in the world." She needs grace, kindness, intelligence, and the unrestrained bloom of life. Most of all, she needs spirit . . . and even though Helen's beast of a husband had done his best to extinguish her light, she still had spirit enough to shine like the blazing Egyptian sun.

Odysseus and Helen had known each other when they were younger. Way back then, Helen wasn't just a beauty, she was heir to the throne of Sparta; the man she married would become the city's next king. So, when Helen came of age, a host of suitors came begging to win the princess's hand. Young Odysseus was sent by his father to do his best to woo the girl . . . but Odysseus hadn't tried because he already loved Penelope.

Helen had always liked him for not treating her like some prize. Of all the young nobles thronging the streets of Sparta, Odysseus was the only one who didn't disturb Helen's sleep by throwing jewellery or poems through her window.

So, when Helen and Odysseus met in Rhakotis, they greeted each other warmly—old friends from old times. Helen invited Odysseus and those who travelled with him to visit her at her house and stay as long as they wanted.

AFTER ODYSSEUS and Penelope went to bed, Paris took a midnight stroll around Helen's estate. The grounds were impressive. During her marriage, Helen had managed the city of Sparta with skill and prudence, while her husband spent all his time on pointless wars. Helen made friends with merchants and traders; without telling Menelaus, she invested in various businesses. By the time she left her husband, Helen was a very wealthy woman. Her property in Rhakotis included orchards, gardens, a stable of spirited horses . . . and a combat training ground.

Paris heard the noise of swordplay while he was still some distance off. He knew the sounds well: a bronze blade slamming into a shield, then into armour, then into a block of solid wood. Someone was striking a wooden practice dummy.

Paris followed the sounds of training and discovered what he'd expected: Helen holding a short-sword and slashing a mannequin armoured in bronze. He'd heard that the girls of Sparta were taught to fight as adeptly as boys. Apparently, too, they never stopped training—not even when they were grandmothers.

Helen stopped striking the dummy. "I know you're out there," she said. "For someone just walking, you make a lot of noise."

Paris chuckled. "I thought it best not to sneak up on someone with a sword. Although I thought Spartans preferred spears."

"I've already finished spear practice." Helen took off her helmet and shook out her sweat-damp grey hair. "What about Trojans?" she asked. "Swords or spears?"

"Usually spears, except royal princes," Paris replied. "We princes prefer swords because you can cover the hilts with jewels."

"Ah, yes," Helen said with a laugh. "Nothing improves your fighting like diamonds jabbing into your palm." She rolled her shoulders to stretch out the kinks, then leaned back against the dummy. "I've heard Troy hasn't gone to war in ages. Have you ever been in a real battle?"

"Just once," Paris said. "And you?"

"Never. A Spartan queen must look like she can fight an army. But Spartan kings make sure that never happens."

"They're afraid you'd show them up." Paris crossed the gravelled training ground and approached a weapon rack. "What about sparring for practice with wooden swords? Do Spartan queens do that?"

Helen smiled. "Spartan queens do lots of things. We can start with a bit of sparring."

<hr>

PARIS'S WIFE Oenone had died of a fever ten years earlier. He'd never found anyone to replace her . . . until that night.

Paris, Helen, Odysseus, and Penelope travelled south along the Nile. Soon enough, Paris caught a glimpse of crocodiles in the river. When Helen saw him watching them, she said, "Don't get ideas about slaying any more monsters. Crocodiles are sacred to the god Sobek; you have enough gods mad at you already."

Paris thought for a moment, then asked, "How well do Egyptian gods get along with Olympus?"

"Some respect each other, some don't," Helen replied. "But there's a story that most Greek gods were forced to stay in Egypt a while. The titan Typhon attacked Olympus, so all the gods except Zeus had to flee. The Greek and Egyptian pantheons lived together while Zeus battled Typhon. After a thousand days and nights, Zeus won the fight, and the Olympians finally got to go home."

"Still," Paris said, "that means that Hera and Aphrodite may have friends among the Egyptians."

"It's possible," Helen agreed.

Paris and Odysseus exchanged glances. That night, they talked until dawn—Paris wise, Odysseus cunning—making plans for what they suspected would happen next.

Days later, they reached Giza. They camped by the Nile and took their time exploring the pyramids, large and small, as well as the sphinx. Luckily, this sphinx was just a huge construction of stone, not a living monster. Paris worried the goddesses who hated him might bring the sphinx to life, but it didn't happen. Perhaps they no longer had enough power to do so.

But when the group returned to their camp just before nightfall, they noticed far too many crocodiles in the river. Penelope made a face and told her husband, "You were right."

Helen said, "I'm disappointed. I'm not surprised when *gods* are predictable, but I expected more from *goddesses*."

Paris and Odysseus just smiled smugly.

***

THE CROCODILES ATTACKED AT MIDNIGHT. They slid from the river and waddled in slow silence toward the camp. But halfway to their target, they discovered a dead horse lying on the sand. Its bloody meat was fresh and tempting. Despite being led by a god's divine will, the crocodiles were normal animals; none could resist taking a bite as they passed.

By the time they reached the camp, the fast-acting poison in the horse meat was taking effect. Few of the crocs had swallowed enough to kill them outright, but all were disoriented and slow. They were easy prey for humans rushing out of the darkness with spears in their hands.

When the massacre was over, Odysseus said, "I've always liked booby-trapped horses."

"Well, I don't," Penelope said, wiping her spear off. "I feel ashamed. It's disgraceful to slaughter a horde of debilitated animals."

"I imagined my first real fight would be more heroic," Helen agreed. "On the other hand, I've lived in Egypt long enough to know what crocs can do. If they hadn't been drugged, they'd have ripped us to shreds."

"Even so," said Paris, "this has to stop. I don't want to spend the rest of my life killing innocent animals."

"What can we do against goddesses?" Odysseus asked. "Not even Heracles could defeat a deity."

"I'm not trying to defeat them," Paris said. "I just want to talk. Work out a truce."

Odysseus rolled his eyes. "You may be wise, Paris, but you're also boring."

"Rhakotis has a temple to Aphrodite," Helen said. "Maybe there's one for Hera too, but I've never bothered to look—it's been a long time since I cared about marriage or childbirth."

"I've tried their temples," Paris said. "The moment I gave Athena the golden apple, I made huge offerings to both Aphrodite and Hera. But it didn't help, did it? I need to talk with them directly."

"Could Athena set something up?" Helen asked.

"They hate Athena more than they hate me," Paris told her. "They'd never do anything she asked."

Penelope looked at Odysseus. "Would Circe know how to talk with goddesses?"

"Who's Circe?" Helen asked.

"A witch," Odysseus said. "Half-goddess herself. We've known her for years—we got shipwrecked on her island, but she and Penelope hit it off."

Penelope patted her husband's arm. "You're lucky you had me along."

Odysseus told Paris, "Circe might be able to help. Can't hurt to ask."

THEY HURRIED NORTH AGAIN, keeping well away from the Nile. When they reached Rhakotis, all four boarded Odysseus's ship—Helen said she wouldn't miss this for the world.

"It's been dull," she told Paris.

"It has," he agreed. They held hands.

WITH PENELOPE CHARTING THE COURSE, they reached Circe's island in less than a week. The witch was happy to see them: "It's nice that I still have friends."

Circe, too, had grey in her hair, even though she was half-divine. *The old world is winding down*, Paris thought. But was that thought Athena's wisdom, or just a projected reflection of his aging self?

When Paris told Circe why they'd come, she said she knew a way to call deities to Earth. "But it's dangerous," she added. "It'll make them angry."

"They're already angry," Paris said. "Can you summon them, please? It's time this was over."

PARIS WOULDN'T LET Penelope or Odysseus attend the summoning. If the goddesses got violent, he didn't want his friends getting hurt. He tried to prevent Helen from attending as well, but she said, "It's so cute that you think I'd listen."

The rite took place at midnight. Herbs were burned and animals sacrificed. Circe danced and chanted for hours . . . until, abruptly, the goddesses appeared: not only Hera and Aphrodite but Athena too.

Oddly enough, it was the first time Paris had seen them. When he was supposed to judge their beauty, none of the three had bothered to talk to him in person. They'd just sent talking birds to offer their bribes: a peacock for Hera, an owl for Athena, a dove for Aphrodite.

But now, Paris could see them all in the flesh: three women who looked no younger than Paris himself. As with Helen, all three women must have been glorious beauties in their youth . . . and as with Helen, they still retained much of their appeal. But the goddesses looked tired, and two of them were furious.

Aphrodite glared at Paris and put up her fists. "You are *so* going to get it."

He stared at her in amazement. "You're going to punch me?"

"You bet!" Aphrodite said. "Ares has taught me a ton of tricks."

"Use a knife, dear," Hera told her, handing Aphrodite a dagger.

Helen struggled not to laugh. Athena met Paris's eyes and merely shrugged.

Paris didn't have a weapon himself. He'd wanted a peaceful parley; coming armed had seemed unwise. Still, Paris had received Athena's gift of skill in war. He thought he could knock the knife from the goddess's hand without much effort.

Instead of that, he knelt before her. He said, "Go ahead, if this is what you want."

"It absolutely is!" Aphrodite said. "You really hurt my feelings!"

"I'm sorry," Paris said.

"Well, I'm not hurt in the least," said Hera. "But I have to protect my reputation. I'm Queen of Olympus. I can't allow disrespect."

"I'm sorry," Paris repeated. He kept his head bent.

"Well, you *should* be sorry!" Aphrodite said. "I'm the Goddess of Beauty. How do you think I feel, being beaten by a Goddess of Owls?"

"Goddess of Wisdom," Athena muttered. "And war. And hand-made fabrics."

"I'm prepared to accept your punishment," Paris said to Aphrodite.

"Fine!" Aphrodite looked triumphant. Then she asked him, "What's a good punishment?"

Paris looked at Helen. Then back to Aphrodite. "What about this: I shall never again feel the burning inferno of love. Perhaps I might feel fondness . . . affectionate warmth . . . rapport and friendship. But not delirious passion. That's right out."

He glanced at Helen. She was smiling. She gave a nod.

Aphrodite said, "Hah! That works. You're totally cut off!"

"And your punishment, Lady Hera?" Paris asked.

Hera was looking back and forth between Paris and Helen. She put on a careful expression. "Well, I'm the Goddess of Marriage and Childbirth, aren't I? So, you horrible, wicked man, I sentence you to never getting married again and never fathering another child."

Paris glanced at Helen. Helen said, "A horrendous curse. But I suppose we'll have to live with it."

"Thank you, Lady Hera," Paris said.

"I'm getting soft in my old age," Hera said with a grimace. "But I'm sick of being the bad guy in damned near every story. If this is my final myth, let me go out not looking like a bitch."

Circe said, "You all want to come back to my place? I've got a bunch of amphoras of wine I picked up on Crete."

"Wine!" said Aphrodite. "Oh, yes, please!"

THIS STORY STARTED WITH A PARTY. It ends with a party, too—the last time a god or goddess was seen on Earth. Afterward, Olympus withdrew; the Age of Legends ended. If the gods still live, their lives are only twilight.

As for mortals, none of us lives happily ever after. Paris and Helen and the others . . . they lived, grew old, and eventually died.

But they lived. That's still something.

Tho' much is taken, much abides; and tho'
We are not now that strength which in old days
Moved earth and heaven, that which we are, we are.

—From *Ulysses* by Alfred, Lord Tennyson

THE CHTHONIC OP

By Tim Pratt

I slithered out from under a pile of split garbage bags into an early morning alleyway. The last thing I remembered was the cool sheets of a room in the Palace Hotel, paid up for the night by a dead man who wouldn't be causing any more trouble, and settling down to sleep with a bellyful of my victim's room service. I never woke up in the same place where I went to sleep anymore.

Rats scurried away from me when I rose, which seemed about right. I kicked trash away with my black wingtips, the ones with the intricate stitching around the toes that make mortal eyes water if they look at the designs too closely. The shoes had a little more heel than they had last time. I groaned from the usual aches of instantiation and patted my trench coat. I had tools in my pockets, so this was a work day. No surprise there. I found my phone—a new model, how about that—and squinted at the screen. Assuming the date was right, I'd been down for almost two years, and hadn't suffered a single nightmare. The Husk must have been happy with my last job. Even I had to catch a lucky break sometime.

There was graffiti on the wall, luminous yellow, so bright the letters seemed to float an inch above the bricks: "Café Tuzan, 8 a.m., blue hair." The map on the phone told me the café was several blocks and fifteen minutes away. Just enough time. The letters on the wall faded as I strolled out of the alley. I checked my pockets more carefully, hoping to get some sense of the job—if it was all stilettos and garrotes, that told me one thing; if it was skeleton keys and chloroform, that told me something else—but I had a little bit of everything this time, which suggested the Husk didn't know the exact nature of the job, or that the parameters were highly variable. I decided to be flattered by the idea that I could handle anything the world threw at me, rather than offended that I might be considered disposable if the problem proved beyond my capabilities.

I walked through an East Bay neighbourhood that was only partway gentrified. It was like seeing a werewolf stuck halfway through its transformation: a check-cashing place a block away from a high-end lighting store, a cavern of a dive bar next to new-construction condos, an antique shop next to a junk shop (the difference was all in the window displays and the price tags). I checked myself out, using a plate-glass window for a mirror, and in addition to the shoes and black trench coat, I had a dark-grey suit, tailored to nip in nicely at my waist. My face was on the young side, with expressive eyebrows and a judgmental set to the lips. My hair was blonde, shoulder-length, wavy, and was going to get in my way later—I'd have to find an elastic band. I had a whole Ingrid-Bergman-meets-Veronica-Lake thing going, really; I was trim and athletic but only about five-foot-two, so I hoped I wouldn't be expected to loom over anyone. Overall I looked like somebody's gender-flipped fanfic of a film noir private eye, minus the beat-up fedora. I'd looked worse.

Café Tuzan was on a corner next to a new-looking wood-oven pizza place and an upscale sex-toy shop, but opposite a dingy body shop and a convenience store with dusty windows. The café itself could have belonged either to the neighbourhood's past or its future —probably a longtime fixture with updated signage and some new furniture, trying to ride the wave of change. Good luck. Time rolls over everybody eventually. I was pretty sure even *I* wasn't eternal.

Most of the tables were taken, some by crusty old-timers with actually-on-paper-newspapers, others by younger people tapping on laptops or tablets or gazing into their phones like they were hypnotic oracles. When I read "blue hair," I'd expected an old lady with a bad blue rinse, but I should have remembered how hair-style fashions had moved on. The only hair in the café that matched the description belonged to a woman who was maybe twenty-five, with a bright-blue undercut and eyes to match. She had a sharp face and dark eye makeup and little silver goat's-head earrings and a pentagram necklace and black nail polish, and *that* didn't make any sense. The Husk didn't typically send me into the service of amateurs with bad dress sense.

But a job's a job, so I sat across from her and waited. She leaned forward and said, "Are you . . . the Tonic Op?"

I didn't laugh in her face because I am a professional. "Chthonic," I said. Sure, it's not a word people use a lot these days, but the ones who are capable of contacting the Husk usually know how to pronounce what they're asking for.

She blushed. "Right, sorry, I . . . I guess I wasn't expecting a woman."

"I never know what to expect myself." I was trying to be

blandly non-threatening, but since I'm neither, it didn't work too well. She was bearing up better in my presence than most humans do, though. Being near me tends to make their back teeth ache and headaches blossom between their eyes, and most of them shuffle away without even thinking about it.

She fidgeted with a cup of espresso. "Right. Do you know, ah . . . why you're here?"

"The Husk didn't brief me, I'm afraid."

"Who?"

"You might know him by another name. My supervisor." The Husk used to be a person, I think—in fact, I think he used to be *me*, or at least perform my role, before something hollowed him out, and everything human was tossed on the fire, leaving behind a shell that talks and schemes and amuses itself.

"Oh. Right. That voice, the one that came from the hearth . . . it was a little . . . husky, now that you mention it." She tried out a tentative smile on me, and I rewarded it by giving her a bigger one in return. Most people can't manage even bad wordplay in my presence. She was tougher than she looked, though I still couldn't figure how she'd managed to call the Husk, let alone commission my services.

"How can I help you, Ms . . . ?"

"Oh! I'm Gabi, Gabi Addison. My problem is a little hard to explain, but . . . a family heirloom was stolen from me, and I need you to bring it back. It's an antique chalice."

"Really?" I'd traced stolen property before, but they were usually artifacts of power, not old cups. "And you called for me? Seems like something a more . . . mundane operative could handle."

"The thing is, my great-uncle Hubert is the one who stole it."

I leaned back. "This sounds like a family squabble. Even more outside my usual purview."

"Well, the other thing is, I *inherited* the chalice from Uncle Hubert." Gabi rolled the empty espresso cup back and forth between her hands. "Last week. When he died. And then, last night . . . he came back. His ghost stole the chalice."

Ah. There we go.

"DEFINITELY AN INSIDE JOB." I walked around the secret vault beneath her grand inherited house and considered the many locked cabinets and the one broken one. "The thief popped open the one cabinet they wanted and ignored the rest, which means they knew what they were looking for."

She didn't get what I was driving at. "Well, yes, this was Uncle Hubert's house before it was mine. We've lived here together since I was a girl, after my parents died. This vault was his—naturally, he knew where the chalice was kept."

I shook my head. "A ghost didn't do this. Ghosts aren't very good at picking things up and carrying them off. They can just about manage to fling a plate across the room or slam a door if they're mad enough. The more coherent phantoms can sometimes possess people and use their bodies, but then they lose the ability to pass through walls. If this vault of yours was secured like you said, with a blood-lock as well as a passphrase, then possession wouldn't work, either."

"So, it's a locked-room mystery, then?" She sounded more amused than annoyed. Gabi was a lot less nervous now that we were on her home turf. Addison House was tucked away in the hills, with views of the bay and the bridges and San Francisco, but this room was below ground and windowless. My sight isn't like other people's, and I could see all the nasty threads of magic meant to keep strangers out, hidden in the floor and ceiling and walls. At least now I had some idea how Gabi had gotten in touch with the Husk. Her family was clearly an old and powerful one, and there were all sorts of conduits and connections and artifacts here that even an amateur could fumble their way through.

"Your uncle Hubert didn't tell you what the chalice does?" I asked, ignoring her question.

She shrugged. "He never wanted to teach me anything. After my parents died in the ... accident ... he was the only family I had left, and he took me in. He said it was dangerous to leave unprotected Addison blood loose in the world. I gradually realized what my family was—the sort of work they did and the way they secured their wealth—but figuring out what that meant or how to make use of it was a different story. I don't know what most of the things locked away in here are for. But the cup must be important if my uncle defied death to take it."

I grunted. "That's the other thing. People like your uncle don't usually get to be ghosts. They live long and pleasant lives by running up debt on a sort of cosmic credit card, and when they die? That's when the bill comes due. His soul should be in the care of my employers by now." I considered. "You actually saw him take the cup?

She nodded, goat's-head earrings swaying. "I heard a commotion and came downstairs to find Uncle Hubert fleeing through the front door, carrying *something*. It was definitely him—he was wearing his funeral robes, the ones with all the little eyes around the hem. I was so startled, I didn't think to chase him, and he got away. Then I checked the vault, and the inventory list told me the chalice was the only item missing."

I made a note to look at that list later. For now, I just slashed out with Occam's Razor. "Are you certain he's *really* dead? There are drugs and other techniques that can simulate death temporarily."

She widened her eyes. "Of course I am! His heart gave out. He was *embalmed*, and we had a memorial service. There's no doubt."

Oh, well. "Was he cremated or buried?"

"Neither," she said. "He was immured in the family crypt."

"I'm guessing that's on the property somewhere? We should take a look."

THE GROUNDS of Addison House were more expansive than they should have been, based on the available geography. There are entities who distort space for purposes of torment, forcing their victims to wander endless forests, or extending hallways and basements into infinite realms, or sending the poor suckers back to the entrance when they finally pass through an exit. Those same beings can be persuaded to expand space in beneficial ways for those who make the proper arrangements. I assumed that was how the Addisons had the equivalent of an English country estate in the Oakland hills. We walked through a formal garden that was going to seed, then through a poison garden (gated, and much better tended), then along a meandering path through a copse of non-native plants, and finally reached a little chapel.

From Gabi's goat's heads and pentagrams, I'd expected one of those tedious modern churches, all inverted crosses and desecrated altars and torn-out Bible pages with obscene marginalia. Those techniques *work*—it's the intention and the will that counts, after all—but the Husk, and certainly his superiors, are a lot older than that nice Jewish carpenter everyone makes such a fuss about nowadays. I always feel a little embarrassed around the adherents who don't understand that Hell is just an aspect of a far more ancient underworld. I am an agent of the silent and the deep, the vast and the buried, the hidden and the shamed—the chasm that waits, and the dark that swallows. My kind appear in as many forms as the human mind can correlate, and all of them are illusory, and yet all of them are also *real,* for our essential nature is that of the fear of the shadowed.

So I was pleasantly surprised to find a shrine in an old style, based on that of an ancient Greek temple—in fact, their church looked like a scale model of the Necromanteion of Acheron, though the tower wasn't quite right. The statues were appropriately weathered, their features blurred into nubs. The important part of the temple must be below ground, in what would have been the chamber of Hades in the original—the ritual entrance to the underworld. As good a place as any for a family crypt.

We descended past another locked portal. This one didn't just sense the blood inside the person seeking to gain entry—Gabi had to actually cut the side of her finger and smear a drop on a particular stone and then whisper a password to it. (Of course, I heard the password clearly. Hearing whispers is one of my skills.) The wall slid open, and I followed her inside, tucking my handkerchief discreetly back into my pocket.

We went down a flight of steps and into a long hallway. Torches burst into smokeless flame as we approached, revealing niches in the walls, each holding a stone box. The corridor smelled of dust and, just faintly, formaldehyde. *Hmm.* She led me to a small circular room, where another stone box rested on a raised platform, in a place of honour. There were dead flowers on the lid and scattered on the floor around the pedestal. Gabi put a hand on the box, gazing down at it solemnly. "The head of the family is immured here until they're supplanted by the death of the next. Then we move their bones into one of the wall niches. Generations of my family rest here."

The words *Mors Omnibus Communis* were carved into the lid. Well, yeah. Everything dies. It's what comes after that this family should worry about.

"May I?" Without waiting for an answer, I pushed the lid of the stone coffin aside, revealing an empty space inside.

She gasped, and from the spike in her pulse, I judged her reaction was genuine. "He—Hubert came back to life? How?"

I took something like a jeweller's loupe from one of my coat pockets and peered into the open—what, sarcophagus? You'd think I'd know the words for all this stuff, but I usually deal with crime scenes, not gravesites. The lens showed me the residue of dark magic smeared inside the box, and I wrinkled my nose at the chemical reek as I leaned in close. I examined the magical stains—it's like doing metaphysical blood-spatter analysis—until I understood what had happened, if not why. "Not brought back to life. Hubert is a walking corpse, but not a mindless one. Technically, he's a ghost possessing a body—it's just that the body is his *own*. His soul is still hanging on, clinging to the meat and bones, even as they rot." I slid the lid closed again. "My employers don't like being cheated out of their due. We should try to figure out what that chalice is for."

BACK AT THE MAIN HOUSE, Gabi showed me the inventory of the family's occult holdings, but the manifest wasn't a lot of help. (Though there were some interesting things locked up in that vault: "Bathory Locket," "Singing Razor," "Void Tincture"—her family really *had* been in service for a long time and earned a lot of trinkets in return.) The latest entry just said "Chalice," and under "Description," the only words were "context-dependent." I knew what that meant. It's the same thing such an entry would say next to a description of *my* appearance.

"See?" Gabi said. "Even in the secret files of the secret vault, my uncle kept his secrets."

"I have another thread I can pull," I said. "I'll be back in a few minutes." I stepped outside (which required walking through several hundred yards of house, of course).

Reaching out to the home office is discouraged—I'm supposed to be an autonomous entity, and the dark powers aren't inclined to make things easy for anyone, even their own agents—but this was no longer just about retrieving a stolen object. It was about retrieving a fugitive soul. I needed to know what I was dealing with.

I took a cigar the colour of old scabs from my pocket, lit up, and puffed. Once the end of the cigar glowed like a baleful red eye, I said, "Husk, what can you tell me about this chalice? Is it some kind of . . . vampiric artifact?"

The smoke shifted around until it resembled the eyeless face of my supervisor. The voice was made of the sound of burning things. "The postulant asked for an artifact that would endow him with eternal life."

I snorted. "That's like asking the bank for a loan that never comes due." Our rulers would extend life, sometimes greatly, but only at a terrible cost of blood and sorrow—plain, uncomplicated immortality was never on the table. "What's the catch? You live on beyond death, but your body rots around you?"

"Not at all," the old creature said. "The blood of two go into the chalice. Both drink. Transference follows."

"Ah. That old gag." Immortality by body-swap—you trade your aging body for a younger model, with the displaced soul stuck in your old form, ready to get murdered, or just die of natural causes. The bosses don't mind that version of immortality because it increases misery in the world exponentially, and besides, the chain of serial possession always breaks eventually, due to mistake or misadventure, and they get to claim the original body-hijacker's soul too. My bosses are patient people, except they aren't really people. "So what? Am I talking to Hubert in Gabi's body?" That would explain some of the weirdness in our interactions. "And Gabi rose from the dead to get revenge or something?"

"You are a terrible detective," the Husk said.

"It was just a theory. What did happen, then?"

"Hubert prepared the chalice. He drank. Before his victim could drink, he died." The old creature chuckled, a sound like crushing a wasp's nest in your fist.

"But the one drink changed him," I hazarded. "Detached his soul from his body for the transfer, but then the soul got trapped inside his corpse, like a fly buzzing around inside a bottle." Interrupted rituals could have unpredictable effects. "So, what, Hubert will try to force her to drink it now, to finish the ritual?"

The Husk said, "You know we cannot see into human minds, and I am unable to guess their thoughts or motivations—I have strayed too far from what it means to be human. That is why *you* are there, Op, instantiated in a mortal body of flesh and bone, to . . . move more naturally among them. But if you are right about Hubert's intentions, such a plan would not work. Both participants must live and draw breath for the ritual to succeed."

"I don't know why Hubert didn't grab her and force her to

drink last night when he stole the thing," I mused. "Unless I'm misunderstanding his motives. Or maybe being inside a dead body has driven him insane."

The cigar went out, smoke dissipating. The Husk only has so much patience for speculation. He's a results-oriented monster.

I didn't have much patience for them, either, to be honest. I decided to track down Uncle Hubert and just *ask*.

"Do you have any idea where your dead uncle might have gone?" I asked.

Gabi pouted at me. "How could I possibly know? You're the detective."

"I'm ... not exactly that. But detectives find out stuff by asking questions, which is what I'm doing. Hubert is a ghost, albeit a weird one, and ghosts are creatures of habit—they maintain coherence by doing the things they did when they were alive. That's why so many phantoms re-enact moments from their lives and appear over and over in the same familiar locations. It helps them remember who and what they are so they don't disintegrate. Just because Hubert has a body doesn't change what he *is*. Did he have any ... forgive me ... old haunts?"

"We didn't have a lot of deep heart-to-hearts about his favourite places," she said. "I guess you could start with the places all the rich old white men around here like. I'll dig around and see if I can find any other leads."

It was a long night. I went to the San Francisco Symphony, the opera house, and many of the finest restaurants in the city, peering through my loupe for signs of necromantic residue. I stalked yachts at marinas on both sides of the bay and went to every museum on the peninsula. No luck. As dawn crept into the sky, I called Gabi from San Francisco. "There must be somewhere else," I said. "Some place Hubert had a sentimental attachment to, or—"

"I went through his study," she interrupted. "Looking for some hint of where he might have gone. I found an old photo of him with Great-Grandma and Grandpapa, wearing these ridiculous old-fashioned swimsuits, at some kind of giant swimming pool complex—I can see part of the walls and the roof; it's like a big greenhouse or something. He didn't keep any *other* photos, so I suppose it must have been a good memory."

"How old was your great-uncle?"

"He just turned eighty in June. His birthday party was *so* dull."

"I think I know the place," I said.

The Sutro Baths opened in 1896, on the western shore of San Francisco, beneath the Cliff House. The place was a wonder, for a time—seven pools, tons of steel, acres of glass, an amphitheatre, eventually an ice-skating rink, and even a hodgepodge of a museum showing artifacts collected by Adolph Sutro in his travels (including a couple of items created by my employers, though Sutro didn't know it). The baths struggled along for years, the maintenance costs always exceeding revenue, and the whole folly finally burned down in 1966. I'd visited the place when it was still in operation—I'd drowned someone in a saltwater pool after hours—and remembered it fondly. I suspected Uncle Hubert must have fond memories, too. He was old enough that he could have visited as a child.

The ocean was grey in the early morning light, and the beach there was deserted. The site of the Baths is in ruins now, just a few freestanding walls and stone outlines full of tidewater. *Mors Omnibus Communis.*

Though some things linger longer than they should. I found traces of necromantic residue and followed them through the ruins until I found Hubert sitting on a low wall, his feet in the saltwater, the hem of his eye-covered robe soaking. I cleared my throat.

"She sent you?" he rasped, without looking around at me. "I called for help, too, but . . . no answer came."

"You're dead," I said. "My employers command the dead. They don't take commands from them."

He slumped even further. "Have you come for the chalice?"

"I was hired to retrieve it, yes. I also have standing orders to collect debts owed to my employers, which means . . . you."

He turned, then. His face was smooth and waxy. The embalming was standing up well even under all his unusual exertions. Hubert reached into his robes and tossed something at my feet: a plastic cup with a jaunty cartoon palm tree printed on the side.

"That's the chalice?" I looked at it through my loupe, and the object burned with bleak magic. Hubert didn't bother to answer me. I picked up the cup, and it transformed into a crystal rocks glass in my hand. Context-dependent appearance. It shifted to suit the surroundings. Or . . . the will? I held the cup up to the sky, thinking of holy grails, and it became a golden goblet. I grunted. "Cute. It goes with everything."

"She isn't what you think she is," Hubert said. "Our Gabrielle. She *pretends*."

"Doesn't everyone? You're pretending to be alive. Though not for much longer."

He tried to run then. That part was fun. That peculiar stitching on my shoes lets me follow people without being noticed, but it also lets me *catch* them, even if they run faster than living muscles allow. They have nastier enchantments, too, including ones that let me kick his ghost right out of his corpse and into his rightful eternity.

I had the chalice. Nothing to do now but return it, as I'd been ordered to do . . . and then return to *my* rightful place.

Hell of a reward for a job well done.

I LIT a cigar on the front steps of Addison House. "Job's done," I said shortly. "Give me ten minutes to wrap things up, then you can extract me." I stubbed the cigar out without waiting for a reply and put the butt in my pocket.

Inside, I found Gabi sipping tea at one end of a dining room table long enough to land a fighter jet on. I sat down in the chair on her left.

"How did it go?" she said, blinking at me from under her long lashes.

"Successfully. But tell me. Why the little-lost-goth-girl routine?"

She looked at me, wide-eyed and baffled, for a moment, then smiled, *really* smiled, her whole face transforming. "Oh, well," she said. "My uncle taught me not to reveal my true self to denizens of Hell. I think he meant, 'Don't show weakness,' but pretending to an excess of weakness can be even more effective. I love being underestimated and having people—or things—trip over themselves to help out poor little me. It's better than the way Uncle Hubert pretended to be lord of all creation to hide how insecure he was. Besides, I like a challenge. If I could fool *you*, the legendary Chthonic Op, I could fool anyone."

"You did have me going for a minute," I admitted.

"Just a minute?" She pouted. "How did you know I wasn't as innocent as I seemed?"

I waved a hand at her. "Your look is pretty over-the-top—the pentagrams and the goat's heads, when that's obviously not the tradition you were raised in. Mostly, though . . . it's that you weren't scared of me. I tend to unsettle people unless they've marinated in the occult for a long time and had their fear receptors burned out. Also . . ." I shrugged. "Pretty much nobody is as innocent as they seem."

"Certainly nobody you're likely to meet in your line of work." She held out her hand. "The chalice, please?"

I opened the bag in my lap, showing her the glint of a golden goblet, then closed it again, amused at the naked greed on her face. "You mean this? Soon enough. Why don't you tell me what really happened with your uncle first? I'm curious, and he didn't have a chance to give me the details before I . . . sent him on his way."

"Just give me the chalice, and be on *your* way." Her impatience was starting to show, like a bit of shrapnel poking through the skin.

"Come on, Gabi. Once I'm done here, I go back to the dreaming void until my next job. Humour me. Give me a story, I give you the chalice."

Her eyes were harder now, and her mouth more cruel. "You were summoned to do a job. I believe I could . . . insist."

"What, go over my head and complain to my superiors?" It was my turn to grin. "If you like. But believe me when I say, the less the Husk pays attention to you, the better off you are."

She sighed. "Fine." She pushed her teacup aside. "There's not much to tell. I was eager to take my place as head of the family, and I didn't hide my ambitions. Uncle Hubert felt threatened by me—reasonably enough, since I threatened him—and he took steps to prevent me from gaining my rightful inheritance. He lit the bone fire in the hearth and opened a conduit to your . . . realm . . . and asked for the chalice. He didn't realize I was listening."

"He didn't check for nieces hiding behind the curtains?"

She rolled her eyes. "He didn't check for listening devices. I had his rooms and the vault wired with voice-activated recorders and motion-sensitive cameras. You can get anything on the internet these days. Hubert did regular sweeps for occult interference but never considered the mundane a threat. Old men forget how the world moves on."

"So you knew he was planning to swap bodies with you?"

"Yes." She shuddered. "The pig rooted through my trash for . . . personal items . . . to get my blood. You only need a drop or two from each person to do the ritual. You can mix the blood with water, wine, anything." Now she looked pleased with herself. Her reluctance to tell me had been artifice, too. She *wanted* to brag. What good is it being clever if no one appreciates it? "Hubert called me down to the vault and showed me the chalice—it was all glittery and jewelled then. He spun some story about how drinking from it would endow me with powers beyond imagining, playing to what he perceived as my greed. I told him I was understandably nervous, given the bad blood between us, and would appreciate seeing him sip from the chalice first to prove it wasn't poisoned. He agreed."

I nodded. "Not realizing it *was* poisoned."

"I poisoned the chalice earlier that day. A colourless, odourless layer of residue, and when he poured in the wine and stirred in the blood, he stirred in the toxin, too. My uncle died gagging and furious." She sighed. "I didn't realize drinking from the chalice would do strange things to his soul. Even when he stole the chalice, I thought he was just a ghost—when I saw his body was gone, I was terrified he'd actually returned to life and that he'd try to complete the ritual."

"He just wanted to keep it from you," I said. "If he couldn't have eternal life, nobody could."

She leaned back in her chair, languorous and self-satisfied. "But he died, and I won. I'm the head of the family now, with all the powers and privileges that entails, and when the time comes, I'll succeed in the ritual where he failed."

"Diabolical, Ms. Addison. And now that I'm off duty, I can have a drink." I reached into my trench coat and unscrewed a gleaming silver flask. "Here's to the new head of the family." I took a deep pull, wiped my mouth, and offered her the flask.

She looked at me with a wrinkle of disgust, then shrugged. She had good manners, at least. She took the flask and sipped. Her expression said she didn't like the taste. "What is that, bourbon?"

"Rye. Very old rye. I've been carrying it around for ages. I poured it out of my old flask, actually." I took a second, far more battered metal container from my pocket and set it on the table.

She stared at my old flask, then down at the beautiful silver item in her hand, then back up at me. "What's going on?"

I took the golden goblet from the bag in my lap and put it on the table. "I picked this up from a street vendor on my way over. Not real gold, or even gold plate, but the world is full of good imitations these days."

The beautiful silver flask began to shift, transforming into a crystal wine glass, a bit of blood and rye still clinging to the bottom. "No. This can't . . . How did you even get my blood?"

"You smeared that all over the temple wall. I just dabbed a bit up with my handkerchief. I figured I could use it to get into the vault or temple without you if I needed to later, but then I found an even better use."

She hurled her cup at the wall, smashing it, and snarled at me. "You're a servant, you're *bound*, you have to obey me!"

"'A family heirloom was stolen from me, and I need you to bring it back,'" I quoted. "That was my mission, and that is what I've done. It's just not *all* I've done. You have to be very specific when dealing with creatures like me." Now I leaned back in satisfaction. "Maybe I didn't underestimate you after all, Ms. Addison. Maybe I estimated you accurately."

"No." She was stubborn to the last. "You're a fool. It won't work. You're not even human, you're some kind of demon—"

"I used to be a mortal," I said. "And this body is flesh and blood, entirely human, even if it was instantiated instead of born." I closed my eyes for a moment, feeling a shimmer inside. "Mmm. It's coming on."

"They'll know! Your masters will realize I'm not *you*!" She stuck her fingers down her throat and then vomited onto the table, which was halfway clever, but pointless. The ritual was done.

"You're going into storage." I experienced a moment of blurred doubling, and then my mouth tasted horrible, and my voice sounded strange. Transference complete. I was looking across the table at my old body, and it looked horrified. "The Husk will thaw you out again eventually, in a year or two or ten, and realize what I did, and dispatch someone to retrieve me, and that will be awful . . . but in the meantime, oh, the *fun* I'll have. Everything dies, so you might as well live it up while you can."

She lunged for me, her hands twisted into claws. It was a good thing she didn't know how to use any of the stuff in my trench coat pockets—she could have done some real damage. As it was, she actually got her hands around my throat and started squeezing before she began to unravel. I stood up from my chair and watched her new body disintegrate into its component parts and then into slurry. The eyes went last. I popped one of them under my heel.

Then I took a deep breath of free air into my stolen lungs and set out to enjoy an unchained world.

THE LITTLE TAILOR AND THE ELVES

By Barbara Hambly

For as long as anybody could remember, Levitsky's Tailor Shop had been in business in the basement of 113 West 34th Street. Solly Levitsky had opened the place in 1941, building it up from pressing pants and doing alterations; by the time his son, Irv, took over in the late sixties, it had expanded into the main floor of the building and included a dry-cleaning establishment as well. Irv's work was excellent, and everyone in the neighbourhood thought very well of him.

Unlike his father, who was big for a Polish Jew—six feet one and built like a refrigerator—Irv, stocky and powerful, barely topped five three, though he wore builtup shoes and invariably claimed five five. Maybe his size had something to do with his temper, and his determination to be twice the tailor his father had been, no easy feat, considering his father's expertise. "It's great, it's great," the Italian businessmen would say, who'd been coming into the shop for years to have their suits made, standing in front of the big three-way mirrors under the fluorescent lighting that made even the dim back rooms of the basement as clear and flawless as day. And, in Irv's opinion, it *was* great: the perfect hang of the iron-gray wool, forty dollars a yard with a hand to it like silk, the precise shaping of the shoulders over just sufficient padding to smooth away the annoying little variations to which mortal flesh is heir—it was a suit you couldn't buy off the rack no matter how much you spent.

But always, as Irv was tucking the final payment cheque into the drawer of the electronic till that had replaced that old cast-iron clunker his father had kept in the shop till the day he retired, he'd overhear them as they went out the front door and up the half-dozen chipped cement steps to where their limos were double-parked in traffic: "You think this is good, Vinnie? You should have seen the one his old man made me back in '58. Now, that was a suit that sang."

And Irv would go upstairs in a bitter temper and slap his wife.

"She's a perfectly lovely girl, Irving." Iris Levitsky put her head down on the kitchen table again, trying to will away the familiar clammy sensation she got in the pit of her stomach at the sound of her mother-in-law's voice. "But would you just tell her what I said about newspapers being best for cleaning windows? Newspapers and ammonia, and never mind all this fancy-schmancy stuff they peddle over the TV. Newspapers and ammonia and good old-fashioned elbow grease." In the front hall, the coat-cupboard door creaked; above the brimming kitchen sink, the tangerine and avocado cotton curtains shifted with the night wind and the sounds of *M*A*S*H* on the neighbours' TV set.

Iris closed her eyes with wretchedness, knowing what was coming next.

"Iris . . . !" She flinched at the singsong whine of anger in her husband's voice.

She raised her head. He was standing in the kitchen doorway in his shirtsleeves with his tie loosened, hands on his hips. People always said he was a short little man, but Iris was tinier yet—her head just cleared the top of his shoulder—and the angry bunch of those heavy black eyebrows filled her with panic.

"I got to tell you, Iris, you embarrassed the hell out of me tonight in front of my folks! What the hell you do around here all day, sit around eating bonbons?" He gestured furiously towards the avocado-green plates that couldn't fit into the sink, lined up like a Manet painting on the harvest-gold Formica of the counter. "I mean, it's eight-thirty, for Chrissake, and them dishes are still dirty! It's not like you gotta go out and work or anything!"

Iris heartily wished she could go out and work or something. She'd been far happier when she'd only been the store's accountant instead of the owner's wife. But she could only whisper, "I'm sorry, honey."

"Yeah, well, I'm sorry, too!" His voice rose, and Iris shrank further back against the table. The first time he'd struck her—the week after they'd come back from their honeymoon—he'd been miserably repentant for days, and it had been nearly six months before he'd slapped her again. Lately, he'd quit going through the formality of saying, "I don't know what got into me." Whatever it was, it had got into him fairly often in the seven years of their marriage so far.

"I'm sorry I'm the one who's gotta be at the store six days a week until seven o'clock at night making sure them *schwartze* girls upstairs ain't robbing the place blind and leaving spots on the customers' clothes, making enough money to have a nice house, a good car, a decent living for you and Melissa, and that I gotta come home after all that and find the dishes ain't done, the house is a pigsty, my daughter's running around with dirt on her face like some wop brat and you sittin' on your can reading a goddamn newspaper!"

He turned furiously away and got a beer from the refrigerator. "I'm gonna be watching TV. And for God's sake, take some time out from whatever the hell you do all day and wash the goddamn windows! I can see the dirt from here!"

His words weren't necessary. Iris had already resolved to turn over a new leaf and wash the windows tomorrow—surely she'd have time between picking Melissa up from school and taking her to her dance lessons . . .

But as she plunged her arms into the froth of suds, Iris recalled that she'd promised to take old Mrs. Callahan to the clinic tomorrow.

For a moment, she wondered whether she ought to call the old lady and cancel, but Jessie Callahan was over eighty, still living alone in her own little house with her four dogs, and the bus ride to the clinic would be hard on her. A guilty glance at the clock showed Iris that it was nearly nine, and Melissa still to bathe and be told her story . . .

Tears of frustration crept down her cheeks as she piled the silverware into the rack to dry. It would leave spots, but those could be wiped off before she put them away, if she had time. Mama Levitsky had also commented on the dirty grout in the bathroom tiles.

Well, maybe tomorrow there'd be time to wash a few windows before picking Melissa up . . .

She dashed a handful of cold water over her eyes, so that

Melissa wouldn't see she'd been crying, as she went to get her daughter a bath.

At the clinic the next day, Jessie Callahan shook her head over Iris's shaky-voiced account of her own failings and her husband's justified anger. "I know I should be better," Iris admitted, looking straight ahead at the harassed Medicare staffers because she knew if she looked at her friend, she'd burst into tears again. "I mean, Irv's mother keeps their house spotless, and she's more than forty years older than I am. But with Melissa, and doing the accounts for the store, I just . . . I just *can't!*"

A small black child, who'd been there with her parents when Jessie and Iris had arrived nearly an hour and a half ago and still hadn't been seen, pelted noisily by. Iris fished in her purse for the package of butterscotch Lifesavers she always carried for Melissa and gave the child one, guessing that the little girl hadn't had any lunch.

"Now, honey," said Jessie Callahan in her soft voice, "there are worse things in the world than a little dirt, and turning your brain into a mushroom and your soul into mould by spending the whole day cleaning property is one of them. Don't worry about it. These things all work out."

Queerly enough, when Iris got home—far later than she'd thought she would, for the clinic had been jammed, and Jessie had had to wait nearly three hours to be seen—she found that she must have dried the silverware after all. The silverware basket and dish drainer were not only empty but hung neatly on their hooks on the inside of the broom-closet door; the dishes were stacked, gleaming, in the cupboard; the silverware grinned brightly at her when she opened the drawer. Behind the tangerine-and-avocado-pattern curtains—and surely the curtains looked cleaner and crisper than Iris remembered them yesterday—the windows sparkled, too.

I must have been tireder than I thought, Iris reflected, *if I don't even remember putting the silverware and dishes away.* She had easily enough time to do the very small amount of laundry which needed doing, and iron Irv's shirts and the fresh tablecloth and napkins Irv always insisted upon, before it was time to put dinner on.

That was the first time it happened and the last time Irv had genuine cause for complaint about her housekeeping.

IT DIDN'T HAPPEN with tremendous frequency after that, at first. But it happened often enough. After the fourth or fifth time that Iris found some particularly daunting piece of housework done— the kitchen floor stripped and rewaxed just before another of Mama Levitsky's unscheduled drop-in visits—Iris started keeping track. It troubled her; she began to wonder if she was developing multiple personalities or having housework blackouts, and she took to running time-and-motion studies on herself until it occurred to her that even if she were doing the housework uncon- scious, that was far preferable to being aware of each mind- numbing chore.

Mama Levitsky still picked holes, of course, and Irv still shouted and threatened, but it seemed to Iris that they had to look harder for faults to find. She continued to drive Jessie to the local Senior Center and the Adult Literacy Resource Center where they both did volunteer teaching, and, weirdly enough, the housework continued to get done.

It was only when Melissa spoke about seeing "little men" that Iris became truly worried and spoke to Jessie about it.

"Ah, I thought that's what might be happening." The old lady smiled. "It's the elves."

"*What?*" Iris stared at her. She'd gone over to cook Jessie some lunch and play cards with her—since Jessie's stroke in the spring of '77, the old lady could barely get around—and they were sitting together in Jessie's neat white kitchen.

Jessie raised her snowy brows. "The elves," she said. "They've been around me as long as I can remember. They did things for Mother, too—Mother cleaned houses out here in Long Island, and there were eleven of us back home, and only me to raise and look after the little ones. But Mother was never too tired to help out her friends or take care of those in the neighbourhood who couldn't take care of themselves. She'd always say that chores like this had a way of getting done. I first saw the elves when I wasn't much older than Melissa . . ."

She nodded toward the little girl, happily tossing a Wiffle ball for the dogs to chase across the neat handkerchief of lawn outside.

"Only glimpses of them I'd get, out the corners of my eyes, usually in the winter, when it got so early dark. It seemed to me then they were three or four little brownfaced men dressed in cobwebs, with long ears like dogs, but that might have been something I made up later or something I read in a book."

She sighed, and shook her head, and reached tremblingly for a spoon to eat the scrambled eggs Iris had made her, but seemed to find it too much effort and put it down again. Iris worried that as she grew feebler, Jessie would be unable to keep the house at all, but so far, it hadn't happened, and she dreaded the day when the old lady would be taken to some kind of state institution because she could no longer look after herself, as much for Jessie's sake as for how badly she'd miss the old lady's company.

"Mother used to say they weren't good folk," Jessie murmured, her arthritic fingers stirring at the spoon—a tiny coffee spoon, with a decorative cartouche at the top saying PERTH—WESTERN AUSTRALIA on it. "Neither good nor evil, she said, but rather like children that never had no mother: queer and selfish and cunning. But leave them out food, in the shop or in the house, and don't put no cold iron above the doors, and they'll be your friends. And that's what I used to do."

"Leave them food?" asked Iris, seeing Jessie's mind begin to drift. "Like some kids leave cookies for Santa on Christmas Eve?"

"Of course, for what's Santa Claus but the memory of some other helping spirit? But these . . . They aren't good folk, having no souls, but they see good in humans and are drawn to it, like cold children to a flame. As they were drawn to Mother." All that complicated erosion-map of facial lines crumpled and changed with her smile.

"And do you know," she went on, "somehow all the dishes did get done at our house, and the food did get cooked, and none of my brothers and sisters ever went dirty, and Mother managed to keep those rich folks' houses spotless, too, be there ever so many of them. I never was afraid of the elves, and I'd bake cookies to leave out for them, but Mother never did let any of us alone in the dark if she could help it. I still leave them cookies, time to time. There's not much to do around this place, now I'm too old to mess it up much. I'm glad they've found somebody else to help. They don't like to be idle."

Iris wasn't sure just what to say to that. Jessie was very old, and her mind wandered, but the fact remained that things got done that Iris didn't remember doing, and Mama Levitsky had less and less cause to complain. That didn't stop her from complaining, of course. In fact, she seemed to complain more. Even after Solly and his wife retired to Miami in 1978, Iris's husband continued to find fault with everything his wife did or didn't do.

A number of things happened in 1978. A big, glossy tailoring and alterations establishment opened on West 35th Street, utilizing, Irv swore nightly in gusts of bourbon, cheap Vietnamese labour who'd work for fifty cents an hour up in the attics. Moreover, fewer businessmen were buying bespoke suits, preferring instead to frequent the high-end designer stores like Neiman-Marcus and I. Magnin. He found himself doing more alterations work and less tailoring as such, and most of the money came in from the dry-cleaning establishment upstairs.

That was the year Iris went back to work. In addition to doing the books—which she'd always done, having been hired for the purpose just out of high school—Irv put her in charge of the dry-cleaning side of the operation. "That way, I can fire those stupid girls who can't do a decent job anyway," he groused, pacing around the kitchen, beer can in hand, while Iris and Melissa stood silent beside the sink where they'd been washing dishes when he'd come in. "Filthy broads, anyway, always off in the back combing their hair or drinking Cokes—Cokes! I caught one of them actually leaving a wet ring on the counter, where customers' clothes go!"

"Did they get Coke on a garment?" asked Iris, shocked. She'd been in the store and knew the girls were pretty conscientious about wiping up crumbs and spills from lunch. Surely, they couldn't have deteriorated that much in a few weeks.

"That ain't the point, stupid!" yelled Irv, losing his temper, and at the sound of his voice, Melissa edged a little closer to Iris's leg. Iris had told Melissa she'd gotten her current black eye from running into a door; she didn't know whether the little girl believed her or not. She always kept a close eye on Melissa and didn't think Irv had ever done more than yell at his daughter, but since business had been steadily worsening, Irv had taken to drinking more beers in front of the TV set evenings and weekends. He'd taken to coming home later in the evenings, too, and by the smell of his breath, the hour or so in between he was spending in the Seventh Avenue Grill.

"The point is them stupid *nafkas* is careless around the customers' clothes! They eat their goddamn greasy hamburgers there, probably on the folding table if I know anything about *schwartzes*! No wonder the place got roaches!"

Iris knew better than to point out that any establishment in Manhattan had roaches, particularly one situated between a Mexican restaurant and a grocery store.

"I shoulda figured you wouldn't know the difference if the store was clean or dirty! God knows what's gonna happen to my reputation—to Dad's reputation—with you in charge there!"

"Melissa," said Iris gently, recognizing the signs of a full-fledged storm brewing, "why don't you go upstairs and run your bath? I'll finish up here."

"The hell she will!" bellowed Irv in a gusty blast of Miller High Life. "You're teaching her to be just as crummy as you, running off and leaving her job halfdone so you can go fix sandwiches and sit around and bullshit with that senile old Mick! My mother was right about you! Well, I'm not gonna have no lazy slob for a daughter, even though I got one for a wife! And if I see so much as one spot, one hair, one pin out of place, I'll teach you to be clean myself, God damn it! And that goes for you, too," he added, turning savagely to his silent daughter, "when your mother's away at work, you hear?"

Nevertheless, Melissa slipped away quietly halfway through Irv's ensuing tirade. Iris remained, taking the shouts and blows in head-bowed silence, reflecting that he did have a point. She was spending a good deal of time with Jessie, now that the old lady was practically helpless. Later she went up to Melissa's room, not turning on the light because she could feel her lip puffing up— she'd have to put ice on it before going into the shop tomorrow— and found the little girl sitting up in bed in the dark.

"Don't worry about Daddy, Mommy," said Melissa softly. "The little men will help me keep house, and then he won't be mad."

Iris hugged her but reflected that it would take more than the elves' housekeeping to prevent Irv from working himself into the furies that seemed to be the only outlet for his frustration with the generally poor condition of the world, his business, and his life.

She wasn't sure at what point she came to accept the elves as a reality and rely on them for their help as matter-of-factly as Melissa did. Perhaps it was during the year which followed, when it became obvious to her that someone was helping Melissa with the housework—a seven-year-old girl couldn't possibly keep everything from the bathroom faucets to the outsides of the upstairs windows gleaming like that. And thankfully, Irv never complained about Melissa or bawled her out for leaving sandwich crumbs on the counter or imagined tasks undone.

This was more than could be said about his attitude toward Iris's performance in the dry-cleaning shop. Nothing was ever clean enough, ever organized enough, ever quick enough, and when it was, it cost too much, and she was wasting money or not treating the customers right. He developed a positive mania about food crumbs attracting roaches, and after every sighting of even the smallest insect, he would comb the shop, searching for crumbs and screaming curses at the top of his lungs. Such performances were usually followed by the dismissal of whatever counter help they had that week, and a hideous shouting-at—if nothing worse —for Iris. Most of these scenes, Iris noticed, came on the days when Irv had been sitting downstairs with nothing to do but watch his miniature television set, or when the few customers that entered sang the praises of old Solly's suits. At one time, early in her marriage, Iris had thought she'd probably get used to Irv slapping her around, but as the years went by, she only grew more and more afraid of him, until she passed each day in stomach-clenched silence, terrified to arouse his wrath.

"It isn't your fault," she whispered one day to the empty shop (that was after yet another girl had been canned) after Irv had pasted her a few for leaving half her sandwich on the desk, then went storming out to the Seventh Avenue Grill. "You keep the place spotless and so beautiful, and I'm grateful. Maybe not having anything really to complain about is what makes him mad."

She reflected, a moment later as she tried to tidy her hair over the bruise he'd left on the side of her face, that she really must be going crazy, talking to imaginary fairies like that. And yet, out of the corner of her eye, she thought she glimpsed something or someone standing just behind her chair, a slip of bony cobweb-clad knee barely visible on the edge of the mirror, a rustly shadow among the whispering plastic ranks of hanging garments. It was November, and almost dark though it was only four o'clock. In the shadows between the alien metal form of the pants press and the cold gleam of the shelf of flatirons for delicate work—and God help her if Irv found so much as a water spot on their stainless-steel smoothness—she wondered if she only imagined the silvery gleam of eyes.

Not human eyes, Iris thought, laying her forehead down

wearily upon her crossed wrists. Her mind wandered back to Jessie, during her last illness at the Shady Rest Home, that thread of a voice coming from the fallen pink face. "Just leave them a little something—they don't need it, exactly, but they like to be thanked," she'd said. "And probably best you don't let Melissa be alone in the shop when it's getting dark . . ."

Her head on her hands in the darkening shop, Iris could see them now, reflected in the long mirror. Two thin shadows, like brown bones wrapped up in grey webs of rags. Between the glare of the lights outside upon the plastic garment bags and the glint of the mirror itself, it was hard for her to tell what she was seeing, especially with her head at that angle. But she thought the taller of the two—who wasn't even as tall as she, at her four feet ten—-crept stealthily toward the desk, where the offending half-sandwich still lay a few inches from her elbow. She had an impression of huge colourless eyes between straggling torrents of hair the colour of ash, eyes blinking down at her like opalescent glass, behind which moved longings and needs foreign to anything she had ever known. A thin brown hand reached out to touch the abandoned food; the smaller of the two creatures clung and whispered . . .

Two, thought Iris cloudily. She had earlier had the impression there were more of them. *Of course. One at least is home helping Melissa with the housework . . .*

She thought of her daughter, finishing her household chores and putting dinner on, while the dusk gathered in the corners of the house and silver-opal eyes gleamed out at her . . .

The terror of the thought jarred her back to wakefulness, gasping with shock.

The shop, nearly dark, was quite empty. A stray, and very small, cockroach scurried out of sight under the baseboard on the grocery-store side. Hastily, Iris removed her pink plastic wrap with "Iris" embroidered on its breast, put on her coat, double-checked the register and receipts, locked up all the doors and windows. She knew she was supposed to sweep up and wipe down the table, counters, pants press, and irons, but even with the radio and all the lights in the place on, she felt the darkness and the silence, and avoided going anywhere near the whispery forest of plastic garment bags, or the shadows which seemed to linger near the sinister bulk of the press. There'd be time to clean up there in the daylight.

At the moment, nothing in the world would induce her to remain in the shop. When she returned the following morning, she couldn't remember whether she'd thrown out the half-sandwich or not, but it certainly wasn't there. After that, she began taking a few extra cookies in her lunch to leave out at closing time, something she'd half-known Melissa had been doing at home for years.

IT WAS the cookies that finally caused the trouble.

Over the years, as his drinking had increased and the profits of the shop had gone down, Irv's mania for cleanliness had increased. Or perhaps, Iris speculated, it was simply that he needed to believe that there was something causing his problems that could be corrected. In any case, he reached the point of forbidding her or any of the girls to eat or drink anything in the shop at all. Since, with the cutbacks in the help as business declined, she almost never got a chance to leave the building for lunch, she took to smuggling candy bars in her purse. After Irv started searching her purse, Iris would bring the candy bars, and cookies for the elves, wrapped tightly in tinfoil and plastic in her coat pockets. She did try very hard not to anger Irv and to keep the shop as clean as his mother once had. At one time—after he broke her ribs—she'd thought of leaving him. But with outmoded accounting skills—Irv never would have the books computerized —and a ten-year-old daughter to support, she knew it would be hard, even if Irv didn't track her down as he said he would.

Irv usually left far earlier than she, to have a few drinks at the Seventh Avenue Grill before taking the subway home, so Iris was able to leave cookies for the elves in the shop before she locked up for the night. She simply got used to the fact that there was never so much as a crumb left in the morning.

How long the situation would have gone on, she didn't know. Maybe forever. But one evening in late October, the telephone in the tailoring shop downstairs rang just as she was preparing to leave, and she ran down to get it—there hadn't been a job of tailoring in weeks. As she did so, she heard the electronic bell on the cleaning-shop door beep, announcing a customer. So, when she finished explaining to the caller that 846-3992 was the number of the Thunderhump Massage Parlor, not 846-3995, she ran upstairs once more and found Irv, standing next to the folding table, staring down at the six oatmeal cookies there in an almost visible cloud of bourbon and rage.

"So, what the hell is this, Iris?" He swung to face her, and instead of roaring as usual, his voice was a deadly whisper. The hand that held up the largest of the cookies was trembling. "You wanna tell me what the hell is this?"

Iris glanced automatically toward the door, but the counter blocked most of that side of the room, and where he stood by the table, Irv was between her and the opening through which she could get to the outside. The next second, the cookie whizzed past her ear like a brown-sugar shuriken and splattered into crumbles against the wall, and Irv was screaming, "You filthy sow! Getting crumbs all over the customers' clothes! No wonder this place got roaches! No wonder we can't get no customers! No wonder . . . !" He lunged at her, caught her by the front of her pink coverall, and slammed her with vicious force back into the shelf containing the steam irons and bottles of benzine.

The shelf cut her back and took her breath away—three irons hit the linoleum with a noise that made her scream. She screamed again as he raised his fist, backed into a corner in terror. "You touch me, and I'm leaving you!"

It was the first time she'd ever said the words, and she wouldn't have if she'd taken the time to think. His face turned so red it was almost purple, dark eyes bulging out in bloodshot webs of veins. "You don't leave me!" he roared. "You don't leave me, you lazy, filthy slut!" He caught up one of the big steam irons, ten pounds at least of tempered stainless steel, in one heavy fist, and lunged at her . . .

———

IT REALLY WAS, Iris reflected, a terrible mess. Blind terror, panic, the inability to breathe or scream or think, the knowledge of murder she saw reflected in those bulging, drunken eyes—and then this. She stood for a long time, a big steam iron in her tiny hand, looking down at her late husband's body on the floor at her feet.

There was blood everywhere. On the pants press, on the forest of plastic-wrapped clothes, on Mrs. Haberman's expensive silk charmeuse dress hanging by the counter . . . Quite a lot of blood on the floor.

The electronic doorbell tweeped. Iris looked up, more startled than anything else, and for a moment found herself staring into the eyes of a very young and flustered blond man in a grey suit who had just dropped an armful of sports jackets on the floor. He gasped, "Holy shit!" and exited.

Iris looked down at the iron in her hand. The iron was covered with blood. So was her hand. She had never realized what that quantity of blood smelled like.

Numbly, she set the iron down on the folding table next to the plate of cookies, wiped her hand on Mrs. Haberman's dress—the charmeuse was ruined anyway—and carefully removed her pink plastic overwrap. Then she went downstairs to the bathroom and washed her hand and her face.

She wondered what they'd do to Melissa while she was in jail. She might, she supposed, plead self-defence, but with the number of times Irv had beaten her up before, surely the judge would merely ask, "Why didn't you leave him?" The judge obviously hadn't lived with Irv.

She didn't feel bad about Irv at all. She knew, as surely as she knew her own name, that he would have killed her.

She wondered if she could make a little candy money in prison by cleaning up other prisoners' cells.

Upstairs, Iris heard the doorbell beep again. That, she knew, would be the police.

It was. Two blue-uniformed New York's Finest, with an extremely shaken-looking young businessman in a grey suit, stood in the gap between the counter and the rest of the shop, looking around them in the deepening shadows of the October evening.

"Are you Iris Levitsky?" asked one of the cops. "This man says there was a crime committed here."

The other cop reached across to the wall and switched on the light.

As he did so, Iris realized that the smell of the blood was gone.

The bright fluorescent glow revealed, in the next moment, that this was because the blood itself was gone. Mrs. Haberman's dress hung beside the counter, spotless, unwrinkled, clean as it had come out of the big fluff-dryer.

Irv's body was gone, leaving not so much as a stain on the green linoleum.

Every iron was back on the shelf, polished like a grinning row of steel teeth; Iris's pink plastic coverall depended neatly from its accustomed hanger; the young man's shirts and sports jackets lay neatly over the spotless counter; not so much as a fleck of blood sullied the garment bags, the pants press, the counter.

The cookies were gone, too. Iris smiled.

NOTE: In 1991, after her missing husband was declared legally dead, Iris Levitsky sold Levitsky's Tailoring and Dry Cleaning to a Korean dry-cleaning chain and used the money to put her daughter through college. Iris and Melissa now jointly own and manage the enormously successful Midnight Magic Housecleaning Service, investing the proceeds in a diversified stock portfolio and funding a small shelter for battered women on Long Island. Melissa has recently opened a shop selling homemade cookies.

A MURDER IN EDDSFORD

By S.M. Stirling

Detective-Inspector Ingmar Rutherston of New New Scotland Yard's Criminal Investigation Department looked up from his copy of the preliminary report as the coach began to slow; he'd had the vehicle to himself for the last three stops. The document was signed *Corporal Bramble, Ox. & Bucks Light Infantry*, but it was as well-written, terse, and concise as most constables could have managed. The description of the dead man's condition made Rutherston's brows rise; the soldier's dismay showed through the flat official prose, as well.

"Peaceful country to all appearances," he mused to himself, forcing his mind to stop worrying the scanty data. "But this Jon Wooton is very dead indeed. Beyond that, there's nothing to be done until I've some fresh information."

He tucked the semaphore-telegraph form into a pocket of his jacket and focused on the view out the window instead. It was a warm afternoon turning into evening, late in August this year of grace 2049 AD. A little white dust smoked up from under the hard rubber treads of the wheels, but the vehicle was well-sprung on good Shropshire steel. The coach was the weekly from the capital, Winchester, to sleepy little Dover over in Kent, much slower than the British Rail pedal-car but stopping at places not so served . . . such as his destination, the Hampshire village of Eddsford.

The landscape of the Downs passed by at a good round trot, long shadows falling from the roadside trees as the sun declined toward the west; rolling chalk hills, green, close-cropped pasture dotted with off-white sheep, fields of grass and clover and reaped grain on the lower slopes, beech-plantations and coppice-woods and low-trimmed hedges where Red Admiral and peacock and tortoiseshell butterflies fluttered. An occasional white-walled farmhouse stood in a sheltered spot, thatched in golden straw, surrounded by barn and stable and cart-shed, wool-store, stock-pond and whirling wind-pump, and gnarled orchards.

Looking about, you'd never dream that the trackless tangled wildwood of Andredesweald lay only a few miles eastward, home to boar and wolf and the odd tiger down from the Wild Lands, and perhaps an outlaw or highwayman now and then. The New Forest to the west was almost as savage, more than it had ever been in the Conqueror's time. Here, the nearest to nature in the raw were hovering kestrels and a buzzard now and then, and flocks of swallows and house-martins crowding the uppermost branches of trees, getting ready for their migration to Africa.

Rutherston smiled at the sight; his father had never seen that without reminiscing about how they'd used the wires strung from pole to pole for roosting when *he* was a young boy in the Old Days.

The detective rolled the window down the rest of the way and peered out, welcoming the fresh air and the scents of baked earth and growing things with the slightly faded, tattered smell that said summer was past its peak, and autumn rains might hit at any moment. A farmer and his workers in the field beyond the road-side hedge were pitching the last of the wheat-sheaves into a wagon drawn by two big chestnut Shires. Men and women and horses alike stopped to look at the high-stepping black geldings that drew the coach, male farmhands with stolid sunburned faces above their smock-frocks, and women in loose pants and blouses and sometimes canvas field-aprons.

A straw-covered jug went from hand to hand as the coach pulled away, and then the pitchforks went back to work. The road dipped down toward the valley of the Rother, showing a glint of sun-struck water in the distance and flatter country southward. Partridges whirred up from the roadside verge . . .

"No, y' daft rassgat!" the driver cursed; probably his assistant levelling her crossbow—she was young and enthusiastic. "Just *your* luck, there'd be some kiddie behind a bush!"

The top of the south-facing slope was planted in undulating rows of shaggy goblet-trained grapevines; beyond, the village proper was bowered in trees and followed the riverbank at a cautious distance, separated by water-meadows and a low bank against spring floods.

And that's the miller's house where the body was discovered, he thought, looking north. *There's the roof through the trees, and you can just see the water from the millrace.*

The assistant tooted again and again on her brass horn, and the driver pulled up to a walk with a *woah-woah, there!* to his team; children and dogs and chickens and the odd passer-by afoot or on a bicycle or on horseback made way, and the usual curious crowd started to gather at the inn. The houses were mostly white-walled, roofed in shingle or thatch, slate or tile, along a street still paved with old-style asphalt and lined with big beeches and horse chestnuts.

The lane opened out into a green at the other end, with the tavern on one side and a stretch of grass in the centre, and a church farther on, near the water-meadows. It was unique in the ordinary manner—a handsome battlemented tower of flint and stone obligingly labelled *1599 AD* over the west door, and other parts that looked to be anything from Victorian to Norman; a Georgian brick rectory stood a little to one side, nearly hidden in oaks and beeches.

The inn was long and low and rambling, plaster over brick, with a higher two-story section in its middle and an irregular studding of chimneys through its mossy shingles. A brass plaque with the royal arms by the door proclaimed that it was a mail-inn, where the coaches stopped for a change of teams and to drop and pick up letters and parcels—usually a profitable sideline for the innkeeper. Three or four shops stood across the green; so did the village post office, flanked by a reading room and small public library marked by its sign and extravagant stretch of window.

A sign also swung from an iron bracket over the main entrance of the inn, showing a Moor's severed head on a silver platter and a branch of dried holly above it. There was a smell of woodsmoke and cooking as households prepared their evening meal, mingling with the homely aroma of middens and the odd whiff from pigs kept behind cottages. A toddler tried to climb into a horse-trough by the side of the street, and a harassed-looking woman in an apron ran out of the door and pulled him inside, smacking him smartly on the bottom while she did so.

The gate to the inn's courtyard opened, and an ostler in a leather apron came out, ready to lead out the fresh team. The driver's assistant unspanned her crossbow with a sharp *tunnggg*, racked it, and jumped down from the seat to open the door as the coach came to a halt. Rutherston sprang down without waiting for the folding step, ignoring a slight twinge where the old wound in his right leg reminded him of that evening in the foothills of the Riff Atlas. She handed down his carpetbags and took a sixpence with a bob of her head before turning to unload the mail-sack and several parcels labelled *Eddsford, Hants.* The ostler and the driver unharnessed the team and led it over into the courtyard.

And a stout man with greying muttonchops and a waistcoat straining over a considerable belly came out of the front door, smiling and fingering the chain of his watch. The taverner's experienced eye flicked up and down the detective's long, lanky form and saturnine, beak-nosed face; quietly expensive but well-worn travelling tweeds and half-cloak; wide-brimmed Panama hat; light cravat of white Irish linen; longsword and belt of good quality but plain and worn; and half-boots. Just a touch of grey at the temples of the yellow hair. And two carpetbags, but no valet . . .

Rutherston smiled to himself as he saw the quick expert evaluation running through the man's guileless blue eyes:

Gentleman, but not rich; still, better than a bagsman or commercial traveller. Not a professor, or a doctor, nor a merchant, surely; and not stopping at the Hall with the Squire. Some King's Man out of Winchester, perhaps, or an officer on leave? Not here for the fishing, though, nei rods . . .

It was accurate enough, and the taverner spoke with precisely calculated deference:

"Mark Eyvindsson—" he pronounced it *Evinson,* in the modern manner "—at your service, sir. I'm landlord of the Moor's Head. Will you be wanting a room for the night, then?"

In fact, what he said sounded more like: *Oi'm the laandlorrd o' the Moo-er's 'Ead. Will ye be wantin' a room fer the noight, then?*

If he'd been born in Winchester instead of just living there the last ten years, the detective might have suspected the innkeeper of deliberately coming it the heavy rustic. But Rutherston had been born in Short Compton in the Cotswolds himself, about a hundred miles north and a little west of here, where the local dialect was just as heavy and only slightly different.

"Detective-Inspector Ingmar Rutherston, of the Yard," he replied crisply. "I would like a room for several days, at least."

The innkeeper managed not to look too startled; several of the oldsters sitting with their pints along the bench beside the inn's door gaped at him; a pipe nearly fell out of one wrinkled mouth. A babble of voices rose and died away.

"Ah, you'll be here about young Jon Wooton; quick work for you to get here so soon, all the way from Winchester. A bad business, sir, a very bad business."

"It usually is when a man's murdered," Rutherston said grimly.

THE INTERIOR of the inn's main room was L-shaped; a long space with tables, a hearth—swept and garnished with pots of flowers now—and a row of windows that looked down on a water-meadow and a stretch of the Rother flowing slowly between willows beyond.

There was a fair scattering of regulars trickling in for a pint or two—it *was* after harvest, after all, the high point of a labourer's year . . . and pocket. A man in a good country suit was talking business with some obvious farmers in cords in the snug, and there was a scattering of everything from cottagers in smocks to tradesmen and their families.

The ones that caught his eye obviously weren't locals; five Army troopers and a corporal, hobelars in green-enamelled chain-mail shirts and leather breeches and riding-boots, with their open-faced sallet helms propped on tables. The longbows and quivers, sword belts and bucklers hung on pegs by the door. They all had mugs of beer before them, and they all looked dusty and tired, as if they'd been on road patrol, which they probably had.

Rutherston walked over to their table as the innkeeper and his staff saw to the baggage and took his hat and half-cloak and his own sword—even on a murder investigation, he wasn't going to wear a long blade inside the village. The soldiers looked up, polite but not more than that—they were the King-Emperor's men, after all. Then he reached into his coat pocket and flipped open the wallet to show his Warrant Card and handed their squad-leader his letter of authorization from the War Office.

That brought them to their feet, saluting smartly amidst a scrape of chairs. The troopers were ordinary enough, strong-built youngsters with open countrymen's faces, distinguished only by one's startling red roach of hair or another's freckles and jug ears. The corporal with the chevrons riveted to the short sleeve of his mail shirt was a few years older than his men. He was about six feet—Rutherston's own height—but broader, with dark blunt features unusual for an Englishman and curly hair so black it had highlights like a raven's feathers.

"Corporal Bramble, Oxfordshire and Buckinghamshire Light Infantry, currently out of Castle Aldershot," he said in a deep, rumbling voice.

The accent was a strong yokel burr but with a slight trace of something different, a yawny-drawly lilt that had a teasing half-familiarity. Then he placed it.

Ah, I've heard something like that from Jamaican sailors in Portsmouth and Bristol, Rutherston thought. *Though he's definitely English born and bred; yeoman-farmer's son, I'd say.*

He'd half-expected a southern-provinces twang; those looks

could be Gibraltarian, but a touch of Caribbean a couple of generations back would account for it just as well.

The noncom went on: "We were told to expect you. I'm to assume this is aid-to-the-civil-power, sir?"

"You are, corporal; dull work, probably, I'm afraid. Your commanding officer has been informed I'd commandeer you; it saves time and trouble. I'll want to talk to you later tonight. You can quarter your men here at the Moor's Head, and I'll handle the requisition slips."

None of the hobelars looked unhappy about it. They'd be spared fatigues and drills, the food and drink would be free but much better than ration-issue, and the chance of finding a girl interested in the glamour of a uniform rather than hard cash was distinctly better here than near a garrison town like Aldershot.

"Thank you, sir. I've a man at the miller's house, of course, guarding the place where we found the body. I'll rotate the duty."

"Good work, that, corporal," Rutherston said, nodding.

It had saved him an undignified scramble, and he had reasons for not heading straight to the scene of the—possible—crime.

"Permission to ask a question?" the noncom said.

The detective nodded, raising a brow.

"You were Army yourself, sir, weren't you?"

Rutherston smiled thinly. *Good. He has a sharp eye, this one.*

He nodded. "Yes; in the Blues and Royals. Tours in the Principality on the Provoland border and out of Rabat and Marrakech. It still shows, eh?"

"It does, Inspector."

"And you're not from this shire, are you, Corporal? A bit further north and east, I'd say."

"My dad's place is just north of Woburn, sir; Jamaica Farm, it's

called, after Granddad. Near Wavendon, if you know Buckinghamshire."

"I do," he said.

Better and better, he thought

That area was northerly and a little wild, though not quite on
the frontier of settlement anymore; that ran just south of
Nottingham these days.

*But still close to the Wild Lands, and still a smuggler's paradise, up
the Ouse from the Wash.*

THE MOOR'S Head wasn't large, but it had all the modern conve-
niences you'd expect so close to Winchester and right next to a
good trout-and-salmon stream; running water in the bathroom on
the first floor, brought up by a hydraulic ram from the river, flush
toilets, and a big copper boiler that supplied plentiful hot water.
The maid had unpacked his bags, all but a small locked case set
on the table, and the sitting room had a pleasant view of the
Rother; the detective found his two rooms to be very comfortable
in a country-inn fashion. Both smelled of clean linen and dried-
lavender sachets, and the alcohol lanterns were bright enough for
reading, even to one accustomed to the capital's incandescent-
mantle gaslights.

Rutherston wallowed gratefully in a tub of the hot water—at
thirty-two, sitting all day in a coach was no longer perfectly
comfortable—and set out his boots and travelling suit to be taken
and dealt with. He took a moment to write a letter as well; Janice
was in her eighth month and naturally hadn't wanted him to leave
town just then.

Then he dressed and came down to an excellent dinner;

grilled trout right out of the river, a pie of veal and ham and truf-fles, sprouts, raudkál, salad, and chips, followed by a fruit tart with cream. There was a glass of a perfectly acceptable local Cabernet Franc to go with it.

Bramble's troopers were plowing their way through much the same, with a roast chicken each added. It reminded Rutherston of the sort of appetite you had when you were twenty years old and spending ten hours a day in the saddle or marching on your own feet under seventy pounds of armour and gear. Instead of his more recent fate, having a city's pavements under his boots, or worse still, an office chair beneath his backside while he filled out endless reports.

Most of the patrons were quiet, talking with their heads together, but the soldiers were merry enough; it wasn't their village, after all. He even caught a snatch of song from them:

"For forty shillings on the drum
Who'll 'list and volunteer to come?
And stand and face the foe today:
It's over the hills and far away . . ."

When he'd finished his own meal, he signed Corporal Bramble over.

"Sit, man. I'm an officer in the police now, not the Blues."

"Inspector."

The big soldier sat, and Rutherston raised his hand for the barmaid—a statuesque blond a decade younger than himself, with a forty-inch bust displayed to advantage by her low-cut blouse and a pouting lower lip that might have been promising under other circumstances, along with the lack of a wedding band.

But you do have one on now, Ingmar, at long last. Keep it in mind. Janice can't see you, but God can.

He'd spent a long time as a foot-loose and fancy-free bachelor, and shedding the habits came a little hard sometimes despite a happy marriage; they crept back while you weren't looking, especially away from home.

"Now," he said, opening his notebook. "Let's get the details. Your report was informative but short."

"You won't be questioning anyone else tonight, sir?" Bramble asked.

Rutherston nodded. "Why am I sitting on my arse waiting for the villains to scarper, you mean?" he said, and smiled at the look of blank innocence the noncom put on. "What I'm doing, Corporal, is letting them get good and nervous. Winchester has seventy thousand people, but here in Eddsford there are six-hundred-fifty-odd, and they all know each other. If anyone runs, they identify themselves for me. If they don't, they'll probably make other mistakes."

"Hmmm, *the guilty flee where nei man pursueth*, eh, sir? My dad's a deacon in our parish," he added in an aside. "You're letting them come ripe, as it were."

"Quite. Tell me what you've seen and heard. Then tell me what you think of it."

The barmaid returned with their mugs. She smiled at the policeman as she put them down, then turned the full wattage on Bramble when it didn't bring any result. He grinned back at her reflexively—he was, after all, still several years short of thirty himself—and then cleared his throat and returned to business.

"Yessir." Bramble's face went blank as he replayed memories in his mind's eye. "My men and I 'ave been on standard road patrol along the South Downs; we vary the route unpredictable-like."

Rutherston nodded as he took a sip of the cool, nutty-bitter ale; it didn't do to make things easy for a would-be Dick Turpin. Open lawlessness like that wasn't likely around here anymore, but it honed fieldcraft and helped hold edge-dulling boredom at bay. He took his gunmetal cigarette case out of his jacket and flipped it open, offering it across the table.

"No, thank you, sir. Never got the habit."

Rutherston lit one himself. They were rum-flavoured *Embiricos* cigarillos from Barbados, and he found the rich, smooth taste soothed and helped him concentrate. The old-timers said tobacco was bad for you, but then, living was ultimately always fatal, and they seemed to have been a bunch of damned old women back then anyway.

"Go on," he said, and opened his notebook to begin jotting down the points.

"We were passing the Mill here on our way back to base—"

"This was early this morning?"

"Yessir, about eight hundred hours. We'd been out since midnight, not seen nothing more dangerous than a badger or a barn-owl, the usual. A woman—the old miller's widow, name of Kristin Wooton—ran out and grabbed me stirrup; there was a man behind her, a wringin' of his hands. She screamed out that her son Jon was dying, and we should get him help. Well, I sent young Jones—that's him, sir, the one with the ears like a bat— back into the village for the District Nurse, then went in to see what I could do."

Corporal Bramble looked hard enough to drive horseshoe nails with his knuckles, but his strong-boned face was uneasy as he went on.

"The man was dying, right enough. Never seen anything like it, sir, and I've seen men die before . . . been stationed over most of the Empire these last ten years. It was like he was *rotting*, sir; hair comin' out in clumps, sores all over his hide. Bleeding from everywhere too, eyes, nose, gums—even his arsehole, begging your pardon, Inspector."

"I've heard the word before, corporal."

A broad white smile, and the man drained half his mug as if trying to wash away a bad taste. His voice was impersonal as he went on:

"Looked like poison to me, sir, and his mother was swearing that he'd been fine the day before, or maybe just a bit peaked. So I sent McAllister—he's the one with the hair like a new penny— over north to the line of rail, they've a semaphore station. Just about then, the poor unfortunate bugger *did* die, and Major Grimsson sent back that I was to hold in place until someone arrived, so I had the body put in keeping, the man's room sealed, and a guard put on it. And then I waited until you got here. Which was quick work on your part, sir."

Rutherston looked down at his notes, tapping the pen on the metal coil at the top of the pad. "It does sound like possible foul play," he said thoughtfully. "The first in this parish since 2012 . . . and *that* was a drunken swain using a hay-knife when he caught his ladylove where she shouldn't have been."

"I don't have any great acquaintance here in Eddsford, sir, but I've heard little good of Jon Wooton. Nothing specific . . . but reading between the lines, like." A pause for another pull at the beer. "Still, you'd 'ave to hate a man right hard to do *that* to him."

Rutherston nodded and finished his beer. "See that your men get a good night's rest," he said.

Meaning, this isn't a weekend pass, so see that they go to bed sober; but there's nei need to say that aloud.

Bramble nodded in turn, obviously following his meaning

effortlessly. He'd never met the corporal before, but he knew the type, a reliable long-service non-commissioned man, steady as a rock in any situation he understood.

What's uncertain is how much imagination he has, but offhand I think he has plenty, just doesn't show it much.

"Tomorrow, we'll start doing the rounds," he said aloud.

Bramble hesitated. "If you don't mind my asking, sir, why do you need me and the lads?"

Rutherston closed the notebook. "I very well may not," he said. "On the other hand, if there's something nastier than a simple impulse killing . . . or someone may run, in which case I'd rather have help quicker on their feet than the usual part-time village Special Constable."

Bramble nodded and grinned. "The one here, name of Edward Mukeriji . . . runs the tobacconist's and sweet-shop, sir, and he was fair stuttering. I see your point."

"And while this may not be your village, you might see things that I don't."

"Ah," Bramble said. "That's a point too, sir."

The words were uninformative, but Rutherston felt that he'd passed some test.

St. Swithun's School For Girls was not far from Eddsford, having been moved out of town when it started up again in the resettlement; a few young ladies in the dark-blue frocks with pleated skirts and white blouses of that revered institution were walking through the village, overseen by a nun in a grey habit.

"Dullafullt," one of them said to a friend, rolling her eyes.

Rutherston had to admit that to a youngster, Eddsford might

indeed seem a little boring, particularly if you'd been stuck there by your parents during the holidays when the other boarders went home. That had happened to him several times, though Winchester College was admittedly much closer to the heart of things.

I'd quite like Eddsford myself if I weren't here to investigate a murder, he thought, taking a deep breath of the cool morning air; it was still fresh at eight o'clock, but he thought it would be another warm day. *It reminds me of home.*

Corporal Bramble stood inconspicuously by his elbow as he used the brass knocker on the door of the clinic, or as inconspicuously as a sixteen-stone man in armour with a longbow and quiver over his shoulder could.

The clinic was just down the lane from the village green; Eddsford wasn't quite large enough to rate a doctor of its own, though one came by weekly from Petersfield, and could be fetched at need. There was a polished plate by the door, also brass, that read: *District Nurse Delia Medford, SRN,* and a modern bicycle with a rather heavy tubular frame and solid-rubber wheels in a stand by the entryway. Roses bloomed in a trellis along one wall, and there were colourful impatiens in the window boxes.

Delia Medford opened the door and responded with a dryly courteous nod to the detective's slight bow. She was a tallish, slender woman in her thirties, with blue eyes, brown hair drawn back in a bun, a no-nonsense expression, and a stethoscope tucked into the breast pocket of her jacket. There was another with her enough alike to be her older sister.

"Detective-Inspector Ingmar Rutherston, ladies," he said, removing his hat and showing his Warrant Card. "Corporal Bramble here is assisting me."

The soldier tucked his helmet under one arm and rumbled "Ma'am," twice.

The nurse gave Rutherston's hand a quick, firm shake. "My sister, Mrs. Alice Purkiss," she said after she'd introduced herself.

The widow Purkiss was a decade older and otherwise very like her sibling, apart from the fact that she wore a conservative knee-length skirt rather than cord riding breeches; the other main difference was her shoes, which *weren't* graced with thick rubber soles.

"I was Jon Wooton's teacher at our little school, Inspector Rutherston," she said. "We thought it would save you time and effort if I came along first thing. I'm retired from teaching now, but I'm still postmistress and run the Eddsford reading room and lending library."

Ah, excellent, Rutherston thought.

He wanted to put off seeing the Wootons until he'd gotten a feel for how the rest of the village regarded them; and these two probably knew everyone's family history since the resettlement, just for starters. Doubtless they were pillars of half a dozen Church organizations and ran the local Whig election committee with an iron hand as well.

Like most such, the office had a waiting room with chairs, a table, and ancient copies of several magazines—*The Illustrated Winchester News*, the *Church Times*, the *British Agriculturalist*, and rather surprisingly, the *Boy's and Girl's Own Paper*.

There was also the inevitable Bible, a tall antique clock ticking in one corner, and hanging pictures of King-Emperor Charles IV, Queen Thóra, the Pope, and the Cardinal-Archbishop of Winchester. A consulting room gave off it, and there were several storage areas in back; presumably, Delia Medmore lived over the shop, judging from the selection of Wellingtons, umbrellas, and mackintoshes at the bottom of the hall stairs, and the tabby-cat looking down curiously from the top.

The body was in one of the storerooms, a tile-floored one with two roll-out compartments for cadavers against the wall and an ingenious icebox-like arrangement for keeping them cold.

"Sir James sends me down ice when I need it," she explained as she pulled on a pair of thick rubber gloves.

Rutherston took up her offer of another pair, a bib-apron, and a mask that smelled strongly of disinfectant, and a little jar of a strong-smelling ointment. He rubbed a touch of that below his nose and handed it around and was glad of it when she pulled out the tray—decay had been quicker than he would have expected, given the refrigeration.

Odd, he thought. *The marks are almost like* burns *rather than* sores. *Blister marks running with clear fluid. As if he'd been touched with a red-hot . . . no, there's no charring. As if he'd been touched with something supremely* cold *instead.*

The nurse might have been examining a gutted chicken at the butcher's, but Corporal Bramble went a little grey beneath his olive tan, and Mrs. Purkiss looked at the ceiling; both stood well back. Rutherston sympathized. The postmortem had left the corpse as gruesome as anything on a battlefield, if neater, and whatever the man had died of was ghastly. Sections of the back peeled away as she moved the corpse.

"I conducted the autopsy," she said. "I usually do them here and pass on the reports to the County Coroner. I confess I was tempted to send for Dr. Kvaran from Petersfield this time, but honestly, I don't think Gudrun could have made head nor tail of it either."

"I'd have brought a forensic surgeon from Winchester if one

had been available, but I agree that it's quite baffling," Rutherston said. "May I see your notes?"

"By all means," she said, handing him a clipboard.

Smith, Jon: age, 27, single male, height 5 ft 11 inches, weight eleven stone, hair, dark brown, eyes, green...

Jon Wooton had been a fairly average modern Englishman... if you subtracted the gruesome lesions that had killed him. The small photograph attached showed him in his late teens, scowling and slouching in a coat with extravagant lapels, but with a certain crude Heathcliffian handsomeness to him. Even allowing for the circumstances, the ensuing decade hadn't been kind.

Rutherston got out his own notebook and began sketching and making observations of the body; he'd seen a good many corpses himself in both his careers, and this one had certain features you didn't often find in a Home Counties village mortuary. After a moment, he tapped his pen in the air above the left shoulder.

"Notice that, Corporal?" he said, pointing to a white scar on the triceps.

Bramble nodded. "Not before, sir; I was sort of distracted. But you're right—he didn't get 'is buckler up in time that round," he said.

Then the noncom followed the pen with his comments: "That's an arrow-wound... so's that... or a square-headed cross-bow-bolt... sword-scars on the right arm. Nasty cut to the leg—he was lucky that time. That there could be a spear 'ead. He didn't get that lot being quarrelsome in the pub of a Saturday night. Not even a pub in Portsmouth or Bristol."

"No record of military service," Rutherston said thoughtfully.

"No, not beyond the usual militia training," the District Nurse confirmed. "He did *say* he'd shipped out overseas as a merchant seaman several times, to Asia and America and the African coast."

"So he *might* have got those fighting off pirates. But," Rutherston said, and turned over the man's right hand.

Even with the skin damage, the hands were definitely wrong for a seaman. Hauling on tarred hemp and sisal and fisting up canvas gave you a layer like cracked horn all across your palms, and you didn't lose it quickly, either; he'd seen that often enough. Jon Wooton's right hand was, if anything, less callused than Rutherston's own, which bore the marks of life-long work with the sword. It did share the "swordsman's ring," a circle of hard skin around the outer side of the forefinger and the inner side of the thumb. There were other scars, too, ones that looked as if they'd been caused by hot metal or acid.

Odd, Rutherston thought. *Those look like blacksmith's marks, or even what someone working in a bleach-powder plant might get. With nothing else to go by, I'd put these as the hands of an artisan in some skilled trade.*

"But he *was* away from home for a good long time?" the detective said.

"More often than not since he turned twenty. Usually about half the year, a month or two at a time; more in the winter than the summer."

"Hmmm. Did he have money?"

"Nothing formal, but he didn't seem to lack for it. Of course, the Wootons are fairly well-to-do; the family has held the lease of the mill since the resettlement."

"Cause of death?"

"Proximate cause was massive exsanguination due to internal bleeding," Miss Medford said.

She unfastened the clips and opened the body cavity. Her sister looked aside slightly, and Corporal Bramble more than that.

"You see?" she said. "The pattern of tissue degeneration is

quite unlike anything I've seen before; very severe mercury poisoning, perhaps—that would account for some of the sores— but there's nei evidence of mercury in the amount you would need. And that should have taken longer. I passed him the street the day before yesterday, and he was healthy enough to scowl and spit then; perhaps a bit pale, but no more. And note how there's no inflammation around the lesions? Simple cellular collapse, I think. There's been no bacterial action to speak of."

"You don't think it was an infectious agent, then?"

"Probably not. I've read of African viruses with similar effects in the old days, and he might have come in contact with those on a voyage, but it's a month's sailing time between Britain and the Guinea coast, and they acted *quickly*. And the *Journal of the Royal Medical Society* lists no known cases since the Change; I have a complete series."

"Had you treated Jon Wooton before?"

"Apart from the usual childhood complaints? Yes." She sniffed audibly. "For a social disease, twice; gonorrhea. Cured by a course of antibiotics from the National Health Centre. One tries to be forgiving, but I cautioned him that I would report any further occurrences to the Ministry of Health."

She slid the tray closed with a snap. They stripped off their gloves and washed up in the stainless-steel sink with strong medical soap, then repaired to a sitting room to one side of the business part of the building; Rutherston took a seat, and Bramble stood next to the door, shrewd dark eyes taking everything in. The furniture was in excellent if subdued and rather plain taste, with a picture on the wall that Rutherston thought might be French Impressionist—salvage art—and a landscape showing Eddsford from the Downs, done in the fashionable neo-Pre-Raphaelite style with a certain amateurish attractiveness. Miss Medford rang a small handbell.

"Tea, please, Aud," she said.

Inwardly, Rutherston raised a brow as a pretty young woman in a dark dress and white apron bustled in and then returned with a tray that had obviously been kept in near-readiness; usually, a District Nurse's salary wouldn't run to a housemaid, and he noticed that Mrs. Purkiss seemed a little constrained. When the tea came—in a beautiful salvaged set of Wedgewood, rather than modern manufacture—he could tell by the scent that it was the genuine black-leaf article from Hinduraj or Sri Lanka, rather than the herbal substitutes most people still used. Asian tea wasn't quite a luxury reserved for the wealthy anymore, but it was expensive even in these days of prosperity, peace, and growing trade, like the cubes of white refined cane sugar in their silver bowl.

He took out his cigarette case and raised a brow. Miss Medford raised her high-bridged nose in turn.

"Not in here, if you please, Inspector," she said in clipped tones. "It's a filthy habit, and I don't encourage it."

He sighed slightly and slipped the gunmetal case back into its pocket; he could have used one now . . . or a stiff whisky-and-soda, despite the hour. Winchester was a city of seventy thousand, and they might have as many as four or five homicides a year, but none like *that*.

She went on: "How do you take your tea?"

"Two lumps and milk, thank you," he said, sipped appreciatively, then buttered one of the fresh muffins. His notebook went on his knee. "You taught Mr. Wooton, Mrs. Purkiss?"

"Yes, for six years—he left school at fourteen."

That was the minimum legal age and usually the maximum for ordinary countryfolk. Rutherston made another note. He'd have expected a miller's son to take another two years; the rural middle-classes, farmers and craftsmen and shopkeepers, usually did. Primary education was free to that level, if not compulsory, and a miller, even if he rented rather than owning the machinery, was usually prosperous enough that he didn't depend on a teenage son's labour to keep the family eating.

The retired schoolteacher seemed to sense his question. "Jon's father died when he was twelve—fell into the gears. His elder brother, Eric, took over the mill, young as he was. Sir James wanted to keep it in the family."

"What sort of a student was Jon Wooton?"

Mrs. Purkiss's lips thinned until they were bloodless. "Quite talented," she said in a tone that tried for clinical and nearly achieved it. "And he continued to study after he'd left school; requested books on interlibrary loan through our reading room here."

"Quite the scholar, then? His interests were . . . ?"

"Late-period pre-Change history, and the sciences. He enjoyed reading, too, which I'm sure you know isn't all that common, particularly if it's not just romances and adventure stories. Very intelligent; even brilliant, perhaps. With more application and self-discipline, I would have recommended him for a Royal and Imperial Scholarship. Father Frances thought the same."

"You liked him, then?" Rutherston said neutrally.

The pinched look grew stronger. "He was a detestable little boy and did *not* improve with age. A sneak, bullied until he got his growth, and a vile bully himself afterwards. When he was quite little, he would try to look in the . . ."

She flushed a little and set her cup down sharply.

". . . the girl's privy."

"Unpopular?" Rutherston asked. "As an older boy or a young man?"

"With all but the *worst* element, louts and . . . girls of questionable taste. He had his cronies. And he would do *unspeakable* things to library books! I had to speak very sharply to him about that and impose fines."

"Ah," Rutherston said with an inward sigh.

Unpopular with the respectable element, and the village Bad Boy. Probably got a girl or two pregnant, too, or gave her Cupid's Measles, and skipped out on some of his trips to avoid the avenging relatives and the Squire and the parish priest.

When they'd left the clinic, the detective put his hat back on— the sun was bright in a sky with only a few piled white clouds— before he snapped the notebook shut and turned to Bramble with a silent question.

"Bad apple, that one," Bramble said. "Knew some wide lads like that back home, but none so bad. From the looks of the knocks he took—and lived afterwards—I'd judge he was a hard man and nei mistake, not just your High Street ruffler ready with his fists or a quarterstaff. Smuggler, probably—treasure trove."

Rutherston nodded. Ruins within the Empire of Greater Britain—which included western Europe to the old German and Italian borders, the Mahgreb west of the Sicilian settlements around Tunis and Bizerte, and theoretically the Atlantic coast of what had been the United States—were, in law, Crown property. Salvage for ordinary materials went on by firms making competitive bids for the rights to a given area, and control of exports gave Winchester influence with the King of Ashante and the Sultan of Zanzibar and his ilk.

Certain types of salvage goods, bullion and jewellery and artwork, were still more tightly controlled. Licences for searching the dead cities for those were dependent on good character, and the government kept the Royal Third. That made violating the law potentially very profitable for interlopers . . . and in the vast tangled wilderness of the Wild Lands northward and on the Continent outside the English settlements, very hard for the authorities to stop. The whole army wouldn't be able to surround the jungled wreck of Paris or Madrid alone.

If the wilderness hadn't been so dangerous, with remnant tribes of Brushwood Men ready to kill and rob unwary travellers—and sometimes, still, to eat them—the problem would have been even worse.

Bramble went on slowly: "There was something a bit odd about the way those two talked about him, sir. Miss Medford didn't like him—not half! You could tell that, but she gave him penicillin for the clap, *twice*, without reporting him."

"That *is* odd, corporal. Not technically *very* illegal, but odd. She'd have to mention it, it would be in the NHS disbursement records . . ."

Bramble frowned as they walked toward the church. "Something rum there. You don't suppose . . . you don't suppose he was having it away with 'er, or something of that sort, sir? She struck me as a born old maid, though."

Rutherston started to wave a dismissive hand, checked himself, and spoke slowly in turn, stroking his jaw: "No . . . but you're right, there's more there than meets the eye." He thought for a moment. "And by the way, do ask questions if you think it would help. I need you for another viewpoint, not just to look formidable."

He sighed. "The usual procedures are of little use here. *Everyone* had access to the victim if it is a poisoning case. There's no clear time element with slipping something into a man's beer, the way there is with bashing him over the head."

The churchyard was well-kept behind its wrought-iron fence, even the older graves from the last century. Like most here in Hampshire, the new sections started with a marble slab on a long mound for the bodies found when the area was resettled from the Isle of Wight in the spring of 1999. By then, the dead in Britain had outnumbered the living by around three hundred to one . . .

It bore a simple: *For the unnumbered and nameless whom we could not aid: Father forgive us. Lord have mercy. Christ have mercy.*

The fifty-two years since showed the usual pattern, a burst in the first years of terrible struggle, then four or five annually, then more again as population built up and the last survivors of the old days approached their threescore-and-ten—according to the *Hampshire Gazetteer,* the village had about six hundred people now, and the parish as a whole twice that. A sexton in his shirt-sleeves with his suspenders dangling was digging a new grave for Jon Wooton, not far from a spreading yew whose dark foliage seemed to drink the sunlight.

The noticeboard beside the doors of St. Mary the Virgin gave the times for services—Mass Tuesdays, Thursdays, and Sunday mornings, of course, as well as the holy days—and the usual exhortations to parishioners to make sure that they confessed and were absolved before partaking. Below that were listed meetings of the vestry, the choral society, the Harvest Festival Committee, the Mothers Union, the guilds—a dozen organizations altogether, some, like the Sunday School, chaired by the vicar's wife.

Rutherston and the soldier removed their headgear and walked through the open door into the cool gloom, with beams of light shining through the stained glass of the windows overhead and a small side-altar to Our Lady of Walshingham. They touched their fingers to the holy water in the font, signed themselves, and genuflected to the altar and the image of the Blessed Mother, waiting for their eyes to adjust. A half-dozen other people were in the church; the usual volunteer middle-aged women and elderly men cleaning and polishing and doing minor repairs, an organist running her fingers through a hymn with the pumps disconnected, a few at silent prayer in the pews, and the vicar himself talking to a deacon.

The detective smiled to himself; together with the sweetness of cut grass from the churchyard, it all had the wax-incense-hassocks-and-choirboy smell of Anglican Rite rural piety; not much different from St Wilfred's back in Short Compton, where he'd been born. He thought of himself as an unsentimental man, but the scent did take him back to the summer Sundays of his boyhood. Janice and he had been back just this Lammas, to watch the Loaf and the corn dollie being carried in and to share a niece's First Communion.

The priest here was a different story from old Father Johnson, though. He nodded to the deacon and came striding over, the skirts of his black cassock swirling around stout walking shoes; Father Frances Broxby was a vigorous man in his mid-thirties, not tall but bull-chested and broad-shouldered, with reddish mutton-chop whiskers and an athlete's corded neck under the clerical dog-collar.

Squire's younger brother, Rutherston reminded himself as they shook hands; he'd consulted *Burke's Peerage and Landed Gentry*, and the Church Registry, of course. The grip was not only strong but callused like a labourer's or a smith's.

That's a bit surprising too. This parish is a reasonably good living.

Topped up by the major landowner, and at his encouragement, by donations from the yeomanry and tradesmen. In theory, the Church didn't allow lay patronage, but in practice, the bishop always consulted about local appointments with someone like Sir James, who owned about half the parish. The everyday work of the Church required the leading family's cooperation.

Frances Broxby has an Oxford Divinity degree, too, but he's not ambitious; he wouldn't have married before he was ordained if he was.

Married men could be ordained in the Anglican Rite and be parish priests, but not those who aimed at Episcopal rank, or, of course, monastics; it was much the same arrangement as for the Ruthenian Catholics, though on a vastly larger scale.

"Come, walk with me, my sons," the priest said. "I think I know what you wish to speak of. A painful duty grows nei easier if we put it off."

Rutherston blinked in the sunlight behind the churchyard. The long meadow there was part of the glebe—the land a parish priest used to graze his necessary horses and a milch-cow for his household and cut hay; the sweet scent from the two fresh stacks was overwhelming. It was also the site where the militia practised with their longbows once a week; the tattered-looking wooden target shaped like a Moorish corsair with a scimitar stood down by the hedge and bank at the end, along with a row of thick shield-shaped wedges of wood on stakes. Two Irish Setters trotted up, grinning and lolling their tongues; the priest bent to ruffle their ears and then led on at a brisk pace until they were on the embankment.

The tree-lined stream bank stood on the other side, with the Rother's surface glittering through the willows, where a few last blackbirds and song thrushes were greeting the morning, and there was a pathway along the top of the earth mound.

"I knew Jon Wooton fairly well," Frances said. "And I regarded him as one of my major failures as a priest."

"Bit of a wild one, Father?" Bramble said. "We get a fair

number of those in the Army. They do well enough, mostly, with some discipline."

Frances looked a little surprised. "Not just that, corporal. Wild young men are common enough, as you say. It was . . ." he hesitated, obviously groping for words. "It was the fact that he was so *intelligent*. So able in many ways. And yet, the *character* was the sticking point. Come."

He turned and walked briskly toward the manse. Rutherston and Bramble exchanged a look that said *this one would do well on a route-march* as they followed him to a long shed-like building behind the brick house, one with skylights of salvage glass.

Frances unlocked it and threw the door open, with a sharp *sit* to keep the dogs outside.

Rutherston felt his eyebrows rise; his nose tingled to strange metallic scents, oily and sharp and pungent. The inside was fitted out as a laboratory-cum-machine-shop. Shapes of brass and steel and glass shone with the gleam of well-cared-for equipment; the detective recognized lathes and drill presses, a still, racks of chemicals, and draftsman's tables, and one corner held a library of several hundred books.

"I supervise a club for some of the parish boys—and a few girls—who are interested in mechanical things and in the sciences," the priest said. "It's a healthy hobby, better than drink, fornication, and poaching, or even an excess of cricket and Morris dancing, and God did not make everyone to work the soil. For that matter, all the land in this area has been taken up, and there are as many labourers as there is employment on the farms. I've been able to find apprenticeships, and a few engineering scholarships, for some of the most able of our young people."

"A worthy effort, Padre," Rutherston acknowledged sincerely. "I presume Jon Wooton was one of your club members?"

"The best of them!" Frances said. "And one of the first. It was the first time he or any of his family took an interest in anything involved with the church, too."

"Ah," Rutherston said, opening his notebook. "Lutherans or Anti-Reunionists?"

"Nei, we've hardly any Dissenters in the parish, not enough for a meeting-house, and none at all in the village. Well, there's Jack Hordursson, our cobbler, but he's an atheist . . . loudly. And the Norbits, they're Buddhists—they got it out of a book. Nei, the Wootons are just indifferent for the most part."

"So you were surprised when Jon Wooton joined the . . ."

"Philomath's Club. Here, let me show you. This is all his work."

He led them over to a bench. Several photographs were pinned above it. Rutherston nodded. They were excellent work; one of the priest, another a family group in front of a watermill, and still another of the District Nurse and her housemaid in front of the clinic.

"Jon Wooton made the camera and developed the negatives. He made several cameras, in fact, some of them every bit as good as one from a factory in Winchester."

Several model machines were racked against the wall, including a small telescope. Another had a brass tube like a miniature hot-water boiler set over a spirit lamp, with an affair of levers and pistons in an arrangement like a grasshopper's legs. The priest undid a cap, poured in water, lit the lamp, and worked valves. After a minute, the machine began to hiss . . . and then, slowly at first, the levers began to work up and down, and the flywheel to spin with a smooth, alien motion.

Bramble took a step back and crossed himself, his eyes going wide. The priest smiled and made a soothing gesture. "Nothing but natural law at work, my son."

"But . . . that sort of thing doesn't work nei more! Not since the Change!"

"Actually, it does, corporal," Rutherston said briskly. "If it isn't the type that needs high pressures. But an . . . what's the phrase, Padre? I should have paid more attention in Classics . . . *they* work."

"A Watt-style steam engine, which functions by creating a vacuum and then using the pressure of the air to push the piston —an atmospheric engine. Wooton made this himself when he was sixteen, just from the plans in a book. And it worked the *first* time."

"That's rare?"

"Take my word for it. *Very* rare."

Rutherston nodded. "There are a few large ones in dockyards to pump out drydocks, and in coal mines up the Severn for drainage. They're not of much use otherwise; they weigh too much and take too much fuel for the work they do. For most purposes, an ordinary waterwheel or windmill is far better."

Frances pointed to several places where the brass rods of the little engine had been bent and then carefully repaired.

"There you have Jon Wooton's genius, and his failing—when I told him that nei great use could be made of the engine under modern conditions, he smashed it and stormed away."

"And who fixed it, Padre?"

Frances passed a hand over his face and sighed. "He did. I had expelled him from the club—and from the sacraments—nine years ago, for reasons which must remain confidential. Then, just two years past, he came back to Eddsford from his longest trip abroad. He'd made a little money, it seems, as a sailor –"

Bramble rolled his eyes slightly toward the ceiling. *Too holy for his own good, this one,* the expression said. Rutherston gave an almost imperceptible nod.

"—and he convinced me that he had mended his ways. Among other things, he offered to help instruct at the Philomath Club here. And did so . . . brilliantly. Until I found him in a compromising position with one of the girls who was a member."

He shook his head. "And he absconded with . . . oh, nothing of value. Some fanciful plans he'd drawn up, and a few books—old works, on technologies that definitely do *not* operate since the Change."

Rutherston nodded. "Evidently, the young man was a disappointment to most people who knew him, Padre. Do you think anyone was disappointed enough to kill him?"

The priest bit his lip. "Inspector, you put me in a very difficult position."

"Oh, I realize that you have to respect the confidences of the—"

The vicar of Eddsford surprised him by chuckling. "No, it's not so much that. It's that there were so *many* people here in Eddsford who . . . ah . . . very strongly disliked Jon Wooton. I hope I'm Christian enough to forgive those who wrong me, but my brother—"

"Frances!"

The voice came from beyond the door; a woman in a good plain dress hurried in with a leather box in her hands; it had a buckled flap with a golden cross embossed on it. "Frances! Mrs. Thordarsson—oh, pardon me."

"Inspector, corporal, my wife, Hrefna Broxby," he said, pronouncing it more like *Refna*. "Yes, dear?"

"Mrs. Thordarsson is failing."

"Ah, then I'll have to leave you, I'm afraid, Inspector," he said briskly, taking the leather box. "Their farm is on the edge of the parish and time presses. Very much a pleasure, and do feel free to call on me at any time."

A youngster in his teens outside was holding the reins of a rather thick-set horse in the shafts of a light two-wheeled carriage; it looked like a prosperous farmer's Sunday showpiece. The priest walked out at the same quick pace, stepped into the seat, gave the other a hand up, flourished the whip, and started off at a brisk trot.

The vicar's wife watched him leave with a smile, then turned to the two men: "Oh, Detective-Inspector," she said. "Sir James asked me to pass on his invitation to visit this afternoon."

After they'd left the churchyard, Bramble nodded slowly to himself. "Think I've got a bit of a handle on this Wooton fellow, sir," he said.

"Yes?"

"Well, he was a right clever lad, eh? And thought he should be a big man . . . and maybe he should have been."

Rutherston frowned. "Then why in God's name didn't he *leave*? Miller is the best thing he could hope for here, in a settled county like Hampshire. And he wasn't even the heir to the lease; there's an elder brother."

"But—" Bramble made a sweeping gesture "—he kept coming *back*, you see? He wanted to make his mark here; not in Winchester or Portsmouth or Bristol or the colonies, but *here*. Where he grew up and with all the people *here*, where it really counts, sir."

"Ah," the detective said. "Now I see your point."

He glanced up at the sun; it was an hour or so to noon. "Let us repair to the Moor's Head until luncheon. If there's anyone in town who knows the gossip, it's an innkeeper."

"Then the Squire," Bramble said. He smiled. "Better you than me, sir."

THE PARK around the manor wasn't particularly large, probably because labour had been scarce until the last few decades, but Rutherston stopped to admire the sight of a herd of fallow deer grazing beneath a beech. They ambled away across greensward studded with crimson poppies and golden corn marigolds as he and Bramble walked in past the gatehouse; the laneway was flanked by clipped shapes of golden yew as it curved around an ornamental pool of several acres, and then through a screen of timber and over a ha-ha into the house gardens, velvety lawns and tall chestnuts and cedars, and banks ablaze with phlox, penstemon, black-eyed Susan, and more. A few gardeners stared or waved tentatively as the two King's Men walked toward the entrance.

Royston Hall itself was seventeenth-century work, for the most part, a rectangular block done in pale stone and four stories high. The grey-haired butler opened the door before Rutherston could knock and took the card he offered.

"You're expected, sir," he said, not deigning to notice Bramble. "If you'll follow me?"

And I don't think he's been a butler all his life, Rutherston thought. *Men rarely have half their left ear chopped off in that line of work. Or get a limp quite like that.*

There was a suit of armour inside the door at the entrance to the hall, a modern man-at-arm's outfit of head-to-toe articulated plate. The model had been fifteenth-century, but the metal was considerably better than any available to medieval smiths.

The detective and the corporal gave it identical considering glances as they went by. It took a good deal of effort to batter good alloy-steel armour into that sort of shape, and it wouldn't be at all healthy for the man inside; the shoulder-flash of the Cordoba Lancers was barely visible, and the visor of the sallet helm had been cut nearly in half, which must have taken a two-handed blow with a heavy axe or a halberd. The butler led them into a room with bay windows overlooking a walled garden; they were open, and a scent of lavender and cut grass drifted in, along with a country-house smell compounded of faint traces of lamp and dog and woodsmoke, tobacco, the old walls . . .

Sir James Broxby was a man of medium height, still slender and lithe at fifty, with amber-coloured hair and moustache, liberally streaked with grey. He would have been handsome if it hadn't been for the slash that had taken his left eye and furrowed the brow above and the cheek below; as it was, he wore the black patch with distinction, and the other eye was bright blue and shrewd beneath the shaggy brow. Rutherston heard Bramble make an *mmmm* sound behind him, and the same thought occurred to him as they shook hands:

Well, that's what happened to the suit of plate.

"A pleasure, Sir James," he told the baronet.

"Mutual, Inspector . . . just a moment . . . Rutherston . . . the Short Compton Rutherstons? The Blues?"

"Yes, Sir James, twice. On the retired list at present, and making my way in the CID—younger son, and all that. Youngest of four sons, actually."

"Ingmar Rutherston . . . the Military Medal down in Morocco some time ago?"

The detective shrugged. "Medals came up from the rear with the rations, and everybody deserved one," he said.

That brought a short laugh and a nod; not precisely agreement, but a meeting of minds on matters which others without their shared experience could never really know. Rutherston opened his cigarette case and offered it.

"Ah, *Embiricos*," Sir James said, taking one. "These alone made the cost of resettling Barbados worthwhile, and damn the Whigs and their Babbage Engine project."

He cocked an eye at Bramble. "You can sit too, corporal."

"I'll stand if it's all the same, sir," Bramble said, taking a position behind the sofa where Rutherston sat; it was rather like having a bear behind the flowered chintz, but reassuring for all that.

"The corporal has been assisting me and doing rather a good job of it," Rutherston said.

"I'm not surprised."

The baronet rang a bell, and a housemaid slid into the room. "Gin and tonic, please, Martha," he said. "And you, Inspector?"

"The same, thank you. It is a warm day."

They made small talk—the weather (good), the state of the just-completed harvest (excellent), the trends in wheat and wool prices (deplorable), Sir James's former command in the resettled areas of southern Spain (great potential)—until the drinks came. Rutherston sipped at his, enjoying the tart astringency, and then opened his notebook as a hint.

Sir James sighed. "Unpleasant business this, all 'round. I confess I wouldn't have been even the least upset if young Wooton had come to grief somewhere abroad, but to have him murdered in my own village . . ."

Rutherston nodded sympathetically. "The Wootons are an old family here?"

The other man laughed shortly and drank, smoothing his moustache with a knuckle. "*Very* old. Gaffer Wooton . . . Jon's grandfather . . . lived here before the Change. So did my family . . . nearby, at least."

Rutherston's brows went up. That *was* unusual. The rescue parties had swept up selected people from all over Southern

England that first year and taken them to the Isle of Wight Refuge to wait out the inevitable die-off after the machines stopped. Most had been farmers, and the others craftsmen or skilled workers of high value. Thatchers, weavers, and blacksmiths and the like . . . and, to be sure, the families of commanders and of their soldiers and of persons of influence on the Refuge. The men in charge had saved civilization here where nearly everything on the Continent from Normandy to Iran had gone down in utter wreck . . . but they'd still been only human, and their power had been near-absolute for a while.

The squire of Royston Hall sighed again. "I don't know how much background you want—"

"The more, the better, Sir James."

"Well, the Wootons got the lease on the mill as soon as this area was resettled in the spring of 1999—my grandfather was Commandant of the region under the Emergency Regulations and got a substantial grant of land when things were privatized, the usual arrangement. Old Tom Wooton did a splendid job; he'd been in the Life Guards with my grandfather, driving one of those . . . what were they called? Not automobiles or trucks, moving steel fort things on bands of metal . . ."

"*Tanks*, I believe."

"Yes. One called after a sword, a 'scimitar,' I think. Old Tom was handy with machinery, and so he was put in charge of renovating the mill—it hadn't been operational before the Change, just kept for appearances, they did a lot of that sort of foolishness then, of course. He married an Icelandic woman—"

Rutherston nodded; that was also common. It had been encouraged, in fact, when the refugees from the northern isles were welcomed into a land gone empty in the second and third years.

"—and his son extended it, added a fulling section."

The detective closed his eyes for a second to search his memory. The mill was on the fringe of the village, but he hadn't heard the distinctive sound of wet woollen cloth pounded by wooden hammers. At his unspoken question, Sir James went on:

"We closed it down about nine years ago. There's not as much weaving here as there was in my father's time—just rough home-spun and blankets, that sort of thing. The cloth trade's been moving off to the West Country and north into your bailiwick lately, and it's cheaper to buy the finer grades. Our Rother really doesn't have enough waterpower for manufacturing."

True enough, Rutherston thought. *Though I wouldn't call Dursley and Stroud and Chalsford our bailiwick, precisely; we just sell them our farmers' wool and wheat and flax.*

He'd never liked the mill-towns. They were too big—Stroud was the most monstrously overgrown and had four *thousand* people nowadays—and they didn't really fit into the Cotswold country he loved.

Winchester and Bristol and Portsmouth are cities, he thought. *Eddsford and Short Compton are villages. Those places are neither fish nor fowl nor good red meat.*

"I turned it into a winery instead and loaned a few of my tenants the money for planting more vines. There we have some chance of competing, what with haulage costs from the colonies. In any case, young Jon took it hard. He'd been full of plans for making the fulling operation more efficient—even adding a spin-ning mill. That we *definitely* wouldn't have had the waterpower for, but Jon was a trifle unbalanced on the subject. We had words on the matter when I pointed out that it *was* my property and the decision was mine. In fact, we both lost our tempers. He swore he'd buy the mill and the freehold of it and I . . . well, I'm afraid I laughed and said he was welcome to do it, any time he had a thousand pounds in cash about him."

Rutherston winced slightly and felt Bramble do the same at some subliminal level. A thousand pounds was what Rutherston made in five years or a corporal in fifteen. There were places, not here in Hampshire but not necessarily right out on the frontiers either, where you could buy and stock a good farm with that much.

Sir James looked at the end of his cigarillo, finished his gin and tonic, and then sighed.

"Well, two years ago . . . by God, he did it."

Rutherston felt his jaw start to drop, and the squire of Eddsford nodded.

"Yes, quite a surprise. But I'd given my word, even if I meant it as a joke, and . . . there he was with a thousand in good Bank of England notes. I had absolutely nei desire to sell family land, but what could I do? It was a fair price, after all; better than fair, even if I did have to put up a new winery. I felt lucky he didn't insist on making a public parade of it; he was always one to kick a man when he had him down, was our Jon."

The detective's pen scribbled over his pad. Unwillingly, he felt a certain admiration for the late Jon Wooton's sheer gall. To come home and beard the Squire that way . . . although it said something reasonably favourable about the landowner, too. If Sir James wanted to, he could make living here impossible for anyone he took against, since he was the largest landowner, the major employer directly and through his tenant-farmers, and Justice of the Peace and Militia captain, to boot. Nobody apart from his own mother seemed to have liked Jon Wooton much, either, which would have made his position that much worse.

Just then, the door crashed open. A woman stood in it, dressed in black silk. It clashed horribly with her greying ginger hair, which escaped in wisps about her long and rather horsey face; she had mismatched features that might have been charming if she smiled, but he had an instant and distinct impression that she didn't do that very often, even apart from whatever was bothering her now.

Relative of the squire, Rutherston thought instantly. *Close relative. Sister, probably.*

Her eyes were red, as if from prolonged weeping, but she glared at Sir James Broxby with open rage.

"You *killed* him, James! How could you!"

The accused man sighed again, closed his eyes for a second, and stood. "I'm rather busy now, Vigdis—"

She turned to Rutherston, who'd also stood by automatic reflex. "Arrest him! He killed Jon because he couldn't *stand* the thought of my being happy, of having a home of my own—"

Something in the detective's face stopped her; she started to weep again, then snatched something from a shelf and threw it. The porcelain shattered against a window, which broke itself; then she turned and stormed out again.

The baronet sat again. "Good *God*," he said quietly. "I apologize for subjecting you to that, Inspector."

Rutherston sat as well. "No need to apologize, Sir James. In my line of work, one often sees people when they . . . ah . . . aren't at their best."

His host rang the bell again. "Another gin and tonic, Martha," he said. "Much gin, little tonic, nei ice. Another, Inspector? Nei? Well, *I* need it, by God!"

He shook his head and went on: "I've been lucky in my wife, my sons and daughters, my brother and our other sisters . . . but Vigdis is, as you can see, a consummately silly woman. And Jon Wooton was rather a swine with women of all classes. Whether you believe me or not, I wouldn't have objected if I'd thought he *would* give her some happiness, but . . . it wouldn't have mattered if Wooton had *ten thousand* pounds coming in every year and a seat in the Lords."

"Of course, Sir James," Rutherston said; quite sincerely, on the whole.

By God, it's a good thing that being a copper is a cure for embarrassment; otherwise, I'd be dropping dead of the English Disease right here. I suspect Corporal Bramble is willing his vital functions to cease immediately.

"Now," he continued. "Jon Wooton bought the mill two years ago?"

"Yes, and that made his brother Eric *his* tenant," Broxby said, escaping to—relatively—impersonal matters with relief. "Another reason I hated to sell; Eric's been a perfectly sound man. Jon immediately cleared out the winery equipment and began extending the old mill building, which at least gave some of our Eddsford people employment. In fact, he swore he'd put in spinning machines as well, even power looms."

Rutherston snorted. He might not like Stroud, but having it close by as he grew had taught him *something* about the economics of the textile trade. Nobody used power looms. Power *spinning*, yes, and some of the processing parts of the fine-cloth trade were mechanized, but when so many cottagers had good treadle-looms and needed work in the off-seasons of the farming year it just didn't pay, especially when people willing to work in factories were so scarce and could demand high wages. Master-spinners put the thread out for weaving through the cooperative guilds, then bought back the cloth for finishing.

"I thought you said there wasn't much spare power from your river?"

"None!" Broxby said, then: "Ah, thank you, Martha," and knocked back his drink as if it were neat whisky. "In fact, there's a Catchment Order enjoining anyone on this stretch from building more dams or weirs. To preserve the fishing, you see. But Wooton would have it that he could install a *steam engine*, of all things! In Hampshire, with not a pound of coal within fifty miles! And they don't pay for anything but pumping out mines even up the Severn, where it's cheap."

Rutherston started to snort again, then remembered the vicar and his Philomath Club and the little model.

But that makes even less sense. He was nei fool, our Jon, and he knew you couldn't get useful work out of one of those machines. Not without a coal mine right beneath it, so the fuel was free! And they took most of the coal in the Old Days; we're working their leavings, or seams too small to be worth noticing back then.

That was the basic lesson of the Change; under the laws of nature as they'd applied since that March 17 of 1998, you couldn't get mechanical work out of heat, not in any really useful amount. Not in an engine, not in a firearm. The detective shook his head. He'd learned the details of it in school, though that had been boringly abstract, especially the bits about electricity—you could visualize a steam engine in your head, but not force flowing in wires.

What really puzzled him was that Jon Wooton, in his own personal and repulsive fashion, was acting as if he were seventy years old and *remembered* the Old World and missed it enough to keep scheming to find a way around the Change. Sir James Broxby braced his elbows on the arms of his chair and steepled his fingers. When he looked over them at Rutherston he was once again the forceful man he'd first met.

"I'm afraid we've presented you with a puzzle, Inspector. You have to determine who *didn't* want to kill Jon Wooton."

"Starting with the District Nurse and his schoolteacher," Rutherston said ruefully.

For a moment, he wished he'd accepted the second drink.

The brow over Sir James's single eye went up. "Them? They *have* been handling his business correspondence with that firm in Portsmouth," he said. "So they can't loathe him quite as much as the remainder of us."

"No, NOT ALL, AS IT SEEMS," Bramble said, frowning intently, as they walked back down the lane to the park gate.

Rutherston nodded. *He's been caught up in the puzzle of it,* he thought, amused. *Natural huntsman, I suppose.*

The big noncom went on: "If Sir James were going to kill a man, he'd do it face-to-face; Jon was younger and knew how to use a blade, too, sir."

Duelling wasn't legal. On the other hand, it wasn't absolutely unknown, either, in the last generation or so.

"There's his sister," the detective pointed out. "The most honourable of men could lose control ... still ..."

Bramble cleared his throat apologetically. "No disrespect to the Squire's sister, but Jon was a man with an eye for the girls from all we've heard, and you'd have to be right desperate to fancy waking up next to her for the rest of your mortal days. *And* he was a good ten years younger."

"Unless it was for revenge."

"Then he wouldn't string her along. Having it away and then dumping her public-like would be revenge in plenty."

"Hmmm," Rutherston said. "I see what you mean. He probably did mean to marry her, then . . . and be a rich man here in Eddsford, with the squire's sister, too. That *might* be enough to overcome Sir James's scruples."

"More likely one of his men's. Did you see that butler, sir?"

Rutherston shot him a glance and got that guileless expression once more.

"Yes, I did. Yes, you're right, corporal, he might be the sort to quietly take care of something the master wouldn't or couldn't . . . but I don't think he'd use poison. Quick stab to the kidneys, and then the body never found, that would be more like it."

"Something to that. But *someone* did it . . . and it would have to have a bit of spite behind it, Inspector. He died hard, did our Jon. Very hard."

Rutherston nodded. "That's the way we have to approach this. Usually, we look for motive and opportunity . . ."

"But everyone in this sodding village hated Jon Wooton, and they all had the opportunity to drop sommat in his beer."

"Exactly. Therefore we'll have to focus on the *means*. Time to go see what may be seen at the Wootons'."

The mill was at the other side of the village; they walked back through the green and along the single long lane, since Eddsford had more length than breadth. With the harvest in, the farmworkers who made up most of the people here were taking time to do repairs and tidying-up; they passed half a dozen parties of thatchers, with householders tossing up bundles of the golden straw to be pegged and trimmed. The trades and crafts were busier than ever, though; they went past a shoemaker—who from the sign also repaired harness and saddles—tapping away with his family working around him, a smithy with its blast of heat and inevitable hangers-on and iron clangour, a tailor's where the treadle-powered sewing machines hummed.

Children were running about, enjoying their last weeks of freedom before the school year started. A mob of the older boys came by kicking a football; one of them sent it across the path of the two men. Bramble stopped it with his foot, bounced it expertly into the air with his toe, bumped it up with his knee, and then head-butted it unerringly to the gangling youth who'd kicked it to him. The tow-headed boy grinned back and then led his shouting mob down a laneway toward the water-meadows.

Rutherston caught a look of mild enjoyment on the noncom's face before it gave way to his usual seriousness. "You may have found His Majesty a recruit there," he said.

"Worse things than going for a soldier, sir," Bramble said. "If you've the inclination."

"True enough."

They passed out of the village proper; beyond it were the allotments—plots of a few acres came along with the rental of a cottage. Many of the villagers were at work there, hoeing and weeding or harvesting vegetables and fruit into woven-withe baskets. Some of them nodded to the two outsiders; others just glanced at them.

"You or I would be grockles in Eddsford if we lived here thirty years, married local girls, and were buried in the churchyard," Rutherston said.

"Probably, sir. Not quite as bad as that where I come from; we weren't resettled until a decade or so later. Still had new folk moving in until around the time I was born."

A few two-wheeled carts went by, loaded high with billets of firewood cut in the coppices; this was the season to start laying it in for the winter. It was also the season for milling some of the recently harvested grain, of course, though not all of it; besides taking time to thresh, it kept better in the kernel. The tall overshot steel wheel was turning as water dropped onto the curved metal vanes from the millrace. That wound out of sight along the hillside and into a patch of dense forest.

Ah, Rutherston thought, looking at a series of heavy metal shapes, forged steel and cast iron; they rested by the newer section of the long rectangular building. *That will be the parts Sir James mentioned from Portsmouth. Odd that Miss Medford didn't mention doing Jon's correspondence.*

In mourning for a brother or no, the world's work had to go on; as they approached, a sling full of sacks was hoisted up to the top story, to be poured into the hopper and eventually emerge as flour —and sacks of *that* were being unloaded into empty wagons from a doorway lower down. The groaning sound of burr millstones turning on each other ran under the rush of the water and the rumble of the big gearwheels meshing. There was a mealy, dusty smell in the air, despite the dampness.

A tall man with thinning sandy hair was overseeing operations. He turned as Rutherston and Bramble approached and nodded at them:

"Been expecting you. I've a bit t' do furst, sir." Then he shouted upwards at his workmen: "Awroi, keep her running! Light on the lever! There's nei way for even biyani like you t' bugger it up now, so don't!"

Rutherston introduced them; the miller had a hand like something carved from bacon-rind and a gravely respectful manner that *might* be hiding resentment . . . or possibly relief. He led them into the rambling, ivy-covered house that stood near the mill and offered refreshment—*nammit* was the word he used for the pound-cake and rosehip tea that his wife brought in and slammed down with a nervous irritation that made the husband wince.

"Where's Mother?" he said to her. "And the kids?"

"*She's* in Jon's room, with his things," she said with a waspish note.

Eric Wooton looked surprised. "How'd she get in? It's locked! There's the guard! She were fussing about it all yesterday and yelling at the so'jer."

"The squaddie's asleep, and she used a strip of tin!"

Oh, my, Rutherston thought, and exchanged a glance with Bramble as they both rose.

Mrs. Wooton the younger was a woman of about her husband's age, somewhere between thirty and forty, with bright blonde hair and sharp, intelligent features and tourmaline-green eyes. She went on with a snap:

"Margrethe and Sally and Tom are staying with Jenny. And that's where *I'm* going now. Call me when your Jon isn't mucking up our lives anymore. I didn't marry *him*, you know."

Eric Wooton winced as the door slammed and trailed after the two King's men down a corridor toward the stairs.

"Jenny's her sister . . ." he sighed, then went on: "You talked with the Squire, I suppose, Inspector? Jon . . . ee allus was a strange boy, off alone with his books or fiddling with some bit of gearwork, but he changed when the Squire closed the fulling mill. First, he goes off to sea; then he comes back with money and big plans, talking all fess about how he'd settle everyone who ever crossed him, and then he goes and buys the mill!"

"Which will be yours now, I suppose, Mr. Wooton?" Rutherston said over his shoulder as they came to a landing.

The square Saxon face went slack. "I hadn't thought!"

The detective blinked. He'd been on the receiving end of a

great many attempts at innocence, and that was the real thing if he'd ever seen it.

And now the poor fellow has more guilt to add to the relief he's trying not to feel, Rutherston thought; the Wootons had ratcheted up two steps on the local social ladder. *Now, how to interrupt his mother—*

Eric Wooton visibly put the dawning realization that he now had his beloved mill in fee simple and rent-free aside and continued:

"I didn't think any good would come of it, nor of those friends of his."

Aha, Rutherston thought. *That's new.*

"Friends?" he said.

"Foreign," Eric Wooton said shortly.

The problem is, foreign *could just mean someone from Warwickshire or even Winchester*, Rutherston thought. *I doubt they were from outside the Empire.*

"And they came by night. Jon would go out and talk to 'em, I suppose he went with them on his trips away, but he wouldn't bring them into the house—not that I wasn't glad of it. Wouldn't want them around my kids. Then when they left, he'd have more—"

Suddenly, he stopped and sniffed the air. Rutherston did, too; there was a hint of smoke, not likely from a hearth in this season, but it could be from the iron stove in the kitchen.

"*Mother!*" Wooton bellowed and tried to bolt past them.

Bramble had his sword out. Rutherston made a gesture, and the noncom sheathed it as they went pounding up the last flight of stairs. The trooper who'd been on guard lay slackly on the floor with a cup beside him; drugged, not drunk or asleep, but Rutherston didn't envy him when he eventually met Corporal Bramble again in his official capacity.

The door had been locked once more; the miller rattled the handle and shouted incoherent pleas, threats, and curses at his mother. Smoke leaked underneath it; Rutherston shoulder-checked the agitated man neatly out of the way, and Bramble hit the oak planks with his shoulder tucked in. That was practical if you had a lot of bone and muscle behind the shove and a mailcoat and padding to protect it. The lock tore out of the jamb with a crunch, and the door banged open.

"No!" a woman screeched.

That was probably Kristin Wooton; at least she was stout and middle-aged. She went for Rutherston with a creditable tackle, but he dodged aside—he'd been a very good Rugby fly-half once—and picked up a jug of water by the side of an unmade bed still marked with the dried blood and fluids of Jon Wooton's hard dying. Smoke turned to steam as he threw it into a metal box where flames ran. Behind him, Bramble had the mother in an unbreakable grip—despite her attempts to kick and gouge—and Eric Wooton was . . .

A wringin' of his hands, Rutherston thought, as he opened a window and waved a pillowcase to disperse the smoke. *If I had to pick a recruit for a commando operation, I'd take Eric's mother, Kristin, over* him *any day of the week.*

The basket held charred papers. And charred photographs as well. The detective picked one up between thumb and forefinger.

For a moment, the shapes made no sense. Then his brows rose as he mentally untangled the interlocked limbs and saw what was going where; he hadn't seen anything like it since a handful of pre-Change magazines were handed eagerly around after lights-out in the dormitory at Winchester College . . . Then the brows rose again, to an almost painful level. These photographs were modern and not posed; they'd been taken at some distance, through an open window—with a camera hooked up to a telescope. It took him a moment to recognize Delia Medmore, and a moment more to identify pretty Aud; facial features weren't the most immediately apparent part of the overall composition.

No wonder his mother had wanted to burn them! Rutherston thought. *And no wonder that Delia Medmore was willing to handle his business correspondence . . . and she certainly had a motive for murder.*

"Good God Almighty," Bramble said in reverent tones.

Rutherston turned, automatically holding the photograph closer to his chest with the back outwards. A large trunk stood by the bed, evidently pulled from beneath it, and with the large, complex, and extremely strong-looking lock hammered off. At a guess, Jon Wooton's mother had done it when she realized that the police were on the doorstep. Part of the contents had gone into the metal waste basket and been set on fire; the rest had been tossed on the bed. They included some diagrams . . . and several neat bundles of banknotes, with many noughts in their numbers. Buying the mill and ordering equipment from Portsmouth hadn't exhausted young Jon's profits from his putative illegal salvage trips by any means.

"I don't want the money!" Kristin screeched. "Take the money! Just don't you slander my Jon! Jon was a good boy!"

No, he was a man, and a very bad one, Rutherston thought. *But that doesn't mean it was all right to murder him.*

Then he looked at the plans. *A steam engine, right enough,* he thought. There was the big rocking beam, the circular boiler, the huge six-foot piston, and the separate condenser. The rest of it made less sense. The channels for water were labelled *cooling system.* Surely the point was to heat the water up, though? And there was no provision for a coal store; simply a rectangular object with pipes running through it labelled *heat source*. And a weird geared arrangement to lower rods into it from above, each fitting neatly into a cylinder.

They were neatly titled *control rods*, with *graphite* in brackets after that and a note: *Test composition? Add fuel elements gradually to check necessary mass.*

"This doesn't make any sense," he said to himself, baffled. "But Jon was brilliant at mechanical things; it's the one virtue he had, and everyone agrees on it. What could—"

He felt his face go pale. "That's *impossible*," he added.

No, he realized after a moment. *It's just very implausible. Anything* else *is impossible.*

"Dammit, I should have known better!" he said softly.

Kristin Wooton's screeches had subsided into sobs. Bramble heard the older man's words.

"Sir?" he said.

"Known that you see what you expect to find!"

"What was it you expected, exactly?" said Bramble, letting the woman down on her feet; she stumbled to a chair and dropped her face into her hands.

"I expected to find a murder."

"The trail's as plain as plain, sir," Bramble said. "Now that we've got one end of it, I can follow it."

The olive face was phlegmatic as usual, but there was a slight sheen of sweat on it. It was near sunset, and they'd been quartering the hanger northeast of Eddsford's mill all afternoon. Half the corporal's squad were helping—the ones with the best field-craft, as Bramble put it.

Or the ones that did the most poaching, Rutherston thought mordantly.

"Best get the rest of them out, then," he said aloud. "We don't need numbers to check on something."

The detective and the non-commissioned officer looked at each other in perfect unspoken understanding; if you were a leader of King's Men, you didn't send them where you wouldn't go yourself. Or send them at all instead of going yourself, if accomplishing the mission was simply a matter of one man walking into danger. He'd been honour-bound to tell the corporal what he thought they were looking for. Corporal Bramble wouldn't let him go in after it alone.

It felt eerily strange to walk through an English beechwood with the smooth grey bark dappled by the sun and feel this way. You were meant to feel like this amid a landscape of arid rock, knowing that hating black eyes were peering at you and quivering-eager hands gripped spears, while the armour was like a vise around your chest and the long clatter of boots and hooves on rock echoed back from the sides of the wadi. His hand ached for the hilt of his longsword, but there was nothing here from which a sword could protect him.

"Here," he said.

Whatever-it-was had been buried skillfully, but you couldn't sink a dozen boxes bigger than coffins into the dirt without leaving *some* trace. Rutherston forced his mind and memory back from a time more than a decade distant, swallowed, cleared his throat.

"This one," he said.

They scrabbled at the duff with their gloved hands. The steel top of the box was still covered in chipped, faded, olive-green paint, with faint black traces where words and code sequences had been stencilled on. The rope handle was modern, though. Rutherston licked his lips again and bent to pull at it. The effort made him stagger, taken off-guard; the weight was far greater than a four-by-three section of stamped steel should be. Bramble stepped nearer and gave him a hand; there was room for both on the loop of hemp.

The lid began to creak upwards. As soon as it was open at all, he could see that the chest had been lined with thick plates of lead and then something else—graphite, he thought. Then he saw what was within, dull-shining metallic wedges, and he jumped back. Bramble did an instant later, and the lid fell back with an echoing *whump*. The softness of the sound meant that the fit must be very good, sealing the boxes air-tight.

Thank God for Jon Wooton's clever hands, Rutherston thought, scraping the back of one hand across his face. *And damn him for a lunatic!*

"Corporal, get your man out to the semaphore line. Code Seven-Seven-Eight, and send it *emergency priority*."

"Yes, *sir!*"

That gave Bramble a reason to run. Rutherston turned and walked instead. He couldn't outrun what waited in those lead-lined boxes behind him . . . and you could never really outrun fear, anyway.

"He wanted to *what*?" Sir James said.

"Build a steam engine," Ingmar Rutherston said.

He looked around the parlour in Royston Hall. Only the essential people were there; the squire; his brother, the vicar; and

District Nurse Delia Medford, SRN. And Corporal Bramble, of course. The sheer *normalcy* of it was inexpressibly comforting, down to the tea-tray the maid had left, and the sheen on the mahogany of the table, the leather of the sofa and chairs, and the large and rather bad oil of William the Great's victory over the Moors at Tenerife that hung by the door.

"That is mad!" the Reverend Frances Broxby said.

The nurse stirred her cup, genteelly holding out the little finger of that hand. She nodded as the detective went on:

"Not if he had the right fuel," Rutherston said. He lit one of his cigarillos and leaned an elbow on the mantelpiece. "Plutonium, I believe it was called, Father?"

The scholarly priest shook his head. "Plutonium—you're all familiar with the name?—plutonium won't *explode* anymore. Even if the chemical explosives to drive the pieces together would work, or the electronic control mechanisms functioned. It won't even get hot enough to melt. And thank God for that. Otherwise, it would have poisoned half of England as it burned through the containment structures."

"Thank God indeed. From my dimly recalled lessons, one sort turns into another sort as it runs down, somehow, and only God and a few boffins know what it is by now."

"Radium, Cobalt-60, other decay products," the priest said quietly. "Wooton's chests probably came from an old power station. Whoever dug it out probably did so under duress and died very quickly."

Rutherston nodded; even if the slave labourers had been Wild Lands savages, it was an unpleasant thought. He went on:

"As you say, Padre. But though it won't melt down, in concentrated form, it will sit there and glow at about seven hundred degrees . . . which is quite hot enough to boil water and to keep doing so for a very long time. I remember that from a course on the Dangerous Substances Act. Generally, we leave the old reactors strictly alone—they're safer repositories for the stuff than anything we can build now."

He could see that the priest followed him, and Delia Medford was unsurprisingly unsurprised; it took Sir James a little longer.

"You mean . . . you mean it would have *worked*?" he said at last, blinking his one eye.

"In theory. In practice, no, and Jon Wooton would have killed everyone in Eddsford trying. It's been looked into exhaustively, back around the turn of the century, though the studies were kept secret. The resources of the whole realm couldn't do it, not with the machines we can make. That stuff is hellish dangerous."

"Good God," the baronet said and drank blindly from his cup, looking as if he'd prefer something much stronger.

"Fortunately, the disposal squad says that nothing significant escaped. The boxes will be put in larger boxes, those will be encased in seamless lead castings, and the whole will be cast into very deep parts of the sea. What the boffins call a subduction zone, where evidently we won't have to worry about it again this side of doomsday."

Father Frances crossed himself. "So there *was* no murder here in Eddsford," he said slowly. "Thank God indeed! Jon Wooton simply killed himself . . . by accident."

All those present signed themselves as well, as the cleric murmured, "Amen."

"And no harm done to the village or the people," Sir James said, with a gusty sigh. "I think, Frances, that a thanksgiving mass is in order . . . not that we need be too specific about the cause." He looked at Rutherston. "And no crime was committed after all."

"Oh, there were several crimes: smuggling, violation of the

Treasure Trove Act, the Dangerous And Prohibited Substances Act . . . but all by the very late, and extremely unlamented, Jon Wooton. So my report will make plain."

There will *be an investigation, but not here and, thank God, by the Special Branch, not me.* Aloud he went on:

"I don't think any of you will be bothered further. Officially, this will be simply a matter of a dead smuggler's buried treasure being confiscated—sensational enough to satisfy village gossip. *Provided* everyone here is discreet."

There were smiles and handshakes all around; Rutherston firmly declined the squire's invitation to dinner.

"My wife expects me back just as soon as possible, Sir James. Otherwise, our first child might be born in the absence of his or her father, and I'd never hear the end of it."

"I could lend you a phaeton and some fast horses . . ."

"Many thanks, but I think I can impose on the military for a pedalcab to Winchester along the line of rail. Miss Medford, shall I walk you home on my way to the Moor's Head?"

Bramble fell discreetly behind as they walked down the drive from Royston Hall. Casually, Rutherston drew an envelope from his jacket and handed it to her.

"I suggest you burn these, Miss Medford," he said. "I glanced at the first, but very briefly."

The spare handsome face of the nurse was calm as she accepted the package. "You don't feel obliged to include them in your report?"

Rutherston lit another cigarillo. "Why should I?" he said with a shrug. "There's no indication of anything illegal . . . on your part; Jon Wooton was evidently a blackmailer, among his many other sins, but that will go with him to the grave. Nothing illegal, or in

Winchester even cause for much remark. I'm a detective, not a priest."

"But Eddsford is my home and where my work is, and I very much wish to continue living here," she said. "Thank you very much, Inspector." She drew a breath: "About the money—"

"Dear lady, I *am* a policeman. Intelligent blackmailers usually try to have as many strings on a victim as possible. It would be just like Jon Wooton to force you to accept part of his smuggling profits. If you feel you should donate to charity, that's none of my affair either."

"Thank you very much, Inspector." They came to the door of the clinic. "And you should stop smoking those things. They'll kill you."

Small children followed the two King's Men as they walked toward the inn, and there was a ripple of nods and smiles from the adults; everyone was happy to have the *murder* settled so quickly, and nobody in their tight-knit little world brought up before the law. The ostler of the Moor's Head had his employer's trap ready, with a good-looking horse between the shafts; it would be an hour's travel to the semaphore station on the rail line, and then perhaps two back to Winchester. Rutherston smiled contentedly and drew the smoke into his lungs.

"She scragged 'im, of course, sir," Bramble said quietly.

"No names, no pack drill," Rutherston said. "Yes, of course. At a guess, she gave him some worthless placebo and assured him it would protect him from the radiation, then told him to pick the pieces up and measure them against some part he'd ordered from Portsmouth or something of that order. From someone who'd healed his illnesses since he was a child, he'd believe it."

"She'd have grassed him up before much longer, any rate,"

Bramble said thoughtfully. "Don't blame her for waiting 'til the last minute, sir, either."

"Not at all," Rutherston agreed.

The two men turned and faced each other. The detective held out his hand; they exchanged a single firm grip, no squeezing nonsense, but a mutual recognition of strength.

"You were of the greatest possible help, Corporal Bramble, and I will say so in my report."

"Thank you kindly, sir."

"And Bramble . . . have you considered what you'll be doing after your current enlistment ends? Promotion is slow in peacetime."

Bramble's square face went a little slack for an instant. "Hadn't thought much, sir . . . might take up a farm in Spain, p'raps. Under me own vine and fig tree. Though farming's a mite too much like 'ard work when you come to think about it."

"Have you considered the police? A good many ex-servicemen do . . . myself, for example."

Bramble chuckled. "Honestly, sir, I can't see meself in a leather bobby's 'elmet, rattling the doors of an evening and chatting up housemaids."

"I meant the detective branch, of course. The pay and pension are reasonable, we can always use good men—and you'd be protecting King and Country just as surely as you would in that tin shirt."

He held out his card. "Take this, think it over, and drop me a line if you want to talk it over a bit more."

Bramble took the card, turning it over in his thick fingers. "I will give it a thought, sir."

Then he grinned. "It hasn't been as boring as road patrol, Inspector, I'll give you that."

Rutherston put a hand on the side of the trap and vaulted into the seat. He tipped his hat to the corporal and waved to the crowd of villagers. They were still waving back as the horse broke into a trot, hooves falling hollow as it trod the shadows of tree and cottage into the roadway.

The detective settled back as the ostler whistled to his horse, smiling as the long peace of Eddsford fell behind and the blue-shadowed line of the Downs rose ahead. The church bell rang as they crested the first hill above the river, calling the villagers to give thanks for God's protecting hand.

And it's no slight privilege, to share the work with Him.

ABOUT THE AUTHORS

KELLEY ARMSTRONG is the author of the Rockton thriller series, standalone thrillers beginning with *Wherever She Goes*, and the Royal Guide to Monster Slaying middle-grade fantasy series. Past works include the Otherworld urban fantasy series, the Cainsville gothic mystery series, the Nadia Stafford thriller trilogy, the Darkest Powers and Darkness Rising teen paranormal series, and the Age of Legends teen fantasy series.

MARIE BRENNAN is a former anthropologist and folklorist who shamelessly pillages her academic fields for inspiration. She recently misapplied her professors' hard work to *The Night Parade of 100 Demons* and the short novel *Driftwood*. She is the author of the Hugo Award-nominated Victorian adventure series The Memoirs of Lady Trent along with several other series, more than sixty short stories, and the New Worlds series of worldbuilding guides; as half of M.A. Carrick, she has written *The Mask of Mirrors*, first in the epic Rook and Rose trilogy. For more information, visit swantower.com, Twitter @swan_tower, or her Patreon at patreon.com/swan_tower.

GARTH NIX has been a full-time writer since 2001 but has also worked as a literary agent, marketing consultant, book editor, book publicist, book sales representative, bookseller, and a part-time soldier in the Australian Army Reserve. His most recent book is *The Left-Handed Booksellers of London*, with *Terciel and Elinor* forthcoming in late 2021. More than six million copies of Garth's books have been sold around the world; they have appeared on the bestseller lists of *The New York Times*, *Publishers Weekly*, *The Bookseller*, and others, and his work has been translated into forty-two languages.

CANDAS JANE DORSEY is the award-winning author of, among others, *Black Wine*, *A Paradigm of Earth*, *Machine Sex and other stories*, *Vanilla and other stories*, *Ice and other stories*, *The Adventures of Isabel* and *What's the Matter with Mary Jane?* (the Epitome Apartments Mystery Series), and YA novel *The Story of My Life, Ongoing*, by CS Cobb. Since the 1980s, she has been a strong presence in the speculative fiction world in Canada as a publisher, editor, and community-builder. In "Going to Ground," she pays respectful homage to, among others, Peter Watts, Eleanor Arneson, James Gleick, and sushi, the world's most nearly perfect food.

JEREMY SZAL was born in 1995 and was raised by wild dingoes, which should explain a lot. He spent his childhood exploring beaches, bookstores, and the limits of people's patience. His debut novel, *Stormblood*, a dark space opera about a drug harvested from alien DNA that makes users permanently addicted to adrenalin and aggression, is out now from Gollancz as the first of a trilogy, with *Blindspace* releasing in November 2021. He's the author of more than fifty science fiction short stories, translated into six languages. He was the editor for the Hugo-winning *StarShipSofa* until 2020 and has a BA in Film Studies and Creative Writing from UNSW. He carves out a living in Sydney, Australia, with his family.

He loves watching weird movies, collecting boutique gins, exploring cities, cold weather, and dark humour. Find him at jeremyszal.com or on Twitter @JeremySzal.

JEFFREY A. CARVER is the author of numerous science fiction novels, including the recently published duo *The Reefs of Time* and *Crucible of Time*, in which Carver returned to his signature series, The Chaos Chronicles. Equally popular are his Star Rigger stories —including the Nebula-finalist *Eternity's End*—and *Battlestar Galactica*, a novelization of the critically acclaimed miniseries. His work takes him to the borderland of hard SF and space opera; his greatest love remains character, story, and a healthy sense of wonder. A native of Huron, Ohio, Carver lives with his family in the Boston area. Visit his blog at starrigger.net.

EDWARD WILLETT is the award-winning author of more than sixty books of science fiction, fantasy, and non-fiction for readers of all ages, including the Worldshapers series and the Masks of Agyrima trilogy (as E.C. Blake) for DAW Books, the YA fantasy series The Shards of Excalibur, and most recently, the YA SF novel *Star Song*. He won Canada's Aurora Award for Best Long-Form Work in English in 2009 for *Marseguro* (DAW) and for Best Fan Related Work in 2019 for *The Worldshapers* podcast. His humorous space opera *The Tangled Stars* comes out from DAW in 2022. He lives in Regina, Saskatchewan, with his wife, Margaret Anne Hodges, P.Eng., a past president of the Association of Professional Engineers and Geoscientists of Saskatchewan. They have a college-age daughter and a much younger black Siberian cat, Shadowpaw, after whom Shadowpaw Press is named. Find him at edwardwillett.com or on Twitter @ewillett.

BRYAN THOMAS SCHMIDT is a Hugo-nominated editor and the national-bestselling author of numerous novels and short stories, including The Saga of Davi Rhii space opera trilogy and The John Simon Thrillers. His latest novel release is *The Complete Saga of Davi Rhii* hardcover omnibus, and his next novel, the near-future hard science fiction thriller *Shortcut*, will be out in early 2022. *Shortcut* has been optioned for film by Roserock Films. His debut novel, *The Worker Prince*, received Honourable Mention on Barnes and Noble's Year's Best Science Fiction of 2011. He is also a screenwriter, songwriter, and musician and lives in Ottawa, KS, with his beloved dogs and cats. He can be found online at bryanthomasschmidt.net.

DAVID D. LEVINE is the author of Andre Norton Award-winning novel *Arabella of Mars* (Tor 2016), sequels *Arabella and the Battle of Venus* (Tor 2017), and *Arabella the Traitor of Mars* (Tor 2018), and more than fifty SF and fantasy stories. His story "Tk'Tk'Tk" won the Hugo, and he has been shortlisted for many other awards, including the Hugo, Nebula, Campbell, and Sturgeon. Stories have appeared in *Asimov's*, *Analog*, *F&SF*, *Tor.com*, numerous Year's Best anthologies, and his award-winning collection, *Space Magic*.

LISA FOILES is the author of the middle-grade fantasy novel *Ash Ridley and the Phoenix*, a story about a young girl and her feisty firebird in a school for magical beasts. The enthusiastically praised audiobook is performed by Lisa herself. Lisa is also an actor, best known as a four-year series regular on Nickelodeon's *All That*. Other TV appearances include an Emmy-winning episode of FOX's *Malcolm in the Middle*, Disney's *Even Stevens*, TNT's *Leverage*, and many more. Lisa is a screenwriter, accomplished singer/songwriter, guitar player, host, voice-over artist, and mom of two cute kids, Chloe and Calvin.

SUSAN FOREST is the author of Aurora Award-winning *Bursts of Fire* (2019), as well as more than twenty-five internationally published short stories. She edits an award-winning anthology series for Laksa Media Groups, was Editor Guest of Honour at Keycon in 2021, and has been invited to co-edit *Life Beyond Us,* coming out from the European Astrobiology Institute. The second novel of her Addicted to Heaven series, *Flights of Marigold* (Publisher's Lunch Selection), confronts issues of addictions in an epic fantasy world of intrigue and betrayal.

MATTHEW HUGHES writes fantasy and space opera. His latest novels are *A God in Chains* (Edge 2020) and *What the Wind Brings* (Pulp Literature Press 2019). His short fiction has run in *Asimov's, F&SF, Postscripts, Lightspeed, Amazing Stories, Pulp Literature, Mythaxis,* and *Interzone,* and in award-winning anthologies edited by George R.R. Martin and Gardner Dozois. He has won the Endeavour and Arthur Ellis Awards, and been shortlisted for the Aurora, Nebula, Philip K. Dick, Endeavour (twice), A.E. Van Vogt, Neffy, and Derringer. He was inducted into the Canadian Science Fiction and Fantasy Hall of Fame. Web page: matthewhughes.org.

HELI KENNEDY is an author, screenwriter, and filmmaker. She has written multiple comic book series and audiobooks based on the BBC America show *Orphan Black.* She also writes AAA open-world video games and has worked on *Far Cry 6* and *Watch Dogs: Legion* for Ubisoft. She has written, produced, and acted in award-winning short films that have screened around the world. When

Heli isn't making up stories, she hikes with her very argumentative husky, Nyla. Or she plays insanely complex board games with a sci-fi/fantasy theme. Instagram and Twitter: @helikennedy.

HELEN DALE is a Senior Writer at *Law & Liberty*. She won the Miles Franklin Award for her first novel, *The Hand that Signed the Paper*, and read law at Oxford. Her most recent novel, *Kingdom of the Wicked*, was shortlisted for the Prometheus Award for science fiction. She writes for a number of outlets, including *The Spectator*, *The Australian*, *Standpoint*, and *CapX*. She lives in London and is on Twitter @_HelenDale.

ADRIA LAYCRAFT, a freelance editor, fiction author, and wood artisan, earned honours in Journalism in '92 and has always worked with words and visual art. She co-edited the *Urban Green Man* anthology in 2013, which was nominated for an Aurora Award, and launched her debut novel *Jumpship Hope* in 2019. You can find her short stories in various magazines and anthologies. Adria is a grateful member of Calgary's Imaginative Fiction Writers Association (IFWA) and a proud survivor of the Odyssey Writers Workshop. Learn more at adrialaycraft.com or follow her YouTube channels, *Carving the Cottonwood* and *Girl Gone to Ground*.

EDWARD SAVIO is a screenwriter and novelist, author of *Alexander X*, Book 1 in the Battle for Forever series, the audiobook of which, narrated by Wil Wheaton, was a number-one overall bestseller on Audible. Born in Connecticut, Edward moved to Los Angeles after university to pursue screenwriting and became a ten-year "overnight success," selling the first of a half-dozen scripts a decade after arriving. His first novel, *Idiots in the Machine*, was optioned by Sony Pictures for seven figures. After three more six-figure deals with Sony and Disney, Savio moved to San Francisco to start a family. And after years of commuting between homes in SF and LA, he chose to shift the focus of his writing toward novels to spend more time with his children. He lives and writes in the home where Danielle Steel wrote her first two breakout novels.

LISA KESSLER is a bestselling author of passionate, page-turning paranormal fiction. She's a two-time San Diego Book Award winner for Best Published Fantasy-SciFi-Horror and Best Published Romance. Her books have also won the PRISM award, the Award of Excellence, the National Excellence in Romantic Fiction Award, the Award of Merit from Holt Medallion, and an International Digital Award for Best Paranormal. Her short stories have been published in print anthologies and magazines, and her vampire story, "Immortal Beloved," was a finalist for a Bram Stoker award. Lisa is also a professional vocalist and host of the *Book Lights* podcast.

IRA NAYMAN is a humourist who often combines comedy with speculative fiction. *The Ugly Truth*, the final novel in the Alien Refugees Trilogy (and his eighth overall), will be published by Elsewhen Press in 2022. Also in 2022, Ira will be celebrating the twentieth anniversary of *Les Pages aux Folles*, his weekly website of social and political satire. Ira was also the editor of *Amazing Stories* magazine for two and a half years. Yes, *that Amazing Stories* magazine.

CARRIE VAUGHN's work includes the Philip K. Dick Award-winning novel *Bannerless*, the *New York Times*-bestselling Kitty

Norville urban fantasy series, more than twenty novels, and upwards of one hundred short stories, two of which have been finalists for the Hugo Award. Her most recent novel, *Questland*, is about a high-tech LARP that goes horribly wrong and the literature professor who has to save the day. An Air Force brat, she survived her nomadic childhood and managed to put down roots in Boulder, Colorado. Visit her at carrievaughn.com.

NANCY KRESS is the author of thirty-three books, including twenty-six novels, four collections of short stories, and three books on writing. Her work has won six Nebulas, two Hugos, a Sturgeon, and the John W. Campbell Memorial Award, and has been translated into two dozen languages, including Klingon. In addition to writing, Kress often teaches at various venues around the country and abroad, including a visiting lectureship at the University of Leipzig, a 2017 writing class in Beijing, and the annual intensive workshop Taos Toolbox, which she teaches every summer with Walter Jon Williams.

JAMES ALAN GARDNER got his Master's degree in Applied Math with a thesis on black holes, then quit university to write SF instead. He is the author of *All Those Explosions Were Someone Else's Fault, They Promised Me the Gun Wasn't Loaded*, and nine other novels. His short fiction has won a number of awards, including the Aurora, the Asimov's Readers' Choice, and the Theodore Sturgeon Memorial Award. In addition to writing, he is a freelance editor, helping writers improve their work before submitting it for publication. In his spare time, he teaches Kung Fu to six-year-olds.

TIM PRATT is the author of more than thirty books, most recently multiverse novel *The Doors of Sleep* and novella collection *The*

Alien Stars. He's a Hugo Award winner for short fiction and has been a finalist for Nebula, World Fantasy, Sturgeon, Mythopoeic, Stoker, and other awards. He tweets incessantly (@timpratt) and publishes a new story every month for patrons at patreon.com/timpratt.

BARBARA HAMBLY has written fantasy, science fiction, historical whodunnits, respectable historical novels, horror, graphic novels, media tie-ins, and Saturday morning cartoons. Recently, she has concentrated on the historical-mystery Benjamin January series. (All of her backlist is available digitally through Open Road Media.) The first mystery of a new series about 1920s Hollywood—*Scandal in Babylon*—has just appeared. She also writes short fiction about characters from her fantasy novels of the '80s and '90s for sale via download on Amazon Kindle Direct or Smashwords. She teaches at a community college. Her other occupations are painting, cosplay, and iaido.

S.M. STIRLING was born in France in 1953 to Canadian parents. He lived in Europe, Canada, Africa, and the US, and visited several other continents. He graduated from law school in Canada, and published his first novel (*Snowbrother*) in 1984, going full-time as a writer in 1988, the year of his marriage to Janet Moore of Milford, Massachusetts, whom he met, wooed, and proposed to at successive World Fantasy Conventions. In 1995, they decamped from Toronto to Santa Fe, New Mexico. He became an American citizen in 2004. Janet passed away in 2021. Stirling's latest books are *Black Chamber* (Roc/Penguin Random House), *Theater of Spies, Shadows of Annihilation*, and *Daggers in Darkness* (Ring of Fire Press), a series of related alternate-history novels set in the 1910s and 1920s, involving Teddy Roosevelt, dirigibles, and spies. His hobbies mostly involve reading—history, anthropology, archaeology, and travel, besides fiction—but he also cooks and bakes for fun and food. For twenty years, he also pursued the martial arts until hyperextension injuries convinced him he was in danger of becoming the most deadly cripple in human history.

ACKNOWLEDGMENTS

This anthology would not have been possible without the generous support of the many people who pledged to back it on Kickstarter. You not only made this terrific collection of science fiction and fantasy stories possible, you've set the stage for more *Shapers of Worlds* anthologies in the future. This anthology only includes guests from the second year of *The Worldshapers* podcast. With luck and supporters like you, there'll be a Volume III next year featuring guests from the podcast's third year—an equally stellar collection of authors. Huge thanks to everyone listed below, and to those who chose to remain anonymous, for helping to bring this book to life.

KICKSTARTER BACKERS

Anonymous, Jordan Theyel, Margaret St. John, Pat, Andrew MacLeod, DCS, David Rowe, Axisor and Firestar, David Edmonds, Margaret Bumby, Martin Beijer, E.M. Middel, Rethyn, Joseph

Geary, Dan-o, Elizabeth Doherty, Adam Eaton, Robert Tienken, Robert Claney, Michael Feir, Anna Fultz, Rich Thomas, Ian Hecht, Max Kaehn, GMarkC, Ina Alexandria Gur, Nancy M. Tice, Arthur Slade, Charles & Sharon Eisbrenner, Joanne B Burrows, Kari Blocker, Aaron Hecht, Margaret Menzies, Sergey Kochergan, Stephen Ballentine, , Robert Cram, Joshua Palmatier, Stephanie Lucas, David Strutton, Eric, Duane Warnecke, Cathy Green, Andrew Hatchell, Charley Kneifel, Amit Hajra, Mary Jo Rabe, Katie Schmirler, Kristi Chadwick, Guenivere McAllister, Gareth Jones, Tony E Calidonna, Mark Newman, Steven Peiper, Julian White, Lawrence M. Schoen, Sarah Ogden, Melanie Marttila, Larry Strome, summervillain, Leah Webber, C. Kierstead, Sarah Spieth, Sandi Pitura, Dino Hicks, Doug Hackworth, K Stoker, Tina M Noe Good, Krystal Bohannan, Fenric Cayne, Jesse Klein, Tara Zrymiak, Kim (miki) Jones, Jakub Narębski (jnareb), PJK, Nancy Casper, Kerry aka Trouble, Lisa Johnson, Brian Bygland, Katherine Magruder, Julia Robart, Haiku Dave, Juli, Sheryl R. Hayes, Peter Halasz, Chris LaHatte, Thomas Bull, Darrow Cole, Emma Ryal, Will Marchant, Steve Mashburn, Alison Armstrong, Jessie M, Joe and Gay Haldeman, Kate Malloy, Chris Wozney, John Woosley, Robert Runté, PhD, Neall Raemonn Price, Yankton Robins, Evan Ladouceur, Adam Rajski, Konstanze Tants, David Perlmutter, Lisa Kruse, Sharon & Mike Sheffield, Lorna Toolis, Henrik Sörensen, Elizabeth Kermath, Helen Dale, Pekka Gaiser, Peter O'Meara, Stu Glennie, John C., Judy Millard, Jess Turner, Patrick Fowler, Cyn Wise, Moira, Brendan Lonehawk, Anonymous H., 'Nathan Burgoine, Jessa Willson, RJ Hopkinson, Llarry Amrose, James McCoy, Chris Gerrib, Rick Straker, Kerry Stubbs, Kerry Stubbs, Dee Danallanko, Simon Matthews, Paul Burger, Nikki Hunter, Annie Schumacher, Emily, Dale A. Russell, Michelle Johnson, MamaJava, Sven Wiese, Michael Fedrowitz,

Lucas K. Law, Pat Hayes, Sara Mitchell, Luis Manuel Sánchez García, Mark Everglade, Tania, Curtis Steinhour, Sir Noah A Waters III, 32nd° F&AM, Lilly Ibelo, Patrick B. Hall, Myth Division, Terry Jacobs, Melissa L Hamner, Rhel ná DecVandé, anonymous, Stephen B. Pearl, GreenShirt52, Jennifer Berk, Mordechai, E. T. Ellison, Mark Laedlein, Amanda W, JB Buoy, Ryan Scarcella, Pedro Correa, Dusan Milatovic, Collin Dutrow, dennisfuzzy1@aol.com, Robbie Bryan, Tashana Landray, Rick Ohnemus, Dan Neely, Ward R. Pederson, Andromeda Taylor-Wallace, John Mead, Meghan Burns, Jermaine Kanhai, Kristen Merritt, Karen Simard, Carol Bachelu, Niklas, Jim Putz, Raul Castro, Anthony Christou, Julia M Haynie, Anonymous, Karen McMahon, Matt Daniels, Katharine Kolb, Dwight Willett, Jeremiah Johnston, Curtis Frye, Robbin Webb, Cindy Cripps-Prawak, Jo Anne Vaughn, SusanB, BethAnn Lobdell, Elyse M Grasso, Jennifer Flora Black, Richard Norton, Stephen Mulrooney, Gretl Claggett, Cathy Seeligson, Daniel Parr, Sachin Suchak, Dr Douglas Vaughan, David Myers, Caroline Westra, Liz M, Ross Emery, J. Svilpis, Tom McG, Simo Muinonen, Clarissa Clement, Fred and Mimi Bailey, David Boda, John M. Portley, Kal Powell, Anne Hueser is fine, dryman, Kevin Hogan, Andrew Bailey, Brent Guild - Victoria BC, Matthew McWhorter, E.L. Winberry, John Burchill, Matthew R Gaglio, Leo Valiquette, Richard D. Grant, Nick B. - Vancouver, Canada, Gordon Rice, Filip Hajdar Drnovšek Zorko, Massive Corporation Games StudioKai Hutchence, Patrick B, David Huggett, Natalie Fagan, Erin Graas, Jenny (Herbey) Cowing, Sean Farrell, Kitt Rose, Marla Kishimoto, Shannon Mason, Debbie Matsuura, Tiffany Hall, Margaret Hodges, Karen E. Bennett, Andy Miller, Krystal Windsor, Paul Keck, Connor Bliss, Gary Phillips, Ernesto Pavan, Erik Håkansson, Bugz, Bill Kohn, Boots Brown, Hayden Trenholm, Lark Cunningham, Carol J. Guess, Mark Jobse, Georgia McGraw,

Dr. D. Hauser, Erik T Johnson, John Miyasato, Brooks Moses, Jim Gotaas, Joseph J Connell, Mark Jobse, A D Peak, Derek Ho, Parker & Malcolm Curtis.

www.ingramcontent.com/pod-product-compliance
Lightning Source LLC
Chambersburg PA
CBHW050842210726
48290CB00004B/1045